T0314557

BUTCHER &
BLACKBIRD

THE RUINOUS LOVE TRILOGY

BUTCHER & BLACKBIRD

BRYNNE WEAVER

zando

NEW YORK

Copyright © 2023 by Brynne Weaver

Zando supports the right to free expression and the value of copyright.
The purpose of copyright is to encourage writers and artists to produce
the creative works that enrich our culture. Thank you for buying an
authorized edition of this book and for complying with copyright laws
by not reproducing, scanning, uploading, or distributing this book or
any part of it without permission. If you would like permission to use
material from the book (other than for brief quotations embodied in
reviews), please contact connect@zandoprojects.com.

Zando
zandoprojects.com

First Zando paperback edition: January 2024

Text design by Pauline Neuwirth, Neuwirth & Associates, Inc.
Cover design by Qamber Designs

The publisher does not have control over and is not responsible for
author or other third-party websites (or their content).

Library of Congress Control Number: 2023948001

978-1-63893-173-7 (paperback)
978-1-63893-174-4 (ebook)

15 14 13 12 11
Manufactured in the United States of America

CONTENT & TRIGGER WARNINGS

As much as *Butcher & Blackbird* is a dark romantic comedy and will hopefully make you laugh through the madness, it's still dark! Please read responsibly. If you have questions about this list, please don't hesitate to contact me at brynneweaverbooks.com or on one of my social media platforms (I'm most active on Instagram and TikTok).

- Eyeballs and eye sockets
- Amateur surgery
- Skin ornaments
- Chainsaws, axes, knives, scalpels—a lot of sharp objects
- Accidental cannibalism
- Not-so-accidental cannibalism
- Questionable use of a mummified corpse
- Lobotomized manservant
- Ill-advised use of kitchen implements
- I'm sorry about the cookies-and-cream ice cream (I'm not really)
- Detailed sex scenes, which include (but are not limited to) cock warming, rough sex, praise kink, anal, adult toys, choking, spitting, dom/sub interactions, genital piercings

- References to parental neglect and child abuse
- Parental loss (not depicted)
- References to child sexual assault (not in detail)
- It's a book about serial killers, so there's some generally messed-up murder and chaos

For those of you who read the trigger warnings and said,
"Accidental cannibalism?! Count me in!"
This one's for you.

PLAYLIST

Click on a QR code to listen:

APPLE MUSIC

SPOTIFY

CHAPTER 1: Ichi-go, Ichi-e
"Stressed Out," twenty one pilots
"Better on Drugs," Jim Bryson

CHAPTER 2: Fun & Games
"Red," Delaney Jane
"Dodged a Bullet," Greg Laswell
"Waves," Blondfire

CHAPTER 3: Ventricular
"Easy to Love," Bryce Savage
"Obsession," Joywave

CHAPTER 4: Atelier
"Territory," Wintersleep
"Castaway," Barns Courtney

CHAPTER 5: Certainty
"Jerome," Zella Day
"Trying Not to Fall," Jonathan Brook

CHAPTER 6: Susannah
"Killer," Valerie Broussard
"Demise," NOT A TOY

CHAPTER 7: Cubism Era
"Demons," Sleigh Bells
"I Don't Even Care About You," MISSIO

CHAPTER 8: Under Glass
"Birthday Girl," FLETCHER
"BLK CLD," XLYØ
"Where Snowbirds Have Flown," A Silent Film

CHAPTER 9: Creance
"Addicted" (feat. Greg Laswell), Morgan Page
"The Enemy," Andrew Belle
"Into the Fire," Thirteen Senses

CHAPTER 10: Dijon
"West Coast," MISSIO
"Heart of an Animal," The Dears

CHAPTER 11: Discordia
"Knives Out," Radiohead
"Walk on By," Noosa
"Drowned," Emily Jane White

CHAPTER 12: Puzzles
"Forget," Marina and the Diamonds
"Shine," Night Terrors of 1927
"Come Out of the Shade," The Perishers

CHAPTER 13: Humanity Eroded
"Blastoffff," Joywave
"Kids," Sleigh Bells
"Shimmy" (feat. Blackillac), MISSIO

CHAPTER 14: Shattered
"Indestructible," Robyn
"Deadly Valentine," Charlotte Gainsbourg
"Love Me Blind," Thick as Thieves

CHAPTER 15: Imprints
"Best Friends," The Perishers
"Novocaine," Night Terrors of 1927
"Sentimental Sins," Matt Mays

CHAPTER 16: Broken Revelations
"Fade into You," The Last Royals
"Between the Devil and the Deep Blue Sea," XYLØ
"For You," Greg Laswell

CHAPTER 17: Beautiful Disaster
"Heaven," Julia Michaels
"Never Be Like You" (feat. Kai), Flume

CHAPTER 18: Detonate
"AT LEAST I'M GOOD AT IT," NERIAH
"Body," Wet
"Crave," Dylan Dunlap

CHAPTER 19: Reservations
"Farewell," Greg Laswell
"Spoonful of Sugar," Matt Mays

CHAPTER 20: Tower
"Dark Beside the Dawn," Adam Baldwin
"Wandering Wolf," Wave & Rome
"Where to Go," Speakrs

CHAPTER 21: Keys

"Look After You," Aron Wright

"Heroin," Lana Del Rey

CHAPTER 22: Finesse

"Vagabond" (feat. Czarface), MISSIO

"Burn the Witch," Radiohead

"Half Your Age," Joywave

CHAPTER 23: Pigment

"Bones," Scavenger Hunt

"Don't Believe in Stars," Trent Dabbs

CHAPTER 24: Plucked

"We Are All We Need," Joywave

"End of All Time," Stars of Track and Field

EPILOGUE

"Lifetime Ago," Greg Laswell

PROLOGUE

Butcher & Blackbird
Annual August Showdown
7 days
Tie-breaker by rock-paper-scissors
Best of five
Winner takes the Forest Phantom

ICHI-GO, ICHI-E

Sloane

Being a serial killer who kills serial killers is a great hobby . . .

Until you find yourself locked in a cage.

For three days.

With a dead body.

In the Louisiana summer.

With no air conditioning.

I glare at the fly-riddled corpse lying beyond the locked door of my cage. The buttons of Albert Briscoe's shirt strain against the bloat of his distended, green-gray stomach. His *moving* stomach, the thin skin undulating over the gasses and maggots that chew through the flesh beneath. The stench of decay, the buzz of insects, the smell of shit and piss that have vacated his body, it's fucking revolting. And I'm not squeamish. But I have standards. I prefer my corpses fresh. I just want to take my trophies and stage my scene and *go*, not hang around and watch as they liquefy.

As if on cue, there's a quiet tearing sound, like wet paper ripping apart.

"No . . ."

I can almost hear Albert from beyond the grave: *Yes.*

"Oh *no, no, no . . .*"

It's happening. This is for killing me, you fucking bitch.

The skin splits open and a white mass of maggots tumbles out, like little orzo pastas. Except a significant number of those pastas is crawling toward me at a glacial pace, looking for a quiet place to complete the next stage of their maggoty life cycle.

"Jesus fucking Christ." I scooch on my bum across the grimy stone floor of my cage to curl myself into a ball. My forehead presses to my knees until my brain aches. I start to hum in the hope I'll drown out the sounds that are suddenly too loud around me. My melody grows louder, and louder, until my chapped lips start to form the occasional word. *No one here can love or understand me . . . Blackbird, bye, bye . . .* I hum and sing until the words fade away, and the melody too.

"I renounce my wicked ways," I say after the song disintegrates among the dust motes and the hum of opalescent insect wings.

"That's a shame. I bet I would like your wicked ways."

I startle at the sound of a man's deep, smooth voice, the cadence of a faint Irish accent warming every note. My curses cut the humid air when my head smashes against an iron crossbar of my small cell as I scurry out of reach of the man who saunters into the thin thread of light from the narrow window, the glass opaque with fly shit.

"You seem to be in a predicament," he says. A lopsided grin sneaks across his face, the rest of his features sheathed in shadow. He takes a few steps into the room to stare down at the corpse, bending to get a closer look. "What's your name?"

I'm on day three of no coffee. No food. My stomach has probably imploded and sucked other organs into the void. A loud chorus of desperately hungry internal monologue is trying to convince me that those are, in fact, little orzo pastas marching toward me, and they might just be edible.

I can't deal with this shit.

"I don't think he's going to answer you," I say.

The man chuckles. "No shit. I already know who he is anyway. Albert Briscoe, the Beast of the Bayou." The man's gaze lingers on the corpse for a long moment before he shifts his attention to me. "But who are *you*?"

I don't answer, remaining still as the man takes careful, measured steps around the corner of the cage to get a better look at me where I'm huddled in the shadows. When he's as close as the bars will allow, he crouches down. I try to hide beneath my tangled hair and folded limbs, giving him only my eyes.

And because my luck is *the worst*, he, of course, is *stunning*.

Short brown hair, artfully disheveled. Strong features, but not severe. A sly smile with perfect teeth and a straight scar that cuts through his top lip, lips that are far too inviting given my current state of captivity, the bottom one a little fuller than the top. I shouldn't be thinking about how I would like to bite it. Not at all.

But I am.

And for my part, I'm fucking *disgusting*.

Knotted hair. Stained, bloodied clothes. The worst breath ever to be breathed in the history of breathing.

"You're not Albert's usual type," he says.

"What do you know about his usual type?"

"That you're too old to be it."

He's right. Not that I'm old, at a mere twenty-three. But this guy knows it as much as I do, that I'm far too old for Albert's tastes.

"And how would you know that, exactly?"

The man's gaze slides to the corpse as a faint look of disgust passes over his shadowed features. "Because I've made it my business to know." He looks at me once more and smiles. "I'm guessing you made it your business too, judging by the quality of the hunting knife stuck in his throat. Handmade Damascus steel. Where'd you get it?"

I sigh. My gaze lingers on the body and my favorite blade before I press my cheeks to my drawn-up knees. "Etsy."

The guy chuckles and I pick up a little pebble in my enclosure just to drop it on the floor.

"I'm Rowan," he says as he extends a hand into the cage. I look at it and toss another pebble, and though I make no move to accept his gesture, he keeps his hand lifted toward me. "You might know me as the Boston Butcher."

I shake my head.

"The Massacre of Mass . . . ?"

I shake my head again.

"The Ghost of the East Coast . . . ?"

I sigh.

I've totally heard of all those names, even though I'm not telling *him* that.

But on the inside, my heart hammers my blood through my veins. I'm just glad he can't see it ignite my cheeks with crimson flame. I know *exactly* the names he's called by, and that he's not all that different from me—a hunter who favors the worst that society can dredge up from the pits of hell.

Rowan finally removes his hand from my cage, his smile taking on a dejected quality. "Shame, I thought you might recognize my little nicknames." He slaps his hands to his knees and rises. "Well, I'd best be going. Pleasure to almost meet you, nameless captive. Best of luck."

With a final, fleeting smile, Rowan turns and strides toward the door.

"Wait! Wait. *Please.*" I clamor to my feet to grip the cold bars just as he reaches the threshold. "Sloane. My name is Sloane. The Orb Weaver."

There's a moment of stillness between us. The only sound to fill the space is the buzz of flies and the steady work of maggots as they consume decaying flesh.

Rowan turns his head, casting a single eye over his shoulder.

And in a heartbeat he's there, right in front of me, his motion so fast it startles me back from the bars but not before he grabs my hand to shake it vigorously.

"*Oh my God.* I knew it. I fucking *knew* they had it wrong. It had to be a woman. The Orb Weaver! Such a cool name. The intricate fishing line, the fucking *eyeballs.* Amazing. I'm such a huge fan."

"Uhh . . ." Rowan continues to shake my hand despite my effort to pull it away. "Thanks . . . I guess . . . ?"

"Did you come up with that name? The Orb Weaver?"

"Yeah . . ." I snatch my hand free so I can step away from this strangely enthusiastic Irishman. He grins at me as though awestruck, and if I wasn't wearing sixty layers of grime on my skin, I'm sure he'd be able to see the blush flame in my cheeks for the second time. "You don't think it's dumb?"

"No, it's so great. The *Massacre of Mass* is dumb. The *Orb Weaver* is pretty kickass."

I shrug. "I kind of think it sounds like a lame superhero."

"Better that than the authorities making something up for you. Trust me." Rowan's gaze shifts to the corpse and back again, his head tilting as he regards me. He jerks a nod once in Albert's direction. "He must have been really acting the maggot. *Get it?*"

There's a long pause, the silence between us punctuated by the hum of insect wings.

"No. I don't."

Rowan waves a hand. "Irish saying, meaning he was up to mischief. But it was a pretty clever joke, given the circumstances," he says, his chest puffed with pride as he hooks a thumb toward the corpse. "Begs the question, though—how'd you wind up in the cage while he's dead with your blade out there? Did you knife him through the bars?"

I glance down at my formerly white shirt and the dirty boot print that hides beneath the splash of blood. "I guess you could say it was a moment of bad timing."

"Hmm," Rowan says with a sage nod. "I might have had one or two of those myself in the past."

"You mean you've been locked in a cage with a dead body and a little infantry of orzo pastas marching your way?"

Rowan looks down across the space around us and frowns. "No. Can't say that I have."

"Didn't think so," I mutter with a weary sigh. I dust off my hands on my grimy denim shorts and take a final step back as I cock a hip. I'm starting to become annoyed at this interloper who seems to be doing nothing more than delaying my slow death by starvation. I'm pretty sure he's a bit nuts and I don't get the impression he's that keen on actually letting me out of here.

Might as well just get on with it.

"Well . . . ?"

"They're making decent progress, the little orzos," Rowan says, more to himself than to me as his gaze remains trapped on the trail of tiny white worms heading my way. When his eyes lift from the floor, they meet mine with an eager smile. "Want to get lunch?"

I level this stranger with a flat glare as I motion to my bloody, boot-printed shirt. "Unless you want to send us both to jail immediately . . . no . . . ?"

"Right," he says with a frown before striding toward Albert's corpse. He rifles through the pockets, coming up empty. When he looks up to the bloated neck, he lets out a little sound of triumph, pulling my blade free before he yanks on a silver chain, the links snapping with the swift assault of his strong grip. He turns his smile toward me as he rises, his fingers unfurling around the key that rests in his palm.

"Have a shower. I'll find you some clothes. Then we'll burn the house down."

Rowan unlocks the door and extends a hand into the shadows of my cage.

"Come on, Blackbird. I'm in the mood for barbecue. What do you say?"

FUN & GAMES

Rowan

The Orb Weaver.

I'm sitting across the table from the fucking *Orb Weaver*.

And she's fucking *beautiful*.

Raven hair. Warm hazel eyes. A spread of freckles over her cheeks and a little nose that's turned a bit red. She clears her throat and takes a long sip of her beer and then frowns, her eyes trained on her glass as she pushes it away.

"You're sick," I say.

Sloane's eyes meet mine with a wary glance before her attention shifts to the diner. Her sharp gaze lands on one table of patrons for only a moment before it floats to the next. Sloane is a nervous one.

Probably justified, all things considered.

"Three days in that hellhole were bound to take a toll. Thank fuck I had water in there." She reaches for the napkin dispenser and pulls a tissue free to blow her nose. Her gaze finds mine again but doesn't stay on me for long. "Thanks for letting me out."

10

I shrug and sip my beer, and I watch in silence as her gaze flicks away to a server who exits the kitchen with another table's order. Sloane asked for a booth midway down the window, pointing to the exact one she wanted when the hostess led us into the room. Now I get why. It's equidistant between the front entrance, the emergency exit by the bathrooms, and the kitchen.

Is she always this flighty, or has her time in Albert's cage got her spooked? Or is it me?

She's wise to be wary.

My eyes stay fixed to her, and I take the opportunity to openly assess my dining companion as she surveys the restaurant. Sloane twists her damp hair over her shoulder and my gaze drifts down to her chest, as it has every two minutes since she walked out of Albert Briscoe's bathroom with a Pink Floyd T-shirt and no bra.

No bra.

The thought echoes through my brain like church bells on a bright Sunday morning.

Her body is curvy and strong, working some kind of witchcraft on her stolen clothes that should look anything but sexy given they came from Briscoe's closet. She even makes his jeans look good, the hems of the long legs rolled to her ankles and the baggy waist cinched with two red handkerchiefs tied together to form a makeshift belt. She knotted the bottom of the T-shirt so it nips in at her waist, showing a sliver of tempting skin and her pierced belly button when she leans back against the booth with an exhausted sigh.

No bra.

I need to get my shit together. She's the Orb Weaver, for Chrissakes. If she catches me ogling, she could pop my eyeballs out of my head and string me up in fishing line before I say the words *no bra*.

Sloane rolls a shoulder, doing little to help my mission to give up my *no bra* mantra. Her fingers find the joint as a little wince of pain creases her features. She frowns when her eyes meet mine.

"He kicked me," she explains, her touch lingering on the top of her shoulder with her answer to my unvoiced question. "My shoulder hit the edge of the cage when I fell in."

My hands fold into tight fists beneath the table as white-hot rage burns in my veins. "Fucker."

"Well, I did stab him in the neck, so I guess it was justified." Sloane's palm slips down her arm and she sniffles, her nose crinkling. Fucking *adorable*. "He managed to close me in before he fell. He even laughed."

The server approaches with two plates of ribs and one of fries, earning a ravenous glance from Sloane. When the plate is set down in front of her she smiles, a little dimple appearing next to her lip.

We thank the server who lingers for a moment in the periphery before Sloane pipes up with confirmation that we have everything we need. When the woman departs, Sloane snickers, that dimple deepening. "Don't tell me you get that so often that it doesn't even register in your brain. That's just depressing."

"Get what . . . ?"

Sloane's gaze darts to the server and I follow her line of sight to the woman who tosses a smile to our table over her shoulder. "Oh my God, it really *doesn't* register. Like, *at all*." Sloane shakes her head and tears a rib free of the steaming rack on her plate. "Well, be prepared, pretty boy. My stomach has been eating nearby organs for the last three days and I'm going to devour these fucking ribs in the most unladylike fashion possible."

I say nothing, riveted to the sight of her perfect teeth as she tears into the steaming flesh that slides off the gray bone. A drop of barbecue sauce gathers at the corner of her lips and her tongue darts out to claim it, and I want to fucking die.

"So . . ." I clear my throat in the hopes my voice won't crack. Sloane's brow furrows as she sinks another bite into the meat. "How come not Blackbird?"

"Huh?" She slips the end of the rib into her mouth and sucks the meat right off the bone to pull it past her lips with sauce-stained fingers. My cock strains against my zipper just watching her cheeks hollow.

Imagine what she could do with that fucking mouth.

I take a sip of beer and look down at my plate. "Your name," I reply before starting on a rib, purely to distract certain body parts that are becoming pretty insistent about what they want. "How come you didn't pick a name with Blackbird? Raven hair, flighty nature, the song . . . I'm going to hazard a guess it's from your childhood, right? I heard you singing it back in the cage."

Sloane's chewing stops for a moment as she regards me with a thoughtful pass of her thumb over her bottom lip. It's the first time her gaze has really settled on me, and it burrows right into my skull. "That's for me," she says. "Orb Weaver is for *them*."

Sloane's eyes have darkened, and with just a blink she's gone from a sexy, runny-nosed, and ravenous beauty to a wicked, remorseless, iron-willed killer.

I nod. "I get it."

I might be the only person who does.

Sloane keeps her unwavering stare pinned on me. "What's your deal, pretty boy?"

"My deal?"

"You heard me. You show up to fuckwit's house, let me out of his cage, burn his house down, and take me for ribs and beer. Yet, I know basically nothing about you. So, what's your deal? Why were you at Briscoe's?"

I shrug. "I came to hack off his limbs and enjoy his agonizingly slow death."

"Why him, though? We're a little far from Boston. I'm sure there are plenty of lowlife drug dealers for entertainment up there that you don't need to come this far for one guy."

A weighted silence thickens the air, both of us paused with ribs heading toward our mouths. A sly smile spreads across my lips as Sloane's face falls.

"You *totally* know who I am."

"Oh my *God*."

"You do. You know what I like to hunt on my home turf. How long have you been a fan?"

"Dear Christ, *stop*."

I chuckle as Sloane drops her forehead onto the backs of her bent wrists, a rib still clutched between her sticky fingers. "Which one was your favorite?" I ask. "The guy I flayed and strung up on the bow of that ship at Griffin's Wharf? Or what about the guy I suspended from the crane? That one seemed popular."

"I can already tell you are the *worst*." Sloane keeps her hands up in a futile effort to cover the flaming blush igniting her cheeks. Her hazel eyes dance despite the glare she tries to shoot my way. "Send me back to Briscoe's cell."

"Your wish is my command."

I look toward the serving station and raise my hand at the waitress who takes all of one second to spot me before she starts heading our way with a growing smile.

"Rowan . . . ?"

"What? You said you wanted to go back to Briscoe's, so back we shall go."

"I was joking, you psycho—"

"Don't worry, Blackbird. I'll deliver you right back to your smelly little cage. I'm sure it's still standing despite the fire. Do you think any maggots survived? You can peck them from the ashes if so."

"*Rowan*—" Sloane's hand darts out and encircles my wrist, leaving sticky fingerprints on my skin. A jolt of electricity crackles through my flesh at her touch. I can barely contain my amusement at the rising panic in her eyes.

"Something wrong, Blackbird?"

The waitress stops beside our table with a bright grin. "Can I get you something?"

I keep my eyes on Sloane, raising my brows as her wild gaze flicks between me and the exits. "Two more beers, please," I say. Sloane's glare turns flat as it alights on me, her eyes narrowed to thin slits.

"Coming right up."

"Like I said," Sloane grumbles as she unfurls her fingers from my pulse. "The *worst*."

I give her a lopsided grin. Sloane's gaze catches on my smile, and her glare softens even though I can tell she doesn't want it to. "You'll love me one day," I purr, keeping hold of her eyes when they reach mine. My tongue passes in a slow lick over the sauce she left on my skin. Sloane's eyes glitter in the warm afternoon light filtering through the diner's windows, that dimple next to her lip a shadow of the amusement she can't quite contain.

"Don't think so, Butcher."

We'll see, my grin says.

Sloane's dark brows flick as though she's issuing a challenge, then she shifts her attention to her food. "You still haven't really answered my question about Briscoe."

"Yes, I did. Hacking limbs. Enjoying agony."

"But why him?"

I shrug. "Same reason you picked him, I assume. He was a piece of shit."

"How do you know that's why I picked him?" Sloane asks.

"Why wouldn't it be?" I reply as I lean my forearms against the aluminum trim on the Formica table. Sloane raises her chin, her expression indignant.

"Maybe he had nice eyeballs."

A laugh bubbles from my chest as I pick up another rib. I let the silence linger, taking a bite before I reply. "That's not why you pry their eyeballs out of their skulls."

Sloane's head cocks to the side, her eyes shining as she assesses me. "No?"

"No. Definitely not."

"Then why would I do that?"

I shrug, not ready to meet her gaze despite the way it beckons me. "The eyes are the windows to the soul, I suppose?"

Sloane scoffs and I look up to catch the shake of her head. "More like 'foster a raven and it will peck out your eyes.'"

My head tilts as I try to decipher her meaning. Very little is known about Sloane, or at least very little makes its way to the press. She specializes in other serial killers and she leaves an intricate crime scene. That's pretty much it. Any other theories the FBI might have about the Orb Weaver are half-baked. From what I've read, the idea of the elusive vigilante being a woman hasn't even broached their little formulaic, predictable brains. Whatever her past and her motivations, whatever she means by her comment, it's all still locked away.

From the second we met, she sparked my curiosity, fanning banked embers into glowing coals, and now she's ignited the first thread of flame.

I want to know. I want the truth.

And maybe I want her to feel the same curiosity about me.

"Did you know I was the one who killed Tony Watson, the Harbor Slasher?" I ask.

She lowers the beer glass from her lips, her movement slow, her eyes locked on mine. "That was you?"

I nod.

"I thought he got into a scrap with someone he was trying to kill."

"That part of the story isn't wrong, I guess. He did get into a scrap and he definitely tried his hardest to kill me, he just didn't succeed." That piece of shit Watson. I beat him until his skull cracked and his body seized, then watched as a final, bloody, gurgling breath spasmed past his broken teeth and split lips. When his body stilled, I left him in the alley for the rats to gnaw.

It wasn't a pretty kill. It wasn't elegant. There was nothing staged or clever about it. It was visceral and raw.

And I enjoyed *every fucking second*.

"Watson wasn't as stupid as I thought. He caught me following him. Tried to ambush me."

A thoughtful *hmm* passes from Sloane's pursed lips. "I'm bummed."

"Bummed why, because he didn't kill me first? Harsh, Blackbird. I'm wounded."

"No," she says on the heels of a barked laugh. "It's just that I had such a cool plan for him. The bodies of his last five kills were already mapped out on my web," she says. Her sticky fingers dance in my direction as though tracing a pattern in the air. She doesn't even look up. It's as though this isn't some giant revelation she just dropped on the table between us.

A map. In the web.

"Not that it would have mattered, I guess. It's not like the dumbass fuckwits at the FBI have figured that out yet. But even so . . . you went and fucked it up," Sloane continues, not looking up from the next bone she tears free of the carcass before her. A heavy sigh spills over the meat that she raises to her lips. "I guess I should be grateful. Maybe I underestimated Watson too. Given Briscoe kicked me into his cage so easily and he was a lazy prick, I'm not sure I would have fought Watson off as well as you did." Her bright, unusual eyes find mine through strands of raven hair that have fallen over her brow as a charming glare flays my blackened soul. "It physically pains me to admit that, by the way. But don't let it get to your head, pretty boy."

A smirk creeps across my lips. "You think I'm pretty."

"I literally just said not to let the Watson thing go to your head.

It applies to your prettiness too," Sloane says with an epic eye roll, one of her eyelids twitching. "Besides, you already know it."

My smile grows a little wider before I hide it behind the edge of my glass. Our gazes stay locked until Sloane finally breaks the trance and looks away, a hint of color infusing her freckled cheeks. "Well, you got to Bill Fairbanks before I could," I say, "so I think we're even."

Sloane's eyes widen, her thick, dark lashes fanning toward her brows. "You were after him?" she asks as I give her a single nod and lift one shoulder. It used to irk me that I lost Fairbanks, even if it was to the Orb Weaver, whom I've considered something of an idol. But now? Meeting the woman behind the web? I would lose to her again to see the way it lights her eyes with pride. Maybe even more than once.

The edge of Sloane's bottom lip folds between her teeth as she tries to anchor her wicked grin against their sharp edges. "I had no idea you were hunting Fairbanks."

"I was tracking him for two years."

"Really?"

"I planned to take him the year before you got him, but he up and moved before I had the chance. Took me a few months to find him again. Then, lo and behold, bits of his body were strung up in fishing line with his eyeballs gouged out."

Sloane huffs, but I can see the spark that flashes in her tired eyes. She sits a little straighter, wiggling in her seat. "I didn't *gouge* them out, Butcher. I *plucked* them. Delicately. Like a *lady*." Sloane sticks her finger in her mouth, pressing it against her cheek as she wraps her lips around it only to snap it out with a *pop*. "Just like that."

I snort a laugh and Sloane gifts me with a beaming smile. "My bad."

Sloane turns her grin to the table before the nerves seem to creep in, and her gaze flits across the room. She takes a few fries, her eyes still shifting over the patrons and exits, before she pushes her plate of ribs toward the table edge.

She's going to take off.

And if she does, I'll never see her again. She'll make damn sure of that.

I clear my throat. "You ever heard of a series of murders in the national parks in Oregon and Washington?"

Sloane's attention snaps back to me with narrowed eyes. A faint crease appears between her dark brows. A little shake of her head is the only response she gives.

"The killer is a phantom. A prolific one. Exacting and very, very careful," I continue. "He prefers hikers. Campers. Nomads with few connections in his hunting area. He tortures them before he positions each body facing east in heavily forested areas, anointed on the forehead with a cross."

Sloane's thin mask falters. She's all predator beneath, scenting a trail. I can almost see her thoughts spiraling in the confines of her skull.

These details are tracks any talented hunter can follow.

"How many kills so far?"

"Twelve, though there could more. But it's been kept pretty quiet."

Sloane's brow furrows. There's a spark in the green and golden depths of her hazel eyes. "Why? For fear of spooking the killer?"

"Probably."

"And how do *you* know about it?"

"Same way you knew who the Beast of the Bayou was. I make it my business to know." I wink. Sloane's gaze snags on my lips to rest on my scar before dragging back up to my eyes. I rest my forearms on the table and lean closer. "What would you say to a friendly competition? First one to win gets to kill him."

Her back rests against the vinyl booth cushion as Sloane drums her chipped, blood-red manicure on the table. She gnaws on her chapped lower lip for a long, silent moment as she lets her attention flow over my features. I feel it in my skin. It touches my flesh. It ignites a sensation I'm always chasing but am never quite able to grasp.

There's never enough risk to scare me. There's never enough reward to satiate me.

Until now.

The drumming of her fingers stops.

"What kind of competition?" Sloane asks.

I flag down the waitress and motion for the bill when she catches my eye. "Just a little game. Let's go for ice cream and we can talk it through."

When I face Sloane once more, my smile is conspiratorial.

Wicked and wanting.

. . . Devious.

"You know what they say, Blackbird. 'It's all fun and games until someone loses an eye,'" I whisper. "And that's when the real fun begins."

VENTRICULAR

Sloane

One Year Later . . .

The need.

It starts like an itch. Irritation beneath my skin. Nothing I do releases the constant whisper of it in my flesh. It crawls into my mind and doesn't let go.

It becomes pain.

The longer I deny it, the more it drags me into the abyss.

I must stop it. I'll do anything.

And there's only one thing that works.

Killing.

"I need to get my shit together," I mutter as I glare at my burner phone for the fiftieth time today. My thumb slides over the smooth glass as I scroll through my short text exchange with the sole contact.

Butcher, it says beneath the photo I chose for Rowan's profile—a single, steaming sausage on the end of a barbecue fork.

I decide not to unpack the various reasons I chose that picture and resort to visualizing myself stabbing him in the dick with the fork instead.

I bet it's such a pretty dick too. Just like the rest of him.

"Jesus Christ. I need help," I hiss.

The man on my stainless steel table interrupts my busy mind as he fights the restraints that bind his wrists and ankles, his head and torso, his thighs and arms. A tight gag traps his pleas in his gaping, fishlike mouth. Maybe it's overkill to strap him down so thoroughly. It's not like he's going anywhere. But the thrashing of flesh on steel irritates me, stoking the itch into a biting torment like talons that scrape at my gray matter.

I turn away, phone in hand, as I scroll back through the handful of messages Rowan and I have exchanged in the last year since the day we met and agreed to this admittedly crazy competition. Maybe there's something I've missed in our limited conversations over the last twelve months? Is there an indication of how this game is supposed to play out? Some way I could be better prepared? I have no fucking clue, but it's giving me an epic headache.

Wandering to the sink, I take a bottle of ibuprofen from the shelf and set my phone on the counter as I tap two pills into my gloved hand, reviewing our text messages from earlier in the week, even though I could probably recite them from memory.

I'll text you the details on Saturday

> How do I know you're not just going to get a head start to win this round?

I guess you'll have to just trust me...

That sounds dumb

And fun! *Gasp* you do know how to
have fun, right...?

Shut your face

My PRETTY face, you mean?

...

Saturday! Keep your phone handy!

And I have done exactly that. I've kept my phone clutched in my grip for most of the day, and it's now 8:12 p.m. The tick of the huge wall clock, which is truthfully mounted on the wall facing the table only to further torture my victims, is now torturing *me*. Every tick vibrates through my skull. Every second scorches my veins with a pulse of need.

I didn't realize how much I was looking forward to this game until the anticipation took root in my thoughts.

The man on my table startles when I turn on the faucet and the water pelts the stainless steel sink. "Calm your tits," I toss over my shoulder as I fill a glass. "We're not even at the fun bit yet."

Whimpers and whines, muffled pleas. His fear and begging both excite and frustrate me as I swallow the ibuprofen and down the glass of water before placing the empty vessel on the counter with a loud thud.

I check my burner phone again. 8:13 p.m.

"Fucking hell."

My personal phone buzzes in my pocket, and I pull it out to read the notification. *Lark*. Her message is just a knife emoji and a question mark. Rather than text her back, I pull my AirPods from my pocket and call her, leaving my hands free for my work.

"Hey, babe," she says, answering on the first ring. "Anything from the Butcher guy yet?"

I bask in Lark's summer sunshine voice for a beat before I let the weight of a sigh leave my lungs. Aside from the wicked work of my hands, Lark Montague is the only thing in this world that brings me clarity when my mind descends into another dimension of darkness.

"Nothing yet."

Lark hums a thoughtful note. "How are you feeling?"

"Antsy." A little sound of thoughtfulness passes through the line, but Lark just waits. She doesn't push or give her opinion of what I should or shouldn't do. She listens. She *hears*, like no one else can. "I don't know if this is an epically stupid idea, you know? It's not like I *know* Rowan. This could be a reckless, impulsive thing to do."

"What's wrong with impulsive?"

"It's dangerous."

"But it's also *fun*, right?"

A thin thread of breath passes through my pursed lips. "Maybe . . . ?"

Lark's tinkling laugh fills my ears as I head to the rows of polished implements lining the counter, the knives and scalpels and screws and saws gleaming under the fluorescent lights.

"Your current idea of . . . fun . . ." Lark says, her voice trailing off as though she can see the scalpel I pick up and examine. "Is it still *fun* enough for you?"

"I guess," I say with a shrug. I set the blade down on the instrument stand alongside surgical scissors, a pack of gauze, and a suture kit. "But I feel like something is missing, you know?"

"Is that because the FBI isn't figuring out the clues you're leaving behind in the fishing line?"

"No, they'll get it eventually, and if they don't, I'll send an anonymous letter. *Check the webs, you fucking idiots.*"

Lark giggles. "*The files are in the computer,*" she says, quoting *Zoolander.* She never fails to chime in with a random yet relevant movie line.

I snicker as Lark laughs at her joke, the shine of her bright light infusing the cool confines of my modified storage container as though she's plugged herself into the electrical circuitry. The levity between us fades as I grip the edges of the tray and wheel it toward my captive. "There's something about this competition that feels . . . inspiring, I guess. Like an adventure. Nothing has really broken through to make me feel excited like this in a long time. And I think—or *hope*—that Rowan would have tried to kill me already if he wanted to. I don't know why, and this is maybe the most reckless, impulsive part of this whole idea, but I believe he feels like I do, like he's looking for something to alleviate an itch that's getting harder and harder to scratch."

Lark hums again, but this time the sound is deeper, darker. I've spoken to her about this before. She knows where I'm at. Relief is harder to find with each kill. It doesn't last as long. Something is *missing*.

That's precisely why I have this piece-of-shit pedo on my table.

"What about this elusive West Coast killer guy that Rowan told you about? Have you found any details on him?"

I frown, my headache needling my eyes. "Not really. I read about one murder that I think might be his from two months ago, out in Oregon. It was a hiker who was killed in Ainsworth Park. But there weren't any details about anointing like what Rowan described. Maybe he's right, maybe authorities are keeping things quiet to not spook the killer." The man on the table lets out a keening wail around his gag and I slap a palm on the tray, rattling the instruments. "Dude, *shut up*. Whining isn't going to help."

"You're sure in a spicy mood today, Sloaney. Are you positive you're not—"

"*No*." I know what Lark wants to ask, but I'm not spiraling. I'm not devolving. I'm not out of control. "Once this competition officially starts up, I'll be fine. I just want to know the details of the first target, you know? I don't deal well with waiting. I need to take the edge off, that's all."

"As long as you're being careful."

"For sure. Always," I say as I wheel the suction machine toward the man as he tries to thrash himself free of the unforgiving leather straps. I press the switch and turn it on as the man's desperate whimpers rise to a higher pitch. A thin film of sweat coats his skin. His wide eyes leak tears from the wrinkled corners as he tries to shake his head, his tongue working against the ball gag strapped in his mouth. My eyes narrow as I take in his tense features, desperation seeping through his pores like musk.

"Got a worthy guest today, huh?" Lark asks as the man's panic bleeds through the connection.

"Sure do." The metal handle of my favorite Swann-Morton scalpel cools my fingertips through the latex gloves, a comforting kiss against my heated skin. The strain of concentration thins my voice to a thread as I focus on positioning the edge of the knife beneath the man's Adam's apple. "He's a total shitbag."

I guide the sharpened tip of the blade through the man's skin, maintaining a straight line as I press down and pass it through his flesh. He screams into the silicone sphere trapped in his mouth.

"This is called the consequences of your actions, Michael." I wipe away the blood that beads along the incision. "You want to talk to underage boys online? Show them your shriveled dick pics? Lure in the neighborhood kids with promises of puppies and candy? Since you like to talk so much, I'm going to take your voice first," I say as I press my scalpel into the void of split flesh on Michael Northman's throat for a second, deeper cut so I can access his vocal and ventricular folds. The suction machine gurgles as it sucks his blood through the control valve gripped in my free hand. "And then I'll take your fingers for every disgusting text and threat you've sent, and I'll shove them up your fucking ass. If you're lucky, I'll get bored and kill you before I get to your toes."

"Jesus, Sloane," Lark says, her dark giggle bubbling through the line. "Yeah, you know what? I think you really should do this competition thing with the Butcher guy. You need to let off some pent-up aggression there, missy."

Yeah, I couldn't agree more.

Michael Northman's final screams flood my kill room as I say goodbye to my best friend and disconnect both the call and my prey's vocal cords. When the surgical procedure is finished, I suture the wound for no other reason but to give him a false hope of survival, instructing Michael to keep his eyes on the clock before I turn to my tray of implements to grab my Liston bone-cutting forceps. Maybe he won't listen to my orders, but I've learned enough about the fragile human mind in this room to know that he'll want something to focus on in the coming hours, and nothing is both more tempting and unforgiving than watching time slowly ticking toward your doom.

I'm about to head back to the man strapped to my table when my burner phone buzzes in my pocket.

> My brother Lachlan is going to draw
> from a hat. He'll text us both with the
> location. As soon as he does, the game
> is on. First one to kill wins. If neither of
> us finds the target within seven days, it's
> a draw. Then I guess we'll have to rock-
> paper-scissors that bitch

A heavy lurch pounds my ribs as my heart rate spikes.

> You have a ridiculous advantage

I watch the dots flicker in our conversation as Rowan types his response to my message.

29

> Trust me when I say that Lachlan wants
> you to win, not me. I have no advantage
> here. He hasn't told me shit

My smile spreads. Michael Northman's desperate thrashing and quickened breaths fall into a hazy backdrop as I tap out my reply.

> I don't know you enough to trust
> you. And if I find out he's feeding
> you info, I'll kick your ass. Just
> laying that out there now so we're
> on the same page, you know?

The chilled air seems heavier in the storage container as I watch the gray circles pulse in the lower left corner of the screen.

> I think I might want you to win now too,
> so I'm okay with that 😌

> You're the worst

> Maybe… but at least you think I'm pretty
> 😔

> Jesus H. Christ

I know I'm smiling down at the device in my hands. I should feel stupid about it. It should feel as dangerous as it is. But the only thing I sense is a relief that settles into my marrow, an excitement that charges the chambers of my heart. It's a current that soaks every cell in light.

I'm about to set the phone down and focus on my captive when it buzzes in my hand with a text from an Unknown Sender, sent to both Rowan and me.

Ivydale, West Virginia

> And good luck, eyeball spider lady, or
> whatever the hell your name is. Just
> think, little brother—your title of loser is
> about to be official.

My grin widens. A text from Butcher comes in on the heels of Lachlan's message.

> See? I told you so. See you in West
> Virginia, Blackbird.

I set down the forceps in exchange for the bloodied scalpel.

When I turn to the man strapped to my table, his eyes are wide with the kind of fear that brings me peace. His face is pale with stress and pain. Blood and saliva slip from the corners of his lips. He tries to shake his head as I twist the scalpel in the artificial light.

"I've got places to be, so I guess we have to cut this short, if you'll excuse the pun," I say before I drive my blade beneath his ear. Blood cascades over the table in a flood of crimson.

"It's game night."

ATELIER

Rowan

"What are you doing?" Fionn asks as he wanders into my room, a carrot snapping in the grip of his molars. "Going on a trip?"

I roll my eyes and gesture to the carrot. "What the hell. Is this a new phase in your CrossFit indoctrination, walking around with raw root vegetables?"

"Beta-carotene, motherfucker. Antioxidants. I'm helping my body eliminate free radicals."

"Take a vitamin. You look like a douche."

"To answer your question, Dr. Kane, Rowan is going on a little hunting expedition with a like-minded soul," Lachlan chimes in as he drops into one of the leather armchairs in the corner of the room. "But in true Rowan style, he's decided to make it into a competition. He roped me into finding some suitable prey that would be enough of a surprise for both of them. So, essentially, he's going to have his ass handed to him like the little bitch masochist he is."

I shoot Lachlan a death glare, but he just smirks over the lip of his glass, taking a long sip of bourbon as he taps a silver ring against the crystal edge.

"Where?" Fionn asks.

"West Virginia."

". . . Why?"

Lachlan barks a laugh. "I'd say because he's trying to claw his way out of the friend zone, but I don't think he's even *in* a zone at this rate."

Fionn takes another crunching bite of his carrot, filling his mouth as he lets out a goofy chuckle like a fucking dumb kid.

So I do what any reasonable, grown-ass man would do to his little brother.

I whip the carrot out of Fionn's hand and then pelt it at Lachlan, hitting him on the forehead with a satisfying *whack*.

My brothers protest in unison and I grin down at my luggage as I stuff another pair of jeans into my carry-on.

"I don't think you've made this much effort for a woman since . . . ever. You haven't seen her in what, a year?" Lachlan asks, not missing a beat.

The sound of Fionn's choked cough fills the room. Lachlan and I watch as he catches flecks of orange in his tight fist. "*What?* A fucking *year?* Why am I only learning about this now?"

"You've had your head in your ass in buttfuck nowhere playing town doctor, that's why," Lachlan snickers. "Come back to Boston, Fionn. Stop wallowing like some Hallmark Movie Sad Man Cinderwhatever and come home to practice some *real* medicine."

"*Prick*," Fionn and I say in perfect unison.

Lachlan grins and sets his glass down on the side table, pulling a pearl-handled switchblade from his pocket before leaning back to unbuckle the extra strip of worn leather from the custom stropping belt at his waist. He loops the metal ring at the slack end of the belt around his middle finger and stretches the leather out, then starts to sharpen the blade on the rough edge of the hide. It's something he's done since we were kids, something that soothes him. Lachlan might enjoy ribbing Fionn and me, but I know he's stressed about our younger brother no longer living in the same city as us, and now about me going off to play some insane death game with a serial killer I barely know. "I'm not wrong," he says after a few passes of the blade over the cowhide. "Nebraska is too far, kid. Besides, you're clearly missing out on all the good details of Rowan's nonexistent, comically sad love life being out there."

"True," Fionn admits. His thoughtful gaze drops to the hardwood as he crosses his arms and leans against the dresser. He's probably assigning numeric values to *knowing the gossip* versus *being out of the loop,* and is weighing the statistical probability of his happiness divided by pi.

Fucking nerd.

"Have you seen her?" Fionn asks as he snaps out of his analytical haze, looking straight to Lachlan as though I'm not even here.

"Only in a few photos." Lachlan takes a sip of his drink as he smirks at my lethal glare. "She's fucking hot. Definitely has a dark side—she likes to take her victims' eyeballs while they're still alive. The feds call her the Orb Weaver. Her actual name is Sloane Sutherland."

"Keep her fucking name out of your mouth," I snarl.

Lachlan's booming laugh fills the room. He raises the hand gripping the switchblade to his mouth as the sound of his amusement floods the space between us. The smartass is undoubtedly reminding me that, out of the two of us, *he's* the one with a weapon at the ready.

If the razor-sharp blade wasn't clutched in his hand, I'd already be punching his fucking smug face.

"Let's say you manage to claw your way into the friend zone, and then by some fucking miracle you get yourself beyond that and into the spider lady's good graces without losing an eye, how would you like me to refer to her?"

"I don't know, asshole. How about *Queen*. Or, *Your Highness*. Fuck off."

I groan as Lachlan's laugh surrounds us again, even louder than before. "*Fuck Off* it is. 'Pleased to meet you, *Fuck Off*. I'm your brother-in-law, welcome to the family, *Fuck Off.*'"

I'm about to launch into Lachlan when my burner phone dings in my pocket.

Making the most of it

There's a photo of Sloane's delicate fingers wrapped around a glass of champagne in business class on a plane, her blood-red manicure shining in the artificial cabin light.

My heart knocks against my ribs.

I can almost feel those nails scraping across my chest and down my abs, wrapping around my cock with deceptive strength. I can imagine the heat of those hazel eyes locked on mine, her breath warming my neck as she whispers in my ear.

Lachlan snickers as though he can read my every thought, and I clear my throat.

> I see you're already on the plane.
> That's...great...

> Indeed I am. And you're clearly not. I'll
> see you if you eventually catch up! I
> won't hold my breath though 😏

My cheeks flush as my thumbs hover over the keyboard.

> Is it too late to call a restart?

Sloane's response is immediate.

> Absofuckinglutely.

A growl vibrates through my chest as I double my efforts to pack, even though I know it won't get me on a plane any faster.

"You okay there, little brother? Or has Fuck Off already killed your target?"

I consider throwing my half-packed luggage at Lachlan's smirking face when his phone rings. Any trace of humor disintegrates from his features like ash falling from a charred log, leaving only cracked carbon behind.

"This is Lachlan," he says. His voice is gruff as he responds to the caller with clipped "yes" and "no" answers, his timbre low. I twist the shirt I'm rolling into a tight coil until my knuckles bleach. My eyes are fused to my older brother, but he doesn't look up from the switchblade he's turning over in his hand. "I'll be there. Give me thirty minutes."

When he meets my eyes, Lachlan's brief smile is grim.

"Night shift?" I ask.

"Night shift," he replies.

By day, Lachlan runs Kane Atelier, his specialist leatherworking studio where he creates beauty from the skin of death. But by night, whenever Leander Mayes calls, my brother becomes the ruthless tool of the devil.

Personally, I enjoy taking the lives of whatever scumbags happen to float my way through the hellish soup of modern society.

Lachlan . . . ? I don't know if he enjoys much of anything these days. He kills with purpose but shrouds himself in cool detachment. Unless he's carving hide with his hands or taking the piss out of me and Fionn, I don't think life matters to him at all.

A pang hits my chest as Lachlan rises from his chair, pocketing his blade and cracking his neck as he threads his stropping belt back into place across his waist. A faint trace of his smile returns when it lands on me.

"Be safe, dickhead," he says.

"You too, asshat."

Lachlan sneers but still claps a warm hand on my shoulder as he passes by. He presses his head to mine for a breath and then he's gone, heading toward the door to do the same with Fionn. Our youngest brother has never been good at hiding his worries. Fionn wears every shade of sadness and worry in his light blue eyes, and he watches Lachlan stride away with aching concern spread across his boyish features.

"See you later, kids," Lachlan says as he strides over the threshold and disappears down the dimly lit hall. "And move home, Fionn."

"Hard pass," Fionn replies, and a chuckle responds from the dark before the heavy door of my apartment closes with a reverberant thud. Fionn turns to me, that anxiety still etched as a crease in the space between his brows. "You sure this trip of yours is a good idea? I mean, how well do you even know this Sloane?"

I drop Fionn's gaze, grinning as I zip my duffel and sling it over my shoulder.

"Not well at all. I've met her only once."

Fionn's nervous swallow is nearly audible. "Once? How did you meet?"

"You really don't want to know."

"This sounds a bit impulsive, Rowan, even for you. I know you've got the whole middle-child thing going on," he says, waving a hand in my direction the way he and Lachlan always do to explain my wild behavior and reckless decisions. "Meeting with some serial killer woman who you've only spoken to once a year ago is . . . not normal."

My laugh seems to do little to reassure him. "Nothing about us is normal, but I'll be fine. I have a gut instinct about her."

The burner phone dings in my pocket.

> I'm about to take off. If this were a race, you'd already be behind

> Oh wait... it IS a race! Look at that. I hope you like disarticulated eyeballs because I'm going to kill this shit, pun intended. Safe travels and get fucked 😘

"Yeah, Fionn," I say with a bright grin as I slide my phone back into my pocket and head toward the door. "I think I'll be okay."

CERTAINTY

Sloane

This is absurd. *I'm* absurd.

I'm sitting in the lobby of the Cunningham Inn, trying to focus on the same page on my e-reader that I've been stuck on for the last five minutes as I deliberate between making a run for it and staying.

What the fuck am I doing with my life?

This is dangerous.

And stupid.

Absurd.

But I can't seem to make myself leave.

My lungs fill with the scent of Pine-Sol and bad decisions as a deep, nervous sigh passes my lips. Giving up on my book, I sit back and take in the quiet lobby where my only company is a morose gray cat who glares at me from a leather chair next to the unlit fireplace. The room is dated but comfortable, with dark oak paneling and an ancient patterned carpet that was once burgundy. The antique furniture is mismatched but polished and gleaming.

A pair of taxidermied owls in midflight stand guard over the sun-bleached reproductions of Rodin paintings and heirloom railway and mining tools scattered across the walls.

I sigh again and check my watch. It's almost two in the morning and I should be tired, but I'm not. There was a lot of rushing around tonight, between slicing up Michael Northman's body and stuffing him in my freezer as I booked a flight out of Raleigh, to packing in a record thirty minutes, to renting a car for my arrival in West Virginia while Lark drove me to the airport. When I lamented that this whole escapade was a stupid idea, her response was: "Maybe, but you do need to get out and make more friends."

"I have a friend," I'd said. "You."

"You need more than one, Sloane."

"But this particular friend? This random Rowan guy? . . . Really?"

I can still hear the chiming cadence of Lark's giggle as she glanced over at my confusion with a gentle smile. "Having another friend who can understand you, the *real* you, is maybe not a bad thing," she said with a shrug, her grin untarnished by the scrutiny of my unwavering stare. "You haven't jumped from the moving vehicle. We're still heading to the airport. So yeah, I guess this random Rowan guy is your friend now."

Maybe I should have jumped from the car.

I groan as I slide farther into the depths of my chair. "Her rationale didn't even make logical sense," I say to the cat as I replay that conversation with Lark, the feline glaring back at me with simmering, judgmental fury.

"Trying to consume its soul, Blackbird?"

I drop my e-reader as I startle, turning toward the source of the subtle Irish accent with a hand clasped to my heart. "Jesus Christ," I hiss as Rowan emerges from the shadows by the door with a smirk. My breath stops short when reality hits me that he's here, *really* here. Rowan looks exactly the same as he did a year ago. I might look a little better than our first encounter, having not spent the last few days in a disgusting cage as a body putrefied a few feet away. I'm not sure if he cared that much about my lack of makeup or knotted hair or chapped lips, considering he spent so much time staring at my tits. The memory makes me blush, and not out of embarrassment.

I swallow down a sudden burst of nerves. "Maybe I *should* consume the cat's soul. Mine just left my body."

"I figured that was how you acquired your freckles. Stealing souls."

"I see you're just as hilarious as the first time we met." I roll my eyes and move to pick up my e-reader but Rowan gets to it first. "Hand it over, pretty boy," I say as he gives me a magnetic grin that fills my senses and douses my worries with a different kind of anxiety. The straight scar through his lip seems to brighten as his smile turns rakish.

"What does my nervous little Blackbird like to read, I wonder?" he teases as he waves the device at me.

A dismissive huff leaves my lips, even though his words crawl into my veins and inject my cheeks with crimson heat. "Monster porn, clearly," I reply. Rowan laughs and I manage to snatch the device from his grip, which only makes him laugh harder. "The sentient dragonman has two dicks and he knows how to use them. A forked tongue too. And a very talented tail. So don't make fun."

"Give me that back. My TV is broken in my room and that's the kind of entertainment I need in my life."

"Get fucked, Butcher." I slide the e-reader beneath my left ass cheek and give Rowan a lethal glare. "Hold on a second. Your TV is broken? When did you get here?"

He shrugs and lets his backpack drop to the floor with a dull thud as he gives me a sly smile, folding his frame into the chair next to mine. "About forty-five minutes ago. You must've been in your room. I left mine to find some booze. I'm your next-door neighbor, by the way."

"Fantastic," I deadpan with an eye roll, which only makes him grin.

Rowan unzips the bag, opening it just wide enough to show the bottle of red wine that rests within.

"It's two in the morning. Aren't all the stores closed?"

"Not the kitchen."

"The kitchen's closed too."

"Is it . . . ? My bad." Rowan pulls the bottle from his bag and cracks the screw-top lid, his gaze fused to mine as he takes a long sip. My eyes narrow to slits when he winks. "Don't tell me you're upset about some petty theft."

"No," I scoff. Gooseflesh erupts on my arm in the brief moment when our fingers interlace around the cool glass as I pry the bottle from his hand. "I'm upset that you're taking too long to pass the bottle over. And you're getting your boy germs all over it. You're probably trying to infect me so I'll be sick in my room with your manpox while you go and win our little competition."

"*Manpox.*" Rowan snorts as I take a long sip and pass the bottle back. He keeps hold of my glare as he takes a drink, the smirk in his expression still gleaming in his eyes. "Well," he says, presenting the bottle with a flourish as he hands it to me, "I've got your girl cooties now, so we're even."

I try not to smile, but it happens anyway, and as soon as that grin sneaks onto my lips it brightens Rowan's eyes as though he's reflecting my amusement back to me. Not just that, but *amplifying* it.

As I settle back into my seat, I realize that it's as though we saw each other only yesterday. It's so easy with him, even when I don't want it to be, just like when we sat in the diner a year ago. Despite how hard I'd tried to force my attention elsewhere, it kept coming back to him. And it's no different now. He lures me in, a pinprick of steady light in the static darkness.

"Any ideas who we're here for?" Rowan asks, breaking me away from the thoughts that have swept me away. I take a sip of wine and eye him with wariness.

"Sure."

"By 'sure' you mean 'not at all,' right?"

"Pretty much. You?"

"Nope."

"How did Lachlan come up with this location, anyway? And how do I know he's not going to feed you information to help you win?"

Rowan grunts a derisive laugh and pulls the bottle from my fingers, taking a long swig before he answers. "Because, like I said, my brother has no interest in seeing me succeed. If I lose, he'll get to rub my face in it for a year, and he'll enjoy every second of it."

When Rowan passes the bottle back to me, he looks around the room, his gaze a careful pass across the features as though he's hunting for hidden cameras or guests he didn't notice. I already know we're the only ones checked in. Aside from the proprietor, a guy named Francis who lives in a well-kept Second Empire–style house that overlooks the inn, we're the only ones on the property. I'm sure Rowan knows this too, but he's right to be careful. "As for how he came up with West Virginia, well . . . let's just say he has connections to certain people who can access certain files of certain government agencies, and some associates who can fill in the gaps."

"That certainly sounds dubious, for certain," I say, grinning when Rowan rolls his eyes at my teasing. "What does your brother do for work?"

Rowan sits back in his chair and taps the armrest as his eyes follow the curves and angles of my face. Their navy-blue caress summons a blush to my cheeks. He looks at me in a way that no one else does, as though he's not just trying to decipher my thoughts and motivations. It's as if he's trying to memorize the smallest details in my skin, to uncover every secret trapped behind my flesh.

"Our hobby," he says when he seems to figure I'm safe to share this answer with. "For Lachlan, it's not a pastime. It's a profession."

I nod. It makes sense to me now how he could have access to information about criminal investigations. Either he works for the military or for dangerous, well-connected individuals.

"So you're sure he's not going to help you cheat," I say.

"If anything, he'd find a way to help *you* cheat."

"I like him already." My smile brightens when Rowan shoots me a fake glare. I take a sip from the bottle and pass it over. "What about you? Do you enjoy the restaurant business?"

Rowan turns a sly smile in my direction. "Have you been looking me up, Blackbird?"

"Like you haven't been doing the same to me," I counter.

"Guilty as charged." Rowan takes a long drink of wine and balances the bottle on his knee. He watches me for a moment before he nods, his smile a little wistful. "Yeah, I do. I love running my own kitchen. I like the pace. It can be frantic, but I enjoy that. I do well with a bit of chaos. Maybe that's why I like you," he says with a wink.

I laugh and roll my eyes. *This man.* He could make anything look flirtatious. "What's with the name?" I ask, and though I skirt around his comment, it doesn't seem to bother him in the least. "Why'd you pick *3 in Coach*?"

"My brothers," Rowan says, his smile taking on that nostalgic quality once more as his gaze falls to the bottle in his hand. "We were teenagers when we left Sligo and came to America. I remember Lachlan buying the tickets. *Three in coach.* It was the start of another life for us."

"Just like the restaurant," I say, finishing the trail of thought he's left for me to follow. His eyes brighten when he nods. "I like that."

Rowan passes the bottle to me. Our fingers graze one another's around the cool glass. Our touch lingers for a moment longer than it should, but for some reason, I find that it's still less time than I'd like.

This is absurd, I remind myself. *You don't know this man.*

I firm up my posture, shift my line of sight to the front desk to give Rowan only the corner of my eye when I drink from the bottle. Walls are good. Boundaries are necessary. He's the kind of guy that will bulldoze right through them if I let my guard down. And this is still a competition, after all. I should only be looking for information that will help me win.

In my periphery, I see Rowan's hand sneaking closer to my chair and I turn to pin him with a glare. The cheeky fucker gives me his most innocent mask.

"What the hell are you doing?"

"I'm going to steal your e-reader. I want to read about the two-dick dragonman."

"I'm sitting on it. Touch my ass and I'll break your hand," I say, failing to contain a laugh as he rhythmically prods my arm.

"I won't. I'll push you over and grab it, then cackle maniacally as I run to my room in triumph."

"Just download the app like a normal person and read it on your phone, weirdo."

"Rock-paper-scissors for it."

"No way."

"Come on, Blackbird. I need some dragonman DP."

He's giving me another poke on my bicep and I'm giggling when a foreign sound enters our domain. It suddenly feels as if we were in a bubble that's just burst. It's not normal for me, and the appearance of Francis by the front desk is a shock to my system. I'm usually so aware of my surroundings. But Rowan had me locked in another realm, as though nothing else existed but us. And for some reason, that felt like a relief, a break from the constant pressure of searching for danger lurking in shadow.

"Hey, man. I hope we weren't keeping anyone up," Rowan says. He doesn't even try to hide the bottle of wine he balances on his knee, his other hand wrapped around the armrest of my chair.

Francis's eyes dart from the wine to Rowan, his lips pressed together in a tight smile. "No, not at all. You're the only guests here. I was just coming to collect Winston Church for the night," he replies as he nods toward the cat still curled on the chair by the fireplace. Francis slips his hand down his pink tie and his eyes bounce between us. "We don't get too much traffic through here, not with some of the newer places popping up in the area. Everyone has an Airbnb now, trying to make an extra buck."

I gesture toward the lobby. "I like it here. It's got charm. Winston looks like he might scratch my face off if I get too close, though."

"Nah, he's harmless." Francis runs a hand through his swoop of dark hair and walks over to the cat who gives him a dirty look and a hiss before he shifts his yellow feline eyes to me. I'm not sure if he wants salvation from Francis or he just wants to continue glaring at me, but his grumbles are lost as Francis heaves his gray body into his arms. "You folks visiting someone in the area? Or just passing through?"

"It's our annual hiking trip," I volunteer. "We pick a new place each year, usually someplace a bit 'off the beaten path,' so to speak."

Francis nods, stroking the cat's head. "There are some great local trails. Elk River is a good place to start. The Bridges is a scenic loop. Just be careful if you head toward Davis Creek. It's easy to get lost. A hiker went missing that way last year and was never found. Wasn't the first time, either."

47

"Thanks, man. We'll make sure to be careful," Rowan says in a tone that politely says *please fuck off now.*

Francis gets the hint and gives us each a nod. "Have a great night, folks. Feel free to call if you need anything," he says, then waves Winston's paw at us before he departs.

Our words of thanks follow him as he disappears down a corridor at the right of the lobby. The sound of a distant door closing reaches us a moment later.

"He looks like he should be trying to pick up girls with a dumbass avatar that looks literally nothing like him as he streams on Twitch or something, not running a hotel in nowhere, West Virginia," Rowan grumbles. He keeps his glare pinned to the hallway as he tugs the armrest of my chair in an attempt to draw it closer.

"What is your problem?" I ask through a laugh as he lurches me closer. "Are you jealous of his pink tie or something?"

Rowan scoffs and shifts that hard stare to me while tugging my chair again. "*No.* Christ. Now give me that dragon dick, Blackbird."

"No way." I manage to slip out of my chair with the e-reader before he can grab me, waving it toward him in a taunt as I back away toward our rooms. "Good night, weirdo. I'm going to bed. Early bird gets the worm, you know. Might plan myself a solo hiking trip to Davis Creek. No boys allowed unless they have scales and a breeding kink."

"Of all the times to forget my dinosaur onesie at home." Rowan sighs, then tilts his bottle toward me before settling back in his chair. His smile is warm, his eyes bright despite the late hour. "See you tomorrow, Blackbird."

With a final wave, I turn and head to my room.

I'm lying in bed, staring at the ceiling when my phone buzzes with a text message.

| Nighty night. Don't let the bedbugs bite.

| I'm pretty sure there are bedbugs.

I grin in the dark. And then I fall asleep.

SUSANNAH

Rowan

On the downside, I still haven't figured out who the hell we're after.

On the upside, neither has Sloane.

Double plus: she *hates* it when I point that out.

I knock on Sloane's door and shove my hands into my pockets, trying to look nonchalant despite the whirling storm of excitement that lights up my chest. When she opens it, her face immediately falls into a dark scowl.

"Expecting someone else?" I ask with a smirk.

"No," she snorts, as though it's the most ridiculous idea ever that some other fella might be wanting to come over at nine o'clock on a Thursday night. I guess the pickings are a little slim in the village of Ivydale. "I just know you're here to gloat."

I let out a theatrical gasp. "I would never." My grin spreads and Sloane's gaze drops to my lips. She likes to pretend she doesn't really want to get to know me, but every time her eyes fuse to my scar, a little crease flickers between her brows. "If you let me in, I'll tell you how I got that scar you can't help but stare at."

The look she gives me is one of pure horror. Blush crawls up her neck and brightens her cheeks. "I was not . . . I didn't . . ." She huffs and raises her chin. "You're the *worst*."

All that fury combined with all that shyness, all her lethal ability wrapped in an easily flustered package. She's so fucking adorable. It takes everything in me not to laugh, and she can tell.

Sloane leans over the threshold, her fingers gripped to the edge of the door as she tries to keep me from seeing inside her room. Her furious gaze scours my face. "I'm a serial killer, you know," she hisses. "I could break into your room while you sleep and suck your eyeballs right out of your head with the industrial vacuum that Francis uses to clean the cat hair from the hideous lobby carpet."

"I'm sure you could, Blackbird. No doubt." My grin spreads and I raise my hands in a truce, though Sloane doesn't seem convinced. "So, you gonna invite me in or what?"

"No, actually." Sloane whips the key card from the holder next to the door and stuffs it in the back pocket of her jeans as she pushes past me. The door closes behind her with a loud *click*. "I've gotta be somewhere."

My feet seem glued to the floor as I watch Sloane stride down the hallway, tossing the strap of her bag across her body as she goes.

"Gotta be . . . *what?*" I jog after her and match her stride, examining her profile as she marches down the hallway with a shit-eating smirk. "'*Be somewhere*'? Where?"

"*Somewhere*, Rowan. Or did you forget this is a competition?" she asks. She tries to hide that growing grin but she can't.

My heart slams my chest wall as I realize she's a little more done up than usual. A white cashmere sweater. Her makeup is the same as she's worn it the last three days since we arrived, with winged eyeliner and black mascara and matte red lipstick, but she's changed out her multiple earrings to a different set of gold pieces, some with stones that shine beneath her dark locks.

My mouth goes bone-dry.

"Are you going on a date?" I ask as we turn a corner and head for the wide stairway that leads to the lobby.

Sloane sighs. "I wouldn't call it a *date*, per se . . ."

"Then where are you going? You know, for like . . . safety purposes and whatnot . . ."

Sloane snorts. "You think I need your protection, pretty boy?"

No. But also yes.

"I should come with you, just in case. Wouldn't want something like Briscoe's to happen again," I say as we enter the lobby.

Sloane draws to a halt and turns to face me. "No, Rowan, you can't come. What if it *is* a date? That would be so awkward." She pats my chest and grins. "Don't worry, I'll fill you in on all the gory details later."

With a final tap on my chest that's really more like a slap, she turns and strides away.

"But . . . I was the one who was supposed to be gloating," I call after her as she reaches the lobby exit.

"Sorry, not sorry," she chimes. She flips me the bird before she slips through the doors, leaving only an echoing thud behind.

I stand in her wake, stunned. A wave of confusion and worry

and jealousy crashes through my chest. In one fell swoop, I've been filled with a fucking ocean of it.

What the fuck?

"Sloane," I call out after her, marching to the door. I thrust it open with more force than necessary and let it hit the door stopper with a satisfying thud of wood against the rubber-coated metal. "*Sloane*, goddammit . . ."

I look left and right. I hold my breath and listen.

Nothing.

My hand drives through my hair. I'm not sure if I'm more irritated that I might be on the losing end of our first game, or that Sloane is on a maybe-date with some wanker from buttfuck nowhere.

I strain to hear anything but crickets, but there's still no sign of Sloane.

"*Fuck.*"

I barrel toward the lobby door and toss it open with more force than necessary as I stalk back into the hotel and head to my room. I pace there for a while as I consider my options. Maybe I should go out and find the local pub and get shitfaced. But what if she runs into someone like Briscoe or Watson? Briscoe must have landed a lucky hit—the bloke was as sedentary as a fucking boulder. But Watson was a crafty bastard. What if she's cornered by someone like that? What if she's trapped and I can't find her? What if she calls for help and I'm pissed drunk at the tavern singing "Country Roads"?

I never expected I'd be pacing my room as I stress over the whereabouts of the fucking Orb Weaver, my heart racing and palms sweaty, worried about whether she might get hurt.

The ding of an incoming text is the only thing that stops me from wearing a hole into the floor.

| I'm fine.

I snort.

| I wasn't concerned.

A complete lie, obviously. I sit on the edge of the bed as I try to resist the urge to resume my track across the room, my knee bouncing.

| Oh good.

| In that case, don't wait up 😈

"What the *fuck* . . ."
I barely temper the urge to hurtle my phone against the wall, electing to clutch it in an iron grip and punch the mattress instead. It's wildly unsatisfying to punch a fucking mattress, by the way.
So I resume pacing.
After a while, I give up on the walking and try to do some research on the local area, but I come up with next to nothing, just like all my efforts over the past three days. The only thing I've found of significance is a handful of news articles. Random stories, nothing to tie the pieces to a suspect. A missing hiker, just like Francis said. Another dead body in a ravine. A car with New

York plates dredged from the Kanawha River. How the fuck Lachlan put together that there's a serial killer in the area, I have no idea. In fact, I'm starting to think he sent us here as a hoax.

I give up and flop on my bed to stare at the ceiling.

It's three hours later when I finally hear the quiet click of Sloane's door closing as she slips into her room next to mine.

Three fucking hours.

Besides the fact that she could have won our game in that amount of time, she also could have done all kinds of *other* things. Been on a date, for one. Maybe she had dinner somewhere other than this hotel with Francis's frozen peas and unseasoned, overcooked pork chops that I'll probably crack a tooth on before the week is out.

. . . Maybe she hooked up with some guy.

A groan rumbles in my throat and I turn over to suffocate myself in the floral pattern of the cheap polyester duvet.

"Rowan, you *feckin' eejit*," I snarl into the indifferent mattress. "This game is already blowing up your feckin' face and it's *day three*."

As if on cue, the sound of music comes from next door.

The volume is low, but I can make out a few of the lyrics through the paper-thin walls, and then the sound of Sloane's voice as she sings along with the occasional bar of the song.

Though I'm relieved she's back in one piece, I still drag a pillow over my head and try to muffle the sound, mostly to stop myself from marching over there to demand she tell me what she was up to, even though it's none of my fucking business and I might not want to know.

The pillow doesn't work, of course. And not just because it's as thin as a fucking tissue. It's probably because I'm straining to listen even though I'm pretending not to.

The song changes and Sloane's quiet voice disappears.

The absence of her presence stretches on, scratching at my skull. Against my better judgment, I roll off the bed and head to the wall that separates us before leaning forward to press my ear to the faded damask wallpaper.

The music is a little clearer, the volume still low. I hear her mattress creak. And then a gentle buzzing sound.

"Jesus, Mary, and Joseph," I whisper, dragging my hands down my face. What I would not give to be in that room right now. Sloane's raspy moan sets my blood on fire. My cock is already rock-fucking-hard.

I'm about to step back from the wall. I really am. I'm starting to lean away when I hear a single word pass her lips.

Rowan.

Or maybe *sewin'*. Or *Cohen*. Or *Samoan*. Can't really be sure. I'll just go with *Rowan*.

My blood is fucking volcanic. My heart thunders. Every cell in my body screams with need. It takes everything in me to start moving away again, but then I hear something strange coming from farther down the wall.

A quiet groan.

I creep toward the source of the sound.

Another groan. A garbled whisper. When I press my ear to the surface, I still catch the faint buzz of Sloane's toy. But much closer is the distinctive sound of someone wanking off.

I recoil from the wall and note the structure. About two-thirds down, toward where it joins the back of the room, there's a right angle where the wall comes farther into the living space. So I make my way there, each step careful and silent.

Heel. Toe. Heel. Toe.

I stop at the protrusion of the wall and press my ear next to the brass frame of a portrait painting.

A man's whisper finds me over the rhythmic sound of a hand pumping an erection. *"Yes, baby . . . just like that . . ."*

Rage floods my veins.

I step back and scan the room for something I can use to destroy the fucking wall before I have to resort to using my bare hands. My gaze lands on the nightstand and sticks there. If inanimate objects had feelings, the brass lamp next to the bed would be shitting itself.

I march over to it and rip it from the plug, gripping its long body like a baseball bat as I turn toward the section of the wall where the pervert is hidden. I'm just about to take my first swing when the eyes of the painting flick open. A real set of human eyes stare back at me and widen with alarm.

"Oh shit," a man's voice whispers.

My instant of shock dissolves into fury as the eyes disappear, leaving dark and empty holes behind. *"Motherfucker."*

I rush the wall and smash the painting with my weapon, lurching halfway into the tiny, hidden room when the thin canvas gives way with nothing behind it. I don't even catch sight of the other man—I can only hear him scurry away like the fucking rat he is.

Sloane's shriek rises above the chaos from the next room over, her string of expletives merging into a cascade of vitriol.

"Rowan Kane, you fucking Irish perverted weirdo WHAT THE FUCK are you doing I'm going to FUCK YOU UP—"

"No, no, no," I protest, though she doesn't hear me over the continued string of swears and now crashes of sound. She must be hurtling her belongings at the wall. My imagination instantly takes me right to whatever vibrator she was just using as a heavy *thunk* slams against the plasterboard. I stumble backward into my room and out to the corridor, the lamp still clutched in my hand as I rush to her room and pound on the door. It swings open before I've even finished the third knock.

Sloane is fucking *fuming.*

"There was a man in the wall," I blurt out.

"I know," she snarls as she shoves me with both hands. "His name is *Rowan Kane* and he has *no fucking boundaries* because he's a fucking pervy weirdo—"

"No, I swear—"

"Were you spying on me getting myself off?"

"No," I protest, but she glares at me as though utterly unconvinced that I'm telling the truth. It doesn't help my case that she's wearing a tiny pair of sleep shorts and a spaghetti-strap tank top, and she's probably able to hear the *no bra* alarm blaring on repeat in my head. "Okay, I *heard* you but I stepped *away* from the wall—"

"Rowan—"

"And then I heard something else," I say, grabbing her wrist with my free hand. I tow her behind me. She squirms and protests, but I refuse to let her go. "You're right, there was someone watching you in the wall. And he took off before I had a chance to see his face, let alone bludgeon it with a lamp."

We stop at the gaping hole where the ruined painting hangs askew and I drop Sloane's wrist so she can peer into the narrow room. She leans in, twisting to assess the exit point to a hidden corridor in the back wall.

"*Motherfucker,*" she whispers.

"Right? That's what I said."

Sloane turns to me, her arms crossed over her chest. I expect to see lingering anger or suspicion, not her eyes dancing in the dim light and the murderous grin that sneaks across her lips. "I fucking knew it."

A heartbeat later, Sloane is marching past me.

"Wait . . . what's going on?" I follow in her wake to stop at her door as she tosses on a plaid shirt, not bothering with the buttons. She slips on her sneakers and whips her sheathed hunting blade from the floor, and then she's pushing past me again to stalk down the corridor toward the staircase. I toss the lamp into her room with a crash of broken glass and jog after her, catching up as she hurries down the stairs.

"What are you doing?"

"I'm boobing boobily, Rowan. What does it look like?"

"You're . . . *what?*"

"Chasing that motherfucker down, that's what."

"*Who?*"

"Francis," she says as she storms through the lobby. "Francis Ross."

All the pieces click into place, the picture coming into view. The car in the river. The plates from New York. When the right victims made the wrong decisions and wound up at the Cunningham Inn, he watched them. And sometimes he killed them.

He watched Sloane. Maybe he would have tried to kill her too.

Rage stains my vision red as we burst out of the lobby and into the night.

The thought that he could have hurt her collides with another realization, stopping me dead in the parking lot as Sloane storms forward on a paved path that winds around the side of the hotel, leading toward the caretaker's house. "That emo wannabe fuck-boy with the pink tie is the killer? And you went on a *date* with that wanker?"

Sloane snorts a laugh but doesn't stop. "Gross."

"Sloane—"

"It's a competition, Butcher," she says as she reaches the corner of the hotel. She doesn't even look over her shoulder as she gives me the finger and leaves me with two parting words: "Get fucked."

Sloane turns the corner with a devilish cackle, her running footsteps consumed by shadow.

"Like hell," I hiss.

And then I take off after her into the night.

CUBISM ERA

Rowan

Sloane's figure is little more than a silhouette as she runs up the hill toward an old black house, the steep peaks of the roof jutting toward the moon like javelins. Wedges of yellow light spill from the windows, down the steep garden and the path that cuts through it, giving me just enough illumination to spot my quarry.

My grin is feral as I eat the distance between us.

I run full-force into Sloane and take her out in a rugby tackle. We twist in the air so I suffer the brunt of the hit. Grass and gravel grind into my forearms as I slide to a halt and roll us over to pin her beneath me.

Sloane's heavy breaths flood my senses with ginger and vanilla. She blows a lock of hair from her eyes and glares at me before she squirms beneath my weight. "Get the fuck off. He's *mine*."

"No can do, Peaches."

"Call me that again, and I swear to God I'll chop your balls off."

"Whatever you say, Blackbird." I grin and give her a swift kiss on her cheek, the feel of her soft and yielding flesh branded into memory the moment my lips touch her skin. "See ya."

I push away and run, the delicious sound of her frustrated protest the most beautiful melody behind me.

My heart thunders and my legs burn as I sprint up the steep hill. I'm nearly at the low wrought iron fence surrounding the house when the sound of an engine cuts through the night.

Francis is running.

I detour and follow the line of the fence toward the driveway where light tumbles down the asphalt from the vehicle in the garage. I reach the edge of the pavement and scoop up a rock from the border just as the garage door slides open and the car barrels out of the building.

So I do what any sane person would do.

I jump on the fucking hood.

Sloane yells my name. Tires screech. I lock eyes with the driver as his panic collides with my determination.

With my body flat against the hood, I grip the edge of it with one hand and smash my rock into the windshield with the other. I don't stop, not as we pick up speed, not even when the car swerves as the driver attempts to dislodge me. I deliver hit after hit. Glass crumbles with my repeated blows. It bites into my knuckles. It slides into my skin when I punch through to the other side and drop the rock to reach for the steering wheel.

A panicked cry rises above the chaos.

"Rowan, tree!"

I pull my arm free of the windshield and let go of the hood to slide off the vehicle and land hard on my side. My grunt of pain is swallowed by a symphony of metal as the front bumper folds around an oak.

I'm on my feet in an instant. Heavy breaths tear from my chest. Rage descends like a red curtain as I watch the slow, labored movement of the disoriented driver within the smoking hunk of metal.

"Jesus fucking Christ, Rowan, are you—"

Sloane's concern is cut short as I wheel on her to snatch her throat in my sticky hand. I crowd her space, push her backward with every step as alarm and defiance churn in her eyes. She grips my arm with both hands but doesn't try to fight me as I force her away from the car. Only when she's off the driveway and shielded by the deep shadows of a tree do I stop. But I don't let her go.

A percussion drums behind me, a metronomic thump drowned by the veil of my heartbeat ringing in my ears as I stare down into Sloane's glassy eyes. The delicate column of her throat shifts beneath my bloody palm.

"Rowan," she whispers.

"*Mine.*"

Her eyes shine in the moonlight. "Okay." She nods in my grip. "He's yours."

I draw her in closer and glare into the inky abyss of her fear and fortitude, not stopping until her warm exhalations fan across my face. The slices lining my forearm burn as her chest grazes the ruined flesh with every breath. "Sloane . . ."

A groan of warped metal and a string of curses end the pounding behind me.

"Stay here," I say, and with one finger at a time, I release her from my grasp.

I take one final look at her, my blood little more than a glistening black smear on her skin, before I pivot on my heel and stride away.

My pace quickens when I spot my prize as he limps from the vehicle. One foot scrapes behind him, a broken arm clutched to his chest. He turns as my footsteps draw closer, his eyes wide as they land on my wicked grin.

"I'm going to love every fucking second of this," I say.

Francis is already begging for mercy when I grasp the back of his shirt. I clutch his hideous pink tie in my fist to strangle him with it but it pulls free of his neck.

I glare at the fabric balled in my fist. Then at Francis. Then back again. "A fucking clip-on? What are you, twelve?"

"P-please, man, let me g-go," he begs beneath me. Tears glass his eyes as I toss the tie onto the driveway and grip him with both hands.

My rage burns my throat but I swallow it down. "Tell me what you were doing in the wall."

His eyes flick to our surroundings, maybe hunting for Sloane, maybe searching for a savior. "I wasn't g-gonna hurt her," he says when his attention lands on me. "I was j-just watching."

His fear is like a drug that invades every cell in my body, every desire coursing through my veins. A slow grin creeps across my lips as he struggles when I shift my grip and catch his throat. "Two things. First, I don't fucking believe you. I think you were going to watch her and then your plan was to kill her. Wouldn't be the first time, would it, Francis."

"No, I swear—"

"Second, and this is the most important part, so listen up,

motherfucker." I raise his trembling body off the asphalt until his ear is next to my lips. "That woman you were watching . . . ?"

My fingers tighten around his throat as he desperately nods. "She is *mine.*"

I'm sure he begs. But I don't hear his pleas. They're fucking useless words that won't save him now.

I drop Francis on the pavement and tumble after him into madness.

My first blow hits his jaw. The next strikes his temple. One fist after the other. Jaw. Temple. Jaw. Temple. I miss and shatter his nose with a satisfying crunch and he wails. Blood spews from his nostrils to coat my knuckles. His jaw breaks next with a pop. Broken teeth slice his lips and fall to the driveway like chips of porcelain. Like memories I want to forget. So I fight them away. I grit my teeth and hit harder.

The scent of blood and piss and asphalt. The gurgle of choked breaths. The slip of his split flesh against my fists. It's fucking fuel. I think of him watching her. I think of her face. And I keep hitting. Even when he seizes. Even when he drowns in his blood.

Even when he dies.

I'm beating on a hunk of ruined flesh when I finally stop. Breaths saw from my lungs as I place one hand on the warm asphalt and stare down at my knuckles where pain throbs with every heartbeat. It's a welcome sensation. Not because I deserve it, but because he did, and I fucking delivered. Destruction with my bare hands. Suffering where it was meant to be found.

Only now does a sliver of fear burrow into my chest.

"Sloane," I call to the shadows.

I'm met with only silence.

"*Sloane.*"

Nothing.

Shit.

Shit shit shit.

A fresh wave of adrenaline floods the chambers of my heart as I lean back on my heels and scan every shade of darkness that surrounds me. The excitement of the kill is washed away as a tidal wave of panic rolls in.

I've fucking scared her off.

She probably ran back to the hotel to grab her belongings and book it out of here. The screech of car tires will likely be the next thing I hear as she leaves and never looks back.

And can I blame her?

We're both monsters, after all.

Different monsters, thrust together in the cage I've created.

Sloane is calculating, methodical. She waits and weaves a web and nets her prey. And while I like to stage a scene from time to time, to display some theatrics, this kill right here? This mess of torn flesh and exposed bone? This is in my *soul*. I'm fucking feral at the core.

Maybe it's best that she gets as far away from me as she can.

Even still, it burns in my chest, a hot needle that's slipped between my ribs to lodge in the very center of my heart. It's a place I never thought could feel pain or longing anymore. But it does.

I drive a sticky hand through my hair as my shoulders fall.

"Goddammit, Rowan, you *feckin' eejit*." My eyes press closed. "Sloane . . ."

"I'm here."

My gaze meets the shadows as Sloane emerges from their grip.

The breath I take feels the same as it does after you dive too deep, unsure if you'll reach the surface in time. The relief is cellular when the air hits my lungs.

I don't move as she comes closer, her steps tentative, her body illuminated by the dim light that spills from the ruined car, her throat still streaked with my blood. Her gaze takes in every detail, from the film of sweat on my face to the swollen flesh of my hands. Only when she's assessed me and stopped by my side does her attention fall to the cooling body on the driveway.

"You okay?" she asks. She looks to me with a flicker of a crease between her brows.

I want to reach for her, to feel the comfort of her unfamiliar touch. But I don't. I just watch.

"He looks like a Picasso," she continues as she nods toward Francis's destroyed face. Her hand flows in his direction with bird-like grace. "Eyes over here, nose over there. Very artsy, Butcher. Embracing your cubism era. Cool."

I still don't answer. I don't know what to say. Maybe it's the mounting physical pain. Or it could be the waning adrenaline. But I think it's just Sloane. The echo of the loss of her and the relief of her presence.

Sloane gives me a faint lopsided smile and lowers to my level, her eyes soldered to mine. Her grin doesn't last. Her voice is quiet, nearly a whisper when she says, "Cat got your tongue, pretty boy? Didn't think I'd see the day."

A breath shudders past my lips as a drop of sweat falls from my hair to slide down my cheek like a tear. "Are you okay?"

Sloane gives a gentle laugh and her dimple appears next to her lip. "Yeah, of course. Why wouldn't I be?" Her words hang unanswered in the air as my gaze drops to the body. Surprise ignites in my chest when her delicate fingers alight on the back of my hand, her touch feather-light as she traces a streak of blood that drips from a split over my knuckle. "I should be asking you that."

"I'm fine," I say with a shake of my head. We both know it's a lie, just like we know her words were too. She was going to leave. I have no doubt.

But she didn't. She's still here. Maybe not for long, but at least for now.

"This is going to take a while to clean up," Sloane says as her hand leaves mine and she stands. Her gaze travels the length of the corpse next to us before it flows to the battered car. "Good thing I've still got a few days off. We're probably going to need it."

Sloane extends her hand and I stare at the lines crossing her palm. Life and death. Love and loss and fate.

"We?" I ask.

"Yeah, *we*," she says. Her smile has a softness to its edges. Her hand moves closer, her fingers spread wide. "But we'd better start with you first."

I slip my hand into hers and rise from the black road.

We leave Francis on the driveway and head to his house in silence. He lives alone, but we're careful nonetheless. We split up and sweep through the home to meet once more in the living room when we're sure it's clear.

"Is this where you were tonight?" I ask as I cast a glance around the room. It's decorated in much the same way as the hotel, with antiques and faded paintings, furniture with worn upholstery but shining wooden framework, the details polished. Sloane nods when my gaze lands on her. "Doesn't really seem like his style."

"Yeah, I thought the same. He talked a bit about his family. He said they've been here for generations. Sounds like he was trapped by the ghosts of someone else's past," she says as she stops at the mantel and leans toward an old railway switch lantern.

"It's the right kind of house for ghosts, I guess."

Sloane turns to me and flashes a quick, faint smile before she nods toward a hallway. "Come on. Let's get you fixed up."

I trail after her like a wraith at her heels. We stop at the bathroom where she motions for me to sit on the edge of the tub as she gathers supplies from the medicine cabinet. She unpacks a roll of gauze, readies bandages with antibiotic cream. When everything is laid out, she saturates a sterile pad with isopropyl alcohol and kneels in front of me to clean the split skin on my knuckles.

"You're going to wind up with some scars," she says as she dabs at the deepest wound, leaving an uncomfortable sting behind.

"Already got some."

Sloane looks up from her work. Her gaze falls to my lip before it returns to my hand, her touch so gentle despite the suffering I know she could mete out, if she wanted to.

I watch in silence as she takes the first bandage from the counter and fits it over the torn flesh before she preps another gauze pad, starting the process over again with the next cut.

"My father gave it to me," I say.

Sloane's gaze flicks up to mine with a question in her eyes.

"The scar on my lip. The one you keep staring at because it's so damn sexy."

Sloane huffs a laugh. Her hair shields most of her face from view as she keeps her attention on my hand, but I can still see the blush through the spaces between her raven strands. "I thought I told you once not to let your prettiness get to your head," she says.

"Just had to check that you still think I'm pretty."

Sloane keeps her head down but gives me a flash of her eyes as they roll. I grin when they fix me with a vicious glare. "I also told you that you're the worst, and that still rings true."

"So cruel, Blackbird. You wound me yet again," I say as I press my free hand to my heart. This wins me a smile before she hides her face away. Sloane places the next bandage on my knuckles and I don't have the heart to tell her they'll probably fall off in the shower I intend to take tonight to soothe my sore shoulders. I resolve to steal the package of remaining bandages when we leave so she won't know.

"Is he still around? Your dad?" she asks to break me away from thoughts of what else might be here worth taking, some little memento of our first game, perhaps.

"No." I swallow. Secrets I never share beg to be released whenever she's around, and it's no different with this one. "Lachlan and I killed him. It was the same night he gave me this scar. Smashed my face with a broken plate."

The motion of her hand slows as Sloane watches me. "And your mom?"

"Died giving birth to Fionn."

Sloane's shoulders rise and fall with a deep, heavy breath. Her bottom lip folds between her teeth as she holds my eyes. "I'm sorry."

"Don't be. Wouldn't have wound up here if everything hadn't happened the way it did," I say. I fold a lock of her hair behind her ear so I can see her freckles. "I have no regrets about where I am."

And there it is. That blush. A pink so addictive that it haunts me. I want to hoard these images of Sloane, her face flushed, her eyes dancing, her smile desperate to be freed.

"You're the worst. You know that, right?"

"Technically, I'm the best. Because I just won."

Sloane might groan, but she can't help but laugh too. "And I'm sure you're going to remind me of this regularly."

"Probably."

"You know, even though I didn't win, which totally sucks, by the way," she says, pausing to narrow her eyes at me before her expression softens into a faint smile, "I had fun. I feel . . . good. Better. Like this is what I needed. So . . . thank you, Rowan."

She smooths the adhesive of the last bandage over my skin with a slow pass of her thumb and then her touch falls away. Then she rises and backs away to stop at the threshold of the door, her hand curled around her arm.

"I'll go start on the driveway," Sloane says, and with a final flash of an unsure smile, she disappears.

I wait for a long moment. Her quiet footsteps lead to the front door and then all sound in the house dies away.

She could slip away into the night. Leave all this behind. Do whatever it takes to never be found.

But for the next three days, every time I think she might disappear, she proves me wrong.

UNDER GLASS

Sloane

You know what I did this morning?

deep sigh

I decorated my toaster strudel

Fascinating. I'm riveted.

Also, toaster strudel? Isn't that meant for hormonal teenagers who need significant quantities of processed sugar to function in the AM? I thought you were a grown-ass man

A man who appreciates mass-produced flaky pastry and icing that can be used to spell "WINNER" in vanilla-ish frosting

| And I'm 100% positive you'll love me
| one day

It's been six months.

Six months since I last saw him. Six months of daily messages. Six months of Rowan telling me about how he's celebrating his win. Six months of memes and jokes and texts and sometimes calls, just to say hello. And every day, I look forward to it. Every day, it warms me up, lighting places that have always been dark.

And every night when I close my eyes, I still picture him in that sliver of moonlight on the driveway in West Virginia, bent on one knee, like he was about to swear an oath. A knight cloaked in silver and shadow.

I think you were going to watch her and then your plan was to kill her, he'd said. Francis begged for mercy in the grip of Rowan's hand. And whatever Rowan said next was just a whisper, but those words unleashed the demon at the heart of him. There was nothing between him and the rage that burned him from the inside. No mask left to hide behind.

"He really beat the shit out of him," I say to Lark as I glance one final time at our latest text exchange before setting my phone aside. I place a bowl of popcorn between us and pick up Winston to plop the perpetually disgruntled feline on my lap. It's been six months since I've seen Lark too. In her typical fashion, she was offered a last-minute opportunity to tour with an indie band and seized it, and has been bouncing around from one small town and hipster city venue to the next. And she looks happy for it. Glowing.

"Was it hot?" she asks as she piles her long golden waves into a haphazard bun at the top of her head. Somehow, it always comes out perfectly messy. "Kinda sounds hot."

"Pretty hot, yeah. Had me worried for a minute, though. I'm used to . . . controlled. And this was raw. Definitely the antithesis of control." My gaze falls to the crocheted throw beneath my legs, one that Lark's aunt made for me the year we left Ashborne Collegiate Institute, when Lark's family took me in and repaid a debt they never owed. I stick my fingers in the little holes between the looped yarn, and when I look up again Lark is watching me, her clear blue eyes fixed to the contours of my face. "I nearly left him there."

Lark's head tilts. "And you feel bad about that?"

"Yeah."

"Why?"

"I don't think he would have left me if the situation was reversed."

"But you didn't leave."

I shake my head.

"Why not?"

My chest aches. It does every time I remember the way he called my name like a broken prayer. The defeated slump of his shoulders is a vivid image in my mind, even now. "He seemed so vulnerable, despite what he'd just done. I couldn't leave him like that."

Lark's lip twitches as though she's holding back a smile. "That's nice." She nibbles at the corner of her lower lip and I roll my eyes. "It's sweet. You stayed. You made another friend."

"Shut up."

"Maybe a future *boyfriend*."

I bark an incredulous laugh. "*No.*"

"Maybe a *soul mate*."

"You're my soul mate."

"Then a best friend. With *benefits*."

"Please stop."

"I can see it now," Lark says, her eyes sparkling as she sits up straighter, one graceful hand held aloft. She clears her throat. "*He can show you the world . . .*" she sings. "*Glittering something shiny . . . 'I think our love can do anything that we want it to.'*"

"You did not just mash up a butchered version of *Aladdin* with *The Notebook*. You have the voice of an angel, Lark Montague, but that is atrocious."

Lark giggles and settles back into the couch as *Constantine* plays on my TV, a familiar backdrop in our limited roster of comfort movies. We watch for a moment in silence as Keanu traps a spider under a glass. "He could come to my house and catch spiders any day," she says as she twinkles her fingers toward the screen. "Dark and broody and grumpy? Sign me up."

"I'm pretty sure you've said that every one of the two hundred times we've watched this."

"It's peak Keanu. You can't blame me." Lark sighs and takes a fistful of popcorn from the bowl. "I'm in a dry spell. You'd think there would be some hot musician types on the road but they're all way too emo. I just want to be tossed around a bit. Manhandled, you know? Call me a dirty little slut and I'm all for it. These cry-into-the-mic types aren't doing it for me."

I snort a laugh and toss a piece of popcorn in the air in a failed attempt to catch it with my mouth. "Don't talk to me about dry spells. I'm going to need a supercomputer to calculate my days of celibacy at this rate."

"Or—and hear me out," Lark says with a slap to my arm when I groan. "You could take a little trip to Boston to visit your Butcher man and see about ending that dry spell. Fill that well, sister."

"Gross."

"Fill it up until it's gushing. *Overflowing*."

"You're disturbing."

"I bet he would oblige."

"We've literally just been through this. We're *friends*."

"And you could be friends with extra perks. There's no rule book to say you can't fuck a friend and still stay friends," Lark says. I try to ignore her and keep my eyes on the screen even though her gaze weighs like a hot veil against my cheek. When I finally look over, her teasing smile has faded into a knowing one. "But you're scared."

I look away again and swallow.

"I get it," she says. Her hand folds over my wrist and she squeezes until I look at her. Lark's smile is sunshine, and she's always ready to share its bright light. "You're right."

My brow quirks. "About what?"

"That you'll probably never meet someone like him again. That he's probably the only one out there like you. That you could mess it up. Or he could let you down. Or that maybe your friendship could go up in flames. You're right about all those worries that are circling around in your head. Maybe all of them are true. But maybe it shouldn't matter, because everyone messes up. We all let each other down once in a while. And sometimes the best things come out of the fire."

My voice is soft when I tell her a simple truth. "You've never let me down."

"What if I do one day? Do you really think you wouldn't give me the grace to correct my mistake?"

"Of course I would, Lark. I love you."

"Then give Rowan a little grace too."

My conflicted sigh does nothing to cleanse a sudden burst of nerves in my chest. Lark jostles my wrist until I roll my eyes. "Okay, okay. If I have a meeting in Boston, I'll maybe see if he's free to hang out."

"You don't have to have some excuse. I bet he'd love to see you. Just *go*. Even if it is just to be friends in person for more than once a year. You miss him, right?"

Christ, I do. I miss his faint accent and his big smile and his ever-present jokes. I miss his teasing and his warmth and how easy it is to just be myself around him, how nice it is to lay the mask aside. I miss the way he makes me feel like I'm not an aberration, but unique.

"Yeah," I whisper. "I do."

"Then go," Lark says as she snuggles herself beneath the blanket and grins at Keanu. "Go and have fun. You can do that more than once annually, you know."

We fall into silence as I think about it.

And I continue thinking about it.

. . . For three more months.

And now I stand huddled in the entryway of a department store across the street from 3 in Coach for longer than any sane person

77

probably would, just watching the waitstaff and the patrons as the lunch rush tapers off to a quieter hum of activity. In true stalker fashion, I've looked up every article about the restaurant since its opening day seven years ago. Every photograph, to the end of the Google search results. Hundreds of reviews. I even found the blueprints from the planning permit submission. I could probably walk the place blindfolded and I've never even been inside.

Maybe it's time to change that.

My bottom lip slides between my teeth as I drive my hands into the pockets of my wool trench and step into the bitter bite of an unseasonably cold spring wind.

Entering the restaurant, I'm greeted by the sound of trendy yet soulless music and a blond bombshell hostess with a sparkling smile.

"Welcome to 3 in Coach. Do you have a reservation with us today?"

A pang of nerves rolls through my stomach as I glance toward the open expanse of dark wood tables and exposed brick. "No, sorry."

"No problem. For how many?"

"Just me."

The woman's gaze rakes over my hair where it's laying across my shoulder before meeting my eyes with a chagrined smile, as though she was caught doing something she shouldn't. "Sure thing. Right this way."

I follow the hostess into the dining room, and before I can request a specific spot, she leads me to a semicircular booth along the back wall rather than one of the smaller tables in the center of the room. She takes the three unneeded place settings away and starts heading toward the kitchen, but a large group enters so she changes course and greets them instead.

The enormity of how stupid this is starts to seep into my veins like wriggling worms. I've let these unfamiliar emotions take over. Things like *longing.* And *loneliness.* It's as though I've been thrown into the ocean, drowning in the swell, and suddenly I realize I could have put my feet down all along. I could have stood up and kept my bearings. It was all just my imagination.

I should just leave. This is dumb. Dumb and so stalkery. Not in a sexy stalker way either. More like a weird, creepy serial-killer stalker way, which tracks. So I need to take off, before—

"Hey, my name is Jenna and I'll be your server this afternoon. Can I get you something to drink?"

I sit back, pretending like I wasn't just edging my way to the end of the booth, and glance up at Jenna. She's even more stunning than the hostess, her face lit with a genuine, broad smile and her thick auburn hair pulled back in a perfect ponytail.

Why am I doing this to myself?

"Alcohol . . ." I say.

Jenna beams, sensing my anxiety. It's something that's always worked in my favor. A woman like Jenna, who unfolds the cocktail menu and suggests a few of her favorite drinks, would never suspect I'd be capable of murdering anyone.

All she sees is a nervous data scientist, weirded out by the beautiful, friendly, outgoing woman who's just ordered me a frozen cucumber margarita that she insists is her favorite. It's true, I am nervous and weirded out, not only by the drink option I apparently just ordered, but by this whole scenario of being an intruder in a space that feels too sacred to bend to my obsessions.

Maybe I need to big myself up. Positive thoughts, remember my strengths and all that shit. Because just as much as I might appear quiet and spooked on the outside, I am also a serial killer who enjoys vivisection and a bit of cartography.

And I also enjoy an annual murder competition.

And I might be increasingly attracted to another serial killer and now I'm not so sure if maybe Lark was right last year, that I'm losing my shit.

I try to latch on to the rational thoughts that are still swimming in the anxiety soup of my head like drowning flies. *Rowan might not even be here today.* Okay, that's a lie, I hacked into the restaurant schedule and he'd marked himself down for lunch service. *So what if he's here? Rowan is in the kitchen. If I got up to leave right now, he wouldn't even know I was ever here.*

I shuffle from the edge of the cushion to the middle of the booth where I'm sheltered by the high and curving backrest. It takes a minute to focus enough to actually read the menu, even though it's short and well structured, but by the time Jenna returns with my bright green drink, I'm ready to order.

And then stew in silence.

And drink in silence.

And eat in more silence.

I take out my burner phone and contemplate texting Rowan, but I end up putting it away when the pressure only makes me more antsy. I opt for a pen and my notebook instead and flip to a new sheet of paper.

I pour my focus into translating the image in my mind into ink. The whole universe can collapse into a single page. Distractions ease, and my thoughts follow the lines of black ink, ideas and conversations existing in strokes of darkness rendered by my hand. Even when Jenna brings the charred Brussels sprouts and coconut curry soup, I barely notice, oblivious to the world around me.

At least, I am until the door opens and a boisterous group of seven enters the restaurant. I look up to lock eyes with a man I've never seen, but one whose features are unmistakably familiar. Dark hair. Full lips slanted in a smirk. Tattoos that climb the side of his neck from beneath his collar. His arm is draped over the shoulders of a tiny brunette woman, the rings on his tattooed knuckles glinting beneath her perfect waves. He's tall and powerfully built. Even with his leather jacket and thick sweater I can tell he's basically a wall of muscle. And with those dark, predatory eyes that sharpen like a blade set to cut me, I know he's trouble.

Big fucking trouble by the name of Lachlan Kane.

I break my gaze away as Jenna returns to my table with my dessert, a fig phyllo Napoleon. "I'm so sorry, but can I get a box for this and the bill, please? Something's come up and I have to get going."

Jenna's smile doesn't falter. "Of course, it's no problem. I'll be right back."

"Thanks."

When my gaze returns to Lachlan, his attention is on a long table in the center of the room where his friends are finding their places, some already seated, others chatting as they take off their coats. But the second I pull my jacket closer across the seat to slide it on, his eyes snap back to mine, amusement coloring their dark hues with the kind of light that sets me on edge.

I drop my focus to my sketch and force myself not to look up as I shrug my jacket over my shoulders and fasten the buttons with a slight tremor in my fingers. Jenna arrives with the boxed dessert and I give her more than enough cash to cover the bill before she heads toward Lachlan's table to gather drink orders. When I hear an Irish accent among the voices, I seize the opportunity to bolt, but not before tearing the drawing of a raven free from the notebook. Some part of me just wants to leave a little piece of myself behind, to exist in a place that means something to Rowan, if only for a moment. Maybe Jenna will throw it away. Or maybe she'll pin it up somewhere in the kitchen. Maybe it will remain here long after I've found a hole to crawl inside to die.

As soon as the sheet is torn free, I'm out of the booth.

I make it halfway to the door with hurried steps before a single word stops me dead.

"*Blackbird.*"

The voice carries across the restaurant and I'm pretty sure *everyone* is now staring at me.

I whisper a curse, taking a deep breath that fills to the bottom of my lungs in a futile attempt to rid my cheeks of a crimson flame. When I make a slow pivot on my heel, my eyes track to Lachlan first, whose smirk is nothing short of diabolical.

And then my gaze collides with Rowan's.

The sleeves of his chef coat are rolled to his elbows, a few flecks of orange dotting the otherwise pristine white fabric. The stains are the same color as my soup, and for some reason that makes the blush smolder even hotter in my cheeks. His black, baggy pants are impossibly sexy and adorable at the same time. But it's his expression that grips my throat in a vise. It's full of shock and confusion and excitement and something hot, something that burns me up from the inside. The combination short-circuits my brain until all that comes out of my mouth is a single, squeaked word. "Hey."

Rowan almost smiles.

. . . *Almost.*

"Meg," he barks, shifting his attention to the front door as he gestures toward me. "What the fuck?"

Meg the Hostess freezes in place, the color draining from her face as though her blood has been sucked out with a straw. "Oh my God, I'm so sorry, Chef. I meant to come tell you but got sidetracked."

Rowan's glare shifts to the exact booth where I was just sitting and then to Jenna who closes in on it with a spray bottle and a rag. The sheet of paper I left behind sits like a damning piece of evidence on the table, stark and obvious against the glossy black surface.

"Do not touch that fucking table," Rowan snaps.

Jenna's eyes widen as they shift between us, her lips folding between her teeth to clamp down around a smile as she turns on her heel and heads for the bar. Rowan watches her for a moment, his frown deepening when she tosses a grin over her shoulder.

His gaze lands on that fucking drawing.

And then it fixes on me.

"Sloane . . ." he says, taking a few cautious steps closer as though trying not to provoke a wild animal. "What are you doing here?"

Dying an agonizingly slow death of mortification, clearly. "Umm . . . eating?"

Rowan's navy eyes glimmer, a fleeting spark igniting in their depths. "In Boston, Blackbird. What are you doing in Boston?"

"I . . . I'm here for work. Meeting. A work meeting. Not like, here in the restaurant, obviously. In town. City. Boston city." *Dear God, make me stop.* I am *burning* hot, my wool jacket trapping my body heat and amplifying it until I'm positive my blood has turned to lava. Sweat itches between my shoulder blades and I try not to fidget, opting to back up a step toward the door rather than shedding my jacket to scratch my skin off.

Rowan's gaze flicks down to my feet and he halts his campaign to inch forward, a crease forming between his brows in a thoughtful frown. "Stay," he says, his voice low and quiet. "We can sit at the booth."

A nervous laugh bursts past my lips, its color darkened by my self-deprecating thoughts. The last place in the world I want to go is back to that booth where I left a drawing like some shy, pathetic middle schooler, confused and lovesick over her first crush.

So I do whatever any pathetic middle schooler would do. I take another step backward toward the door and lie my face off. "I've gotta get going, actually. But it was great seeing you."

I flash Rowan an apologetic smile before turning to stride toward the exit only to be stopped short by Lachlan, who's standing as a sentry between me and my escape. He raises a glass of whiskey to his lips and takes a sip around a devilish grin. I was so caught up in seeing Rowan and battling with my emotions that I didn't even notice him receive his drink, or rise from the table, or block my access to the door.

Shit.

"Well, well," Lachlan says through his shit-eating grin. "*Fuck. Off.*"

Rowan growls behind me. "Lachlan—"

"If it isn't the elusive Sloane Sutherland," Lachlan continues, swirling the ice in his glass. "I was beginning to think you were a figment of my brother's overactive imagination."

"Sit down, Lachlan," Rowan grits out. I glance over my shoulder to where he stands rigid a short distance behind me, his hands folded into tight fists.

"Whatever you say, little brother."

Lachlan raises his glass in a mock toast before sauntering off in the direction of my booth.

"Touch that fucking table and I will rip your goddamn hands off and use them to wipe my ass until the day I die," Rowan snarls.

Lachlan stops, turning slowly to give his brother a devious grin before he shrugs and starts back to his own table, passing close enough to the seething chef to clap him once on the shoulder and whisper something in his ear. Rowan's eyes darken, but they never leave mine. Even when my gaze darts around, every time it lands on him, he's there, waiting.

"Sloane—"

A blast of animated conversation enters the restaurant on the cool draft from the open door.

"Rowan! You're done for the day?"

I turn to watch a gorgeous blond woman enter the restaurant with two equally beautiful friends close on her heels, both of whom are engaged in an animated conversation full of laughter and confidence. The blonde strides straight for Rowan. She never wavers on the stilettos that accentuate her bare, tanned legs, her skin glowing as though she's just returned from some expensive spa vacation. She tosses Rowan a wide grin, oblivious to the tension she's just shattered in the room, the shards of it cutting me to the core.

"Hi, Anna," he says. Those two words seem full of resignation as the woman wraps an arm around his shoulder in a hug he doesn't return, though she doesn't seem to notice. When she lets him go, she turns, spotting me for the first time.

"Oh, I'm sorry, I just kind of barged in, didn't I?" She offers me what seems like a genuinely apologetic smile. I can tell she's trying to assess whether I'm a disgruntled customer, or maybe a food critic, or a vendor here to supply meat or vegetables, not that I look like the gardening type.

No, Anna. I'm clearly here to die of embarrassment.

"Anna, this is Sloane." Rowan pauses as though considering how he should elaborate on how he knows me, but nothing comes. "Sloane, this is my friend Anna."

"Hey, nice to meet you," she says, her expert smile transforming from apologetic to welcoming. "Are you going to join us?"

My throat is raw. My voice comes out a gravelly rasp, grating compared to Anna's smooth, bright tone. "No, but thanks for the offer. I've gotta get going."

"*Sloane—*"

"Nice seeing you, Rowan. Thank you for lunch, it was lovely," I say, rattling the box of fig Napoleon that I have the urge to throw into the nearest flaming dumpster where the rest of my life belongs.

I meet Rowan's gaze for only a moment, and I regret it as soon as I do. The resignation that was in his voice moments ago has found its way to his eyes, swirling with desperation and dismay. It's a terrible combination that turns the ache in my heart to a sharp, piercing pain.

I give him a final, fleeting smile, not waiting to see what effect it might have. The urge to run is so strong that I have to think about each hurried step I take to the door. There's probably not much dignity left for me to salvage, but at least I can force myself to walk.

So that's what I do. I walk away. Out the front door. Down the street. Not knowing where I'm going. Not remembering when I throw away the box of dessert. Not aware of when the first hot tear of embarrassment falls across my cheek.

I keep going, all the way to Castle Island, where I stop at the shore and look out across the dark water. And I stay there for a long time. Long enough that the walk back to the hotel seems like an endless trudge, like all my energy has been spent.

As soon as I walk through the door, I fire up my laptop long enough to rebook my flights to the earliest departure the next morning, then I slide into bed and fall into a restless sleep.

Can we talk?

I'm just getting on the plane.
Maybe when I get home?

Yeah of course, just let me know. Safe travels

Hey, you make it home okay the other day?

Yeah, sorry. Just been chaotic.
Work is full-on. I'm in meetings all day but I'll text you when I can

I'm sorry, my week got a bit out of control.

And I'm sorry for just showing up to your restaurant and not contacting you first. That was weird of me.

Each one of the past ten days since I got back from Boston has passed in a haze, and every time my phone has chimed with a message, my heart has rioted with a burst of nerves. I've been working myself up to get to this moment, but as I press send on my most recent message and place my burner phone face down on my lap, I'm already wondering if I should try to recall the text before Rowan has a chance to read it. I'm still staring at my carpet, wading through the depths of indecision when the phone buzzes on my lap.

It wasn't weird. I wish I'd known you were there. I wish you'd stayed.

I turn the phone off and set it on the coffee table, then drop my head into my palms and hope that they can absorb me into another world.

One where I don't have to feel anything.

Because revenge is easy.

But everything else is hard.

CREANCE

Rowan

I watch from behind the elm across the street as the kid I paid knocks on the yellow door of 154 Jasmine Street. The door opens a moment later and she's there, confusion etched on her beautiful face as she looks down at the paper bag the kid thrusts in her direction. I can't make out the question she asks him, but I catch his little shrug before I dart behind the tree to avoid Sloane's gaze as she scans the neighborhood. My grin spreads as I listen intently for the sound of the door closing and the kid's shuffling footsteps as he leaves the house to approach my hiding spot.

"All done, mister," he says as he grabs his bike where he left it leaning against the tree.

"She ask who it was from?"

"Yup."

"You tell her anything?"

"Nope."

"Good lad." I slip the kid fifty dollars and he stuffs the bills into the back pocket of his jeans. "Same time tomorrow. We'll meet at the mailbox down the street, yeah?"

"Cool. See ya."

With that, the kid takes off on his BMX, one hundred dollars richer to spend on candy or video games or whatever the hell twelve-year-olds buy these days. He's going to make out like a little demon if he sticks to our arrangement.

Give her the bag. Stick to the script. Fifty for the delivery, fifty when it's done.

I pull out my burner phone, bringing up my most recent text exchange with Sloane.

I wish you'd stayed, my last message said. And she didn't reply.

That was over a week ago. It's been almost three weeks since she was standing in 3 in Coach with a look of absolute mortification in her eyes, as though she'd dumped her heart out on the floor just to have it stomped on. It fucking burned through me in a way I never expected. I thought I might convince her to stay and talk, but the timing could not have been worse with our friends coming in for Lachlan's birthday lunch. In typical Sloane fashion, her first instinct was to take off, a feather in a north wind.

I can't let her pull away any further, or she'll slip through my fingers and I'll never get her back.

I'm peering around the tree trunk toward the house when the phone vibrates in my hand.

| Orzo...?

I lean against the bark and grin down at my phone.

| Did you deliver orzo pasta to my
| house??

| I have no idea what you're talking
| about.

| But…since it's there, you might
| as well get it out.

| And if there's parmesan in the
| bag, you should probably start
| grating that.

| Oh and mince some garlic too, if
| there is any.

| Are there mushrooms? Maybe
| wash those.

| Asparagus goes well as a side. Is
| there asparagus?

The phone rings and I force myself to wait for a moment before accepting the call.

"Can I help you, Blackbird?"

"What are you doing?" Her voice is wary, but I still detect the faint trace of amusement beneath her trepidation.

"I'm not sure what you mean."

"You delivered food to my house?" There's a pause. I imagine she's probably checking the windows, looking for any sign of me. "I have food, Rowan."

"Good for you. I think that qualifies you as a fully fledged adult."

I can almost hear Sloane's eyes rolling, can nearly feel the heat of the blush creeping into her cheeks, if I could touch that dusting of freckles that speckles her skin.

Her long, steady exhale is the only sound between us. Sloane's voice is melancholy and quiet when she asks, "What are you doing?"

"What I should have done the other day. I'm cooking with you," I say. "We're going to make it together. Put the phone on speaker and start grating the Parmesan."

Another pause weighs the thread between us until it feels like it'll snap.

My voice is low, the amusement burned away when I say, "I wish you would have stayed, Blackbird. I would have taken you back into the kitchen. We could have made something together."

"You were busy. I was . . . intruding."

"I would have made time for you. You're . . ." I swallow before I can say more than I should. "You're my friend. Maybe someday my best friend."

The silence stretches on so long that I pull the phone from my ear to check if the call disconnected. When Sloane's voice comes through the line, it's little more than a whisper but still cuts louder than a scream.

"You hardly know me," she says.

"Really? Because I bet I know the darkest parts of you better than anyone. Just like you know the darkest parts of me. And despite that, you still want to hang out with me. Most of the time, anyway." I smile when Sloane's breath of a soft laugh travels through the line. "So, I think that makes you my friend, whether you like it or not."

There's a long beat of silence, and then the sound of a drawer opening, cutlery rustling in its confines.

"I'm supposed to grate this whole block of cheese? It's the size of a small baby."

I know I must look ridiculous, grinning like a fucking lunatic next to a tree, but I don't give a shit. "How much do you like cheese?"

"A lot."

"Grate enough to make a baby head."

"Are you serious?"

"You said you like cheese. Get to work, Blackbird."

An unsure "okaaaay" filters through the line, though I'm sure she's talking to herself and not me. The metronomic sound of the hard Parmesan against the metal teeth of the grater sets a gentle percussion to my thoughts as I try to imagine what her kitchen might look like, Sloane standing at the counter with her raven hair tied back in a messy bun and some cool-as-shit old T-shirt tied at her waist. I could be in there with her, coming up behind her, trapping her against the counter, my cock pressed up to that fuck-ing round ass that I just want to bite, and then—

"After I've grated an infant's head's worth of cheese, what should I do next?" Sloane asks as the sound of the grater continues in the background. For a second I wonder if I might have moaned out loud.

I clear my throat, suddenly blanking on the ingredients I put in the bag for her. "Uhh, wash the asparagus and trim the ends off the stalks."

"Okay."

The grater continues with a steady beat. I run my hand through my hair and resolve to pull my shit together. "So, you said you were in Boston for work. A meeting?"

"Umm . . . yeah."

"What kind of meeting?"

"Investigator meeting."

"That sounds . . . terrifying."

Sloane lets go of a quiet laugh. "Yes and no. They're not investigators like *police* investigators. It's what we call study doctors who run our trials at their clinics. An investigator meeting is where we train them and their staff on the study. The meetings are only a bit scary if you have to present. Being on stage in front of a bunch of doctors can be a bit intimidating. There could be fifty people in the audience, there could be three hundred. I've done lots of them but sometimes I still get nervous when the tech guys put the mic on me."

"A mic? Like the whole Madonna, Britney Spears–type thing?"

Sloane giggles. "Sometimes."

So much for resolving to pull my shit together.

The thought of Professional Sloane in a fucking curve-hugging pencil skirt and a Madonna mic, standing on stage as she bosses around a bunch of doctors with her raspy lounge-singer voice is the fantasy I never knew I needed.

I'm a fucking goner.

"Cool, cool . . ." I say, shifting my stance as my cock practically begs me to march up to her door and fuck her on the kitchen counter. "Can I come watch?"

Sloane laughs. "No . . . ?"

"Please?"

"*No*, you weirdo. You cannot come watch."

"Why not? It sounds both hot and educational."

Her husky laugh warms my chest. "Because it's all confidential, for one. And for two, you'd distract me."

My heart lights up with fireworks. "With my pretty face?"

"Pfft. *No*." That *no* is totally a *yes*. I can virtually see the burn of her blush through the phone line. I wish I could FaceTime her, but Sloane would know where I am, standing across the street like a smitten fucking fool, too nervous to scare her off to actually go to her door but too desperate to be near her to really care. "I have a baby's head's worth of cheese. I'm doing the asparagus now," she says, her voice soft.

"When you're done with that, put some salted water on to boil."

"Okay."

The chopping starts in the background, reaching through the absence of Sloane's voice. I close my eyes and lean my head against the tree as I try to imagine Sloane with her hand expertly wrapped around the handle of a knife. I don't know why that's so fucking sexy, but it is. Just like the thought of her on stage with her little Madonna mic. Same as the image of Sloane in the booth at my restaurant, bent over a sketch.

"Why do you work there?" I ask abruptly.

"At Viamax?"

"Yeah. Why not art for a living?"

There's a pause before she snorts. The flush on her throat and down her chest must be absolutely crimson. "I'm not really going to make money selling bird sketches, Rowan."

I'm surprised she'd go there, after the way she looked toward the booth at 3 in Coach as though she wanted to take a flame-thrower to that drawing she left behind and probably the whole fucking restaurant. But as much as she's going straight to this moment that clearly embarrassed her, it's still a deflection. "But you could. You could do other art, if that's what you want."

"It's not." Her firm words ring between us like she's waiting for them to settle into my head. "I like what I do. It's different from the career I envisioned for myself when I was young. Like, who does, right? Not many of us end up as dolphin trainers or whatever." She snickers and pauses again, but I don't press her this time, content to wait her out. "Art brings up bad memories sometimes. I used to love painting. I'd paint for hours. I started experimenting with sculpture too. But things . . . changed. Sketching is like the foundation. It's all that was left when the rest burned down—the only thing I still enjoy. Well, that and my webs, which feel like art to me."

These might be only tiny pieces of Sloane, but I'll hold on to them nonetheless. My art was never so tarnished that I couldn't bear to create it. It makes me wonder what would strip art from Sloane so thoroughly that she can no longer paint or sculpt, reduced to monochrome.

"I always wanted to be a chef," I offer. "Even when I was young."

"Really?"

"Yeah." I look down at my shoes as I recall the kitchen of my childhood home in Sligo, eating around the small table with my brothers, the three of us usually alone in the dark, unwelcoming house. "Lachlan would find a way to bring home food. I would cook it. And our little brother was a picky little shit at that age, so I got pretty good at creating decent flavors from limited resources. Cooking became a kind of escape. A safe place for my mind to run free and explore."

"Culinary art. Literally."

"Exactly. And my ability to cook probably made hard times at home a little easier." At least my father's drunken or drug-induced rages weren't made worse by hunger. There were a few times he controlled himself long enough to shove me into the kitchen and demand dinner rather than strike me down. Cooking became a kind of armor. Not foolproof, but a barrier at least. Something to soften the blow. "I was lucky, I guess. It survived. Eventually, it became another mechanism for me and my brothers to build a better life."

Sloane pauses, her voice melancholy when she says, "I'm sorry you and your brothers went through that. But I'm happy for you that your art survived."

"And I'm sorry you don't enjoy your art anymore."

"Me too. But thank you for teaching me yours. I may have only grated a baby's head's worth of cheese, but . . ." She pauses to take a deep breath, as though mustering up courage. "I'm having fun."

I gasp theatrically. "*No*, you can't, that wasn't part of my plan."

Sloane giggles and I grin my way through the rest of the preparation of the dish. We stay on the line as she eats and insists I find something to snack on so she doesn't dine alone. All I've got is a granola bar that was squished in my carry-on, but I eat it anyway as we talk about random shit. Raleigh. Boston. Food. Drinks. Everything. Nothing.

I leave when she's finished eating, only moving from my hiding spot when I know she's occupied at the sink.

The next day, I come back. I wait behind the tree as the kid delivers the bag of groceries. He earns another hundred bucks. Sloane calls me and we make roasted feta shrimp and polenta. I bring a premade salad so I can eat with her. We talk about work. About fun. A little about Albert Briscoe and the aftermath of our serendipitous visit to his house. Several murders have been pinned on him, and Sloane seems pleased. I might have nudged the police in the right direction, but I don't tell her that.

On the third day, I hide behind a different tree a little closer to the house where I can hear her when she opens the door. Sloane peppers the kid with questions but he holds out. Gotta hand it to him, he's pretty dependable. When I peer from behind the trunk, I can see her frustration, but she clearly doesn't want to freak the kid out either. As he collects his bike, I ask him what he's going to do with all this cash, and he tells me he's saving for a PlayStation. Before he goes, I give him an extra two hundred bucks.

Sloane makes steak, a beautiful Wagyu filet mignon, with charred Brussels sprouts on the side. She's the most nervous about this one. I know she doesn't want to fuck it up. But she doesn't. Sloane sends me a picture—it turns out a perfect medium rare. She hums through every bite. We talk about our families. Well, I talk about my brothers. She doesn't have much to say about hers. No siblings. No close cousins. Her parents keep in touch on her birthday and Christmas but that's it. They're too immersed in their own lives and I don't get the sense she wants to share. Maybe there's just not much worth remembering about them. And I get that, better than most.

The next day, I hide behind the tree for a long while and watch her house. At one point, she opens the door, takes a few steps outside. She looks down the street, her brow furrowed. I shift out of view when her gaze pans in my direction as she assesses the other end of the road. But there's no kid. No groceries.

She steps back inside, locks the door. The curtains sweep away from the window only to fall once more.

After a few more minutes, I walk away. I'm in my rental car, already driving toward the airport when a text buzzes on my burner. But I force myself not to read it. Not until I'm back in my apartment in Boston.

Because I know if I do, there's a chance I'll tear the fucking door off the plane to get back to Jasmine Street.

A few hours later, the phone is clutched tight in my hand when I pour a generous shot of whiskey over the cracking cubes of ice. It's not until I'm settled in my favorite leather chair with my shoes kicked off and my feet up that I look at the screen.

Forcing myself to wait is a delicious torment. Alcohol burns down my throat as I open the unread message from Sloane.

| I missed you today.

| I also realized I can't cook for shit
| without you. I don't think I'm a fully
| fledged adult after all.

I smile and take a long sip of my drink before I set it aside and tap out my reply.

> I missed you too. Next time you're back in Boston for another one of those meetings we'll make fig phyllo Napoleon in the restaurant.

At first I'm not sure she'll reply, given the late hour and how long I've left it to send a response. But almost immediately I see those three dots flicker, and then:

> I'd like that

My eyes close as my head settles against the leather. I smile as I think about her face today as she stood on her front porch and looked in both directions for the delivery that didn't come. Disappointment has never looked so damn sweet.

My phone buzzes in my hand.

> See you in a few weeks for the game.
> Friends or not, I'm still going to kick your ass. Just so you know…

I smile in the dim light.

> I'm counting on it.

DIJON

Sloane

There's an art to cornering a man like Thorsten Harris.

The first trick is to approach him in a place where he feels confident, one where he thinks he's the apex predator in his little pond because he's successfully hunted there before. Like this place, Orion Bar, an upscale cocktail lounge within what I already know is Thorsten's preferred range. It's just far enough from his home that he feels like it's an adventure, just close enough to his house to make luring his prey there viable.

The second step in the process is to learn what he likes. What excites him. What he loathes. In Thorsten's case, he enjoys red wine, impeccable cooking, and expensive things. Not always *nice* things, in fact they're often gaudy and pretentious, but expensive nonetheless. As for what he hates? Bad manners. And yams, apparently. Then take all that knowledge and start to build a rapport with him.

And the last step is the tricky part: you have to make him believe you're smart enough to be an interesting conquest—you might be prey, but you're worth the risk to take a trophy. But you also have to come off as just dumb enough that you would willingly accept his dinner invitation at his home tomorrow night, even though he's essentially a stranger.

. . . Or, you can throw all that out the window and just be Rowan Kane.

A motorcycle helmet drops onto the empty space next to me on the white leather couch.

Instantly, my blood turns volcanic.

"Fancy seeing you around these parts," Rowan says as he plops down next to it with a shit-eating grin.

I give him a dead-eyed glare in reply.

My ferocity only earns me a wink before he's leaning forward with his arm extended over the coffee table toward the man sitting across from me.

"Hi, pleasure to meet you. I'm Rowan."

"Thorsten Harris, pleasure is all mine," my well-dressed, older companion says as he accepts the handshake. I've spent the past four days trying to avoid this exact scenario in my attempts to corner Thorsten, who Rowan now knows is our annual target, though he doesn't seem to know *why*.

I thought I had finally escaped Rowan when I slipped out of the hotel and his rental car was still in the parking lot.

Clearly, I misjudged him.

And he is fucking *elated* about that.

"I'm sorry to interrupt," Rowan barrels on, ready to light the fuse for every cannon in his arsenal of charm. He aims his fucking flawless smile at my prey, his skin bright and flushed, probably from the excitement of successfully chasing me down. "I saw my friend's car here as I was passing through and it's just been so long, I thought I should stop in and say a quick hello to her."

And then he turns the full force of his charm attack on me. "Hello, friend."

"What a deep joy it is to see you here, Rowan. I'm so thrilled." I take a long sip of my wine before I give him a tight smile. The silence between us stretches. Thorsten shifts in his seat and I suppress a groan, aware that I'm already pushing Thorsten's boundaries for manners. "Would you care to join us?" I ask woodenly. My smile has a vicious edge that clearly says *fuck the hell right off.*

And Rowan says, "I would be delighted."

Within one minute, Thorsten has poured him a generous glass of expensive Chianti.

Within five, Rowan has him whooping with laughter and clapping his hands.

Within ten, Thorsten is nearly tripping over himself to invite Rowan along to our dinner at his home tomorrow night, something I've spent all evening orchestrating as a solo venture.

Two hours later, we're leaving the swanky bar side by side in Thorsten's wake, tomorrow's dinner plans etched in stone.

And I'm seething.

"I have to hand it to you," I whisper as Thorsten gets into his car and we wave him off. "Your grocery delivery trick to my home was very cute. You nearly had me fooled there with that cooking-together thing."

"*Fooled?*" Rowan's eyes roam over me, bright and wry. "Not sure what you mean, Blackbird."

"Fooled into thinking that you weren't going to turn around and become a monumental *pain in my ass* at the first available

103

opportunity for this season's game," I say. He bellows a laugh and I fold my arms across my chest as I glare up at him. "You are a *cheat*."

"Am not."

"You've been following me around relentlessly to figure out who we're after rather than looking on your own."

"It's not in the rule book that I can't."

"We don't have a fucking rule book. But we should. Rule number one: do your own fucking research."

"Why, when I can have so much fun following you?" Rowan's smile only grows more devious when I growl in my most accurate Winston impression. "So . . . who is that guy anyway?"

I huff and roll my eyes before I pivot on my heel and stomp toward my rental car. "You are the *worst*," I hiss as Rowan pulls open the driver's-side door for me. "You and your"—I wave a hand in his direction as I slide into my seat—"skullduggery."

Rowan snorts as he leans down into my vehicle, his face so close to mine that I feel his every breath on my cheek. I try to ignore the way it twists my belly with a different kind of fury. "*Skullduggery.* Should I take this as a sign that you've moved on from dragon smut to pirate porn?"

"Maybe I have."

"You know, you're kind of adorable when you're indignant."

"And you are still the *worst*," I snarl as I tug my door free of his grip.

He manages to move before I slam it on his hand, but I still catch his teasing laugh and his parting words: "You'll love me someday."

The next day is not that day.

No, not when Rowan invites himself to my breakfast-for-one at the hotel restaurant. Nor when he shows up in the mall as I shop for an outfit, even though he does carry my bags and help me pick out a cute little retro-style halter dress. It's just a ploy to gain an advantage, after all. Crafty fucker. And *someday* is definitely not today when I park at Thorsten's grand, secluded home in Calabasas and Rowan's rented motorcycle is already there. He's leaning against it, hot as sin in a black leather jacket, his gaze raking from my toes to my eyes with a look that sets me on fire, and he knows it.

"Evening, Blackbird," he says as he pushes off the side of the bike.

"Butcher."

Rowan draws to a halt in front of me as I cross my arms and cock a hip. "That's a pretty dress. Someone help pick that out for you? Whoever they are, they clearly have impeccable taste."

"Great taste. Absolutely zero boundaries."

He grins. "I'm so happy we're on the same page."

I give him my most dramatic eye roll and am about to launch into him when the front door swings open and Thorsten stands on the threshold with his arms spread in greeting.

"Welcome, my young friends," he says, looking ready to host illustrious guests. His white hair is perfectly coiffed. His burgundy jacquard dinner jacket shimmers in the setting sun. The smile he flashes us has a hidden, sharp edge. "Please, do come in."

He steps aside and motions for us to enter the palatial home.

We start with cocktails in the living room where first-edition books and ceramic figurines and paintings surround us, and I take the time to appreciate the art as Thorsten gives us a tour of his collection, his most prized possessions carefully labeled. Even after he's moved on, I stare for a long while at a signed drypoint and etching print by Edward Hopper called *Night Shadows*. The sketch shows a man from overhead as he walks alone on a city street, the lamplight casting deep shadows around him. Something about him seems sinister. He could be stalking. He could be *hunting*. And when I look left and right, I see the narrative emerge from the art that engulfs me.

To my left, a black-and-white photograph by Andrew Prokos called *Fulton Oculus #2.* The image evokes the feeling of an all-seeing, ominous eye made of steel and glass.

To my right, a painting by John Singer Sargent of a woman sitting at a dinner table. She faces the viewer, her hand wrapped around a glass of red wine. A man sits next to her at the far right of the image. But he's not looking at the viewer. He's looking at *her*.

Beyond that, a print of *The Waltz*, by Félix Vallotton. It depicts couples dancing, but they seem almost ghostly. The woman in the lower right corner looks like she's asleep.

After that . . .

I look at Rowan and place my cocktail on a coaster and leave it on the side table, untouched. He's immersed in conversation with our host and doesn't notice me.

But Thorsten does.

"Drink not to your taste, my darling?" Thorsten asks with a tight smile.

"It's delicious, thank you. Just saving myself for your wonderful collection of wine," I reply with a bow of my head.

His smile seems more relaxed when he sets his own drink down and declares it's time to move on to the main event.

"I can't tell you how elated I am to have a professional chef grace my table this evening," Thorsten says, leading us to the dining room where classical music plays on a low volume and candles flicker among the dark flowers of an elaborate centerpiece. He points me toward a mahogany chair covered with plush red velvet, pulling it away from the table and pushing it back in as I sit. "And his lovely companion as well, of course."

"Thank you," I say, dropping a demure smile to my place setting. I don't know anything about antique bone china, but I'm willing to bet Thorsten would have an absolute fit if any of it were smashed.

I file that thought for later.

"And such a lovely couple you make. How did you meet, anyway?"

"Oh, we're just friends," I say at the same time that Rowan says, "An expedition in the bayou."

We give one another a pointed look as Thorsten laughs. "Seems like you might have differing opinions on the subject of your relationship status."

"Well, it's hard to compete with the stunning waitstaff and Rowan's adoring socialite regulars," I say with a sickly sweet smile.

"No one competes with Sloane." Rowan's eyes anchor on mine, dragging me into the depths of a navy sea. "She just hasn't realized it yet."

Our gazes stay locked for a heartbeat that feels too heavy in my chest. But the suspended moment is cut too short as Thorsten chuckles, the pop of a wine cork breaking the connection between us. "Perhaps tonight she will. Let us take inspiration from the art of cuisine. For as Longfellow said, 'Art is long, and time is fleeting, and our hearts, though stout and brave, still, like muffled drums, are beating funeral marches to the grave.'"

Rowan and I exchange a glance as Thorsten focuses on pouring his wine, and I manage to roll my eyes and catch Rowan's fleeting grin in reply before our host can look our way.

When my wine is decanted into an etched crystal goblet and Thorsten has settled into his chair, he raises his glass for a toast. "To new friends. And for some of us, perhaps one day more than just friends."

"To new friends," we echo, and a sliver of unexpected disappointment finds its way beneath my skin when I realize I'd hoped Rowan might repeat the last line of the toast instead.

Our host takes a sip of his wine and I do the same, figuring it must be safe enough to drink if he's taking a long pull. He holds up his glass and grins at the ruby wine. "Two thousand fifteen Tenuta Tignanello, 'Marchese Antinori' Riserva. I do love a nice Chianti," he says. He takes another sip, closing his eyes on a deep breath before his lids snap open. "Let us begin."

Thorsten picks up a little bell next to his place setting, its tinkling melody flooding the dining room. A moment later, a man enters with slow, careful steps, pushing a silver serving cart toward the table. He appears to be in his late thirties, tall, athletic with broad shoulders that stoop as though the muscles have recently forgotten they have a job to do. The yellowing remains of healing bruises rim his vacant eyes.

"This is David," Thorsten says as David places a plate of hors d'oeuvres before me. David doesn't look up, just trudges back to the trolley where he fetches a plate for Rowan. "Mr. Miller can't talk. He had a terrible accident recently, so I have taken him under my employ."

"Oh, how very kind of you," I say. My stomach twists with discomfort. I figured Rowan might have worked out who we're dealing with since yesterday, but when I look up at him, the first hints of regret start to seep beneath my skin. My eyebrows hike when he meets my eyes. *Haven't you figured it out yet, pretty boy?* I try to convey with nothing more than my widened eyes.

He tilts his head and gives me a fleeting, quizzical expression, a reply that simply says, *Huh?*

Nope. He definitely has not figured it out.

That twinge of regret starts to burn.

When Thorsten's plate is set down, David leaves. "Goat cheese crostini with olive tapenade," Thorsten declares. "Enjoy."

I try not to let my sigh of relief seem too obvious as we start the first course. It's legitimately pretty good, maybe a little salty, but at least it's a decent start. Rowan charms Thorsten with compliments that seem sincere, and the two talk about possible refinements that would elevate the dish. Rowan suggests fig to bring sweetness into the balance, and I keep my attention on our host to escape Rowan's heavy gaze. It rests on my cheek, searing my skin like a brand when he mentions the fig phyllo Napoleon from the dessert menu at 3 in Coach.

I play along with the conversation, nod and laugh at all the right places, but really I'm not paying that much attention—I'm too concerned with how I'm going to communicate anything to Rowan with the power of my facial expressions alone.

When the course is done, Thorsten summons David again with the bell, and he collects our dishes to return with gazpacho. This round is fine, nothing special, but Rowan seems pleased, and the two discuss the tomato varieties that Thorsten grows on the property.

"I would love to see your garden," Rowan says after Thorsten details the other herbs and produce he nurtures in the backyard.

Thorsten's pleasant mask slips, a feral gleam igniting in his eyes before a blink carries it away. "Oh, I'm sure that can be arranged."

Rowan grins, but this is his smile of secrets, and it's one I know well. At least he's aware that we're in the presence of another murderer, so I guess that's a plus. I'm momentarily hopeful that maybe Rowan does know who Thorsten is after all, and he's just been keeping it under wraps in the hopes of winning this round of our competition.

But when Thorsten uncorks a fresh bottle of wine, topping up both our glasses but not his own and watching with predatory interest as Rowan takes a long sip, I know my hopes have been dashed.

I guess I should be happy. This is shaping up to be an easy win. In reality, however, my anxiety has my chest feeling as if I've been plugged into a power grid. I'm grateful for the hideously ornate tablecloth that shields my jittering legs from view.

Rowan takes another generous sip of wine as the culinary discussion continues. Thorsten summons David to return for the empty soup bowls, relaying explicit instructions to bring back the salad course from a specific shelf in the kitchen. He's repeating the steps to David for a third time when Rowan catches my eye over the lip of his wine glass with a questioning flicker in his brows, as though he's asking what the fuck is going on.

Lobotomy, I mouth at him, trying to make it look like I'm scratching my forehead when I tap it and nod toward David. Rowan's head tilts and I roll my eyes, gritting my teeth. *Lo-bo-to-my.*

Rowan's head tilts in the other direction, his brow still furrowed but a hint of a grin playing at his lips. He subtly points at me, and then at himself. *You love me?* he mouths.

I smack my head.

"Everything all right, my darling?" Thorsten asks as David departs for the kitchen.

"Oh yes, of course. I just remembered something I forgot to do at work before I left. But it's fine, I'll do it in the morning." Thorsten smiles at my excuse, but it's brittle around the edges, uncertainty bleeding into his mask. "*Late* morning at this rate. This wine is going down a treat," I tack on with a charming smile. He watches as I bring the glass to my lips and swallow, though I don't let any of the liquid into my mouth. The deception seems to appease him and I set my glass down, folding my hands in my lap.

Thorsten's restraint buckles as the approaching trolley squeaks in the hallway, a beaming, ravenous grin claiming his features as his refined mask peels away. But Rowan doesn't notice. He just smiles at me, swaying slightly in his chair, a glassy sheen coating his half-lidded eyes.

"You look so pretty, Blackbird," he says as David enters the room with three covered dishes on the trolley.

Blush flames in my cheeks. "Thank you."

"You always look pretty. When you came to the restaurant, I said—" Rowan hiccups twice, then drowns the next one with a gulp of wine—"I said, '*Sloane is the most beautiful girl in the world.*'

111

And then my brother called me a '*feckin eejit*' because I could have all the pussy I wanted in Boston but instead I've taken a vow of obstinance—"

"Abstinence."

"—*abstinence* over a girl who doesn't want me."

I'm pretty sure the blush has set fire to my skin and the source of the flame is my incinerated heart.

Thorsten grins in my periphery, clearly entertained by our dinner conversation. My lips part, a held breath burning in my chest. All I manage to say is a single word: "Rowan . . ."

But his attention has dropped to the dish set before him.

"Beef Niçoise," Rowan chimes with a delighted smile as he takes up his knife and fork. I glance at Thorsten who watches Rowan with rapt attention. "I love beef Niçoise."

"Yes," our host says as he lays a folded piece of paper-thin rare meat on his tongue. "Niçoise."

"Rowan—"

"I'm so curious to know your thoughts, Chef," Thorsten barrels on. "This is my special take on the traditional version."

"*Rowan*—" I hiss, but it's too late. Rowan's already scooped a forkful of salad into his mouth, his eyes closing as he savors the chopped lettuce and green beans and cherry tomatoes and . . . beef.

"This is fantastic," he says, slurring his words. He spears another forkful of salad with an unsteady hand and jams it into his already-full mouth. "Homemade Dijon dressing?"

Thorsten beams under the compliment. "Yes—I used an extra half teaspoon of brown sugar, as the meat is gamey."

"So good."

I swipe a hand down my face as Rowan manages to shovel one more bite into his mouth before he passes out face down on his plate.

There's a beat of silence. Thorsten and I stare at the man sleeping on a bed of salad with thinly sliced rare human steak hanging out of his mouth.

When Thorsten meets my eyes, it's as though he's coming out of a euphoric haze.

He thought I was drinking my wine. When I wasn't drunk enough, he probably thought he could easily subdue me.

He thought wrong.

I hold Thorsten's confused gaze as I push the stem of my wineglass over, toppling it onto my plate. The crystal shatters, chipping the china, flooding the salad with blood-colored wine.

"Well," I say, as I sit back in my chair, laying my hand on the surface of the table with the watered steel blade clutched in my palm. "I guess it's just you and me now."

DISCORDIA

Rowan

My first conscious thought is a single word, one that slurs past my lips as if it's stuck in viscous syrup.

"Sloane."

My second thought is the awareness of the steady beat of music. At first, I was convinced it was my heartbeat, but I was wrong. A man's angelic voice floats above light drums and a dreamy guitar melody that reminds me of the desert at sunset.

Sloane hums along with the music that swirls around me. As she sings along about cooking someone and squashing his head, I realize I recognize the melody. "Knives Out." Radiohead. Sloane's raspy, rich voice fills my chest with relief. I know she's okay, thank fuck. Because I am *not* okay.

Screams fill the room and I open my eyes. A vaguely familiar candelabra comes into view, laden with gaudy crystals. I try to focus on them as the rest of the table swirls at the edges of my vision.

"Just . . . hold . . . still . . ." Sloane says, gritting out every word over the man's garbled cries. "I'd say it would hurt less if you stop struggling, but that's a total lie."

The man screams again and I turn my head toward the sound. It might be the hardest fucking thing I've ever done. My head feels like it weighs a hundred pounds.

The screeching reaches a fevered pitch. Sloane's back is to me. She's straddling the terrified man seated in the chair at the head of the table, shielding him from view. Some of the evening comes swimming through the soup of wine and sedatives clouding my thoughts. *Thorsten.* The man is Thorsten. And he *fucked me up.*

"Just a little snip. There you go."

The screaming stops abruptly and Sloane's shoulders sag with disappointment.

"Wuss."

She reaches behind her without turning around, her gloved fist covered with blood, and drops a severed eyeball next to another already resting on the bread plate next to my head.

I retch.

Sloane whips around at the sound. "*In the bowl*, Rowan. Jesus Christ." She tears her gloves off as she climbs off the man and hauls my torso upright so I can vomit into a stainless steel bowl next to my face. Her hands hold tight to my shoulders as red wine and dinner vacate my stomach. "Better out than in. Trust me," she grumbles, her tone dark.

"Fucker drugged me," I manage to grit out when the heaving finally stops and I wipe my mouth with a napkin, my hand clammy and shaking.

"Sure did."

"How long have I been unconscious?"

"A couple of hours," she replies. She passes me an unopened bottle of water with one hand, drags the bowl away with the other. Sloane looks toward the door to the hallway, hesitating. "I need to ditch this but David is freaking me the fuck out."

"Has he threatened you? If he's fucking threatened you, I swear to God—"

"No, not at all," Sloane says, pushing me back down on the chair when I try to stand. My body pitches to one side. She tries to smile, I think, but it comes out like a grimace. "He seems pretty harmless."

"Then what's the problem?"

"He's eating. In the kitchen," she says.

I shake my head, not following what she's laying down.

"The next courses. The . . . food."

"That's what most people eat. Food."

The color has drained from Sloane's face. "Yeah . . . most . . ."

"I don't get it—"

"*You ate a fucking person,*" she blurts out.

I blink at Sloane once before pulling the bowl back to heave again.

"Oh my *God*, Rowan, it was really gross. You stuffed it in. Couldn't get enough."

I retch.

"You passed out while chewing. I had to scrape it off your tongue so you wouldn't choke."

I glare at her through watery eyes before vomiting again, though thankfully there's not much left to get rid of.

"Did you know it was a rump roast? I tortured Thorsten until he told me. I had to dig *human ass* out of your *mouth.*"

"At least you didn't fucking *swallow it*, Sloane. Why the fuck didn't you stop me?"

"I tried, but you just went for it. Don't you remember?"

Shit. I do remember.

I remember a lot more than that.

Sloane watches me a little too closely. She's not as apathetic as she tries to appear. The longer I stare, the more her indifferent mask crumbles, and a faint blush rises beneath the freckles dusting her cheeks and nose.

This fucking girl. Panicking because I gave her a glimpse into how I feel. Clearly nervous about a conversation she's desperate not to have. Ready to fly.

And I would do anything to keep her around, even if it means taking a hammer to my own heart.

"No." I shake my head as my gaze drifts toward the centerpiece. "The last thing I remember is David coming through the door with the trolley. I don't recall anything after that."

When I glance up, Sloane's lips twitch. It's almost a smile. Her eyes are a little softer.

Fuck.

Just as I suspected. She's fucking relieved.

I'll absorb the venom of this burning sting. I drop my head into my hands. She'll never know I remember every second of my embarrassing, unrequited confession. I'll never forget the way her skin flushed such a pretty shade of pink when I said she was beautiful. I would have crawled across the table to kiss those plump lips when they pursed as I spilled my secrets between us.

I need to get it through my fucking thick skull. She will never want more than this. But I refuse to lose her. Sloane is the only person in the world who can look at my monster and find a friend. And I know she needs a friend just as much as I do. Maybe more.

"Are you okay?" she asks, her voice barely more than a whisper.

"Yeah. It's just the drugs," I lie again. I make a vow right this instant that it will be the last lie I ever tell Sloane Sutherland. "I feel like shit."

Truth.

"I imagine you do. I know how it goes," she says. She pulls the bowl away when she seems reasonably sure I'm done. "Well, not the eating people part. I don't know about that."

I give her a half-hearted glare that only serves to brighten her smile before she turns away and carries the bowl to set it in the hall, muttering to herself about dealing with it later. There's a groan of pain from the end of the table and I'm a little grateful for something else to focus on besides the burn in my throat.

I look toward Thorsten. And for the first time, I really focus on the scene around me.

"Orb Weaver," I whisper, my breath catching in my chest at the beautiful horror of an intricate web that shimmers in the candlelight. "Sloane . . . how?"

Her smile is bashful as she pushes away from the table with a shrug. "I had time to kill."

Sloane walks toward Thorsten. His head hangs against his chest as blood drips down his face from the lightless caverns where his eyes once were. He stirs a little and groans before he fades back into unconsciousness.

"Nearly done," she says, patting him on the shoulder as she

stops to examine the pattern of fishing line behind him that extends from the floor to the ceiling.

Some lines intersect, others layer behind one another. Some are a thicker gauge than others, the thinner lines tied in delicate knots to hold the heavier thread in specific angles or approximations of curves. At different points and depths there are thin pieces of flesh hanging from the web.

Sloane withdraws a pair of latex gloves from a box on the table, then a tape measure and two pieces of precut, thinner-gauge fishing line. She hums to the music playing from her own playlist through a portable speaker as she ties the first of the two threads up on the web above Thorsten's head, using the tape measure to distance out one meter from the first string to place the second. When the measurements are done, she returns to the table, meeting my rapt attention with a devious grin.

"You might want to look away, pretty boy," she says, pinching the edge of the bread plate to slide the eyeballs closer to her end of the table.

"Fuck off. I'm not squeamish."

"You sure?"

My stomach is *not* sure.

"*Usually* I'm not squeamish. I'll be fine."

Sloane shrugs and plucks one of the eyes from the plate with careful, delicate fingers. "One hundred percent positive?"

"I'd rather watch you make skin ornaments and eye baubles than go to the kitchen and check on Lobotomy David. Let's just go with that."

"Fair enough."

Sloane heads back to the web, carefully winding the first of the two measured strings around the eye to trap it in the clear filament.

"You really did all this in a couple of hours?" I ask. The hem of her dress drifts higher up the backs of her thighs as she works at tying the line in knots. My dick hardens just imagining how the curve of her ass would feel in my hands, the softness of her flesh in my palms.

"I make each layer at the hotel first. It's easier to glue them to drop sheets and then roll them up so I can peel them off when I get here," she replies as she nods toward several scrunched-up pieces of paper-thin plastic on the floor next to the wall. "I knew I wanted to stage him in the dining room, so I found the measurements from the realtor's records."

Sloane approaches to retrieve the other eye, gifting me another shy smile before she heads back to the web with her prize. Just as she did with the first eye, she winds the thin strand of fishing line around the orb and ties it into her masterpiece before standing back to survey her work.

"*Voilà!*" she exclaims into Thorsten's ear, but he doesn't wake. She watches him for a moment, nudging his bloody arm where it's tied to the chair. When he remains unconscious, she sighs and turns to face me. "He's not very tough, this one. This is the fifth time he's passed out on me."

"To be fair, you did gouge out—"

"*Pluck*, Rowan. I *plucked* his eyes out."

"You did *pluck* out his eyes. Though I dunno, Blackbird . . . that eye hole on the left looks a little gouge-y."

She leans toward Thorsten with a scowl, scrutinizing the empty eye sockets as I bite down on a grin. "His left? Or my left?"

"His left."

"Fuck off, it does not look *gouge-y*," she says. Her doubt turns into a scowl as she looks back over her shoulder and catches the amusement in my eyes. "Dick."

I laugh and try to avoid the tape measure as she chucks it at my head, though I'm still too drunk and drugged to avoid being hit in the arm. When I meet her eyes, she tries to look pissed, but she's not. "You said before that it's a map," I say as I rub my forearm. She nods. "How?"

Sloane grins and comes closer, pulling off her gloves as she looks down at me with bright hazel eyes. That dimple winks next to the corner of her lips as she holds out an upturned palm. "I'll show you, if you think you can stay upright without puking on me."

I slap her palm and she laughs but holds it out again, and this time I grab it. The room swirls as I stand. I'm not so convinced I'll be able to keep my shit together, but Sloane just waits, patient and steady. Her grip is an anchor. When I stop swaying, she's still there, ensuring that every step I take is a firm one as she leads me to her work of art.

"This is the scale," she tells me as she points to the eyes set one meter apart above Thorsten's unconscious head. "One meter equals ten kilometers on this map."

Sloane pulls me closer. Heat radiates from her body to warm her ginger and vanilla scent. She leads me to the edge of the first layer of fishing line and then lets go of my hand to step behind me.

Her fingers wrap around my upper arms as she rises on her tiptoes to look over my shoulder.

"It's hard to do, but try to imagine it in three dimensions. One layer is for streets. One is for wetlands. Another is for soils," she says. She lays a delicate hand on each side of my head and shifts me so I can see the layers on an angle, where severed flesh is neatly tied at specific points in the web. "If those idiot investigators would take each section of the design and layer it into ArcGIS software, they'd have enough to make a topographic map. The piece from his chest in the center of the web is this house. Every other little bit of Thorsten represents the last known whereabouts of missing persons he's taken or killed." Sloane's arm rests on my shoulder as she points to a piece of skin wound in fishing line. Her breath warms the shell of my ear, triggering the rise of goose bumps on my neck. "That's for a man named Bennett who he killed two months ago. I took it from Thorsten's bicep. *B* for *Bennett*."

I glance at Thorsten, who's starting to stir once more. His sleeve has been cut off, a patch of flesh raw and exposed from where the skin has been peeled away.

"This is so much work," I say as Sloane slips her hands from my head and moves to my side.

She glances at me, a hint of pink rising in her cheeks before she smirks and rolls her eyes. "You probably think I should take up crochet and acquire twelve cats and start yelling at the neighborhood children to get off my lawn."

"Never." I turn toward her and hold her wary gaze. "Well, maybe the *yelling at neighborhood children* part. I'll always condone that. But this, Blackbird? This is *art*."

Sloane's eyes soften. A faint smile tips up one corner of her lips. I could so easily lean down and inhale her scent. I could kiss her. Run my hand into her raven hair. Tell her I think she's brilliant, and cunning, and so fucking beautiful. That I have fun with her. That even though I feel like complete shit right now, I'm disappointed this year's game is nearly over, because I hate watching her walk away. What we have now? It's not enough. I want more.

But I'm afraid that trying to push for it will only drive her away. With the way she took off at the restaurant and how long it took to coax her back, that's a risk I'm not willing to take.

I take a step back and mask my thoughts behind a cocky grin. "I am surprised you don't already have twelve cats, though. You seem like the cat-hoarding type to me."

Sloane wallops my arm and I laugh. "Fuck you, pretty boy."

"You could make so much money as a cat litter influencer on Instagram."

"I was going to let you do the honors and kill this pretentious fuckwit, but I totally take it back." With a final glare that has no real venom behind it, Sloane turns and heads back to the table to pull on another pair of latex gloves before picking up a scalpel. Thorsten stirs and moans, but he's not fully conscious until she twists the cap from a vial of smelling salts and holds it under his nose.

"Please, *please* stop—"

"You know what, Thorsten . . . or is it Jeremy? That's your real name, right? Jeremy Carmichael?" Sloane stops next to his shoulder and looks at her web, reaching up to tap one of the eyes that gazes across the room. "You remind me of someone I once knew."

Thorsten's cries grow more frantic as Sloane trails the tip of her blade across his neck. A light scratch lines his skin and I smile as he thrashes. I know her typical process and her next moves. She'll notch a precise cut into his jugular with a single strike and then leave him to bleed out in his chair.

The final slash of color in her perfect canvas.

"This man, he lured people in with promises of safety and care only to deliver the opposite," she says as she stares down with disdain at Thorsten's shaking body. "A lot like you, really. You lured us in with the promise of a meal and nice company only to drug and deceive us. It just didn't work out entirely the way you hoped, did it."

"I'm begging you, I'm sorry, truly, I—"

"Did David beg you to stop when you decided to play Lobotomy Barbie with his face? I bet he pleaded with you, and you loved the sound. But the funny thing is, Mr. Carmichael, you and I have something in common. I'll tell you a little secret," she says. A devastatingly beautiful smile creeps across her lips as she leans close to his ear. "I love the sound when my victims beg too."

"No, no, you don't understand . . . *David! David, help me!*"

His pleas for help go unanswered as Sloane backs away and returns to the table to exchange her scalpel for her Damascus blade. Thorsten's head swings from one side to the next as he loses track of her whereabouts beneath his desperate, sputtering cries. But Sloane doesn't make a sound as she creeps closer to her prey. She moves like an owl in flight, fluid and silent and graceful. Predatory and powerful.

"The man you remind me of, he presented such a civilized mask to the world, yet underneath, he was a devil. He promised the best education. The best opportunities for students gifted in the arts. He promised a safe place to learn and the best chance for getting into the most exclusive universities for those of us whose parents were wealthy enough to pay the price. And since mine were never around, they didn't notice the price I truly paid."

For all the times I've thought my soul was little more than a fucking stone, Sloane Sutherland proves me wrong.

Her words echo in my head until my imagination takes me to every dark and terrible possibility. My heart hits every bone on its way down to the floor. All that's left behind is a black space that burns hotter with every hollow beat.

"I could take it," she says. "I could cope. I had an end in sight. And in a way, I *was* learning. I was learning how to keep my rage and darkness beneath a mask so I could carry on in the world. So I kept my mouth shut as I gave pieces of myself away. But you know the one price I could not pay?" she asks as she stops behind Thorsten. Her smile is gone. She stares straight ahead, her eyes nearly black in the dim light. Her voice is low and drips with menace when she says, "The price I could never pay was Lark."

Ice infuses my veins. A chill spreads through my arms. It sluices down my spine.

"She was the only person I cared about. When I found out what he was doing to her, what she had been hiding, I did some hiding of my own. That same night that she confessed someone else's sins to me, I waited in the shadows. I made a vow in the dark. That I would wipe out everyone like him that I could find. That I wouldn't stop until I found the worst, the darkest, the most depraved, and I would erase them from the world, one at a time. And I promised myself that I would never let anyone hurt some- one I cared about ever again."

Sloane's arms raise on either side of Thorsten's head, the handle of the knife gripped in both hands, her skin bleached over her knuckles.

"This is me keeping my promise," she says.

The music crescendos through the speakers. She is a fucking virtuoso, surrounded by her masterpiece. She waits for a single word from the man beneath her, holding out for the perfect note.

"*Please*—"

Sloane plunges the blade into Thorsten's stomach.

"Since you asked so nicely, let's spill the filth from your guts together," she grits out, dragging the sharpened steel upward through his abdomen to the melody of his blistering scream.

Blood and viscera flood from the straight line carved into Thorsten's flesh. Heavy breaths saw from Sloane's chest as she whips the knife free, a flick of crimson to stain the carpet with the twist of her hand. Thorsten's wail slows until it falls silent beneath Sloane's menacing, watchful glare, and with a few final, ragged breaths, he dies strapped to his ornate chair.

An electric charge surrounds us. The aroma of hot blood perfumes the air. Candlelight flickers on the web. Every detail sharpens, as though the universe has narrowed to this single room.

And Sloane the goddess of chaos at the heart of it all.

There's a shiver in her blade. My gaze tracks a slow path up the length of her arm. Her shoulders tremble, her attention sharpened on some faraway memory brought too close to a murky surface from another place in time. I know it because I feel it sometimes too, the way I feel it in her now. It's bleeding into her lightless eyes.

Neither of us should be trusted. She could turn on me while she's caught in this lethal fog. But when I see the first tremor in her lips as a tear slides across her freckled cheek, I know I'd take any risk for Sloane.

I approach with careful, measured steps. She doesn't move as I fold my hand around her wrist and pry the handle of the blade from her grip. I lay it on Thorsten's bloodied lap and she hasn't as much as shifted on her feet, her gaze still caught in another moment of time.

"You're okay. Lark is okay," I whisper as I slide one arm across her back. When Sloane doesn't react, I fold my other arm around her too, until she's caged in my embrace. "You did good."

There's no change in her, not even when I tighten my arms or lean my head on her shoulder.

"I'm okay too," I continue. "Though I might need some antacid. Something about that homemade Dijon dressing just isn't sitting quite right. Not sure what it could be."

Sloane lets out a breath of a laugh and leans some of her weight against my chest. Wherever she's gone, I know in this moment that I can bring her back.

"David might have some pointers for me. Sounds like he's having no trouble with dinner."

"It's really bad, Rowan," she says into my shirt, her voice muffled. "When I went into the kitchen to get the bowl, he had half a sausage link hanging from his mouth."

"That doesn't sound so bad—"

"It was *raw.*"

"Okay, yep. That's pretty bad." I swallow down the uncomfortable protests of my stomach and cleanse the imagery from my mind with a deep breath of Sloane's ginger scent. I don't want to let go, but time is always working against me when it comes to her.

It works against me almost as hard as she does.

Sloane tenses in my embrace and I let her go before she can pull away. "We should probably check on him," I say, shifting my attention away when she looks at me with a question in her furrowed brow.

"Yeah, I guess we probably should."

Sloane shifts around me, her gaze lowered as she leads the way out of the dining room. When I offer to take the metal bowl, she refuses, claiming I might spill it on the walls and give her twice the amount of cleanup work, but I don't think that's the full reason. Maybe she just feels guilty for not telling me about Thorsten earlier. Maybe she needs something else to focus on. Or maybe, just maybe, it's because she meant what she said. That she cares.

I mull over her reasoning as I follow Sloane down the corridor, the bowl held as far from her face as she can manage without the risk of spilling. Her steps slow until she stops and lingers just before the threshold to the kitchen. When I halt at her side, she looks up at me with a grimace, her nose crinkling, a little spattering of blood dotting her cheek like a crimson echo of her natural freckles. If I could, I would tattoo it right into her skin.

Fucking adorable.

"It's too quiet," she whispers. "I don't like it."

"Maybe he wandered off."

"Or maybe he's in a meat coma."

"Christ. Too soon."

We lean forward and peer through the door.

David is sitting on the counter, his legs swinging and his gaze vacant as he spoons what seems to be cookies-and-cream ice cream into his mouth straight from the tub.

"That's a relief," I say as I let go of a held breath.

"He's living his best life." Sloane's shoulders drop and she watches David for a moment before heading into the room with careful steps as though not to spook him. He tracks her movement as she stops at the sink to ditch the contents of the bowl before dousing everything with bleach, but he doesn't move, just keeps slowly digging into the pint of ice cream.

I lean against the doorframe and cross my arms as I watch Sloane work at the sink. "When did you figure out who Thorsten was?"

"Pretty much right away." She shrugs, her focus still caught on her hands as she washes the bowl more thoroughly than it probably requires. "I heard about a cannibal killer in the UK from a few years ago who hadn't surfaced recently. When Lachlan gave us the location and I looked into disappearances nearby, they fit the same profile as the victims in his previous location. After that, I went through local real estate purchases from the last few years and, bingo, found him."

"Did you consider at any point that you might want to clue me in about a cannibal inviting us over for dinner?" I ask.

Sloane shrugs, her attention still not shifting to me. "Maybe. Mostly only when I was scraping human meat off your tongue. Up until then, no, I can't say that I did. You insisted on worming your way into my dinner invite, after all."

"Christ."

She giggles, clearly delighted with herself. Her eyes shine with amusement when she turns to me as she dries her hands with a paper towel. "Worked out pretty well in the end, wouldn't you say?"

"Not really."

Sloane grins as she heads toward David, whose focus is consumed by the ice cream in his grasp. She shoots me an unsure glance before she stops by his swinging legs. "Hey, David. I'm Sloane," she says. He doesn't acknowledge her words, just watches her as he slides a spoonful of ice cream into his mouth. "Maybe we should take a break from the food, what do you say?"

Sloane's smile is sweet, her movement fluid and graceful as she grasps the tub with one hand, the spoon with the other, then gently pulls them from David's grip. He doesn't protest and relinquishes both items at her request.

"Well," she says as she saunters closer to me, her dimple a shadow of restrained amusement as she keeps her eyes fused to the plain white tub in her hand. She's still reading the homemade label when she draws to a halt in front of me. "I might never look at ice cream the same way again."

"I don't want to know."

"Ingredients: cream—"

"Sloane—"

"Sugar—"

"I'm begging you," I say, but as soon as *beg* leaves my lips, Sloane's grin ignites. My stomach flips in the most uncomfortable way.

Sloane clears her throat. "'Semen, milked April tenth to April thirteenth.' That's an interesting substitute to salt—"

I push past her and vomit in the sink to the sound of her traitorous laugh. Christ, I thought there wasn't anything left, but I was wrong. It takes a long moment to recover myself before I can rinse my mouth and the sink, my breath and balance both unsteady.

"Chrissakes. What a fucking weirdo," I say as I wipe a thin film of sweat from my forehead and turn to face Sloane where she stands next to David with her arms crossed and a shit-eating grin spread across her lips.

"Yeah, he was a strange one."

"I'm still not sure if I'm talking about Thorsten or you."

Sloane giggles and shrugs. "Maybe it's fun to see the perfect pretty boy a little messed up for a change."

My dark glare only seems to amuse her further. "I think you've already seen that plenty," I reply as memories of last year's game bubble to the surface. I can still recall Sloane's touch as she bandaged my bloody knuckles, can still feel the warmth of her fingertips on my skin.

"That was different," she says. "That was you in your natural element. This is . . . definitely not that."

I huff a breath of agreement but say nothing further.

"But, you do kinda owe me extra for this year's win," Sloane says as she wanders closer.

I give her a suspicious glance as I lean against the stainless steel sink. "How do you figure?"

"Saving you from choking, for one thing. I thought that was kinda obvious," she replies with a shrug. She stops just out of reach as she gnaws the edge of her lower lip. "I think I need to make a claim."

"A claim?"

"A victory claim."

"Hold up," I say, shaking my head. "I didn't make a victory claim last year when I beat that piece of shit into the ground for spying on you."

"To be fair, you also kinda spied on me."

I scoff, but it sounds forced. "Did not."

"No? The way I remember it, you were pretty much *in the wall*, that's how hard you were listening to me getting myself off."

"I was listening to that pink-tie motherfucker getting himself off to you. So, no."

"Sure," she says with a flat glare. She turns toward David, watching him for a long moment before she spins on her heel and levels me with ferocity in her green and gold eyes. "David."

My gaze travels over to the vacant expression of the man who sits on the prep table, his legs still swinging in circles. "What about him?"

"Give him a job."

I snort a laugh. "A job." Another loud laugh whooshes from my chest before reality sinks in. *She's fucking serious.* "What the fuck?"

"You heard me. A job." Sloane's eyes narrow when I shake my head. She takes a step closer and pins me with a murderous glare. "We can't leave him like this."

"Sure we can. He should be glad he didn't get eaten. He's in the clear. Dodged a bullet. Or a fork," I say.

"And now he's got nothing. You could give him a place to work. A purpose."

"Have you noticed that we're in Cali-fucking-fornia? I live in *Boston*, Sloane. How the hell am I going to get him from here to there without arousing suspicion?"

"I dunno," she says with a shrug, her expression unconcerned by this dilemma she's dropped in my lap. "If he hasn't been reported missing by anyone, you could just . . . take him."

"It's not like Winston. I can't just put him in a cat carrier and bring him with me."

Sloane sighs and tries to tamp down an eye roll she's desperate to unleash. "I didn't find anything about a missing person matching his description in the area in my research. If Thorsten wanted a long-term servant, he probably took someone whose absence wouldn't be missed by anyone. You could just claim he's your brother. It's not like he's going to tell them any different."

"This is an epically bad idea, Blackbird."

"Then drop him off at the hospital and drive away. If his reappearance hits the news, you could reach out, offer to set him up. Just say you were so moved by his story or some shit."

"I'm not." I look over at David, who watches me with no spark of interest or awareness. "No offense, mate."

He doesn't respond.

I drag a hand down my face and pin her with a pleading gaze. "Look, Blackbird, it's sweet what you're trying to do for him. Really. But this is a huge ask, and he might be better off here. I'm sure he's got family *somewhere*, people who need to know where he is and who will want to take care of him. We don't even know what he can and can't do now, thanks to that Thorsten fucker."

"I bet he could wash dishes." Undeterred, Sloane turns from me and approaches David. Her hand folds around his wrist and he looks down at her touch. "Come with me, okay?"

With a few gentle tugs, David slides off the table and follows Sloane. I make room for them to stop close to me at the commercial dishwasher. She takes a few plates and hands them to David before she guides him to the rack, her smile encouraging, that fucking dimple filling me with equal parts warmth and dismay.

"Can you help me with the dishes, David? You just put them in the rack and then open it like this." She demonstrates how to open and close the freestanding machine before guiding him to fill the rack, which he does a little more quickly than I expected. He successfully navigates all the next steps with her encouragement, and when the cycle is finished he takes the clean dishware out and leaves it to cool on the counter. "That was awesome. See, Rowan? He got it no problem."

I resist the urge to groan when Sloane's bright smile alights on me. "For godsakes. You look like a kid asking for candy."

"Please? Super please. Big extra pleases with cherries on top," she says as she stops in front of me. Her dainty hands curl around my biceps in an uncharacteristically forward touch, her blood-red nails like talons against my skin. "I'll even give you a victory claim to make up for last year. Whatever you want."

I swallow and resist the urge to either maul her or run away. My feet stay planted as my eyes narrow with skepticism. "Whatever I want?"

She nods, but her brow furrows as though she's just starting to realize what she's gotten herself into.

My slow smile is wicked. "You're one hundred percent sure about this."

Her face scrunches. My grin stretches.

David burps.

And just like that, my smile disappears. "Fucksakes. I'm going to regret this, aren't I."

Sloane bounces in place.

"I'm going to collect," I warn.

"I know."

"And you're helping me clean."

"I thought that much was obvious, seeing as how I just washed your puke bowl."

I let loose a heavy, lengthy sigh. "Fine," I say on a groan, and Sloane beams. She bounces in place. There might even be a squeak. I don't think I've ever seen her bounce or squeak, and I'm not sure it's so much about David as it is about convincing me into something that she really, *really* wants.

"Thank you," she breathes.

In one hop, she kisses me on the cheek.

And then she's gone, the echo of her touch fading as though it was never real, just imagined. But I think I catch the wisp of blush on her cheek as she turns away. I think she hides it from me as she gathers supplies to start cleaning. In fact, I know it. It's in the shy smile she darts in my direction before she lowers her head and leaves for the dining room.

It takes a few hours of cleaning to erase our presence from Thorsten's house. When we're done, I keep David occupied in the kitchen by loading the same three racks of dishes over and over, and then I walk Sloane outside.

We stand in silence, both of us looking up at the few stars whose light penetrates the pollution from the city sprawl beyond the dark hills. It was only a few hours ago that it felt like the universe had collapsed in on us. All its power was honed in a single blade. And now we're a fleeting breath of time beneath starlight.

It's Sloane's voice that breaks the night.

"I think we're officially best friends now," she says.

"Oh yeah? Do you want to go do karate in the garage?"

Sloane grins at her feet. Her dimple is a shadow in the porch light. My heart is still turning over when her smile fades.

"I lied, by the way," she says.

I wish she'd return my gaze, but she doesn't. She can't bring herself to. So I take a second to memorize the details of her profile, because I know the hardest part is coming, just like it did last year, just like it did in the restaurant.

"Lied about what?" I ask.

Sloane swallows, the only sound between us.

And then her head turns, just enough to give me her eyes and a melancholy smile that tips up one corner of her lips, the faint trace of her dimple coaxed into view.

"Boston. I wasn't there for a meeting."

Her words echo in my head, and before I can absorb them or ask what she means, she hikes her bag higher on her shoulder and walks away.

I don't just hate this part. I fucking *loathe* it.

"See you next year, Butcher," she says, and then she slips into her car and disappears into the night.

I lied too, I want to say. But I just don't get the chance.

PUZZLES

Sloane

"More boobs."

"Seriously?"

"More. Boobs."

I look down at my black dress and back to the laptop screen where Lark has her hands under her breasts, pushing them up.

A deep sigh passes my lips. My heart has been hammering for the last hour.

And just think! Only another hour to go.

My heart rate doubles.

"Go big or go home, Sloaney!" Lark chimes through the laptop speaker. "Boobs!"

A conflicted groan rumbles in my chest. "Okay . . ."

"That's the spirit!"

I let out an unsteady laugh and head to my luggage to get what Lark calls the emergency dress. It's a curve-hugging, vintage-inspired oxblood velvet cocktail dress with black scalloped lace detailing that skims the low-cut neckline. It fits like a second skin.

I change out of Lark's view and slide on a pair of simple black pumps, taking in my reflection in the floor-length mirror next to the TV. I feel like a retro movie pin-up girl. With a deep breath and a final slide of my hands over the ripples in the soft fabric, I step into view of the camera.

"That's the one," Lark says with happy claps as she bounces on the edge of her bed back in Raleigh. "One hundred percent. Hair down. Do some old Hollywood waves. Gold star! Two gold stars! One for each boob."

She totally would gold star my tits if she was here in the room. She's always carrying around gold star stickers, mostly for the children she works with as a music therapist when she's not on the road performing, but she's not afraid to whip them out for adults too.

"Are you nervous?" she asks as I pick up the laptop and take it to the bathroom with me so I can start on my hair.

"No, of course not," I deadpan as Lark raises a skeptical brow on the screen. "I'm fucking terrified."

And excited. And rattled. And a little bit nauseous.

It's been almost eight months since I've seen Rowan in person. For the first six months, we talked nearly every day, in one form or another. Sometimes just short texts. Sometimes just a meme, or an article the other person would enjoy, or a funny video. Sometimes, they were long video calls. But lately, since he's been working on opening a second restaurant location, it's tapered off. Though I respond right away when he messages, it sometimes takes him a week to send back a short reply.

Superficially, it seems like the ideal situation for me. There's less pressure. I'm not used to having people around. Even when Lark and I became close at boarding school, it took me a long time to be comfortable around her. She's kind of like Rowan in the way that she wore me down, worming her way past the defenses I've held around my solitary nature. Her light is unstoppable. It pierces through every crack. And now, after the years that have passed since we met, I miss her whenever she's gone.

Like I miss him.

"He's going to be floored by those boobs," Lark says.

I snort a laugh. "Wouldn't be the first time." My smile quickly fades as I plug in my curling iron and run some styling cream through my hair with my fingers. "I need more to go on than just tits."

"You have murder too, he likes that."

I roll my eyes and stare her down through the screen. "Boobs plus murder don't equal a relationship, Lark. That math ain't mathin.'"

We fall into silence as I start the first curls. She's joking about the murder part, of course. I know that. And I know how I feel about Rowan. The more we talk, the more we laugh and play, the more I can't picture my life without him. But I am scared as fuck. More scared of wanting something beyond a friendship with Rowan than I've been of anything else I've done in my weird, unconventional life.

There's really not much that scares me, as though that sensation has been dulled. So why this? Why does this heat my skin and slick my palms and charge my heart with galloping beats?

I know why.

Because aside from Lark, no one has stayed around. Not even my parents.

What if I'm not worth keeping?

"Hey," Lark says, her soft voice a lifeline in the undertow of dark thoughts. "This is gonna be great."

I nod. My eyes stay fused to my reflection as I twist another curl around the hot metal.

What if I've got this all wrong? What if everything I feel is all in my head? What if he's been avoiding me? What if I'm unlovable? What if something unfixable is wrong with me? What if I try for something more with Rowan and I fuck it up? What if he never wants to see me again? I could just leave now. What if I do? What if what if what if—

"*Sloane.* Get out of your head and talk to me."

Tears glass my eyes when I turn them down to the screen. I swallow the ache that's building in my throat.

"He's got a big life, Lark. Lots of friends. He's got another restaurant that's almost ready to open. He's got his brothers. I just . . ." I shrug and run a thumb beneath my lashes. "I don't know if what I have to offer compares to all that, you know?"

"Oh, Sloaney." Lark presses a hand to her heart. Her lip wobbles but she puts on a determined expression as she takes hold of her laptop and brings the camera closer to her face. "You listen to me. You're *amazing*, Sloane Sutherland. You are brilliant, and so brave, and loyal to the ends of the earth. You set your mind to something and you fucking get it done. You work hard. You're funny. You make me laugh when I don't think I can. Not to mention, you're smoking hot. Gorgeous face. Gold-star tits."

My laugh comes out strangled. I set my curling iron down and grip the counter edge as I shake my head and try to breathe past the sting in my nose.

"You had to find comfort in being alone because you've had no choice. But as much as you like it, you're also lonely," Lark continues. "I know you're scared, but you deserve to be happy. So put some of that bravery to use for yourself for a change. Rowan would be lucky as all hell to have you."

I bite down on my lip and stare at my bleached knuckles.

Lark sighs. "I know what you're thinking, sweetie," she says. "It's written all over your face. But you are not unlovable, Sloane. Because *I* love you. And he might too, if you give him the chance. He did say that sweet stuff about you to the cannibal guy, right?"

"Yeah, but he was loaded and not really in the best headspace, you know? Plus, it was a year ago. He doesn't even remember he said that stuff."

"Maybe so, but he did ask you to come all that way to see him, didn't he?"

"I owed him a win. Plus, it's his birthday in two days, I couldn't really say no."

"Sweetie," she says with a shake of her head, "Rowan could have asked someone else to accompany him if he wanted to. He asked *you.*"

She's right, he could have asked someone else. When he called last month to claim the win I owed him from West Virginia, he'd said he wanted to have fun at the annual Best of Boston Gala for a change. *"You're the only person I can have real fun with,"* he'd said when he FaceTimed with the request.

I could have pushed back. The timing isn't ideal—I have to leave for a meeting in Madrid first thing tomorrow morning. But I didn't push back. Honestly, I was relieved to hear his voice after weeks of next to nothing. I told him I'd keep my end of the deal and then I changed my flights so I could leave for the meeting from Boston instead of Raleigh.

And now here I am, getting ready to spend the evening with Rowan, with no idea what to expect.

I take a deep breath and release my talon grip on the counter edge. "You're right."

"I know. I usually am," she says. I meet Lark's gaze through the screen and she gives me a wink. "Now do that hair, put on some makeup, and go have fun. You deserve it."

The kiss I blow to Lark is caught, and she pretends to press it to her cheek before sending one back to me. She gifts me with her megawatt smile and then disconnects the video call. When she's gone, I put some music on, a playlist of Lark's songs mixed with others that remind me of her. And I think of her. Of everything she said. How much richer my life has been since she became part of it.

I'm ready to go, sitting on the edge of the bed with a bouncing knee, when Rowan texts to say he's downstairs in the lobby.

One last check in the mirror, and then I'm walking out the door, my clutch gripped tight in my hand. The elevator ride is the longest of my life. When that door finally opens, he's the first thing I see across the hotel lobby, his broad back facing me and his head bent.

My phone buzzes in my bag. I pull it out and read the message.

<blockquote>I'll be the pretty boy in a black suit</blockquote>

> I can see that. But I'm not sure
> how I'm going to keep it from
> getting to your head if you look
> that good

Rowan's head snaps up and he turns to face me. He's so beautiful it steals the breath from my lungs. His hair is swept back, his suit perfectly tailored, his shoes polished, his momentary shock eclipsed by a bright smile. He pockets his phone as he strides across the lobby, his eyes never straying from me.

When he stops within reach, his eyes flow over every inch of my body, unabashedly drinking me in. I feel his gaze everywhere it touches. My lips, crimson red. My hair, the waves held back on one side by a sparkling, starburst barrette. My neck, sprayed with Serge Lutens Five O'Clock au Gingembre perfume and decorated with a simple gold necklace. My breasts, unsurprisingly, and his attention lingers there for a moment before sweeping all the way down to my toes and back up again.

"You look . . ." He shakes his head. Swallows. Shifts on his feet. "You look gorgeous, Blackbird. I'm so happy you're here."

He closes the distance between us and wraps me in an embrace, and I fold my arms around him in return, my eyes drifting closed as I take in a deep breath of his scent, warm sage and lemon and a hint of spice. For the first time in the last few hours, my heart slows even though it still hits my bones with heavy beats. Something about this feels foreign yet right, somehow.

Rowan releases me from his embrace but holds my upper arms in his warm palms. And then his lips are pressed to my neck where my pulse surges. My breath catches as the kiss lingers for a moment just long enough to etch itself into my memory for eternity.

There's an electric charge in the air between us as he pulls away to look down at me with a lopsided smile. How a man can simultaneously look so cocky while blushing I have no fucking clue, but it's intoxicating. "Would have kissed your cheek," he says as his fingers trace my skin where his lips were pressed, "but I didn't want to ruin your makeup."

My lips tighten around a grin that begs to be set free. I know he can see the way my eyes dance with surprise and amusement. He eats it up. "What's your angle, pretty boy?"

"To make you blush, of course." He gives me a wink and then takes my hand, seemingly clueless to the cacophony of thoughts that riot through my head at the simple touch of his palm to mine. "Come on. Car's waiting. We're going to have a fun night, Blackbird. Guaranteed."

Rowan leads the way to the lobby doors and the circular driveway where a blacked-out Escalade is parked, a driver waiting by the rear passenger door that he opens as we approach. Rowan keeps hold of my hand as I step up into the vehicle before he walks around to the other side, and then we're off to the Omni Boston Hotel at the Seaport, the venue for the gala.

"This is very fancy, Butcher," I say as I run my hand over the leather seat. "We could have taken an Uber, you know."

Rowan catches my hand and holds it on the empty seat between us as I try not to let surprise flicker across my face. "I'm not taking the most beautiful girl of the night to the social event of the year in a fucking Honda Accord."

"What's wrong with a Honda Accord?" I ask as a flurry of butterflies dances across my rib cage. "I drive one."

Rowan scoffs and rolls his eyes. "No, you don't. You drive a silver BMW 3 Series."

"Stalker."

"You're overdue for an oil change, by the way."

"Am not."

"Liar. The car has literally been telling you *Change my fucking oil, you heathen* for the last three weeks."

I guffaw a laugh and whack Rowan on the arm. "How do you know that?"

He grins and shrugs. "Got my ways." His phone dings in his jacket and he lets go of my hand to read the message with a frown. "Anyway, I thought it would be nice to splurge for a change. It feels like I've been stuck with my head down, dealing with problem after problem between the two restaurants. I could use a fun night out with my best friend."

My heart lurches in my chest as though it's suddenly facing the wrong way around. Like *everything* is. The hand-holding. The kiss on my pulse. Maybe I read too much into these small gestures.

What if everything I feel is all in my head?

I clear my throat and straighten my spine, folding both my hands over the sparkling clutch that rests in my lap. "How is it going with the new place?"

Rowan tilts his head side to side, his focus on the phone screen as he taps out a reply. "Not too bad. A lot of work. We're still on track to launch in October, but the electrical upgrades have been a bitch."

"How's David? Still doing well?"

At this he huffs a laugh, locking his screen before he pockets the device. "Great, actually. I've had Lachlan look again recently for any missing persons reports fitting his description, but there's still nothing. And David's been a solid helper. He's steady with the dishes. Reliable. Got him set up in a new group home since the last time we talked—this one brings him over and picks him up for every shift when one of the kitchen staff can't give him a ride. It works really well."

"I'm glad," I say with a smile as I sweep my waves away from my shoulder, a motion that Rowan follows with keen interest before he trains his gaze to the city streets passing by his window.

"Me too. At least one thing is going right at 3 in Coach. It feels like everything else has been a bloody circus the last few months. I know it's part of the nature of the business—shit just breaks and has to be fixed. Stuff inevitably goes wrong. It just . . . feels like a lot lately."

I lay a hand on Rowan's wrist and he glances down at the point of contact before meeting my eyes with a furrowed brow. "Hey, at least you've got this award tonight. Third year running, right? I know it's been shit to manage, but you're still doing it right."

Rowan's expression softens, and for the first time, I notice the subtle hints of stress in his face, the hint of dark circles beneath his eyes.

"And if something really goes south, I know what will help," I say with a sage nod as his head tilts.

His eyes dip to my dimple and narrow.

"Beef Niçoise salad."

Rowan groans.

"With homemade Dijon dressing."

"Blackbird—"

"And maybe some—"

"Don't say it—"

"—cookies-and-cream ice cream for dessert."

He pokes my ribs and I squeak out some sound I've never made before. "You know I have not been able to eat ice cream since then?" he asks as I giggle with the onslaught of jabs. "I used to love ice cream, *thankyouverymuch*."

"It's not my fault," I wheeze as he finally lets up. "I was just ensuring you were informed of the ingredients, in case you wanted something sweet to follow your one-of-a-kind dining experience."

"Sure. Very believable."

The vehicle slows and turns into the venue drop-off, drawing to a halt in front of the glass building where other gala attendees arrive with their shimmering gowns and fancy suits. I tug at the hem of my dress where it hits just below my knee, as if that will magically lengthen it. The driver has my door open, waiting for me to accept his hand and step out of the vehicle, but I don't.

"It's not black-tie," Rowan says as his hand slips between my back and the seat to prompt me toward the door. "And I guarantee that you could wear a potato sack and still be the most beautiful woman here. The dress is stunning, Blackbird. Perfectly you."

With a final, unsure glance at Rowan, I take the driver's hand and slide out into the fresh air, the scent of the sea thick on the spring breeze. Rowan's hand is on the small of my back as soon as we exit the vehicle, and my heart leaps into my throat and sticks there with every step we take.

The ballroom is decorated with bright white linens and colorful tropical flower centerpieces, and we find our seats in the center of the second row of tables from the stage that's framed by lights in shades of deep pink and blue. Several bars churn out drinks and groups of people laugh and chat near their tables as background music plays through the speakers around the perimeter of the room. A band sets up instruments on a lower stage at the opposite side, where a dance floor gleams beneath the dimmed overhead lights.

We grab drinks and mingle as we make our way through the growing crowd that snakes between the tables. There are introductions to Rowan's friends and acquaintances. Restaurateurs, lawyers, professional athletes. Regular customers. Irregular fans. Rowan is in his element, shining, glowing brighter than the splashes of color that shift overhead. His smile is easy, his laugh warm. His energy is infectious. Even though he's capable of killing any one of them without remorse, he still puts people at ease, his mask infallible.

It might be Rowan's element, but it's definitely not mine.

Small talk is usually easier for me when I'm hunting, because I have a purpose, a plan to lure someone in. I find it hard to relate to people when I know they're not shitbags who deserve to be relieved of their eyes. But with Rowan, it feels easier. He helps me make the first connections to other people. To find a common ground. *Your new album is doing great—did you know Sloane is close friends with Lark Montague?* Or, *Sloane is going to Madrid in the morning for a meeting, weren't you there last year?* And then I'm off and running, integrating like I'm more than just a plus-one. He helps me to the boundaries of my comfort zone without pushing me over the edge.

And the whole time, his gentle touch is an anchor. My lower back when we stand. My elbow or my hand when we move. And throughout dinner he continues to check in even though we're sitting right next to one another, with a smile or a glance or a single finger that glides over the inside of my wrist. When his name is called, he goes on stage and collects his glass teardrop trophy for Best Restaurant during the awards ceremony and even then he finds me with a wink and a lopsided grin.

And the ache buried deep in my chest burns hotter with every moment that passes.

When dinner is finished, the band starts up. Some people migrate to the dance floor; others stay to chat and mingle around their tables. Rowan heads to the bar to get us another round of drinks and becomes caught in conversation along the way. Likewise, I find myself swept away with the stories and anecdotes of our table companions who have remained behind.

But my eyes stray to the tall, beautiful man who sucks all the air from the room like an inferno.

He knows my darkest secrets. I know his. We can be monsters, and maybe we don't deserve the same things that other people do. Happiness. Affection. Love. But I can't seem to stop the way I feel when I look at every facet of Rowan, from his brightest light to his deepest, most dangerous dark. Maybe I don't deserve it for the things I've done. But I want it. I want more with him than what I've got.

Suddenly, I'm excusing myself from the table and weaving my way toward him before I even know what I'm going to do. His back is to me, my fresh glass of champagne in one hand, a glass of whiskey on ice in the other. He's speaking to a couple and another man, one he introduced to me as an investment broker. I stop just behind him, and when there's a break in conversation I lay a hand on Rowan's sleeve, my mind seemingly cleaved in two, like I'm watching myself from outside my body.

"Hey, I'm sorry," he says with a sheepish smile as he passes me the flute. "We got chatting about business."

"Of course, I didn't mean to interrupt." I start to retreat but Rowan catches my wrist. He says something about it not being an interruption but I absorb only one or two key words beyond the music and the deafening percussion of my heart. I swallow, my eyes snagged on his lips before I finally manage to lift them and meet his gaze. "Would you like to dance? With me . . . ?"

Rowan's momentary surprise evaporates as his attention flicks to the dance floor, a spark igniting in his eyes as his lips lift at one corner. It reminds me of the devilish little smile he had at Thorsten's when the cannibal suggested a visit to the tomato garden. When Rowan's eyes meet mine once more, they glimmer. "Absolutely," he says. He pulls my drink from my hand and places our beverages on a nearby table before leading us through the crowd.

As we near the dance floor, the band finishes one song and starts another, the pace slower but still energetic enough to be more than a shuffling dance, the tone romantic. Some people leave to refresh their drinks. Others pair up. I think for a moment that Rowan might detour back to the table or turn around to gauge my reaction, but he doesn't. He forges ahead with my hand clasped in his until we're on the floor among the couples, facing one another.

"You're probably going to be annoyingly good at this, aren't you," I say as his right hand slides across my hip, his left holding my right hand aloft, his grip warm and steady.

Rowan grins down at me and begins to lead us in movement. Nothing fancy, nothing showy. Just synchronicity, like we fit to one another, to the music. "And you'll still be better at it than me, won't you."

I smile and Rowan's grin grows brighter, then I raise our joined hands in a signal he understands. He guides me through a little spin, letting me out, reeling me back in closer with a chuckle. "Maybe. Or maybe we'll be just the same," I say, and I hold his eyes for as long as I can before my gaze drifts away over his shoulder.

The song plays on and I feel every little change of motion and charge in the air. Rowan's hold on my back becomes an embrace. My hand on his arm shifts to hook around his shoulder. His chest touches mine with every inhalation. When his breath warms my neck where my waves are swept back, my eyes drift closed. My head tilts. I want another kiss there, right where my pulse surges, so I know it's not just a moment of the past, an anomaly.

"Sloane . . ." he says close to my ear as we make a gradual turn.

"Yes," I whisper, that simple word unsteady on a ragged breath.

"Are you ready to have some real fun?"

My eyes flutter open. Rowan's voice is steady and clear. Devious. Not like mine, breathy with want and rioting desires.

I say nothing as I pull back enough to show him the confusion and questions lodged in my furrowed brow. That devilish smile is back, sneaking across his lips. A smile of secrets.

"The bald man with the glasses and the red tie. You should be able to see him across my shoulder," he says.

My gaze scans the dance floor and lands on a trim man in his mid-fifties in a well-cut designer suit. He dances with a woman about his age, her blond hair set back in a sleek updo.

I nod.

"His name is Dr. Stephan Rostis." Rowan's lips graze my ear as he then whispers, "And he's a serial killer. He's killed at least six of his patients over his fifteen years in Boston. Maybe more when he was living in Florida. And we can take him out together. Tonight."

My steps become wooden and small. The pieces I'd put together in my head are suddenly split apart and rearranged into another picture. *I got it all wrong. It was just in my head.*

I was wrong about everything.

Our steps slow and stop. Rowan pulls away and looks me over, excitement still radiant in his eyes. "I've got a great plan. He never stays late at these things. We can grab him and come back here without our absence being noticed. Perfect alibi."

"I . . . um . . ." Thoughts die before they land on my tongue and I clear my throat to try again, hoping I can infuse my voice with strength that just won't come. "I'm not really dressed for the occasion," I hedge, looking down at the red velvet shimmering in the flash of lights.

"I'll do all the messy stuff."

It's the first time that I can think of when I've not been excited at the prospect of killing another killer. It's just not what I expected, I guess. Not where I wanted this evening to go.

"Hey, you okay?" Rowan asks. "I thought the color of your dress was an inside joke—you know, blood red and all—but I'll make sure it doesn't get damaged, of course."

My heart is crinkling like paper crushed in a fist.

"But if you don't want to . . ." he continues, his voice fading as worry and maybe disappointment weigh down every note. He seems to realize we haven't been aligned at all when he says, "I thought when I said we could have some *real fun* that you knew what I meant."

"No, I actually didn't get that. But I can see it now."

The pause between us feels a thousand years long. Rowan's thumb lifts my chin, my focus still trapped on my dress until I'm forced to meet his eyes.

Confusion is etched between his brows. His gaze scours my face—my flushed cheeks and glassy eyes, my lips that are set in a tense line.

"You . . . you didn't know that's what I meant?" he asks.

"Shockingly, *I want to have real fun* doesn't reliably transfer into *I want to murder someone together,* unless I missed something in Google Translate."

"And you still came?"

I swallow and try to look away, but he won't let me. He's taking up all the space in every one of my senses, and no matter how much I want to be sucked into a void, Rowan anchors me right here.

Clarity and disbelief twine within his changing expression. He's trying to put his own broken puzzle back together, a new picture emerging.

"Holy shit . . ." His whispered words are barely audible over the voices and music that surround us, but I feel them, as though they're thorns embedded in my skin. His grip on my chin firms and he steps closer, looming over me, his eyes bouncing between mine. "Sloane," he whispers. "You're really here."

I'm not sure what that's supposed to mean. But I don't ask. Not as his gaze lingers on my lips when they part on a shaky exhalation. Not when his other hand slowly reaches up to sweep the waves from my shoulder, his fingertips an electric murmuration on my skin as they trace the slope of my neck.

He leans closer. His eyes don't leave mine. His lips are just a thread of space away . . .

And then his phone rings with the sound of a siren.

"*Fuck*," he hisses, his curse spilling across my lips. He draws away, the would-be kiss lost to another dimension, another Butcher and Blackbird who finally collide.

But in this realm, Rowan's hand falls from my face as his eyes press closed. He withdraws the phone and accepts the call.

"What is it?" he says as he tries to hold his frustrated sigh back from the caller. "What do you mean '*exploded*' . . . ? Jesus feckin' Christ. Is everyone okay . . . ?" Rowan runs a hand through his hair, the swept-back style now disheveled. His eyes land on me with dark and focused intensity. "I'm on my way. Comp whatever meals you have to."

"That didn't sound good," I say with a bittersweet smile when he disconnects the call.

"I have to go. *Right now.* I'm sorry."

"I can come and help—"

"*No*," he says, his voice unexpectedly firm. His hand finds my arm and holds on, an apology for his sharp tone. "The stove in the pastry section just literally blew up. Thank fuck no one is injured. I don't want you anywhere near that. I can't, Sloane."

I nod and try to smile. "I'm sorry your night took a turn."

"Me too. I'm so fucking sorry," he says with a deep crease between his brows as he shakes his head. "Stay and have fun. I'll take an Uber to the restaurant and text you the driver's details so you can take our ride back to your hotel when you're ready."

His hand folds over the back of my neck and he presses a kiss to my forehead. The touch echoes long after his lips are gone.

My chest aches when he takes a step backward and lets his hand fall to his side. Rowan's smile is faint, his brow furrowed. "Bye, Blackbird."

"Bye, Butcher."

I watch as he backs away, nearly bumping into couples on the dance floor, his eyes fused to mine until he forces himself to turn. And still I watch, my feet rooted to the floor and my hands clasped together, a statue among the lights and movement that swirl around me.

Just as he reaches the doors, Rowan turns. His eyes find mine. I give him a fleeting smile. He runs a hand down his face and a fierce, determined expression is left in its wake. He takes two steps in my direction but halts abruptly, his shoulders falling as he pulls his phone from his jacket pocket. With a final, defeated glance in my direction, he accepts another call and turns on his heel to stride away.

Five minutes later, a text buzzes on my phone with the contact details for the driver.

I leave as soon as it comes.

When I get back to the hotel, I run through my nightly routine and slide between the crisp linens, falling asleep almost instantly, as though my head and heart have run a marathon. I'm up just before my alarm, checked out within forty-five minutes of waking, heading to the covered walkway between the Hilton Hotel and Logan Airport when my phone chimes in my hand.

I miss you already

Emotion clogs my throat. I stare at the screen for a long moment before I tap out a reply.

I miss you too

Are we still on for August? No pressure if you can't, truly. I know you have a lot going on

I fully expect he can't make it. Who would? With a new restaurant under construction and a popular one that appears to be falling apart at the seams, it would be reasonable to expect he would want a year's reprieve. Would I be devastated? Sure. But would I understand? Of course.

Blackbird...

The dots of his incoming reply keep me motionless on the walkway.

I will blow this restaurant up myself before I miss it. I'll see you in August.

> And change your oil, you bloody
> heathen!

I pocket my phone and swallow the burn creeping down my throat, and then I keep going, ready to plow through these next few months. Maybe ready to try again.

What if I just try again?

What if I do.

HUMANITY ERODED

Sloane

Four Months Later . . .

"Damn. Am I too late? Did you win?"

Rowan shoots a fleeting glance my way as I approach on the worn path, dust coating my sneakers in a roan-colored film. His arms are crossed over his chest, the sleeves of his T-shirt straining against his taut biceps. There's a flash of trepidation in his eyes, their scrutiny cataloging the details of my face before he turns his attention back across whatever lies beyond the rolling hills of prairie grass.

"Nope. Didn't win."

"What are you doing?"

"Trying to psych myself up."

My head tilts with a question, but Rowan doesn't look at me. I follow his line of sight when I stop at his side.

"Whoa . . . That's just . . . Yikes."

I take in the dilapidated two-story Texas farmhouse set beyond the gentle rise of the hills, letting my gaze roam the battered and bleached wood of the siding, the shattered and boarded windows on the second floor. A hole on the right side of the roof gapes at the sky like a screaming maw calling to the thunderstorm that darkens the horizon. There's an assortment of junk on the covered patio—broken chairs and boxes, diesel cans and tools, the items strewn on either side of a clear path leading to the screened front door.

"Well . . . that's a homey place," I say.

Rowan hums a low and thoughtful note. "If by *homey* you mean *nightmarish*, I agree."

"Are you sure he's in there?"

Maniacal laughter and a man's piercing scream precede the growl of a chainsaw that starts up inside the house.

"Pretty sure, yep."

The screams and the unhinged laughter and the roar of the chainsaw crack through the air that suddenly seems too heavy, too hot. My heart rate spikes. Blood hums in my ears, a steady percussion to the symphony of madness.

"We could just go for beers," Rowan says above the chaos emanating from the house. "That's what normal people do, right? Go for beers?"

"Yeah . . ."

Part of me thinks that's a wise idea, but I can't deny the excitement that floods the chambers of my heart with adrenaline. Harvey Mead is an enormous brute, a beast of a man, and I want to take him down. I want to nail him to the floorboards of his horror house and carve out his eyes, knowing I'm the one who stopped him from ever taking another life. I want him to feel what his victims felt.

I want to make him *suffer*.

Rowan releases a heavy sigh, glancing down his shoulder at me. "We're not going for beers, are we."

"Sure we are. But *after*."

Another desperate scream slices through the air, startling a murder of crows and a lone vulture from the thin copse of trees to the left of the path. They don't go far, probably already aware that the sounds in the house signal an upcoming meal.

The pitch of the chainsaw rises and the scream grows weaker. There's a hazy quality to the anguish in it. A hopelessness. This isn't a scream that begs for mercy. This is only pain, little more than a reflex. Humanity eroded, stripped away, reduced to an animal caught in the clutch of distress.

Harvey Mead's maniacal laughter dies. The cries of his victim grow thin until they fade away. The chainsaw continues, its pitch climbing and falling as it works, until finally it ends too, blanketing us in stark silence.

"New rule," I say as I clear the gravel from my throat and turn to face Rowan. He stares down at me, his cheeks flushed, his navy eyes burning like the core of an alkane flame. Though he nods, I can't find any excitement in his expression, his lips set in a grim line as a crease deepens between his brows. "If you catch him first, I get to take something."

Rowan nods again, just once. His presence bleeds into my space. His heat. His scent. Sage and pepper and lemon envelop me.

"Just one," he says, his words raw as though their edges have been debrided. My breath catches as he raises a folded hand to my cheekbone, drifting his thumb across my lashes as my eyes close. Everything seems more vibrant in the momentary darkness—the silence from the farmhouse, the scent of Rowan's skin. His gentle touch. The thrum of my heart. "Just one," Rowan says again as his hand lifts away. When I open my eyes, his gaze is trapped on my lips.

My voice is a thin whisper. "Just one what?"

"Just one eye." Rowan drags his hard stare from my face as he turns toward the decaying farm. "I want him to suffer. But I want him to see every moment of it."

I nod. A flash of lightning illuminates the black backdrop of an encroaching storm, followed a breath later by the crack of thunder. "No matter who wins, we'll make sure of that."

Pulling my Damascus steel blade from my belt, I turn to stalk toward the house, but Rowan's fingertips graze my forearm, their featherlight touch igniting a current in my flesh that stops me abruptly. Our gazes collide and my heart folds in on itself. No one has ever looked at me like this, with so much caged worry and fear. And for the first time, it's not fear *of* me.

It's fear *for* me.

"Be careful, Blackbird. I just . . ." Rowan's thoughts fade away on the sudden breeze as he glances toward the house. He shakes his head, drops his attention to my dirty sneakers before returning his gaze to me. "He's a big bloke. Probably keyed up right now. Don't take any chances."

A half smile tugs one corner of my lips, but it changes nothing in Rowan's severe expression.

One long look. One held breath. A handful of heartbeats and a lightning flash.

Then I walk away, Rowan's footsteps drifting in my wake as we make our way to Harvey Mead's house.

The path snakes between two low hills, opening to a yard of scrub grass that surrounds the buildings. To the right of the house, the land dips to a shallow ravine of shrubs and what must be a small creek that's probably not much more than a trickle of water beneath the August sun. Between the house and the ravine is a small garden surrounded by chicken wire and tinkling charms of broken glass to scare the birds away. To the rear left of the house are outbuildings. A chicken coop. An old workshop with a low, flat roof. A barn that stands as a foreboding fortress between the house and the storm that rolls toward us. The skeletal remains of warped and rusted cars jut from between the trunks of Texas ash and desert willows.

I stop at the edge of the yard. Rowan draws to a halt at my side. "Great curb appeal," I whisper.

"So much better up close. The doll's head really adds character," he whispers back, nodding to the decapitated head of a 1950s-era Chatty Cathy doll staring back at us from the porch with soulless black eyes.

"I'll take it if he throws in the"—I lean forward and squint at a patch of gray fur stuck beneath a shattered rocking chair—"the . . . opossum?"

"I was going to go with cat, but sure."

I straighten, turning to Rowan with my fist held between us. "Sloane—"

"Rock-paper-scissors. Loser takes the front door," I say with a dark grin.

Rowan regards me for a long moment before he shakes his head with a resigned sigh. His fist finally meets mine.

On a silent count of three, we make our choices, my scissors losing to Rowan's rock. He frowns.

"Two out of three," he hisses, grabbing my wrist when I start toward the steps.

"For *losing*? No way. Go to the back door and enjoy your advantage, weirdo." I smile and crinkle my nose like it's no big deal, even though Rowan can feel my pulse surging beneath his palm until I pull free.

I don't look back as I focus on making it up the front steps alive. My chest burns to turn to Rowan, to stay with him and hunt by his side, but I don't.

When I set a heel on the cracked planks of the stairs, I see Rowan in the periphery as he finally stalks toward the rear of the house.

With every silent step I take, I survey my chaotic surroundings, careful not to lose my balance or knock something over. There's no sound from the house, no movement past the screen door, no menacing shadows illuminated by a flash of lightning. The first drops of rain hit the covered porch just as I reach the door, bouncing off tin cans and debris in a metallic melody.

I open the screen door just enough to slip inside, the quiet squeak of the rusted hinges absorbed by a crack of thunder that rattles the walls.

The scent of food and decay and mold blend in a nausea-inducing swirl as I start down a narrow hallway. A living room sits off to the left, with old furniture and original features covered in a film of dust. Flowered wallpaper peels from the walls and flutters in the breeze of the storm as it finds its way through open doors and broken windows. There's a partially mummified body sitting in an armchair next to the fireplace, her legs covered with a crocheted blanket and a Bible laying open in her skeletal hands. Her long, white hair lifts from her shoulders, a set of dentures still clinging to her slack jaws.

"Old Mama Mead, I presume," I whisper to her as I take a few cautious steps into the room until I'm standing before her. "I bet you were a total bitch, weren't you."

Knowing that Harvey Mead follows the worn path of many other serial killers with a fixation on a controlling, overbearing, and likely abusive mother doesn't make him any less dangerous.

But it certainly does give me some ideas . . .

I lean in close and grin at the leathery skin and hollow eyes of the woman in the armchair. "I'll be seeing you soon, Mama Mead."

With a wink, I firm my grip on my knife and leave the room, heading across the hall to the staircase that leads to the second floor.

The creaking steps are muffled by thunder and rain. It seems impossible that the house could be so devoid of human sounds after the brutal killing that just took place, but the only things I can hear are my heart and the storm.

When I arrive on the landing of the second story, the rain grows louder, the scent of it washing away the stench of the main floor. I wait for a moment, watching, listening. But nothing comes. No clues emerge about Harvey's whereabouts as I pause before the mouth of a corridor.

I start inching forward.

First, I arrive at a bedroom filled with boxes. Magazines.

Newspapers. Yellowed manuals for cars and tractors. Taking a turn in the room yields no worthwhile insights.

I reenter the hallway and head to the next room, a bathroom with a cracked pedestal sink and a shower curtain clinging to the interior of a claw-foot tub, its formerly white plastic speckled in black mold. There's no blood on the floor. No tracks. No unusual smells or sounds.

The next room I enter is the primary bedroom. Of all the rooms I've seen, this is the cleanest, though it would be a stretch to call it pristine. The window is filmed with dust and grime but it isn't broken. The bed is a simple wrought iron frame, the sheets rumpled, a few clothes strewn across its surface and the floor. I check the room, but there's no Harvey Mead here, so I don't linger, deciding to go through his meager belongings once he's dead.

I leave the room.

The next bedroom is across the hall. The sound of rain pelting metal containers dampens my footsteps as I step inside the small room. A hole in the ceiling gapes at the sky, cutting through the shattered beams of the attic. Lightning flashes overhead. Rain falls into the house to fill a series of metal pots and ceramic containers jammed against one another on a sheet of clear plastic that covers the floor. Surrounding the edge of the hole are bones that dangle from strings of wet yarn like wind chimes. Vertebrae twist and knock together in the breeze, rivulets of water streaming from their bleached bodies and wings.

I watch for a moment, pondering the psychopathy of the man who strung them here before I exit the room to head to the last door on the opposite side of the hall at the very end of the corridor.

This door is shut. I stand next to it for a long moment with my ear pressed to the wood, my blade clutched tight in my hand. No sound comes from within. No sound comes from downstairs either, though I'm not sure I'd be able to hear anything from the lower floor unless it was a confrontation. The thunder rages. The rain drives against the roof in wavering curtains.

A pang of worry fills my chest for Rowan. Maybe it's best that I haven't heard him, but I also haven't heard sounds of Harvey's suffering, and that lodges like a thorn deep beneath my skin. At this rate, I don't care who wins. I just want Harvey dead.

I shake out my wrists to let the excitement and tension and fear slide from my limbs, and then I grip the handle of the door and push it open.

"What the *fuck* . . ."

This is not what I expected.

Three monitors sit on a desk piled with papers and strewn with pencils. The screens display the feeds from eighteen cameras. The barn. The workshop. The back door. The kitchen. A darkened room where I can't make out any features. A brightly lit room where a dismembered body lies piled on a plastic-covered table, blood and flesh dripping onto the tile floor.

I see Rowan, entering the living room.

And then I see Harvey, stalking down the hall toward him.

The blood drains from my limbs. Ice infuses my skin.

"Rowan," I whisper.

I yell his name as I run from the room . . .

. . . straight into Harvey Mead's boot.

SHATTERED

Sloane

Water pelts my throbbing face. Nausea swirls in my stomach. Blood coats my tongue. The world spins around me. Rolling. I'm rolling down a steep hill. Rolling and *falling*.

I land with a shattering crunch on my left shoulder, the wind vacating my lungs through a silent scream. I gasp for air that won't come. My chest seizes. Rain and flashes of light blind me as I blink at the sky, the first winded breaths finally drawing into my panicked lungs.

A set of boots lands nearby with a heavy thump, approaching to stop next to my head. Rain washes congealed blood from the black leather. I open my mouth to groan Rowan's name when a hand twists into my hair and tugs me from the comforting scent of earth and wet grass.

I come face-to-face with Harvey Mead.

Rivulets of water cascade from his bald head to drip from his brow and fall across his expressionless face. He stares right into me. I glare back into the abyss of his dark eyes.

And then I spit in his fuck-ugly face.

Harvey doesn't wipe my saliva away. He holds me steady, letting the rain carry the bloodied streaks down his pockmarked skin. A slow grin pulls his lips back to reveal decaying teeth in a smile that's unnervingly disconnected from the rest of his apathetic mask.

He drops me but keeps his hold of my hair as he drags my weakened body around the side of the house. My head throbs. My face pulses. Tears sting my eyes with every tug on my hair, the pain in my shoulder radiating up my neck and into my limp arm. My feet scrabble on the grass and mud and debris, but I can't get any footing with the way he keeps my head down low. I scratch at him and hit his leg with my good hand but he's far too large to feel any impact from my futile fight.

We stop at a set of cellar doors. Harvey unlocks a rusted padlock and pulls the chain through the handles before opening one door and tossing me inside.

I hit the dirt with a grunt, my first breath filling with the scent of shit and piss and fear.

The contents of my stomach spill across the floor.

It isn't until I've stopped retching that it registers that I'm not alone. Someone is sobbing in the dark.

"Adam," a woman says through desolate cries. "He killed Adam. I h-heard it. He *k-killed* him."

She keeps her distance, repeating her words in a desperate chant that seeps into every crack and crevice of my chest. Brother or lover or friend, whoever this Adam was, she loved him. And I know what it's like to bear witness to the suffering of someone you love. I understand her grief and powerlessness better than most.

"Yes. He killed Adam," I reply through strained, panting breaths as I pull my phone from my back pocket. It buzzes in my hand with a message, but I turn on the flashlight first, aiming it toward the floor between me and the naked woman crouched against the wall as she recoils from the light. "And I promise you, Adam will be the last person Harvey Mead ever kills."

I'm not sure if that gives her any reassurance or closure. Maybe one day it will, but right now her loss is too fresh and the wound too deep. Her quiet sobs continue as I turn my attention to the screen when a text message comes in.

> Sloane

> SLOANE

> ANSWER ME

> WHERE ARE YOU

The dots of another incoming message start flashing as I type out a reply.

> I'm okay. Locked in cellar. Right
> side of house

Rowan's reply is immediate.

> Hold tight, love. I'm coming

I read his message twice before I lock the screen and bite down on my lip. My nose stings. An ache burns in my chest. Maybe it's just an Irish expression, but I still hear it over and over in Rowan's voice, as though he's right here in my head.

Hold tight, love.

"What's your name?" I rasp out as I turn my attention to the crying woman who huddles against the brick wall. She's about my age, slim, covered in streaks of dirt across her naked frame.

"I-I'm Autumn."

"Okay, Autumn." I set the phone down so the flashlight shines toward the ceiling and start unbuttoning my shirt. "I'm going to give this to you but I need your help to get it off."

Autumn hesitates for a moment before approaching with tentative steps. We don't talk as she helps guide the fabric over my dislocated shoulder, and though she backs away momentarily when I let out a cry of pain, she perseveres to free the shirt from my body. The fabric is soaked and muddy, and it might not keep her warm in the cool cellar, but at least she'll be covered.

She's just doing up the last button when an ax splits through the cellar doors.

"*Sloane,*" Rowan's desperate voice yells, carrying above Autumn's terrified scream and the wind and the driving rain. "Sloane!"

A raw ache grips my throat. My eyes fill with tears as I grab my phone and scramble closer to the doors. "I'm here, Rowan—"

"Stand back." With a few more hits, the doors splinter and fall into the dark with the lock and chain. Rowan's hand appears in the dim light.

"Take my hand, love."

There must have been stairs in here once, but they've been removed, and I have to jump to grab Rowan's palm, slipping on the first attempt with the rain and sweat on our skin. He repositions himself to lie on his belly, leaning farther into the darkness.

"Both hands," he demands, offering his palms to me.

"I can't."

A flash of lightning illuminates Rowan's face, searing it into my memory forever. His lips are parted and I can almost hear the sharp intake of breath as his gaze snares on my misshapen shoulder and missing shirt. His features are anguish and fury painted in light and rain. Beautiful and haunting and terrifying.

Rowan doesn't say anything as he reaches for me. When I jump, he catches my hand and grips it tight, hauling me up enough to grasp my elbow and pull me from the cellar.

As soon as I'm on the ground, I'm crushed in his embrace, trembling in his arms. I fist his soaked shirt. His scent envelops me and I want to hold on in this moment of comfort, but he forces us apart to look into my eyes.

"Can you run?" he asks, surveying my face. His eyes never settle as I nod, roaming my expression as though hunting for the truth. "You trust me?"

"Yes," I say, my voice breathy but sure.

"I'm going to keep you safe. Understand?"

"Yes, Rowan."

We look at one another for a final moment before he picks up the ax and grasps my hand. He looks back down into the cellar and it seems that he only realizes now that anyone else was down there with me, despite Autumn's continuous cries and pleas to be pulled free.

"Stay here," he says down into the pit, brooking no argument despite her elevated appeals. "If you keep quiet and hidden, he'll think you've already run and he'll leave the cellar alone. We'll come back for you as soon as it's done."

"Please, *please* don't leave me—"

"Stay the fuck here and be quiet," Rowan barks, and he drags me away without another glance into the cellar, ignoring the despairing cries that follow as we run toward the back of the house.

We stop at the corner and pause as Rowan leans forward to scout the path to the barn. When he seems satisfied, he squeezes my hand, turning enough to look at me over his shoulder. He nods once and I've barely returned the gesture before he's leading us across the debris-riddled backyard to the decaying barn. He enters the structure first through the open door, his ax raised, but the building is empty aside from tools and pigeons and an ancient John Deere tractor. Only once he's satisfied that it's safe does Rowan pull me deeper inside to stop against a wall at a point equidistant between the front and rear exits.

Thunder rattles the windows and the tools that hang from the planked walls. Rowan drops his ax to the dust with a dull thud. There's a breath of time between us when we just look at one another, both dripping wet and covered in mud and grass.

And then his hands are on my cheeks to hold me steady, his breath hot on my skin as his eyes travel across the details of my face.

A thumb passes over my forehead and I wince. A finger follows the slope of my nose. He traces my upper lip and I sniffle, the taste of blood lingering at the back of my throat.

"Sloane," he whispers. It's not for me to acknowledge. It's confirmation that I'm here, and real, but broken. Rowan keeps me close to the wall, shadowing me with his body, his hands drifting down my neck, lifting my chin to check every inch of my throat for injuries as I tremble in the dark.

"Your shirt—"

"I gave it to the girl. He didn't touch me that way."

Rowan's eyes flash when they meet mine. He says nothing in reply, just drops his attention to my injured shoulder where an angry bruise already colors the joint in the first streaks of purple. With a warm palm on my good shoulder, he turns me so I'm facing the wall. He assesses the injury with a careful touch. Though I try to stay silent, a tight cry still escapes when he moves my arm from where it's tucked against my side.

"Can you put it back in place?" I whisper when he turns me to face him once more.

"It might be broken, love. You need a doctor."

I blink away the sudden tears that fill my eyes as Rowan drops to a knee, inspecting my ribs, tracing each one. They're sore from the fall, but not broken. Rowan just ignores me when I try to tell him that, as though he won't be satisfied until each one is checked with a pass of fingertips over bone. When he's done, his hands lay on my hips, a long, tense breath covering my belly with heat that I feel down to my very core.

"I'm sorry," he whispers. He presses his forehead to my stomach, his arms wrapping around my legs to hold me close.

For a moment, I don't know what to do. I'm immobilized by the sudden current that fires through my trembling flesh. Every exhalation against my skin makes my heart beat faster until it's a hammer against my bones. And then my hand lifts, my body taking control without my mind, knowing something I don't—that it's the most natural thing in the world for my fingers to glide into his hair. My nails trace over Rowan's scalp and he sighs, pressing his forehead harder against my stomach as I do it again and lose myself to the cadence of a simple touch repeated.

The heat of his breath climbs from my navel, between my breasts, over my heart, following my surging pulse as Rowan slowly rises from his bent knee. I can't bring myself to take my touch away. My fingers slide from his damp hair until my palm rests on his cheek and the stubble that rasps against my skin. Rowan leans into my touch. He brings his hand to rest over mine as though I might fade away if he lets go.

"Sloane," he says, his eyes soldered to my lips. My name is a whisper of salvation and suffering as he says it again. A thick swallow catches in Rowan's throat. "I can't lose you."

"Then you'd better kiss me," I whisper back.

Rowan meets my eyes. His hands warm my cheeks. We're just a breath of space away from one another, and I know everything will change once his lips touch mine.

And it's true.

Everything transforms with a kiss.

Rowan's lips are soft but the kiss is firm, as though there's no room in his mind for doubt or uncertainty. He knows what he wants. Maybe he's wanted it all along. Maybe I'm the only one who needed the time to come around.

The heat between us builds in every sweeping touch. I open my mouth when his tongue traces the seam of my lips, and with the first caress of Rowan's tongue over mine, every thread of restraint between us unravels.

I lose myself in desire. It crashes into me, as though it was always hiding behind a crumbling wall.

And once it's unleashed, it consumes me.

Urgency takes over. Rowan's hand threads into my hair and he crushes me to him. I moan when he sucks my bottom lip into his mouth. My hand grips the back of his neck and I dig my nails in until he growls and drives his tongue deep into my mouth, demanding more from a kiss that's already sparked an inferno of longing in my veins.

I forget all about who we are. Where we are.

Why we're here.

A sudden scream has us instantly parting to stare at one another with wide eyes and ragged breaths. The terrified pleas for help are drowned by the sound of a chainsaw sputtering to life.

We lean out of the shadows enough to see Autumn run full speed around the side of the house, coming straight for the barn. A second later, Harvey appears, chasing her down with the chainsaw gripped in both hands. Despite his heavy, blocky frame, he's gaining on her as she stumbles through debris with her bare feet and naked legs.

We slip back out of view and Rowan flashes me a devastating, feral grin.

"Be right back, Blackbird."

He folds a hand around my nape and presses his lips to mine in a final, quick kiss, and then he lets go to retrieve his ax from the floor.

"What are you doing?" I hiss.

Rowan rests the handle of the ax against his shoulder and huffs before giving me a wink. "Getting revenge for hurting my girl, of course."

The hard edges of my heart melt a little with those words, and Rowan grins as though he can see it. Without another word, he turns away, stalking closer to the door to crouch behind a set of metal toolboxes as I back up until I'm sheltered by the engine of the tractor.

A second later, Autumn comes tearing into the barn, heading for the back door, every step punctuated by a panicked wail.

Harvey Mead rushes into the room after her. And everything that happens next is in slow motion, a beautiful choreography of revenge.

Rowan surges forward. He swings the ax upward in an arc that sweeps so low to the ground it stirs the dust. The blade connects with the chainsaw in a brutal strike. The chain breaks from the guide bar. It whips into Harvey's face and he lets out a furious roar. The machine sputters as he drops it and stumbles to a disoriented halt. He raises a hand to his bloody face in reflex, not yet aware that Rowan is already rounding on him for another strike.

The ax splits his kneecap with a wet crack. Harvey cries out in pain and falls to his other knee as Rowan tugs the blade from the bone.

"Let's see how much you enjoy this when you're on the receiving end," Rowan grits out, and before Harvey can fall to his side, Rowan kicks him in the face, his heel a loud thud when it connects just between Harvey's thick brows.

Harvey falls to his back, stunned and groaning, barely conscious. His blood-streaked head wobbles from one side to the next in a cloud of dust. Rowan stands over him and tightens his grip on the handle of the ax. Rage and focus sharpen the features of his beautiful face. Malice flashes in his eyes as he glares down at his enemy. "This is going to be so fucking satisfying," he says, looming over Harvey with a lethal smile. He raises the ax.

"*Wait*—" I say as I step away from the safety of the tractor. Rowan stops instantly, though it looks like it takes everything in him to do so. "Don't kill him yet. You promised me a turn."

A dark grin sneaks across my face as I approach. Rowan surveys my expression with a flicker between his brows, an unvoiced question passing between us that I answer with a wider smile.

"But feel free to keep him occupied," I say, and then I head toward the house.

Autumn's screams have gone blessedly silent in the torrent of the storm that still rains down on us. It will be slow going for her on foot with no shoes, but she'll find help eventually if she follows the creek or double backs to the front of the house to take the path that leads to the gravel road. It's a fair distance to the nearest neighbors and the road doesn't see much traffic, but we can't bank on the remoteness working in our favor. I know we can't stay too long.

Just long enough to have a little fun.

I don't linger in the house, working quickly to collect what I need before heading back to the barn.

A string of expletives greets me as I near the old building. Rowan appears amused by the colorful vitriol as he hammers a metal spike through Harvey's hand to keep him trapped against the ground, a similar implement already impaling his other palm. Rowan is so consumed by his work that he doesn't notice me until I'm standing at the door.

It takes him a second to process what he's seeing before he barks an incredulous laugh.

I drop what I'm carrying with my good arm and raise a finger to my lips around a fit of giggles. Tears cling to my lashes as hysterics threaten to consume me. I'm quite pleased with myself, I have to admit. This might just be one of the best ideas I've had in a long time. And I want to make the most of the impact, so with a few choppy hand motions, I manage to communicate that I want Rowan to block me from Harvey's view. He nods and stands between us as I maneuver through the shadows, creeping closer with my coveted prize.

When I get to Harvey's feet, I lay my little gift on his ankles and start sliding it up his legs.

Harvey groans when I graze his injured knee. He looks down the length of his body and meets the vacant eyes of his mother.

Harvey Mead lets out a blood-blistering scream.

"You've been a terribly bad boy, Harvey," I say in my best imitation of an old woman's voice as I continue sliding the corpse toward Harvey's face. He struggles, trying to kick it off, but Rowan intervenes and holds his good leg down.

"Good boys don't chop people up with chainsaws."

Another desperate scream. He's absolutely losing his shit and can't do anything about it.

I take my sweet, sweet time. I enjoy every second of Harvey's torture, slowly dragging Mama Mead up his torso as strained breaths saw from his chest. His pulse pounds in his thick neck. Sweat beads across his creased forehead, dripping down his temples as he shakes his head.

Mama Mead and Harvey finally come face-to-face.

"I think you deserve to be punished."

"This is very dark," Rowan says behind me, though he doesn't sound like he's complaining.

"Shush, you. Mama Mead's got some things to say." I jostle the corpse's head around as Harvey screams and squirms. The dentures fall out of her mouth to land on his face and he enters another dimension of fear. "Oops, my bad."

I set Mama Mead down on his chest so I can grab her brittle wrist, keeping my injured arm out of the way as Harvey tries to thrash her off. Her curved fingers stroke his face before I hook them into the corner of his mouth. *"Hold on, son. I just want to crawl inside and have a look around."*

Harvey lets out a keening wail.

And then he gasps for air, *gulps* for it as though it won't go in, his face a contorted grimace.

"Uhh . . ."

The veins in Harvey's temples protrude. His flesh turns red and then rapidly drains of color. His lips turn blue.

"What the . . ."

A rattling breath leaves his chest. His eyes go dim. His pupils fix to the ceiling and dilate.

"Did he just have a heart attack?" Rowan asks. He stops by Harvey's unmoving head to stare down at his bloodied face.

My shoulders fall with disappointment. "This is so uncool, Harvey."

"You literally scared him to death. You should be proud."

"I had so much more in me." I give Mama Mead a petulant shove and she rolls off Harvey's unmoving chest. "Do you think we should give him CPR?"

179

"If you want to, but I call dibs on not doing mouth-to-mouth."

". . . Dammit."

Rowan grins when I look up. He walks around Harvey's head, stopping beside me with his hand outstretched. "Come on, Blackbird. The adrenaline's going to wear off soon and that shoulder will really start aching then. We'd better burn the place down and get going before that bird finds her way to help. Then I'll get our things sorted at the motel and we'll be on the road."

I place my hand in Rowan's and he pulls me to my feet. The scar through his lip lightens a shade as he smiles down at me. My gaze travels over his face, and I want to remember every detail, from his dark brows to his navy eyes and the faint lines at their edges, to the tiny mole on his cheekbone and the shine on his wet hair. Most of all, I want to remember the warmth in his kiss when he presses his lips to mine.

All too soon, he's pulling away, but not without taking my hand as he leads us toward the house.

"On the road," I say, his words finally surfacing from the haze of adrenaline. "On the road to where?"

"Nebraska. To see Dr. Fionn Kane," he says. "My brother."

IMPRINTS

Rowan

Sloane sleeps next to me in the passenger seat, a blanket I stole from the hotel covering her body, her black hair swept over her swollen shoulder. Her bra strap holds an ice pack in place over the joint, and though I know it probably melted an hour ago, I haven't had the heart to replace it in case I wake her.

When I look at her, I can't seem to pry one emotion away from the others. They all intertwine when I think of Sloane Sutherland. Fear is fused with hope. Care with control, with envy, with sadness. It's fucking *everything*, all at once. Even the desire to turn this feeling off locks with the need to nurture it. The totality of it devours me.

And it only grows with every passing moment. Sloane bleeds into every thought. When we're apart, her absence is an entity. I worry for her. I dream of her. And yesterday, I almost lost her. Killing bound us together, and it's a compulsion neither of us can live without. This need, and now this game between us, consumes me as much as she does.

My obsessions push me to a cliff I'm bound to fall over, and there might not be an end to the drop once I do.

Sloane stirs and groans, and my fucking heart starts rioting. Maybe it hasn't stopped since that first day in the bayou when she walked out of that bathroom at Briscoe's, all wet hair and flushed, freckled skin and that Pink Floyd T-shirt tied at her waist. Every time I think of her, my heart reminds me I'm not as dead on the inside as I thought after all.

"Easy, Blackbird," I say as she groans again, more of a whimper this time that claws at my guts. I lay a hand on Sloane's thigh, maybe to reassure myself as much as her. "Just a few more hours."

She shifts, every painful movement etching a crease on her skin until her eyes are squeezed shut. The blanket falls down to her waist when she finally makes it to a straighter position but she doesn't seem to notice, and when I pull it back up for her she gifts me with a faint, grateful smile. I pass her a bottle of water and a handful of pain meds before she has the chance to ask for them.

"I feel like hell," she says, her eyes drifting closed once more as she swallows the pills. When I respond only with a thoughtful *hmm*, she gives me a sidelong glance. "You can say it."

"Say what?"

"That I *look* like hell too."

I chuckle and her eyes narrow. "I'm not saying that. No fucking way." I look back to the road, saluting a magpie that flies over-head, trying to keep my attention on the horizon even though the weight of Sloane's piercing stare on the side of my face is like a hot brand on my skin. "What? I think you're beautiful. Like some kind of vicious, battle-hardened goddess of vengeance."

Sloane snorts. "Goddess of vengeance, my ass."

182

I glance over in time to catch one of her epic eye rolls. Before I can stop her, she's got the visor pulled down and flips up the cover for the mirror.

A shriek fills the little hatchback.

"*Rowan*—"

"It's not that bad, once you get used to it."

"*Get used to it?* There's a fucking *boot print* on my face." She leans closer to the tiny mirror, turning her head side to side as she inspects the bruises of distinct tread marks on her forehead and two black semicircles beneath her lower lashes. When Sloane turns to me, her eyes are glassy with unshed tears.

"Blackb—"

"Don't you *Blackbird* me. That can-can motherfucker stamped my fucking forehead. I can even see the Carhartt logo on it," she says, her voice taking on a watery quality as she draws closer to the mirror before turning back to me, a tear spilling over her lashes as she leans over the center console and points to the circle in the center of her forehead. "See? Right there. *Carhartt*. Why couldn't he have just punched me in the face like a normal person?"

"Probably because he wasn't a normal person, love. I thought the chainsaw was a big clue." I wipe one of her tears away with my thumb. Her lip wobbles and I want to simultaneously laugh and burn the world until I find a way to resurrect that arsehole so she can kill him again. "It won't be there forever."

"But I have to go to the bathroom," Sloane says, managing to wrestle her voice under control even though her face is still the picture of distress. "How am I supposed to go anywhere without drawing attention to myself?"

I don't dare offer the option of finding a private bush on the side of the road to squat behind. She's clearly reached a limit to her stress and I'm not keen on being stabbed while driving.

"There's a rest stop in ten miles. I'll sort you out."

Sloane watches me for a long moment, and though her expression is still weary and pained, it softens just a little before she settles back into her seat. "Okay."

My chest aches. *She trusts me.*

I swallow, dragging my attention back to the road. "Okay."

Silence descends as Sloane gnaws on her lower lip, watching out the window as farm fields slip past. I turn up the music now that she's awake in the hope it might calm her when I sense the tension rolling from her motionless frame. Sometimes, it feels like having a wild thing in my grasp when she's with me. She's just like her nickname, ready to take off with the first gust of wind. I've never wanted to earn trust before Sloane. I've never cared about keeping it on a personal level, not for anyone but my brothers. And suddenly, Sloane's trust is one of the most important things in the world to me. I know if I lose it, I'll never get it back.

And that scares the shit out of me.

"What if I need surgery?" Sloane whispers.

I offer her a smile, but it doesn't seem to reassure her. "Then you'll have surgery."

"People will ask questions."

"My brother will take care of that. But we don't even know if it's necessary. Let's see what Fionn says when he takes a look."

Sloane sighs, and I lay my hand back on the blanket covering her thigh, unsure if this is too much when I don't know where we stand. But her good hand slips into mine, and my heart jumps into my throat with a heavy beat.

Not so dead on the inside after all.

"Does Fionn know too?" she asks, her gaze angled away from me toward the open expanse of land and sky.

"About our . . . hobbies? Our game?" She nods, and I give her hand a light squeeze. "Yeah, he knows."

"But he's a doctor. Our idea of fun is kind of the antithesis of his life's work."

I shrug before I give a nod toward the sign for the upcoming exit. The tension in her hand eases. "Let's just say my brothers and I didn't have the most conventional upbringing even after we left that shithole of my father's house. Between Lachlan's ruthlessness and my recklessness, Fionn has no blinders on when it comes to the darker shades of life. He's chosen his own path like we always hoped he would. But he accepts what Lachlan and I have become, just like we accept him."

"Your path," Sloane says. "How did you find it?"

"You mean the restaurant?" I ask, but when I glance at Sloane she shakes her head, her gaze honed on my face like she's absorbing every nuance. "After my father attacked us for the last time, when Lachlan and I killed him, I realized I didn't feel what I probably should about doing something like that. Most people would feel guilt. But I felt a rush of excitement when it was happening. Accomplishment when it was over. There was peace in knowing he would never come back. And when I met someone else that reminded me of him a short while later, I realized there was nothing stopping me from doing it again. There was always a next person. Someone worse. Eventually, it became a kind of sport, to find the worst person I could and wipe them off the planet forever."

Sloane hums a thoughtful note and turns her gaze toward the gas station ahead. I want to know the same kinds of things about her. How did she get to this? What happened before and after her first kill? Does she really have no one other than Lark? But with Sloane, I already know she shares when she's ready, not when she's asked. I can only hope she'll be a little readier now.

We pull into the gas station and I park far from the building where she's less likely to be spotted, cutting the engine before I turn to her. "I'll leave the keys with you, just in case."

Sloane's gaze flicks to the dash and back to me. Something softens in the pain still rampant in her bloodshot eyes. "Okay."

"I'll be right back."

She nods, and I nod in return.

I try to take as little time as possible in the gas station, scooping up water and soft drinks and an assortment of snacks, along with a few things that will hopefully make Sloane more comfortable. I'm pleasantly surprised when the vehicle is where I left it, Sloane watching every step I take from behind the windscreen. Her deep breath and flicker of a smile don't go unnoticed when I open her passenger door.

"I thought this was fitting," I say. I snap the tag from a distressed gray trucker cap before handing it to her. *Sounds like bullshit to me*, the cursive script says across the front.

"Accurate," she replies, centering it on her head before she takes the cheap aviators I pass to her next, clutching them in her good hand.

186

"This next part is probably going to hurt like a bastard." I pull a button-up shirt from my bag and she lets go of a heavy sigh, frowning at the creased fabric. "We'll cut it off when we get to Fionn's."

Sloane makes no argument, just glances down at her injured arm that lies limp and useless over the blanket before she gives a single nod.

I remove the melted ice pack from beneath her bra strap first, watching as her eyes press closed and her lower lip slides between her teeth. When I take her injured hand and guide the sleeve past her wrist, she lets out a pained whimper, a flush climbing up her neck and into her cheeks. I keep going, even though I know I'm the one causing her to suffer just by helping her put on a fucking shirt. I try to push away the thought that the whole thing is because of me, this whole stupid game, her busted shoulder, her battered face. But I tamp those thoughts down because she needs me, and the only thing that matters now is to get her help.

Once I slide the shirt over her bad shoulder, the task becomes easier. She's able to twist her body enough to get her other arm in without too much trouble, and then I drop to a crouch to do the buttons up for her.

"Thank you," she whispers through ragged breaths as I start the first button. I glance up at her face, a pretty flush brightening her cheeks beneath a thin film of sweat. "That sucked."

"You did good," I say. My fingers graze her stomach near her pierced navel as I thread the next button through the hole. I didn't mean to touch her but I have zero regrets, especially when she responds with a little shiver. Her exposed skin pebbles, and when I look up, Sloane's hazel eyes are fused to mine, her pulse humming in her neck as my gaze falls to her throat. I'm faintly aware that my fingers are slowing around the third button, the need to touch and taste her skin dulling every other thought behind a hazy film of desire. My cock strains against my zipper and I let my gaze travel down the slope of her collarbone, resting on the smooth skin of her chest as it rises and falls with rapid breaths. I follow the line of her bra to where the edge of the shirt is folded open, exposing the stained white satin.

And then I stop dead, all the world narrowing to the point of her nipple.

Her *pierced* nipple.

I can distinctly make out the shape of a heart around the firm peak and a tiny ball on either side.

That was *not* there the first time we met. I *know* that. I know it because my internal monologue was punctuated by the words *no bra* every two minutes from the second she walked out of that bathroom at Albert Briscoe's.

I think my hands have stopped moving. Can't really be sure. I'm just staring at that little heart as my mouth goes dry and my cock goes hard as fucking stone.

A sudden flicker of motion breaks the spell as Sloane unfolds the sunglasses with a snap of her wrist.

"Something caught your eye, pretty boy?" she asks.

Those lips. That dimple. *That fucking smirk.* She slides the sunglasses on with a wink before her hazel eyes disappear behind the mirrored lenses, and then she's slipping past me, all curves and sass as she tugs the shirt down enough to cover her bra before she saunters away to the gas station.

Goddamn.

I am going to have so much fucking fun punishing her.

It's ten minutes later when she returns to the hatchback and I'm still sitting here with a raging hard-on, immersed in fantasies of how I'm going to torture her into telling me everything about those nipple piercings. My dick has no hope of calming down with that faint grin still plastered on her face.

"You good?" she asks when she pulls off her sunglasses and slides into the passenger seat. Her eyes flick to mine as she tugs the seat belt across her body.

"Great. Yep. Just great."

"You sure? You want me to drive for a bit? You look a little . . . distracted. Wouldn't want something shiny to grab your attention and you run us off the road."

I shoot her a glare as I key the engine and shift into drive. "Christ alive. Let me just survive the next two hours and then we're going to have some words."

And I feel like that's what I barely manage to do. *Survive.*

As soon as we arrive at Fionn's house, I'm ready for a stiff drink. It's barely noon. I text my brother as soon as we're parked, but he doesn't answer, so I assume he's immersed in some of his workout shit and head around the side of the vehicle to collect Sloane. Her bruises have darkened and she looks exhausted, which I guess isn't surprising, but she bites down on any complaints as I help her out of the car and up the front steps of Fionn's white-and-red Cape Cod home.

I ring the doorbell.

We wait.

I pound three times on the door.

We wait longer.

"Fucking Fionn," I hiss. "He's probably playing Metallica full blast on his headphones as he does eight thousand burpees, the little shit."

Sloane glances up at me, her pain now infused with worry. I give her my best attempt at a reassuring smile before I press a kiss to her temple.

"He knows we're coming. It'll be okay. He won't let us down," I say as I wrap a hand around the doorknob.

Unlocked.

I roll my eyes—of all people, Fionn Kane should know better. "For such a smart guy, he's a fucking dumbass sometimes."

The house is quiet as we step inside. It's quaint as fuck. Definitely Fionn in his peak "Hallmark Sad Man Cinderwhatever" era, just like Lachlan said. There's even a lace doily on the coffee table.

Leading the way farther into the living space, I start heading toward the kitchen where I can see a rear door to the backyard. "*Peckerhead*," I call out to the silent house. "Stop dicking around."

Something cracks me across the skull. Stars explode within my vision.

"Dick this, motherfucker!"

A woman's screech precedes a second hit that whacks my hand where I clasp it to the sore spot on top of my head. I manage to grab the weapon and rip it free of her grasp. Sloane is yelling behind me, a series of *whoa, whoa, whoa*s, as I wield the club with one hand while I try to keep Sloane behind me with the other. Except, the club isn't really a club, but . . . a crutch . . . ?

"*Who the fuck are you?*" a small, twentysomething, dark-haired banshee of a woman yells, hobbling into my field of vision as she takes a swipe at me with her remaining crutch. I hit it out of her hand and it spirals across the hardwood, but the little demon manages to stay upright. I'm about to jab her chest with my crutch in an attempt to push her over when she whips a hunting knife from behind her back, the blade nearly as long as her arm. "I said, *who the fuck are you?*"

"Me? Who the fuck are—"

"Did you do that to her face?" she snarls. She points the tip of her blade between me and Sloane, who's now by my side with her good hand raised in a placating gesture. "You did that?"

"*No*, Jesus—"

"I'll cut you—"

"How about everyone just settle down. I think this is all a simple misunderstanding," Sloane says as she takes a careful step closer to the little banshee. "What's your name?"

The banshee's dark eyes dart to Sloane and stick there. "Rose."

"Rose. Cool, okay. Nice. I'm Sloane."

"You look like one of the bally broads kicked you in the face in clown alley," Rose says.

Sloane blinks. Her mouth opens, then closes, then opens again. "I . . . I honestly have no idea what that means. But he didn't do it, I swear."

"Right, sure," Rose scoffs, her eye roll nearly as good as Sloane's. She takes a hobbling step closer, but the cast thuds on the floor and she grimaces. "He just nudged you with his foot, did he? Just a love tap? You don't need to protect this piece of shit, honey. *I'll fucking cut his balls off,*" she growls, pointing the tip of her blade toward me. I try to knock it with the end of her crutch but she dodges my swipe before Sloane steps between us.

"No, really. See? Carhartt logo. *Right there,*" Sloane says, tipping the brim of her hat up to point at the circle stamped on her forehead. She waves her hand behind her in the general vicinity of my feet. "He's more of a Converse guy."

"Where's the motherfucker who did that to your face?"

"He's dead."

"Then who the fuck is this crutch-stealing fleabag?"

"He's Rowan," Sloane says, gesturing at me again.

Rose narrows her eyes as though this is insufficient information.

"He's my f-fr . . . boy. Guy. A man-guy. I'm . . . with. Here."

I snort a laugh as Rose's face scrunches. "*Man-guy,*" I echo. "Real smooth, Blackbird."

"Shut up," Sloane hisses as she glances over her shoulder at me as though she's unsure if she should relinquish the details of Fionn being my brother. I hike my eyebrows in reply and press my lips shut. "Little help before I get knifed?"

I shake my head. "Man-guy shutting up, as requested."

Sloane groans, her eye roll putting Rose's earlier efforts to shame. I swear her eyes even go in different directions before she turns back to the woman with a blade up in her face. "Look, I'm in need of some medical help, obviously. Fionn is a doctor, right? He also happens to be this crutch-thieving fleabag's brother."

Rose's suspicious glare slices between us. She deliberates for a long moment before she pulls a phone from her pocket, her knife still pointed in our direction and her eyes straying from us only long enough to select a contact to call. I can hear the faint ring as she presses the phone to her ear, then my brother's muffled greeting.

"There's a beat-up chick here with a tall guy claiming to be your brother. He stole my fucking crutch," Rose bites out. She falls silent as Fionn says something in the background, and her eyes then fix to me like lasers. She jerks her chin once in my direction. "He's asking to confirm your childhood nickname."

Blood drains from my extremities as my gaze darts to Sloane. I shake my head. "No."

That seems to delight the hellcat—Rose's responding smile is fucking feral. "Great. Then I knife you in the balls."

"Yeah? Hobble over here and try it," I snarl. I try to poke her with the rubber end of the crutch but Sloane bats it away.

"For fucksakes, you two. I've got a messed-up arm here. I need a doctor," Sloane says, shifting side to side at the waist to give a demo of her limp appendage. She turns enough to give me one sad-puppy eye. The longer she stares at me, the more my resolve crumbles. Her lower lip juts out in a pout, and even though it might be fake, I know I'm a fucking goner. "*Help me*, Man-guy."

A long groan rumbles in my chest as I drag a hand over my face. "Fuck. Fine." Both women watch me with unwavering stares, their eyebrows hiked in anticipation. "*Shitflicker.*"

They face one another. There's a moment of blessed silence.

And then a fit of giggles.

Rose relays my response back to Fionn and I hear him cackling on the line before he gives her some clipped instructions and disconnects the call. She pockets her phone and sheaths the blade as Sloane tugs the crutch free of my grip and passes it over to her.

Great. These two are going to be best friends now. Just what I need.

"Okay, Shitflicker. I guess you passed the test. Fionn will be home in fifteen to sort you out."

"Hold on a second. You haven't told us why the fuck you're here," I say as Rose rakes a dismissive smirk over my features.

"Maybe I'm Fionn's Girl-chick, Mr. Man-guy Flick-a-shit."

Sloane snorts a laugh. I take her good elbow, guiding her to the couch as I keep my glare pinned on Rose. "God help us all."

Rose hobbles away on her crutches, muttering something about "worse than the circus," whatever the fuck that means. I watch as she makes her way to the dining table, and when I'm satisfied she won't chase after us with a crutch and a knife the size of a machete, I refocus on Sloane. I help her drag some pillows under her left side so she can find a comfortable position on the overstuffed couch, but I know what it's like to be so exhausted you're desperate to rest, yet so in pain that it seems like a distant reality. When she seems as settled as she can manage, I kneel in front of her and sweep her raven locks back from her face.

"Drink?" I ask, and she nods, her eyes pinched with the pain that settles in as her adrenaline wanes. "What do you want?"

The space between her brows crinkles as her pretty hazel eyes hold mine, her pain tugging at my chest.

"I want . . ." She trails off as her eyes dart away and back again. Then her dimple peeks out at me. That fucking thing is like a beacon of mischief. I barely manage to suppress a groan. "I want to know how the Shitflicker name came to be."

"Sloane," I warn.

"Was it your own shit you flicked, or someone else's? Regularly? And like . . . why?"

Her diabolical mask falters when I lean forward and brace a hand to either side of her knees. "You're lucky you're injured."

Sloane gives me a smug little grin. Fuck, I want that smart

mouth and those plump lips wrapped around my cock so badly it aches. "Oh yeah?" she snarks. "Why's that?"

I drift closer still. Push into her space. She resists the urge to sink deeper into the cushions as her breath hitches. My hand folds around her throat, one finger at a time pressing into her skin, her pulse like music beneath my palm. She shivers when my lips graze her earlobe. "Because I'd bend you over my knee and spank that perfect ass of yours until it glows. And then do you wanna know what I'd do?"

She gives me a shaky nod. Three uneven breaths. "Yes," she whispers.

"I'd teach you a lesson about *wanting*. About wanting to come so badly you have to beg for it." My cock hardens as Sloane's blood surges against my fingertips. "And once I was sure you'd learned that lesson, I'd teach you about wanting to *stop* coming so badly you beg for that too."

Sloane's hummingbird pulse sets my blood on fire, her faint ginger scent marred by sweat and blood and her lingering fear. I wonder if she realizes how easily I could crush her delicate windpipe. I wonder if she thinks about how she's caught in the grip of a killer who is just as deadly as she is.

"You're trembling, little bird."

In a flash of movement, I let her go and tower over her. My cock begs for relief as I take in her blushed cheeks, her rapid breathing. Her fingers graze her neck, a light trace of motion across her pinked flesh as though she misses my touch.

When her eyes meet mine, I give her a dark grin, one full of confidence. Full of promises. "Maybe you should start practicing your begging, love. Might not bring you back a drink otherwise."

Sloane's unsteady exhalation is answered by my wink before I turn and stride away. It's hard to not look back. Flushed and flustered Sloane might just be my favorite version of her yet.

Of course, I do look back, because I can't help myself. Just one glance. A sly smirk that I throw over my shoulder, and I burn the image of her undisguised want into my memory.

When I get to the kitchen, I take my time to rummage for drink options, settling on the bottle of Weller's Antique Reserve bourbon, not because it's what I actually want, but because it's the most expensive bottle of alcohol in the house and that little shit Fionn deserves to have his pricey booze stolen after the nickname fiasco. Rose is sitting at the dining table, the lights dimmed and a row of cards laid before her.

"I didn't take you for the solitaire type," I say as I set the glasses on the counter and pour the first drink. Her glance at me is fleeting.

"Tarot."

"Clearly," I say flatly.

Her gaze flicks up to me again, a faint smile tipping up one corner of her lips as though in apology for missing the joke with her distracted focus. "Want a reading?"

"Hard pass. Not keen on tempting ghosts or some shit. Don't need more bad luck."

Rose shrugs, flips over a card from her deck. "Suit yourself."

She examines the cards. A crease deepens between her brows as her eyes shift from one to the next. Another dog-eared card is flipped, her silence drawn out with her assessment of its hidden meaning.

"So . . ." I say, and she doesn't look up as she turns another card. "You're staying with my brother? How long have you two been going out?"

"We're not."

"I thought you said—"

"—that 'maybe I'm his Girl-chick'?" Rose doesn't look up as she snorts a laugh. "Yeah, 'Man-guy' didn't sound real solid either. No offense."

I glance to where Sloane sits in the living room with her left shoulder slumped, her focus on the phone balanced on her right knee. "None taken," I mutter.

"How long have you been"—her eyes slice up from the cards and roam over me—"pining . . . ?"

My hand drags down my face as I groan. Something tells me there's no bullshitting Rose. "A long-ass time."

Rose looks down at her cards and nods sagely. "Yeah. Thought as much. Well, you're welcome, in that case."

"For what?"

"My serendipitous presence in this charming abode," she says, sweeping a hand toward the living space. "Fionn has the primary bedroom. I have the first guest bedroom. That means you, my friend, get to share a bed with your Girl-chick over there."

A burst of both excitement and nerves floods the chambers of my heart. I run a hand through my hair and look toward Sloane as she scrolls through her phone. I'm not sure if she'll want that. Or if I should take the couch. Or if I can make myself take the couch. Or maybe I should just sleep on the floor. But I'm also no saint, so there's no fucking way I'm doing that.

"Fuck," I whisper.

Rose snorts. "Exactly. Shoot your shot, bro."

I shake my head and grin at the little she-devil, but her attention is absorbed by the cards spread before her in the shape of a cross on the left, a line on the right. Her head tilts. Her brow furrows. Her fingers dance above the row of images, their meanings unfamiliar to me. "So, you got her into this whole fucked-up-shoulder, bootprint-face situation?"

"I . . . I guess. Yeah."

"Some kind of . . . game . . . gone wrong?"

The bottle nearly slips from my hand. I set it down next to the glasses and take a step toward the table. "What?"

"A game," she repeats without looking up. She points to a card of a man wearing a wreath and riding a horse, another wreath encircling the pole in his hands. Her gaze travels over the remaining cards. "A game of life and death. There's suffering. Secrets and deceptions. Illusions," she says, her voice grave as her thumb touches the edge of a card whose title at the bottom says THE MOON.

"I thought I took a pass on a reading," I say in a wary voice that's little more than a whisper.

"You did. The cards disagreed." Rose shrugs. "They do that."

I find myself at the opposite end of the table, my eyes fused to Rose as she taps a finger next to the top card in the row on the right, a metronomic tick of time.

"The Tower," she says. Her finger rests on the faded gold lightning that strikes a stone tower. "Destruction. Or liberation. What does it mean to you?"

Her eyes are nearly black in the dim light as they settle on me. My mind reeling, my only answer is a shake of my head.

"A tower of stone," she says, not looking from me as she taps once on the card. "It should be strong. But built on an unstable foundation, it just takes one lightning strike to bring it down. Chaos. Change. Pain. And when your world crumbles around you, the truth is revealed."

"And what . . . you think what happened to her is the lightning strike?"

Rose looks away to Sloane, a thoughtful frown passing through her expression before she turns her attention back to me. "I don't know. Maybe it is. Or maybe that strike is yet to come."

And though her gaze shifts away when Fionn comes striding through the door, Rose's words remain like barbed hooks snagged deep into my thoughts. They refuse to let me go.

I make introductions. I go through the motions of explaining what happened, answer all my brother's questions as he examines Sloane's shoulder. We don't linger in the house, and within twenty minutes, I'm gathering her up to bring her to Fionn's office. But when I look at Sloane, it's Rose's questions that still remain. Maybe they were always there.

Did I ever really free her?

Or will I be her destruction?

BROKEN REVELATIONS

Sloane

My head lies in Lark's lap as her fingers rake through my hair. She rocks in time to the melody of her unsteady voice. *"No one here can love or understand me . . ."* she sings. Her voice wanes to a shaky hum.

I know I've done something I can never take back. Something I would never want to, even though most people would feel regret. But I don't. I feel relieved. I've finally opened the gate where a monster lay rattling its bars on the other side, begging to be freed. Now that it's out, there's no way to close it back in.

And I don't want to.

"My parents will fix this," Lark whispers as she presses a kiss to my hair. "I'll tell them what you did for me. They'll help us. You can come home with me."

My hands are wet. Sticky. I raise them into a sliver of moonlight from the window. They're covered in crimson blood.

When I lower my hands, I see the body on the floor. The artistic director of Ashborne Collegiate Institute.

And my one wish is that he'd rise from the afterlife so I could do it all over again.

"*I'll arrive late tonight . . .*" Lark sings, "*Blackbird, bye, bye.*"

"Blackbird," a different but familiar voice says. I surface from the murk of memory and dreams that never let go. When I open my eyes, Rowan is there, sitting on the edge of the bed. His hand sweeps the hair from my face. "Just a nightmare."

I blink and take in my unfamiliar surroundings. Light spills from the en suite bathroom to illuminate a slice of the guest room, decorated in hues of deep gray and white and pops of yellow that lose their cheerful brilliance in shadow. Moments come back to me from the haze of strong painkillers. Memories of agony as Fionn rotated my arm. The pain in Rowan's eyes as he held my hand and reminded me to breathe. The relief of the bone sliding back into place. The way Rowan rested his head next to mine when it was over, as though every moment had carved a deep slash across his heart. When he rose and looked at me, there was both distress and regret in his eyes, and I couldn't tell which one was worse.

And even now, they still linger in his eyes.

"What time is it?" I ask as I sit up a little with a groan. My shoulder aches, but there's a certain comfort in having my arm strapped across my body in the sling.

"Eleven thirty."

"I feel gross," I say as I look down at my leggings and the button-up flannel shirt that I've just slept in for the last few hours. I haven't showered in well over a day, not since the morning of Harvey's house of horrors. It's as though he haunts me through the film that coats my skin.

"Come on." Rowan offers a hand to help me sit. "I'll start you a bath. Might help some of the soreness."

He leaves me at the edge of the bed and heads to the sliver of light, as though he knows I need a minute to get my bearings. I hear the faucet squeak, the water rush into the tub. For a long moment, I just linger in the dimly lit room until I conquer my inertia and join Rowan in the bathroom.

I say nothing as I stop at the vanity to stare at my reflection and try to will the tears away despite the sting in my eyes and the knot in my throat. Deep purple bruises follow the curve of my eyes, the imprint of Harvey Mead's bootprint even more vibrant in my skin than it was when I first saw it in the car. Dried blood still rims the edges of my nostrils. My nose is sore and swollen. Fortunately, however, it's still in the right place. Which is good, because I already look like a fucking dumpster fire and I don't need a broken nose to add to the current shitshow.

"Ready," Rowan says as he switches the water off for the bath. When I don't answer, he comes closer, his reflection drawing to a halt in the periphery. I don't take my eyes from my ruined face. "I'll get Rose to help you."

"No," I whisper. Tears gather on my lash line despite my best effort to keep them at bay. "You."

Rowan doesn't move for a moment that feels stretched thin. When he approaches, he stops behind me, the weight of his gaze so heavy on my reflection that I can feel it through the glass. "Beautiful."

An incredulous laugh that sounds more like a sob escapes my lips. "I look like shit," I say as the first tear falls. I know I shouldn't care as much as I do. It's only temporary. In a few weeks, this will be nothing more than a memory, probably even a funny one. But the problem is, I *do* care, no matter how hard I try not to. Maybe I'm just tired from the pain and the stress and the hours on the road. Or maybe it's just hard to see that my vulnerability isn't just trapped on the inside. It's staring out at the world in full color. It's staring at *him*.

"You're beautiful to me," Rowan says. He reaches from behind me to chase the tear from my skin with his thumb. The next pass of his caress follows the swoop of the bruise beneath my eye. "That color right there, how many things can you think of that are that color? It's rare."

He grazes my bruise again, his touch so soft that I don't feel pain. My lip trembles in the mirror. More tears well in my eyes. "Eggplant," I say, my voice tremulous. "It's the worst vegetable."

Rowan's huff of a laugh warms my neck and sends a current through my skin. "It's not. Celery is the worst vegetable."

"But eggplant is mushy."

"Not when I make it. I promise you'd like it."

"I have an eggplant face. That's basically a dick face. A mushy dick face with a Carhartt logo."

Rowan shifts the hair back from my shoulder and lays a gentle kiss on my cheek. I don't have to see his reflection to feel his smile as his lips linger on my skin. "This is not having the intended effect. Let me try again," he says, amusement warm in his voice. His other arm wraps around me to unclip the first of two buckles for my sling. My wince of pain is met with another kiss. "That color doesn't remind me of eggplant, for what it's worth. It reminds me of blackberries. The best berry, if you ask me. It reminds me of irises. They have the best scent of any flower. It reminds me of night, just before dawn. The best time of day." The other buckle clicks free and I close my eyes against the pain as Rowan slides the sling from my arm.

"But—"

"You're all the best things to me, Sloane. No matter how many bruises are in your heart or on your skin."

When I open my eyes, it's not my marks I see. It's not the swelling or the scrapes or the blood. It's Rowan, his navy eyes fused to mine, his arm banded across my waist as his other hand traces slow patterns on my skin.

I place my good hand over his, wrap my fingers around his knuckles where scars crisscross over bone. Then I lift his hand away, every nuance of his expression absorbed by my watchful gaze. I guide his fingers to the top button of my shirt and let my hand rest on the tense muscle of his forearm.

No words are shared between us. Just the connection of our eyes in the mirror, one that doesn't waver.

Rowan frees the first button. The second. The third. The fourth is low on my sternum. The fifth reveals my upper abdomen. The sixth the jeweled bar at my navel. Still he holds my eyes as he works the seventh and eighth buttons free. A slice of skin down the center of my body glows in the light that bathes us from above the mirror.

My pulse pounds. I could see it in my neck if I was willing to break my gaze away. But I'm not. I keep holding on as Rowan's fingers curl around one edge of my shirt.

He folds it open, exposing my breast to the warm air. Then he does the same with the other side. And still our gazes remain locked. It's not until I swallow and raise my brows that he finally lets his eyes fall to my body.

"Jesus . . ." he whispers. "Sloane . . ."

My flesh is a mess of scratches and bruises, all the marks darker and more obvious than they were hours ago. His gaze drifts over every inch of my exposed skin as though I'm something precious yet damaged, a broken revelation. It might not be how he expected, but I know he's imagined me like this before, bared and vulnerable to his gaze, his touch. Just like I've imagined him. But it's different to feel it in the heavy silence that stretches between us. I couldn't have expected the way my blood would charge through my flesh, or the way the whole world would shrink to this pinpoint, this moment in a mirror.

Rowan's gaze rests on my throat, his navy eyes nearly black, his pupils consuming the color until only a thin band of blue remains. It traces a line down the center of my body, his attention so slow and deliberate that it feels like a touch against my skin. It flows over the ridges on my sternum. It veers left and slows over my heart. It traces the rose gold piercing encircling my peaked nipple. Gooseflesh rises on my arms and I shiver as his gaze crosses my chest to the other side and the matching piercing on my right breast.

"Something caught your eye, pretty boy?" I whisper.

"Yes," he says, his voice pained. "God, yes, Sloane. All of you."

Rowan drags the shirt down my uninjured arm first, then takes his time to pull it from my swollen shoulder, his eyes remaining steady on the reflection of my body. The fabric falls away and pools at my feet. He takes a deep breath before he hooks his thumbs into the waistband of my leggings and pulls them over my hips. His fingers wrap around my ankle to raise my foot from the cool tile and tug the fabric free of one leg and then the next. When he rises to his full height behind me, I can see every strained breath in his chest, every thump of his heart as his pulse surges in his neck.

"I need to get my shit together," he mutters, his voice low and gritty, the words not meant for me. He holds out a hand for me and I take it. "Come on. Into the bath before I fucking die."

I drag my feet as he tugs me toward the cloud of white bubbles shimmering in the tub. "Would that mean I'd get an extra win?"

"I'm about ready to forfeit every game, Blackbird," he grumbles. "I don't think we need to go to the extreme of killing me off just yet."

We stop at the edge of the tub. Rowan keeps hold of my good hand as I dip one toe into the warm water. When I take my first step in, I glance up, expecting to catch him focused on the details of my body. But he's not. His eyes are on mine, a crease notched between his brows as though this whole experience is excruciating.

"You okay?" I ask as I steady myself with his hand and place my other foot in the water to stand in the small tub, my faint smile serving only to deepen his frown.

"Not really."

"You're doing great."

"Shouldn't I be telling you that?"

"Probably."

"Just get in, for the love of God."

"I am in."

Rowan drags his free hand down his face. "How do you still have the energy to take the piss out of me?"

"I always have the energy for that. Your suffering is my number one priority." My smile starts out bright but falters when Rowan's gaze shifts from me to the corner of the room as though he can't bear to keep his attention on my face for a moment longer. "What is it? Rowan . . . ?"

"I've been suffering for four years, Sloane. I'm begging you here. Get in the fucking bath."

My eyes don't stray from his profile as I slowly lower myself into the water. Every inch that I fall, I hope he'll meet my eyes, but he doesn't, as though he suddenly can't. Like he's put himself into a box that wasn't there just a moment ago.

"Technically, three years," I say, trying to resurrect the levity between us as I submerge myself until the bubbles consume my chest, only my shoulders and upper back visible above their diaphanous embrace as I curl forward and hug my knees.

Rowan's long exhalation is unsteady above me. "Four years."

"Harvey's place was three—"

"That was yesterday. That means we're in year four now. And it feels like eighty."

"Okay," I say with a teasing grin that he doesn't see. It takes a moment before he squats down to my level. My gaze is still fused to him, and he still avoids it.

Rowan takes a facecloth from where he laid it out at the edge of the tub to saturate it in the bathwater. He's careful not to touch me beneath the surface. He withdraws the cloth and slides it across my uninjured shoulder to cleanse the grime from my skin with slow strokes, and though I stay perfectly still on the outside, my thoughts churn with the force of a hurricane.

I swallow, still unable to look away from Rowan. My voice sounds small when I say, "So . . . four years?"

Rowan's eyes darken, their focus snagged on the motion of his hand as he sweeps the cloth across my skin. He doesn't graze me with his fingertips, not even once, despite repeating the motion of the cloth until the water in it cools. "You already know. I told you at Thorsten's."

My heart lurches. Rowan dips the cloth through the cloud of bubbles and into the water, this time grazing my hip in a fleeting touch that might have been intentional. Before I can be sure, the cloth is out of the water and sliding over my spine.

"You . . . you remember that?"

Rowan doesn't answer. I don't think he will. So when he dips the cloth into the water for a third time, I grab his wrist beneath the surface, and finally his eyes meet mine.

"Hey," I say, my voice gentle. "I'm right here."

"Sloane . . ." Rowan presses his eyes closed and takes in a long breath as though hoping to wash away the pain. When he meets my gaze, he looks just as agonized as he did a moment ago. "If I touch you again . . ." He shakes his head. "It took everything in me just to get you undressed without bending you over at the bathroom counter and fucking you until you beg me to stop."

My cheeks pink, but I try on a cocky smile, one that only darkens the agony in Rowan's eyes. "Not sure I see the problem with that idea at the moment."

"You're injured."

"Just my shoulder. And my face. Okay, my ribs are a little sore too, but I'm fine, really. Hazards of the job, right?"

"I need to look after you. It's my fault you're like this. The game was my dumbass idea."

"*Hey*, do not shade the game. It's the most fun I've had since . . . maybe ever. As long as I can remember. It's the thing I most look forward to every year," I say, the amusement slipping away from my voice with every word spoken as the truth rises to the surface. "*You* are the thing I most look forward to, Rowan."

He swallows, his expression a thin veil over whatever conflict is chewing him up on the inside. When he shakes his head, the sting of sudden, restrained tears burns in my nose. Maybe his suffering isn't what I wanted, as much fun as that seemed just a few heartbeats ago.

"I wanted to play," I continue, my voice still sure even though I don't think it will be for long. "I was scared when we started, afraid that I was making a huge mistake. But finding someone who could understand me for all the shattered pieces beneath the mask? I needed that. Before you came along, something was missing. *You*, Rowan. You were missing. You made it safe to feel seen. Safe to play on our terms. Safe to have fun, even though our fun might not be everyone's idea of a good time."

His jaw clenches, like it's a struggle to not bite out his next words. "That is the problem, Sloane. It's not safe. It's the farthest thing from it." When I open my mouth to argue, Rowan grasps my chin with his hand to trap me in his stern glare. "I almost lost you," he says, every word punctuated by a pause, as though he's trying to push each one into my head.

"I am right here," I reply in the same cadence. My fingers fold around his, guiding his palm to my heart to lay it flat against the surging beat. "*Right here.*"

"Sloane—"

I've had enough of words.

I close the space between us and press my lips to his. He stalls with shock and I squeeze his hand where it's still damp and hot on my chest, my tongue a demand against his lips. *Let me in.* I realize at this moment that I've always been *in*, in Rowan's thoughts, in his plans, maybe even in his heart, and now it terrifies me that he could suddenly shut me out.

He kisses me back, but it feels tentative, like he's trying to keep me away even though he doesn't want to.

I drag his hand across my skin. His breath shudders when I stop at my breast, the piercing at my nipple resting in the center of his palm. A conflicted groan escapes Rowan's control. His hand presses harder to my flesh. But the kiss is still not the same as it was in the barn, not when it felt like we'd escaped one fate to fall into a better one.

So I move his hand. I pull it to my sternum. Glide it down my skin. Let his hand slip into the water, slow and gentle over my navel. I know he likes that piercing too. I could see it in his eyes when he watched me in the mirror.

Our kiss breaks when I keep going lower. His breath floods my senses, the hint of bourbon a phantom between us. I inhale the scent and trap it in my lungs as my pulse hums in my ears.

I press Rowan's palm to the apex of my thighs and hold it there.

He sucks in a ragged breath.

"Sloane . . . is that . . ."

My hand floats away as I let him explore. His fingers find my clit and the triangle piercing there and I bite down on my bottom lip at the burst of sensation. He then moves down to the symmetrical outer labia piercings where the bars on each side are capped with small titanium balls. By the time he reaches the fourchette piercing, he's nearly vibrating with tension.

"Out of the fucking bath," he growls as he grips my good arm and hauls me to my feet. A wave of water sloshes over the edge of the tub and soaks the bottoms of his jeans, but he doesn't seem to notice.

"But I just got in, as instructed, I might add."

"I don't fucking care."

I give him an innocent smile, one that earns me a sharp and heated glare. "I thought you said you needed to take care of me."

"And that's *exactly* what I'm going to do."

The moment my second foot is out of the tub and touches the bath mat, he lifts me into his arms. He doesn't give me a towel, doesn't wrap me in anything but his embrace. Fat drops of suds slide from my body and drift to the floor as I soak his shirt.

Rowan yanks the door open with more force than necessary and marches toward the bed.

"But I'm no fucking angel, Sloane."

He sets me down on the edge of the bed and steps away. His chest strains against his wet shirt with every breath. Arms folded, he glares down at me where I sit, my legs crossed, my good arm clutching the injured one to my body as the water cools my skin.

"Show me," he demands.

My brows hike as my heart tries to spear itself against my ribs. "Show you?"

"You heard me. Get up on that bed and spread your legs and show me."

"I'll make it wet—"

I don't even get my last word out and he's in my face, barely an inch away, his hands bracketed to either side of my hips. "Do I look like I give a fuck? Do you *really* think I care?"

My skin tingles as though begging for his caress, but I'm sure he knows it, can sense it in every ragged breath that passes my lips. He's careful not to touch me with anything but the fire burning in his eyes.

"I'm done running around this, Sloane. I've wanted you for four years. And you're going to show me what I've been missing."

Rowan doesn't move as I slowly uncross my legs and release my hold on my body to brace myself with my right hand. I slide up farther on the bed and he looms over me, his fists pushed into the edge of the mattress and his eyes hooked to mine until he seems satisfied that I've made it far enough. When I stop in the center of the bed, Rowan stands straight and crosses his arms once more, his jaw clenched.

"Spread your legs, Sloane."

His eyes stay fused to mine as I let out an unsteady breath. My left heel slides across the mattress, then my right, my knees still bent and my upper body braced off the mattress with my elbow. Rowan's eyes still haven't left mine even though I'm bared to him, as though he's torturing himself, denying himself of his desire to look down.

"Wider."

Heat surges in my core as I shift my legs a little farther apart. An ache builds beneath my bones, an emptiness that begs to be filled. Every demand Rowan makes is fuel, every word incendiary.

"*Wider*, Sloane. Stop trying to hide from me, because I promise you now, it's not going to work."

I swallow. My legs spread to the point of discomfort.

A beat of time passes before Rowan's gaze unlinks from mine to travel down my body. I feel it in every inch of flesh, the weight of his desire as it travels over me, his thinning restraint like fire beneath my skin. His attention settles on my exposed pussy as the muscles of his forearms tense.

"The clit piercing. Tell me."

He doesn't look up when I pause. He just waits, watches. "I was eighteen," I say. "It was my second body piercing, after my navel. It hurt, of course, but not as bad as I thought it would. Once it healed, it helped, I think. With orgasms."

"You couldn't orgasm before?"

"I don't know. I didn't have the right . . . situation . . . up until that point. But it felt like it gave me control." I remain still as the muscle in Rowan's jaw jumps. His eyes are dark, hooded. He knows just enough about my past to cement the gaps in his knowledge with his own imagination. "The labia piercings I got when I was twenty. I liked the way they looked. I know they're small, but somehow they remind me of armor. Maybe that doesn't make sense."

"It does," he says as his eyes anchor to mine.

I give him a faint smile that fades in a heartbeat. "The last one, the fourchette, I got that a few months before I met you. It just made me feel more confident. And I thought a partner might like it too."

Rowan's eyes are a lightless void, his voice a deep and gravelly rasp when he says, "Did they?"

My gaze travels across the room to land in the shadows. I don't look at him when I shake my head. "I don't know. I haven't been with anyone since I met you."

Those words are met with silence. They hang in the air. They consume the oxygen in the room. When my gaze lifts from the shadows, it collides with Rowan's and I see it, the exact moment his restraint detonates.

"Why not," he demands.

I shake my head again.

"I told you already. *Stop hiding.* It's not going to work with me, not anymore. You want this? You want me? Then fucking *tell me,* Sloane." Rowan's arms unravel from his chest. His hands lie on my knees, steady on the tremor in my bones to capture the tectonic shift that's cracking me apart. "You fucking tell me, so that you know when I ruin you for all other men, it's what you asked for. *Tell me*—"

"You," I say. Every breath shudders through my lungs. "I met you. I didn't want anyone else. Just you. I only want you."

There's no amusement or relief in his eyes, only predatory intensity. He looks at me the way a tiger would a lamb.

A meal to be devoured.

The mattress dips as he shifts one of his legs onto the bed and then the other to kneel between my spread calves.

"Remember what you just said when you think you can't

possibly come again. Because you will. We've got four fucking years to make up for." Rowan sinks down between my thighs, his calloused palms wrapped around my tender flesh to keep me bared wide open. Every exhalation warms the moisture gathered at my entrance. His eyes still hold mine from the length of my body, a gravitational pull I can't escape from. "Pick a safe word. Do it now."

I swallow. *Hard.* "Chainsaw."

His breathy laugh is a burst of warmth against my core. "How fitting, love. Now be a good girl and find something to grab on to"—he says, then passes one long, slow lick over my center— "because I'm about to destroy you."

BEAUTIFUL DISASTER

Rowan

I told her I'm no angel.

I don't think she believed me.

But she's about to discover that I'm the devil she never knew she needed.

I flick my tongue over the curved metal bar just below her clit as my thumb circles her sensitive nerves with just enough pressure to leave her wanting for more. Sloane bucks from the mattress and gasps a breath when I suck the piercing into my mouth. The scent of her arousal mixes with the lingering soap on her skin. I'm already nearly mad with the need to sink into her tight heat.

"Rowan," she whispers. My free hand slides up her body to toy with the heart that surrounds her peaked nipple. I trace the curves and the tiny balls at each end of the bar before I give it a gentle tug that elicits a shudder. Her responsiveness makes me smile, but her restraint has got to go.

"I didn't quite catch that, love." I latch on to her clit and roll my tongue across the bud and the metal bar until a loud moan finally passes her lips. "That's better," I say when I let her free of my mouth.

"They'll hear us," she whispers. "Fionn and Rose."

"Good. We'll show them how it's done. Give Fionn something to think about. Maybe he'll get over himself and make a move on Rose."

Sloane's laugh becomes a cry of pleasure when I plunge my tongue into her pussy to taste her sweet, hot arousal, letting it cover my senses and burn into my memory. My fingers trace the symmetrical rows of titanium balls and bars that frame her entrance and she squirms before I drag my tongue through her lips and return to her clit to dip a finger into her pussy. Her eyes are closed, her head tilted back against the pillow. Her good hand grips an iron rung of the headboard as she bites down on her lip.

My finger curls to stroke a slow path over her inner walls. She writhes and sinks her teeth down into her flesh. *That definitely won't do.* I give her breast two gentle slaps in quick succession and she immediately lets go of her lip to suck in a needy breath.

"I still can't hear you."

"*Rowan,*" she whimpers.

Sloane writhes when I give her another little slap. Her pussy soaks my hand as I pump my finger in slow strokes. "Did you want something, Blackbird? You're going to have to speak up."

"More," she says, louder this time. "I need more."

I add another finger and a louder moan slips past her lips. But she's still holding back. "You're going to have to do better than that if you want to come."

A shiver wracks her body as I blow a thin stream of air over her exposed flesh.

"Please, Rowan. *Please*," she rasps.

"I'll tell you what," I say. She meets my waiting gaze, her eyes hooded with lust. "Since you asked so nicely, I'll give you this one and let you come. But you'd better find your voice quick, little bird. Because we've only just started, and I will keep this up as long as it takes until I'm satisfied that you're not hiding from me. By the end of this, you'll scream. That's a fucking promise."

A strained whimper wrestles free of Sloane's chest.

I slide my free arm beneath her hips and raise her ass off the mattress.

And then I devour her.

I pump my fingers and curl them to stroke the most sensitive flesh of her channel. My tongue dances over her clit until I take her piercing between my lips and give it a gentle tug. She bucks and moans and whimpers, but Sloane is going nowhere but right to the edge. And I keep her where I want her for as long as I want her there. I thrust my fingers in deep and hold them steady, denying her the orgasm building in her core.

"One more thing, love," I say as she lets out a petulant whine. "Keep your eyes on me."

Sloane's blown pupils fix to my face and I smile.

"Such a good girl."

Unblinking, I suck her clit into my mouth, press my lips to her flesh, bear down on her to push her closer to coming undone. She cries out and tightens her grip on the iron bar of the headboard. Her pussy cinches around my fingers and I grin against her clit.

I let her go again.

"Oh, and another thing—"

"*Rowan*," she barks, and I chuckle a dark laugh against her skin. My eyes hold hers as I flick my tongue with languid strokes against the triangle piercing, earning a shiver of need from her. "For fucksakes, please just let me come. No more 'other things.' No more stopping."

"*No more stopping*," I repeat. The devilish gleam in my eyes is met with a flash of wariness in hers. "As you wish, Blackbird. I'll make sure to *not stop*, as requested."

For a final time, I seal my mouth around her, licking and sucking and nibbling until she's a writhing mess in my hands, her arousal smeared across my face and her inner thighs. Her cunt pulses around my fingers and she comes apart with a strangled moan, her back bowed from the damp sheets. I keep the pressure on until I'm sure every second of her pleasure is spent, until she's boneless and breathless.

I slip my arm from beneath her to place my palm on the soft skin of her belly as I withdraw my fingers from her pussy and rise on my knees. Maybe she doesn't yet realize how long she's going to be at my nonexistent mercy, but at least she knows I'm not done.

I loom over her. Her eyes stay fused to me as I trace the tip of my glistening finger over her lips.

"Open," I command. She does, her tongue pressed against her lower lip, waiting. I lay my fingers on the slick heat and she closes her lips around them, taking me straight to something I've imagined many times already—the fantasy of her mouth warm and wet around my cock. "Suck it off."

Sloane's eyes flutter closed with a moan that vibrates in my fingers as she pulls hard on the flesh. Her tongue swirls over my skin. A shiver racks through me and her eyes snap open, narrowing on me, a subtle smile filling her cheeks.

"You know what you do to me, don't you. You want to torture me just as much as I do you," I say as I pull my fingers free against the suction of her mouth.

"Maybe," she breathes.

"This is one game you won't win, Blackbird." I give her a dark smirk as I shift backward off the bed.

With one hand behind my shoulders, I pull my shirt off, tossing it to the floor. Sloane's eyes roam across my body to take me in. And I let her. I fucking welcome it. She likes to remind me not to let my prettiness get to my head, but I know what I am and what effect I can have. I'm muscle and scars blended with scripts and swirls of black ink. The same way I look at her and find beauty in the marks that are only temporary, she looks at me and I know she feels the same. There's art in our scars. There's wonder in the way we can heal.

"Something caught your eye, pretty girl?"

Her throat strains as she swallows. I feel the heat of her gaze as it drags up my body to collide with mine. "Yes. All of you."

"Oh good," I say as I unfasten my belt and unzip my jeans to pull them and my briefs down, freeing my erection. Her eyes drop to my cock as I wrap my palm around it to pass my hand over my length in a slow stroke. She licks her lips. I can see her pulse pound in her neck, even in the dim light. "Wouldn't want you to be disappointed."

Sloane huffs an incredulous laugh. "Impossible." And then she meets my eyes, her expression serious. "You're beautiful, Rowan."

This time, it's my turn to blush.

I'm sure she sees it. It's in the way her gentle smile flashes and fades away. But if she thinks a smile and compliments are supposed to make things sweet, it's not going to work.

I wrap a hand around her ankle and open her wider to me as I climb back onto the bed. "Are you on contraception?"

"Yes," she replies as a deep blush creeps across her chest. "I have an IUD."

"Good." I notch the head of my cock to her entrance, roll it across the fourchette piercing. *Fucking hell.* She's going to feel like heaven, just like I always knew she would. "Because I'm going to fucking fill you until you're overflowing with my cum."

My eyes drift closed as I run the crown of my erection over her labia piercings, up one side and back down the other. A deep, unsteady breath fills my lungs as I deny myself a moment longer. I want to savor the anticipation.

Sloane's hand finds my wrist and her nails dig into my skin. When I open my eyes, I find desperation staring back at me. She doesn't just want this as much as I do. She fucking *needs* it. "Fuck me, Rowan, please. Destroy me."

My restraint snaps.

"Then look down. Watch how well you take me."

I push into her tight heat, just enough that the crown is enveloped by her warmth. She watches just like I demanded, breaths sawing from her lungs. A whimper passes her lips when I remain still, all my attention honed on the way her body fits around mine, the piercings glinting so beautifully in the dim light.

I slide my cock in a little deeper then withdraw just an inch, her pussy clenched around me. "Goddamn, Sloane. Look at how desperate your cunt is to be ruined. So fucking tight it doesn't want to let me go."

With every shallow thrust, I push deeper, pausing whenever Sloane tries to throw her head back on a moan. I want her to watch. To never fucking forget this moment. So I wait. Whenever she tries to look away, whenever pleasure pulls her from me, I bide my time until her focus is back right where I want it. On me. On *us*. And when she finally stays riveted to where our bodies are joined, I spread her legs wider and thrust deeper until I finally bottom out, my hips flush against her flesh.

I stay there, my hands fastened to her waist, my gaze raking from where I'm buried deep in her pussy to her beautiful, bruised body. My focus lands on her face and I drink in every change in her expression as I pull out to the tip of my erection to thrust all the way to the base. Sloane's responding moan is loud, desperate. She grasps the headboard and I do it again. This time she's louder still.

"That's my girl," I say, meeting her dark and hooded gaze with a rakish grin as I lean forward. My hand folds around her throat. "Be as loud as you want. The whole goddamn neighborhood could hear you and I wouldn't give a fuck."

I slam into her with long, powerful strokes, my cock rolling over that piercing with every pass, making me feral with want. I'm flooded with her. Her scent and her raspy moans. Her pulse as it surges against my palm. The sight of her body beneath mine. The feel of her cunt gripped tight around my cock. She's everywhere, in every drop of my blood, in every spark of thought, and I want to fucking destroy her for it. To shatter her just like she's broken me. Because she brings me to my fucking knees. I want to ruin her so that she's *mine*, my beautiful disaster. My wild creature. My goddess of chaos.

And I fuck her like that's exactly what I'm going to do.

I rut into her. Hard. Deep. Unrelenting and merciless. She strains against my grip around her throat, veins protruding in lines up her neck. I tell her all the ways I'm going to take her. In her mouth. In her perfect pussy. In her tight little ass. I'm going to fill her up until I'm *everywhere* inside her. Just like she's everywhere in me.

And she fucking loves it.

Her arousal perfumes the air. She pleads for more. She begs me not to stop. And I don't, not for a single second. I firm my grip around her throat with one hand, press my fingers to her clit in circles with the other and slam into her, over and over until she cries out my name and clenches around my erection as she comes apart. And I'm right behind her. An electric current rolls across my spine and my balls tighten and I'm spilling into her, shaking, my heart a riot of deafening drums in my ears. I push as deep as she can take me and relish the flutter of her pussy as it milks every drop of cum.

I want to stay buried here, to gather her up and press Sloane's sweat-slicked body against mine as I fall asleep with her cunt wrapped around my cock.

And I will.

Later.

I pull out slowly, inch by inch, riveted to the sight of our glistening arousal as it coats my cock. Sloane's arm is slung over her eyes as she tries to recover her breath. It's adorable, really. She probably already thinks I've destroyed her.

She's wrong.

I lean down and seal my mouth over her pussy. My fingers work her swollen clit. I'm rewarded with a shocked yelp of my name as I plunge my tongue into her pulsing channel.

"*Rowan*—"

Her muscles contract and our cum floods my mouth. I smile against her flesh as I collect our spend on my tongue.

Then I prowl up the length of her body.

Sloane's hazel eyes flash, the bruises setting off the green hues in her irises as they dance between mine. I think the realization is finally setting in. This isn't even close to over.

It's only just begun.

My weight rests on my forearms as I hover over her. I tap one finger to her lips.

Tap, tap, tap. Open wide.

Sloane's lips part. I spit the cum into her waiting mouth.

"Swallow."

She does, her eyes not leaving mine, not until I crush my lips to hers.

This kiss is raw. There's no barrier left between us now. It's Sloane stripped down to little more than carnal want. It's the way I've felt so many times when I've been with her. Like I'm made of nothing more than desperate need. Our teeth clash. She bites down on my bottom lip and a tang of iron bleeds into the flavors of sweetness and salt.

"You taste that, Blackbird?" I ask when I pull away just enough that I take up all the space in her field of vision.

"Yes," she whispers.

"You know what that is?"

She has the good sense to shake her head. I smile.

"An appetizer. And now it's time for a fucking feast."

I slide back down her body to settle between her trembling thighs as I snake a hand beneath her back to raise her pussy to my mouth.

And just as I promised, before the night is through, she screams.

DETONATE

Sloane

I can't sleep, even though my mind is more relaxed than it's ever been and my body is exhausted.

It might have something to do with the cock buried in my pussy.

I think I *could* fall asleep like this, wrapped in Rowan's arms. There's never been a safer place. And I love the idea of drifting off like this, still connected in a way I don't want to be with anyone else.

But I can't. Because despite how tired I am, I *want* him.

He unleashed something in me, cracking me open to reveal layers beneath that I didn't know existed. It's not like I haven't had good sex before, but nothing even close to what it was with Rowan. He takes in a way that's giving. He seems to know exactly when to push and how far. And in the end, it's fervent. Uninhibited.

And I already want it again, even though our hosts would probably hate us for it.

Every time I think about facing Rose and Fionn tomorrow

morning, heat burns in my cheeks. We were so loud. *Both of us.* I screamed Rowan's name more than once. He roared mine as he came in my mouth, my hair twisted around his fist.

When I finally begged him to stop making me come, he gathered my limp, spent body in his embrace, piled pillows around my injured arm, and then slid back into my pussy to the sound of my gasp. I felt the smile in his lips against my neck when I whispered a disbelieving curse.

"Go to sleep, Blackbird," he'd said, then placed a kiss on my neck before laying his head down on the pillow. "Or don't, up to you. But I'm going to sleep like a fucking rock with my cock buried deep in your perfect pussy."

How the fuck was I supposed to sleep after he said that?

And now here I am, desperate for movement, for friction, and not wanting to wake the man whose cock is balls-deep in my cunt.

"Jesus," I whisper.

I thought at first that he would soften and slip free, but that has not happened. I'm not sure how long it's been, maybe twenty minutes, but it feels like a fucking eternity. If I could just *move*, get some relief from this aching need between my thighs . . .

I'm going to be awake all night at this rate.

Nope. That will be torture. Which he'd probably love.

A thin, determined breath of air threads past my lips.

I shimmy my left arm through the nest of pillows until I'm able to press my fingers to my clit with a sigh of relief. My shoulder is too sore to move easily, but it doesn't need to be perfect, not with Rowan's cock filling my pussy. I'm halfway there already, I just need a little pressure.

I start swirling my fingers over the sensitive bundle of nerves, rolling my touch over my piercing as I bite down on my bottom lip. A moan begs to slip free. Moisture slicks my fingers. As I touch myself, I think about all of Rowan's fantasies he whispered while he fucked me—about taking me in a public place, about spreading me wide on a table at the restaurant and devouring me, about using my toy in my pussy as he fills my ass with cum.

A little whimper escapes my lips.

I go still. Hold my breath. Nothing changes in Rowan's hold or the cadence of his exhalations. No indication that I've disturbed him.

When I'm sure nothing has changed, I resume the slow circles.

"Sloane."

I go completely still, a breath caught in my lungs, my fingers still pressed against my clit and piercing.

"You seem to be up to something. Want to tell me about it?"

"Umm . . ."

Rowan props himself up on an elbow so he can gaze down at the side of my face. "I thought we talked about hiding." He shifts his other arm from where it's draped across my waist and lays his palm on my elbow. I shiver as his lips graze my ear. I don't need to see him to know his face is lit with that teasing grin of his, the one he wears so often when we're together. He's always trying to get under my skin. Just like now. This was probably his plan all along.

I scoff, disgruntled.

He laughs. "I have some ideas. Let me give you my theories."

His palm slides down my forearm, over my wrist, engulfing my hand. He presses my fingers harder against my clit and I squeeze my eyes closed as a burst of sensation overtakes me.

"I think you couldn't fall asleep. You were thinking about how good it felt to be fucked the way you deserved. Admittedly, it was probably a little hard to fall asleep with my cock lodged deep in your greedy cunt, wasn't it?"

Rowan pulls out slowly and slides back in until his hips are flush with my ass. I'm already trembling. He does it again and then bites my earlobe, not hard enough to hurt but with enough force to make me gasp.

"I just asked you a question, love."

"Y-yes," I say, and I'm rewarded with a kiss and a harder press of his fingers against my throbbing clit. "Couldn't sleep."

"Was that so hard?"

I shake my head, even though it might be a lie. If he knows, he doesn't call me on it.

"I think you couldn't get out of your head all the things I told you I was going to do to you. You've been wondering if they were just fantasies, or promises. And when you couldn't stop, all those ideas running through your head became need. You *need* to be fucked, even though you're so goddamn tired. And you need to know what's real."

He's in my head. It's terrifying and exhilarating. I've been on my own for so long. And now he's in every thought like he's always been here.

He was right when he said there's no way to hide from him anymore. He didn't just open my cage, he shattered it, and the first breaths of freedom burn in my lungs.

"Yes," I admit, with more confidence this time. "It's all true."

Rowan's long exhalation drifts across my shoulder, raising goose bumps in my skin. I know without asking that he's relieved he doesn't have to pull an answer from me, that as much as I trust him with my body, I trust him with my thoughts and hopes and fears too.

"Stay right here," he demands with a press of his hand to mine in a request to keep going.

He slides out of me and the mattress dips as he shifts away. I twist enough that I can watch what he's doing as he heads toward our luggage. It's the first time I've actually seen his back, and even in the dim light from the en suite I can see that his skin is marred with several wide, long, scars, but something else spreads across his shoulders.

My heart climbs into my throat and threatens to dump itself on the bed.

"*Rowan . . .*"

He stops, turning his head to watch over his shoulder as I sit up and look more closely at the black ink that flows over the thick muscles lining his spine. He twists as far as his neck allows to follow my line of sight but can only see the tip of one wing.

"Is that . . . ? Did you . . . ?"

"Did I get the raven you left on the table tattooed on my back?" His smile is teasing, but there's a hint of shyness in it as he finishes my thought. "Yeah. Appears to be the case."

I swallow the vise that threatens to choke me. "Why?"

His grin widens and he shrugs before turning away to rifle through one of the bags. *My* bag.

"For one thing, I couldn't really take the original with me. Might get damaged." He lets out a little sound of triumph and faces me. My mouth is still hanging open with this revelation when I take in what he's holding—my vibrator in one hand, my bottle of lube in the other. "Seems like I still need to clear up a few things for you."

Rowan prowls toward the bed. My heart ricochets against my ribs like a pinball.

"Turn around. On your knees."

I swallow. "You're very demanding."

Rowan smirks. I give him one final, heated glance before I do as he says and turn my back to him.

"Don't even pretend you don't enjoy it," he says as he comes up behind me on the bed. He takes my good hand and folds it around one of the crossbars of the headboard, then positions my hips where he wants them, nudging my knees wider with one of his muscular legs. "Your pussy gives you away. It's dripping for me, Sloane."

"You were right. You're no fucking angel."

He slides the toy through my lips and presses it to my entrance. "Damn straight. And neither are you." He guides it into my pussy and back out again in several shallow strokes before turning the vibration on. "I told you I was going to fuck your mouth and I did. I told you I was going to eat your pussy at the restaurant like it's the best goddamn meal I've ever had, and I will. And I told you I was going to fill your ass with cum as I fucked you with a toy. And you know what happened when I said that?"

"No," I say on the heels of a gasp as he works the toy in deeper thrusts.

"Your cunt gripped so tight around my cock that I thought I'd fucking explode. You were soaked. Dripping down your thighs."

The cap snaps open on the bottle. Lube drizzles down my ass and over the pleated hole. "Have you done this before?"

"Kind of—it was the other way around."

He presses his thumb to my hole, massaging the rim as he continues the rhythm of the toy.

"And you loved it."

I nod again. "Yes."

"Good," is all he says, his tone definitive as he pushes his thumb into my ass to the sound of my gasp.

He loosens my tight ring of muscle, relaxes me into the sensation until I'm pushing back on him in a silent request for more. And then his thumb is gone, replaced with the lubed head of his cock as he glides it over the tight hole, pressing it against me until it slips past the resistance. He pauses as I breathe through the foreign sensation of fullness and then picks up slow and shallow thrusts, each one delving a little deeper against the vibration of the toy.

"Now that we've established that everything I told you is a fucking promise," he grits out as he intensifies the rhythm of his thrusts, "we should probably clear up your other question."

I'm shaking, sweating, lost to some mindless dimension where all I know is the feeling of intense pleasure twined with a hint of discomfort, but one I welcome because it only adds to the euphoric haze that consumes me. Rowan has picked up an unbroken cadence of deep thrusts and I don't think I can even remember my own name, let alone something I said a few minutes ago. "Question . . . was . . . ?"

I hear the smirk in his huffed laugh. Jesus fucking Christ. I'm incapable of stringing together a simple sentence and this man is fucking me relentlessly while probably able to recite the entire year-by-year history of the Napoleonic Wars.

Rowan leans closer, slows his thrusts, covers my back with the heat of his body. One of his hands finds my breast and he rolls my nipple between his fingers as he blows a thin stream of cool air across my neck to make me shiver. "About the tattoo, Sloane," he says, his voice saccharine. "You asked me why I got it."

I whimper as a deep thrust pushes me closer to an intense orgasm that's nearly within reach. "Right . . . uhh . . ."

"Any guesses?"

My forehead presses to my arm as I let out a strangled cry. ". . . like me . . . ?"

"Because I '*like you* . . .'?" Rowan cackles an incredulous laugh. "*Like. You.* Seriously . . . ? *Christ*, Sloane. You are fucking brilliant but also the most willfully oblivious person I have ever met. Do you really think I just *like you* when I framed a drawing you left for me on a scrap of paper you tore from a notebook? The one I hung in the kitchen so I can look at it every day and think of you? Do you think I just *like you* when I tattoo it on my skin? I play this fucking game every year and tear my heart out watching you walk away, only to do it all over again, and I *like you*? You think I just *like you* when I fuck you like this?"

The pace quickens. Rowan's hot palm caresses my breast. He pistons into me. I cry out his name and he fucks me harder.

"I would kill for you, and I have. I would do it again, every damn day. I'd turn myself inside out for you. I would die for you. I don't just *like you*, Sloane, and you fucking know it."

Vicious thrusts throw me over the edge. Stars shatter across my vision. A sound I've never before made spills across my lips as the orgasm breaks me apart.

I don't unravel. I *detonate*.

Rowan's arm folds around my waist and he holds me close as he comes, my name dulled by my heart as it thunders in my ears.

His breath is still ragged, his chest shuddering when I turn off the toy and he whispers against my neck, "I don't just 'like you,' understand?"

I nod.

Rowan's fingers trace my jaw, soft and slow, a touch I lean into when his palm stops to rest against my cheek. "And you don't just *'like me'* either, do you."

It's not a question. It's not even a demand. It's a need to be freed from a place where he thinks he's been alone.

The key slides into the lock as Lark's words echo in my mind above the riot of heartbeats.

Put some of that bravery to use for yourself for a change.

All the *what ifs*, I set them aside. All except one.

"No," I whisper. "I more than like you, Rowan. I think about you all the time. I miss you every day. You appeared one moment and nothing has been the same since. And that scares me. A lot."

Rowan presses a kiss to my shoulder as his thumb glides across my cheek. "I know."

"You're braver than me."

"No, Sloane," he says with a low chuckle as he pulls away. "I'm just more reckless, with less sense of self-preservation. I'm scared too."

I watch as he climbs off the bed to head to the en suite only to return with the washcloth and tissues. He takes time to clean my skin with gentle strokes, his attention caught on the movement of his hand and his brow creased as he seems deep in thought.

"What are you scared of?" I ask when the silence stretches so long that it feels as if it's tugging on my bones.

Rowan shrugs, not looking up when he says, "I dunno. Having my eyeballs sucked out of my head with an industrial vacuum is a recurring nightmare. Not sure how I came about that one." When I slap his arm, Rowan's stoic mask finally cracks into a faint smile. But it slowly fades, and he doesn't answer until it's gone. "I'm scared of you destroying me. Me destroying you."

I blow out a dramatic breath. "Going straight for destruction, huh? Not the easy stuff to be terrified of, like the fact that we live in different states, or that we're both crazy busy at work, or like, I have one friend and you apparently hang out with the entire city of Boston. Nope. Straight for *destroy*."

His smile returns, but I can still see it in his eyes, how fear clings to his thoughts, finding its way into mine too. "None of those are insurmountable things. We just have to do what normal people do. Talk and stuff."

"We don't have a good track record of normal-people stuff." I point to my face. "Exhibit A. We could have gone for beers."

"Then we'll get good at it. We've just gotta practice."

Seems simple enough, doesn't it. *Practice.* Get a little better most days. A little stronger. It's hard to imagine how to climb past these obstacles that seem like mountains when you're standing in their shade. But I'll never climb if I just keep standing still. And Lark was right, I have been lonely standing in the shadows.

So I keep asking myself the same question: *What if I try?*

I don't let my mind wander to an answer. Because the real

answer is, *I don't know.* I've never really tried and meant it before, not like this.

Don't answer the question. Just try.

That's what I think when I look at my reflection in the bathroom mirror. It's what I think when I come back to the bed and Rowan helps me into a tank top before putting my sling back on. It's what I think when I lie down next to him. He watches me openly, and I watch him back. His eyelids are heavy, just like mine, but he refuses to look away. And still I think, *Just try.*

I shimmy my right arm from beneath me and raise a fist between us. "Rock-paper-scissors."

"What for?"

"Just do it, pretty boy."

He gives me a suspicious grin, and then he meets my fist with his. On the count of three, we make our selection. Rowan goes with rock. I go with scissors.

I already know that rock is chosen the majority of the time in games of rock-paper-scissors. I looked it up after the first time I met Rowan and he suggested it in the event of a tie-breaker. And I already know that Rowan almost always chooses rock.

"What did I just win?" he says.

"You can ask me anything, and I'll answer you honestly."

His eyes flash in the dim light. "Really?"

"Yeah. Go on. Anything."

Rowan chews at his lip as he deliberates. It takes him a long moment to settle on a question. "You were going to leave when we were in West Virginia and I killed Francis. Why didn't you?"

The image of Rowan kneeling on the road bursts to the forefront of my mind. I've thought about it so many times, the way he rained relentless blows on the man clutched in the grip of his madness. I'd watched from the shadows, and as Rowan slowed and stopped, I backed away. Leaving was the smart thing to do. He was clearly unhinged. Dangerous. He'd grabbed me by the throat only moments before, and even though I was afraid, I still trusted him. Part of me knew he pushed me away from Francis and the car to hide me in the shadows. And when it was over, my mind screamed at me to run, but my heart saw a broken man on the road, struggling to find himself in the haze of rage.

And the first word to pass his lips was my name.

I hadn't made it more than two steps backward. I never even turned away.

"You called out for me. It sounded like loss. I . . ." I swallow, and his touch finds me from the shadows, a trace of tingling warmth that flows up my arm and back down again. "I knew you didn't just want me to stay. You needed me to. I haven't been needed like that in a long time."

His gentle caress finds my cheek, a contrast to the violence that carved scars into his knuckles that night. "It's probably pretty obvious by now, but I'm glad you stayed."

"Me too." I lean closer and press my lips to his, relishing his familiar scent and the warmth of his presence. When I pull away, I say, "Can I ask you a question, even though I just lost rock-paper-scissors?"

Rowan's laugh precedes a kiss to my temple. "I think I can give you a freebie. Just one, though."

"I remember you whispering to Francis before you beat him. What did you say?"

The pause of silence between us stretches on, and for a moment

I think he's not going to answer. Rowan slides his hand beneath my pillow and pulls me closer until my head rests on his chest, his heartbeat a comfort in the dark.

"I said the same thing that I told you just before I killed him," he finally says. "That you're mine."

When that piece of the puzzle snaps into place, it aches a little, like my heart has to crack to make room for it to fit. It doesn't seem like it could be true, but maybe Rowan really has been sure about us all along, about what we could be and what he wanted. He was patiently waiting for me to catch up.

I press a kiss to his chest and settle my cheek above his heart. "Yeah. I guess I am."

My eyes drift closed, and the next time I open them, the room is washed in the dawn light that creeps in through the slatted blinds.

I'm still wrapped in Rowan's embrace, his legs intertwined with mine and his arm slung across my waist. He's fast asleep. I take a moment to just watch the twitch of his eyelids and the steady rise and fall of his chest, and then I untangle myself from his limbs and slide away. When I'm done in the bathroom, he still hasn't moved, so I get dressed in silence and leave him to sleep.

The scent of coffee and sugary batter pulls me down the hall. When I make it to the dining room, Rose is already there, her dark hair looped over her shoulder in a loose braid and a plate of waffles set before her. She looks up as I approach and gives me a bright smile, her big brown eyes welcoming.

"Morning," she says. "There's more in the kitchen. Help yourself."

"Thank you. And I'm so sorry."

"For what?" Rose says around a mouthful of waffle. Her gaze darts around and she squints at me like she's trying to work out if I stole something from her in the night.

"For being . . . *loud.*"

Rose just shrugs and drops her attention to her plate of food. "Honey, I've lived in a literal circus since I was fifteen. I could sleep on the Tilt-A-Whirl if I had to."

I snort a laugh and head to the kitchen, pulling two mugs from the shelf to fill them with coffee. "The clown alley thing from yesterday makes more sense now."

"Well, whatever was going on," she says with a goofy, exaggerated wink as I meet her eyes across the kitchen island, "I didn't hear a thing. But *him*, on the other hand . . . he looks a little worse for wear."

I turn as Fionn enters the dining room in his pajamas, his hair disheveled, eyes half lidded. He heads straight for the fridge and pulls a bottle of probiotics from a row on the door. When I glance at Rose, her smile is wicked.

"Good sleep, doc?" she asks. "I slept like a *rock*. Not sure about Sloane and Rowan though."

Fionn gives her a dark look. But there's a banked heat in it too.

"I'm sorry," I say, my cheeks heating with fire beneath my skin. "You've been so kind to take us in on zero notice. We didn't mean to keep you up with the whole uh . . . pent-up . . . um. Stuff."

"Don't worry, Blackbird. He'll be just fine. Dr. Blueballs is just a little jealous."

Rowan approaches in a pair of low-slung sweats and nothing on top but a delicious spread of muscle and ink. My blush heats a second time as he stops by my side to lay a kiss on my temple.

"Put a shirt on, loser," Fionn grumbles as Rowan slaps him on the back and pushes past him to grab the milk.

"Why? I figure it's good to remind you periodically that even though you spend hours a day on your burpees, I can still kick your ass."

Fionn looks as though he wants to argue that point, but his gaze darts over his older brother's muscled and scarred body before he seems to rethink that idea. "I thought I said something about taking it easy," he argues instead. "Getting rest. No rough . . . sports."

Rowan's grin is nothing short of diabolical. "We weren't playing sports. We were having sex."

Rose cackles at the table and stuffs another bite of waffle into her mouth. "Amazing. I love these two. Can they stay?"

"*No.*" Fionn glares at Rose and then Rowan before shifting his attention to me, his expression taking on an apologetic quality. "I'm sorry. Under normal circumstances, definitely. But that prick over there," he says, hooking a thumb toward Rowan, "he's going to make my life hell for the nickname thing until he gets it out of his system. I need sleep at night. And so do you. In fact, you should probably take a couple of weeks off work until you're out of the sling."

"I've still got another week of vacation," I reply. "I haven't taken a sick day in almost two years, so it shouldn't be a problem."

"I'm going to write you a doctor's note anyway, just in case. I want you to wear the sling as much as you can. And schedule some time with a physical therapist. No heavy lifting, *no sports*," he says as he darts a pointed look to Rowan. When Fionn's gaze returns to me, his brow furrows with worry. "Do you have someone who can help you at home if you need it?"

"She does," Rowan replies before I have a chance to even mention Lark's name. "She's got me."

My gaze bounces between Rowan and his brother. Disbelief and nerves and excitement twine together like rope in my chest. "You're coming to Raleigh?"

Rowan sets his coffee on the counter. His blue eyes hold mine, the shade of the deep sea beneath the sun. There's no teasing smile to light his skin, no amused smirk that dances across his lips when he steps closer and stops in front of me. He watches the motion of his fingers as they trace the contours of my cheek.

The rest of the world falls away.

"No, Sloane," he says. "I'm taking you home. To Boston."

RESERVATIONS

Sloane

"Oh my God. It's *you*."

I look to my right where Lark stands at my side, expecting that this is probably a fangirl moment. Lark might be signed with a smaller indie record label, but she still has a significant following and it wouldn't be the first time she was recognized while we were out together.

But when I return my gaze to Meg the Hostess, she's staring straight back at me.

Flame engulfs my cheeks. "Umm . . . hi . . . ?"

"I'm so sorry. When you came the last time, I totally got sidetracked and forgot to tell Rowan." Meg's pretty blue eyes widen as she shakes her head. "I still feel terrible."

"Well, I hadn't made a reservation, so you have nothing to apologize for."

"But you have a standing reservation at 3 in Coach," Meg says with a sweet, knowing smile. She pulls a thumbtack from her podium and passes me a sheet of paper.

Table 12 is PERMANENTLY RESERVED for:
—any reservation under the name Sloane
Sutherland
—a beautiful, black-haired woman with hazel
eyes and freckles, 5'8", probably alone, shy,
looks like she wants to run
Inform Rowan immediately of any
reservations under this name or any guests
fitting this description.

And then, in red text as though it was added at a later date:

IMMEDIATELY. I AM NOT FUCKING AROUND.

The word *IMMEDIATELY* is underlined six times.

"That's so cute," Lark says as she lays her chin on my shoulder and reads the note, pointing to the red text. "It sounds like he's going to cut people up for you. That's so Keanu-mantic."

I snort a laugh as I pass the paper back to Meg. "First of all, *Keanu-mantic* is so not a word. Secondly, Keanu doesn't cut people up in a red-flag romantic kind of way."

"He does in *John Wick*."

"Sure. For a *dog*. I wouldn't call that romance, Lark."

Lark shrugs before she beams a smile at Meg. "Table for two, please, for Sloane Sutherland, black-haired, freckled, five-eight beauty who looks like she wants to run."

Meg takes two menus from her podium and grins as she motions us forward. "Follow me. I'll let Chef know you're here as soon as you're seated."

Lark squeaks and grips my wrist as we follow Meg to the booth I sat in the last time I was here over a year ago. She can probably feel my pulse hammering into her hand. I stayed with Rowan for two weeks after extending my time off from work, as Fionn had recommended. And those two weeks with Rowan just weren't enough.

My body was still bruised and sore when I left for Raleigh to pack up my things and rent out my furnished house. I made arrangements at work to go fully home-based and spent my evenings and weekends dismantling my storage container kill room that I've barely used since we started this game. It's been three weeks since I saw Rowan, and my heart is nearly ready to burst through my chest as the seconds tick down to the end of our separation.

I don't know if this is going to work—living with him, working from home every day, being in a new city, trying to build this foundation we've made into something more. But I'm going to try.

"You're hella excited," I say to Lark, trying to divert attention from my own blistering anticipation as we weave through the busy restaurant. The lunch rush has passed, but there are still more full tables than empty ones, even if many of the patrons have finished main courses and have moved on to desserts.

"Of course I am. My bestie is in *l-o-v-e* and I get to meet her man for the first time."

I snort. "I never said anything about *love*."

"Didn't you sneakily install a security camera in the kitchen?"

"That's *stalking*, not love."

"To-may-to, to-mah-to. And clearly, he adores you too. He

knows my baby," she says, gesturing toward the booth as Meg lays the menus on the table. "A perfect Sloaney choice. Sheltered and equidistant between the exits."

Oh my fucking God. She's right.

Lark slides onto the padded seat and Meg disappears to grab Rowan from the kitchen, and I'm still standing off to the side like a dumbass, staring at the table like I've never seen one before.

He permanently reserves the booth he knows you would want at his popular restaurant. He beats the shit out of an emo pervert for watching you masturbate. He has some random neighborhood kid bring you groceries.

Who the fuck are you kidding? You don't just "more than like" this guy.

Lark's head tilts and a crease appears between her brows as her gaze travels across my face. "You okay there, Sloaney? You look broken."

I'm about to say something. I open my mouth, manage a stuttered start to a sentence that never materializes. It dies on my tongue when I hear the subtle Irish accent rise above the conversations of diners and the clang of cutlery on plates, glasses on tables.

"Blackbird," he says loud enough to carry across the noise. When I look over, he's striding past tables of patrons, looking much like he did the last time I came to 3 in Coach, his chef coat rolled to his elbows and a white apron tied around his waist. But this time, there's no look of shock, only a warm smile and his arms spread wide. "Get over here."

I glance at Lark and her grin is electric, her eyes dancing. She jerks her head in his direction, and even though I know I probably look like some lovesick teenager, I can't help it. My heart is pounding its way up my throat. If it had its way, I'd already be running in his direction.

I might not run, but I still walk. *Fast.*

When we meet in the middle of the restaurant, Rowan grasps my face between his palms and takes a moment to just absorb the details of my expression, as though he's savoring every nuance. He's radiant, clearly in his element in this space, his eyes bright and crinkled at the corners with the width of his smile and the depth of his relief.

The kiss we share doesn't linger. But its heat does, infusing every cell with both comfort and the need for more than we can take in this moment.

"You look so much better," he says when he pulls away.

I shrug. "A little sore still, but getting there."

"Trip was okay?"

"Winston hated every moment of the drive from Raleigh. I think I'm going to hear his growl in my sleep for a week, but he's settled down now that he's in your place. He seems a bit weirded out, but I'm sure he'll adjust in a day or two. I left my stuff on the floor in the living room, so I'm ninety percent certain my cat will have all the luggage shredded in retribution by the time we get back."

"*Our* place," Rowan corrects, and loops an arm over my shoulder to guide our way back to the booth. "*Our* cat. I can't wait to be kitty litter influencers together; what a great side hustle. We're gonna be *rich*."

I bark a laugh and roll my eyes. "You're the worst.

"You'll love me someday."

One of my steps falters.

Today is that day.

Maybe yesterday too. And the day before that. Maybe for a while, in fact.

I can't tell exactly when it started, but I don't think it will ever stop.

I take Rowan's hand where it lies over my recovering shoulder, the joint still a little tender but getting better every day. When I look up at him, I try to repress a smile but fail. "Yeah. Maybe."

Rowan doesn't call me out, doesn't prod for more, but I know he can see it in me as though it's written in the constellation of dots on my skin, even when I try to force my gaze away.

"Told you so," he whispers as he presses a kiss to my temple.

Lark slides out of the booth and gives Rowan a hug as though she's known him for years, and the two fall into easy conversation from the moment we're seated. And though I pretend to be immersed in my menu, I'm not. I'm watching Lark and Rowan with a heart fuller than I ever thought it could be. The only two people I love in this world are sitting right next to one another, forging the first moments in a friendship, a foundation that will hopefully only grow with time.

I might not have a lot of people, but I have Lark and Rowan, and that's enough.

We share a meal together. A bottle of wine. We split the fig phyllo Napoleon for dessert and sit with our coffees until the last guests have departed and the restaurant shuts down to prepare for the dinner shift. There's no lull in conversation. There's no shortage of laughter. And when it's time to leave, we make plans to get together again over the next few days while Lark is in town—live music, dinners out, maybe a sailing trip around the harbor. As we make our way to the exit, Rowan gives me a wink, like this is all part of his grand plan to lure Lark here.

We hug her goodbye at the door and Rowan winds up with a gold star sticker on his cheek before Lark dances away.

"Come on, need your help," he says, taking my hand when Lark turns a corner two blocks down, heading for her hotel. Rowan tows me along in the opposite direction. "Very important job, Blackbird."

"What job?"

"You'll see."

"Are you going to leave that sticker on your face?"

Rowan scoffs. "Of course. Makes me prettier."

Four blocks and one turn later, Rowan pulls me to a stop. Though I ask him what he's doing and where we are, he evades my questions. Instead of answering, he maneuvers behind me to fold his palms over my eyes before he nudges me forward. I'm about to give him some little jab about how I'm not going to walk across the entire city of Boston blindfolded when he guides us to a stop and we turn to the left.

"Ready?" he asks.

I nod.

He lifts his hands from my eyes.

Before me is the front of a brick building where a new black awning with globe lights stretches over an outdoor seating area that doesn't yet have chairs on the freshly painted deck. The interior is finished, the luxurious details of the furnishings and dark wood tables mixed with the exposed brick and unexpected pops of teal-blue decorations. Massive ferns wave gently in the breeze of the air-conditioning system hidden among the industrial network of black steel beams and ductwork on the ceiling. It's beautiful and elegant, yet comfortable.

And across the full front of the restaurant, stretching over the door and the awning, a massive sign in block letters.

Butcher & Blackbird.

"Rowan . . ." I take a step closer, staring up at the sign and the stylized wrought iron raven and meat cleaver incorporated behind the first few letters. "Are you for real?"

"You like it?"

"It's incredible. I love it."

"Well, that's a relief, considering we're two weeks away from opening. Reservations are booked up past Christmas. Would have been awkward to cancel." With a flash of a grin, he takes my hand and tows me toward the door where a large poster details the upcoming grand opening and the contact details. He unlocks it and holds the door for me to step inside, the scent of fresh paint and new furniture greeting us. "Still need your help, though."

As we head toward the kitchen, Rowan points out details, decorations that reflect his brothers' influence, like the selection of Weller's bourbon behind the bar for when Fionn comes for the opening, or the branded leather coasters that Lachlan made. But I am *everywhere* too. In the huge black leather wing, the intricate feathers spread across a wall above the booths, the exact spot where I would want to sit. In black-and-white paintings of ravens by local artists, a butcher's knife or meat cleaver incorporated into every one.

It's not just me. It's *us*.

I pull Rowan to a stop in the center of the room. His eyes dart across my face and down to my neck as a burning swallow shifts in my throat.

"You . . ." is all I manage to squeak out. I gesture between us and then to the room. "This . . . ?"

Rowan tries to bite down on a laugh as a knowing smirk sneaks across his lips. "Eloquent. Is this another 'man-guy' situation? Can't wait to hear what you come up with, Blackb—"

"I love you, Rowan," I blurt out. I take only a moment to register the shock in Rowan's expression before I barrel into him, wrapping his solid body in my embrace. His heart hammers beneath my ear as I press my face to his chest.

His arms fold around me, one hand threading into my hair as he lays a kiss to the crown of my head. "I love you too, Sloane. So fucking much. But the restaurant was probably a giant clue."

I laugh into his chest and shimmy a hand between us to catch a tear before it falls. "I kinda got that vibe. Not sure what tipped me off. Might have been the sign out front."

Rowan pulls away, his hands warm around my shoulders. When he stares down at me, I see everything I feel reflected back at me in his faint smile and soft eyes. There's relief knowing I *can* love and be loved, after years wondering if I was so broken that there was room only for vengeance and loneliness in my heart. And I think I see the release of that burden reflected in Rowan's eyes too.

"Come on," he says after pressing a quick kiss to my lips. "I still need your help."

Rowan leads the way to the kitchen where brand-new commercial appliances and stainless steel counters gleam beneath the recessed lights in the freshly painted ceiling. He heads first to a row of hooks where aprons are hanging and tosses one to me before he disappears into a walk-in fridge.

"What are we doing?" I ask as he returns with ingredients stacked on a tray that he sets on the counter next to me.

"Building a spaceship." He grins when I give him a flat glare. "Cooking, clearly. I'm still fine-tuning the lunch menu for opening week. I need your help tweaking it."

"I thought we'd already established that cooking is not my strong suit."

"No, we established that you cook perfectly well, we just need to do it together."

And we do.

We start with simpler things, like making a red wine vinaigrette for one of the salads and prepping vegetables for a soup. Then we move on to harder things—pork loin with shallot rings, a salmon fillet with cream sauce. And watching Rowan share his art with such passion and confidence is like injecting an aphrodisiac directly into my veins. My desire for him grows more powerful with every moment that passes, and he's so immersed in what he's doing that he doesn't seem to notice any of the signs.

It only makes me want him that much more.

We sample the dishes we create together and Rowan presses the gold star from his cheek to the top of a fresh page in a stained, dog-eared notebook where he jots down ideas and feedback on everything we make. And then he declares that it's time for dessert, the course where he needs the most help. When I try to protest that I'm full, he laughs me off.

"I know you can take more," he says with a smirk, then strides off in the direction of the fridge.

He returns with another tray of ingredients, but this time the pavlova and crème brûlée and chocolate cake have already been made. They just need to be assembled with their presentation and sauces, which Rowan does with speed and precision before he sets them in front of me on the counter. He then takes a step back and lets his gaze flow down the length of me. I feel it in the center of my body, as though he pulls an invisible string that tightens my core until it aches.

"Face the counter and pull your dress up, Sloane."

My panties instantly dampen, even before my brain has fully processed his words, as though my body knows what's about to happen before my mind does. I suck in an unsteady breath and my mouth pops open, but I don't know what to say.

Rowan raises his brows and flicks his gaze toward the counter. "You think I didn't notice the way you tugged your dress down before you leaned over to show me your tits when we were making that white wine sauce? I *always* notice you, Sloane. Now do as you're told."

I shudder out my held breath, grasp the hem of my dress, and drag it up my thighs as I turn and face the stainless steel counter, its polished edge cold against my heated skin. Rowan's warmth envelops my back as he steps behind me to run a calloused palm up my leg and across the globe of my ass.

He pulls my panties to the side and notches his cock to my entrance, then slides into me with a single stroke to the sound of my gasp.

And then he just stays there, unmoving, lodged to the hilt in my pussy.

A whimper catches in the back of my throat. My clit throbs, begging for friction, my cunt desperate for motion. I try to move forward and back again, but there's nowhere to go between Rowan's unyielding strength and the sharp edge of the counter against my hips.

"No," he commands when I try again. "Relax, Sloane."

A strangled moan passes my lips. "How the fuck am I supposed to do that?"

Rowan chuckles, nonplussed by the fact that desire is burning me up, every cell torched with the need for more than he's going to give. "Just try. See where it takes you."

My pulse drums a galloping rhythm, my breaths are shaky and uneven. When I stop trying to move, Rowan lays his chin on my shoulder and takes up a dessert spoon.

"Such a good girl you are, Blackbird," he coos into my ear as he slides the spoon through the crème brûlée and brings it to my parted lips. "And good girls get rewards."

The creamy dessert and tart berry topping land on my tongue with a burst of flavor. Rowan remains still as I savor the taste.

"Did you like it?" he asks.

"Y-yes."

"Missing anything?"

"I . . ." Fuck, I don't know. I can't think clearly with his cock thick and hard in my pussy, my arousal slick at my entrance, my clit demanding relief. When I shake my head, he seems to understand that I don't mean "no," but that I can't be sure.

"Close your eyes. Try again."

I do as Rowan asks and close my eyes. The scents of sugar and fresh berries flood my nostrils, aromas I didn't truly notice the last time. Rowan traces the edge of the spoon across my lips to paint my pink skin in flavor before I open for him.

"What do you taste?" Rowan whispers against my neck.

"Cream. Vanilla. Caramelized sugar. Strawberries and raspberries," I reply, my eyes still closed. It feels like I'm floating, not outside of my body but in places within it that I've never seen or felt before. There's another realm inside that I didn't even know existed. It's as though I'm disconnected from the rest of the world, yet more present in it than I've ever been. Every sensation becomes clearer in the absence of extraneous noise.

"What's missing?" Rowan tries again.

"Nothing. But . . ." I shake my head. Rowan's hand glides down my arm in reassurance, that this place and my words are safe with him. "But it's not unique."

"You're right," he replies. An indulgent kiss lingers on my neck as his cock twitches within me. I notice every motion he makes, from the way his lips lift from my skin to the rise and fall of his chest against my back. "It's not unique. It's like every other crème brûlée in the city. It needs something different. Something new."

"Thorsten Harris probably would suggest—"

"*Blackbird*," Rowan says, punctuating his warning with a bite to my earlobe. "Do not even think about finishing that sentence, or there'll be hell to pay."

My eyes remain closed as I grin. "I like your version of hell."

"You say that now. But I could stay in this tight little cunt of yours for hours, and I think you'd feel differently if I spent all that time not letting you come." Rowan shifts his hips, just a hint of movement that ignites my desperation for more. "Now be my good little bird and name me the most random fruit you can think of. The first thing that springs to mind."

I don't even really think about it. I just speak. "Persimmon."

There's a beat of silence. Rowan relaxes behind me, as though the pent-up tension in his chest has spirited away.

"Yes. Persimmon. That's an excellent idea, love."

And then he slides out of me.

I open my eyes and turn around as he takes a step back, tucking his erection back into his briefs before he tugs his pants up. My breaths come in shallow pants as I take him in. There's heat and desire in his eyes, but he keeps it banked. Not like me. I know my desperate need for more is written all over my face.

"I thought you said good girls get rewards," I say, my voice low and husky.

A slow smile tips up the corner of Rowan's lips where his scar brightens in a straight line through his skin. "You're right. I did say that. Go out into the restaurant and sit on your table."

"Which one is mine?"

"You'll know."

He tosses me a wink and starts to gather the unused ingredients onto the tray. I watch for a moment before he nods toward the door and tells me he'll be there as soon as he's done.

I head out into the dimly lit space and toward the booths beneath the black wing mounted on the wall. When I glance between the front entrance and the sign for the emergency exit by the bathrooms and the door to the kitchen, it's obvious which one

I'd choose—the booth that sits just beneath the vertex of the spread wing.

When I slide onto the seat, there's a line of text in a simple cursive script, branded into the surface of the wood. *Blackbird's Booth,* it says.

My finger traces each letter as I look out at the space and take in every detail from this vantage point. I'm still absorbing the warmth spreading through my veins when I hear the *swoosh* of the kitchen door.

"I thought I said for you to get *on* the table," Rowan says as he stalks in my direction. I glance from him to the windows lining the front of the restaurant and back again. Anticipation rushes through my veins on a flood of adrenaline.

"But—"

"*On,* Sloane. Now."

Fire crawls beneath my skin as I gesture toward the front of the restaurant. Rowan stops next to the booth with a stern expression that states he's clearly unwilling to entertain any protest I'm about to make, not that it will stop me from arguing. "I just saw a woman walk by with her groceries," I say. "She does not want to see that. No one does."

"Of course they do. And even if they didn't, there's an important detail that you might be missing: I don't. Fucking. Care. So are you using your safe word?"

"No."

Rowan's hands press flat to the surface as he leans closer, pinning me with an unwavering stare. "Then get on the fucking table, Sloane."

I climb onto the surface with my back facing the row of

windows as heartbeats hum beneath my skin, keeping my eyes on him the whole time. When I'm settled, Rowan slides onto the padded bench until he's directly in front of me. My gaze is trapped in his, our connection unbroken, neither of us moving. He seems to enjoy that I'm waiting for his instructions as much as I enjoy obeying them.

"Pull your dress up to your waist," he says, his eyes dark and brimming with lust. I do as he says, but I take my time, dragging the hem across my skin. "Spread your legs wide."

Rowan's gaze stays riveted to my damp panties and the outline of my piercings beneath the fabric as I spread my thighs as wide as my hips will allow. He grasps my knees and prompts me back a little closer to the center of the table.

"Remember what I told you?" he asks, not taking his eyes from the apex of my thighs.

I nod. "That you were going to devour me on a table in the restaurant."

"Damn straight, Blackbird. And this is a meal I've been fucking dying for."

Rowan stretches my panties to one side, lowers his head, and feasts.

He wasn't lying. There could be people walking by. They could be staring in the window. They could be at the table next to us and he doesn't fucking care. He ravages my pussy like it's the last meal he'll ever have. He lavishes every piercing with attention and sucks on my clit. He plunges his tongue into my cunt and moans. He tightens his fingers on my thighs in a bruising grip that only ratchets up my desire.

And if anyone is watching, I don't care either.

I grasp Rowan's hair in a tight fist and hold him against me to grind my pussy into his face. I'm rewarded with a throaty growl and two fingers plunged into my cunt, the immediate rhythm and his expert touch pushing me closer to coming undone. My ass squeaks against the wood as he surges forward and consumes me, body and soul.

I come apart with a cry of Rowan's name, soaking his fingers, coating his face. And he leaves me no time to recover from the intense orgasm before he drags my panties down my legs and tosses them to the floor. The moment they're gone, he's tugging his pants and briefs down and sliding into me.

"Fuck, Sloane," he grits out with the first full thrust. I can already tell it won't be long before I'm coming apart for a second time. "I've missed you so fucking much. It's been hell here without you."

"I'm right here," I whisper. I rake my fingers through his hair with one hand and glide my touch beneath his chef's coat to trace the muscles of his back with the other. He leans away enough to pull the thick fabric over his head and I press my touch to every taut muscle and jagged scar.

Rowan bands an arm across my back and yanks me off the table, never breaking our connection as he pulls me down to straddle him on the bench. "You're going to take my cock as deep as you can. You're going to ride it the way you want until you come all over it. And these tits," he says as he unzips the back of my dress and pulls the low neckline down along with the cups of my bra, "you're going to bounce these glorious fucking tits in my face."

I grip the top of the booth with one hand and lean closer to guide my breast to his waiting mouth with the other. He sucks on my nipple and rolls his tongue across the piercing, his moan a vibration in my flesh as he pinches the other one to a firm peak.

I glide on his erection, filling myself with his length. I want to make this pleasure last. I want to savor every long stroke of his cock, every grind of my clit against his flesh as I take him deep, every touch of my piercings against sensitive nerves. But he drives me right to the edge with his kisses on my breasts and the filthy demands he makes every time he surfaces from my skin. *That's right, baby, take me deeper in that tight little cunt. You're going to be dripping my cum down those pretty thighs all the way home.*

My orgasm shatters my vision with a burst of stars as I press my eyes closed and scream. I break apart as Rowan thrusts up, hitting even deeper as he spills into me, his hands gripped tight to my hips as he holds me down on his pulsing cock. Our foreheads are pressed together, our breath shared, our gazes fused. When we finally come down from the euphoric fog, I smile and trace Rowan's cheeks with my fingertips.

"I missed you too."

Rowan sighs, and I realize this is the first time I've seen him truly relaxed since I got back. He lays a kiss to the tip of my nose. "Let's go home and do this again. And again, and again, and again." He guides my hips up until he slides free, his cum leaking from my entrance.

"Napkin?" I ask as I dart a glance down to my legs.

Rowan traces a line up my inner thigh. Two fingers gather the milky rivulet and slide up to my pussy, his eyes already dark with desire as he watches my reaction.

"Fuck no," he rasps as he finger-fucks the cum back into me

with slow thrusts. I shudder and moan, my sensitive flesh already desperate for more. "I meant what I said. You'll be walking home with that mess on your thighs, little bird."

After a final, deep thrust and a roll of his thumb over my clit that has me gasping and clutching his shoulder, he withdraws his fingers and raises them to my lips to suck them clean. When he's satisfied, he gently guides me to the end of the booth and pulls his clothes back into place before following.

We stand for a moment, hand in hand, looking at the space and the windows where thankfully no one has stopped to watch us in our sanctuary, the one that always seems to surround us when I'm alone with Rowan. I let my eyes travel over the space, and when my attention flows in his direction, I feel Rowan's gaze pressing against my face like a gentle caress.

"I'm so happy you're back, Blackbird," he says as he pulls me into his chest and wraps his arms across my back.

I close my eyes. We shift in our embrace, moving together like two dark creatures intertwined, flowing with the current of the world around us.

"I'm not going anywhere," I whisper. "Just home with you."

TOWER

Rowan

It feels like I've walked through hell the last two weeks to get to this exact moment—opening night of Butcher & Blackbird.

We've had the normal pre-launch growing pains. Issues with the POS system. Problems with suppliers. The usual things, but nothing major—just a lot of shit that adds up. But 3 in Coach has been another beast entirely. Equipment breakages. Electrical problems. Faulty appliances. It's like an endless pain in my ass, when it should be running smoothly. I've tried to brush many of the issues off to stay focused, but the stress is still there, and there's not even been time to let off any steam like the Butcher of Boston normally would. If I could just pick off an easy target like some shitbag drug dealer, I know I'd feel so much more at ease. There's just no time.

But thank fuck, the one bright light is Sloane.

If she's bothered by my long hours or my exhaustion and stress, she doesn't let on. I know she's worried about me, but there's no irritation or demands for more attention and presence than I can give right now. In fact, she seems to be thriving, even though it's hard for me to believe.

"I feel terrible, you coming all this way, upending your life, and I'm barely even here," I'd said as I stared through the dark toward the ceiling when we laid in bed two nights ago. But what I didn't say was how worried I constantly feel that this isn't going the way I envisioned at all. I've wanted Sloane for years, and now that she's finally here, it gnaws at me that I might not be giving her what she needs. What if I'm just coming home every night to fuck enough stress out of my system that I can fall asleep but not providing anything tangible in return? Is that what I'm doing?

"I'm happy," she'd replied simply, as though it should be obvious. "I like solitude, Rowan. I feel safe when I'm alone. Maybe not always with that furbag over there looking like he wants to shred my face off," she'd said as she flailed a hand toward the bedroom door, "but Winston aside, this is good for me. I don't feel lonely. Actually, it's the first time in a long time that I don't."

She had pressed a kiss to my cheek as though punctuating her point and then she fell asleep where she always does, resting on my heart. But I stayed awake long after that, with a single question rolling through my mind:

What if she's lying?

I blow out a deep breath and refocus on the task at hand, namely not burning the pan-fried foie gras for the appetizers as Ryan, the maître d', enters the kitchen for a time check for the next course. *Two minutes.* Two minutes and the first guests will be eating at Butcher & Blackbird. Two minutes until the next step in my career becomes reality.

I place the foie gras on the toasted brioche prepped by the

sous-chef, Mia. We dress every plate, five in total, and place them on the pass for the server who's already waiting, and we're immediately on to plating up the next orders that are already cooking.

Then we hit our stride.

Soups. Appetizers. Salads. Fast and nimble. Plate after plate. I keep watch on the table numbers but there's no 17, and that table is permanently reserved for Sloane.

I glance at the clock mounted on the wall.

7:42.

A pang of worry hits my ribs and twists my guts. She's forty-two minutes late.

"Is Sloane here?" I ask when Ryan enters the kitchen with one of the servers.

"Not yet, Chef."

"*Feckin' Christ*," I hiss.

Mia chuckles next to me on the line. "Put the Irish accent away, Chef. She's just late."

"She's never late," I bark with a glare.

"She'll be here, don't worry."

I want to call her, but I can't stop, not even to check my phone. I'm in the middle of the first round of main courses with more appetizers coming in as the restaurant fills to capacity.

My heart claws through my chest and chokes up my throat.

This isn't like her.

She was lying. She's fucking miserable here.

She's gone.

Something's happened. She's been in an accident. She's hurt or harmed or fuck, arrested. She'll wither away in a place like prison. That would be worse than death for a woman like Sloane. Can you fucking imagine?

Shy and acerbic Sloane Sutherland, surrounded by people twenty-four hours a day, never able to find a safe space to hide?

"Hey, Chef. Sloane's here," one of the servers says casually as she picks up two mains from the pass. She darts away with the plates before I can even release my barrage of questions on the breath I've been holding.

But it's enough relief to re-energize my efforts and recharge my spiraling focus.

The team and I plow through the service and I pay special attention to table 17, not knowing which of the six orders for that table is hers. And then the onslaught gradually wanes, and as we finally move into desserts, I unwrap the apron from my waist, thank my hardworking kitchen staff, and head into the front of house.

Smiles and applause and half-drunk, sated faces greet me as I enter the dining area, but my eyes immediately find Sloane where she sits surrounded by my brothers, Lark, Rose, and my friend Anna, the latter of whom she seems to be growing closer with. Ryan passes me a champagne flute as other servers float from table to table, handing complimentary glasses to the patrons.

"Thank you so much for coming tonight," I say as I raise my glass in a toast. My gaze pans across the room, snagging on Dr. Stephan Rostis where he sits at a table with his wife before I force myself to look away. *Fuck*, that would really make my night to cut that asshole up. My smile brightens at the thought. "Without your support of 3 in Coach, this next venture of Butcher & Blackbird would not have been possible. I also want to thank my hardworking and dedicated staff, who have done an incredible job not only tonight, but in the run-up to opening."

Applause rises around me as I shift my attention to Sloane's table. She sits between Rose and Lark, who have both made the trip for opening night, my brothers on either end of the curved bench. "Thank you to my brothers, Lachlan and Fionn, without whom I know I wouldn't be here. We might give each other shit, but they've always had my back. You know I love you boys."

Rose leans close to Fionn and whispers something in his ear. He grins as he makes a flicking motion with his finger and thumb.

"Well, I *kind of* love you. Really I just tolerate you most of the time. Especially you, Fionn," I clarify to the sound of laughter.

Then I turn my attention to Sloane.

She's so fucking beautiful in that dress she wore the night of the Best of Boston gala, with her dark hair pulled across one shoulder in shining waves. Candlelight from the small votive dances in her hazel eyes as she smiles. Nobody's ever looked at me the way she does, with an intoxicating mix of pride and secrets that only we share. The rest of the room disappears as I just soak it in for a moment.

When I speak, it's only to her.

"To my beautiful girlfriend, Sloane," I say as I raise my glass in her direction. "Thank you for putting your trust in me. For putting up with my shit. For putting up with my *brothers'* shit." The crowd laughs and Sloane's smile broadens as the blush creeps up her neck. "When I was young, I collected every lucky charm I could find. I carried a rabbit's foot around everywhere. Don't ask Fionn where I got it, he'll never shut up," I say, and laughter surrounds us again. But Sloane doesn't laugh, she only flashes a melancholy smile as she stays hooked on the past beneath my words. "I couldn't understand why those talismans never changed my luck, so I stopped believing. But now I know. I was saving it all up to meet you, Blackbird."

Her eyes shine as she presses a kiss to her fingertips and offers it to the space between us on an upturned palm.

"To Butcher & Blackbird," I say as I raise my glass. The crowd echoes my toast and we drink, the round of applause that follows easing my pent-up worries about our success.

I spend time checking on guests, most of whom have been regulars at 3 in Coach and were given preference on the limited opening-night reservation list. Excitement follows me from table to table. They're enthusiastic about everything from the interior design to the cocktails to the dinner menu. I know it's a winner. I can feel it in my bones.

And maybe all this insanity from the last few months was worth it.

The last table I stop at is the booth beneath the center of the raven's wing.

"I'm proud of you, you little shit," Lachlan says as he folds a tattooed hand over the back of my neck and presses his forehead to mine, just like we've done since we were kids. "You did good."

"Yeah, you're not so bad. I guess we'll keep you," Fionn pipes up as he slaps me on the shoulder harder than necessary. Rose stays seated with her leg still trapped in a cast, so I lean down to press a kiss on each of her cheeks. Anna gives me a beaming smile and a brief hug before she returns to her conversation with Rose, the little banshee entertaining the table with her never-ending tales of circus life. From Lark, it's a fierce embrace and a string of effervescent compliments as Lachlan watches her with a look of vexation. When I finally get to Sloane and slide in next to her on the padded booth, a combination of relief and exhaustion punches through the mask I feel I've been wearing for far too long. She wraps her arms around me as I lay my chin on her shoulder and run a hand down the soft velvet covering her back.

"You're not just a pretty face," Sloane says as I let out a laugh in her arms. "It's amazing, Butcher. It's perfect. And I'm sorry we were late." She turns her lips to my ear, then whispers, "It was Lachlan and Lark's fault. I think they hooked up but I'm confused, because it seems like they fucking hate each other."

"Somehow, none of that feels like a surprise seeing as how Lachlan is involved," I reply before I kiss her neck and pull back enough to see her eyes. She smiles when I trail my fingers through her hair. "I should be saying, 'Let's go out and party once everyone's gone and we can place bets on whether or not they'll hook up again,' but really I just want to steal your e-reader and curl up in bed with some pirate porn and then fall asleep for a thousand years."

Sloane rolls her eyes and looks away as I grin. "You need to catch up. I'm on the hitchhiker smut now."

"Then let me borrow your e-reader."

"Get fucked," she says, and presses her lips to my cheek before tucking herself beneath my arm and threading her fingers between mine. "In a loving way, of course."

I settle in just long enough to feel the calm of her touch and the company of family and friends before I'm back in the kitchen, helping Mia and the team prepare dinner for the staff to share. And then the whirlwind of chaos that I crave and thrive on ebbs away, leaving peace in its wake.

It's well after midnight when Sloane and I get home, and it feels like I'm barely even into the bed before I'm asleep.

The next morning is a Sunday—technically my day off, though I usually end up working in some capacity. Sloane is already awake, coffee brewed, her laptop open, her eyes fixed to the screen as she shovels Froot Loops into her mouth. Winston sits on the opposite end of the table, staring her down as though trying to communicate his simmering judgments telepathically. I pick him up as I walk by and he growls as I plop him on the floor.

"What the fuck are you eating?" I ask as I trace a touch across the pulse in her neck as I continue my trek to the blessed coffee machine.

"Individually dyed Cheerios, clearly. Took me all morning," she snarks.

I grin, though she doesn't see it. "That smart mouth is going to get put to good use as soon as I'm caffeinated."

"Are you threatening me with a good time?"

"More like promising. And speaking of good time," I say, pouring the rest of the coffee into the largest mug I own before starting a fresh pot, "did you see Dr. Rostis there last night?"

"Ooh, I did, yeah. Didn't get a chance to talk to him. Maybe we should make him into next year's game instead of enlisting Lachlan to identify a target."

A twinge of worry wracks my body with a shiver. I still see Sloane trapped in that cellar at Harvey Mead's house, his boot print an angry red mark on her face, blood dripping from her nostrils in the rain. The flash of lightning across her misshapen shoulder is still vivid in my mind. I dream of that moment too often. It fucking haunts me. "Or maybe instead of a competitive game this year, we can play together. We could hunt him as a team."

Sloane snorts a derisive laugh. "Are you afraid of losing again, pretty boy?"

"I'm afraid of losing you."

Sloane turns to me then, a scrutinous eye flowing over my face. Her gaze softens into something akin to pity. It's probably due to the dark circles under my eyes and my haphazard hair and longer-than-usual stubble. She catalogs every detail before she sits back in her chair. "Rowan, I'll be okay. This is what we do. What happened with Harvey was my own careless mistake."

"Why did you make it?" I press. I already know the answer. She knows I do.

Sloane swallows. "Because I thought he was coming for you."

I head toward the table and she opens an arm to me, wrapping my waist in her warmth and laying her head against my side when I halt next to her. "I don't want to stop," I say. "But there's a lot more risk involved when we work against one another rather than together."

"True, but it's also so fun when I kick your ass."

A sigh leaves my lungs, a hint of frustration in a puff of air. "Sloane, I can't handle worrying about you right now. I don't think I can take that stress on top of everything else. I can barely manage to keep a day-to-day, normal life with you together, let alone *that*."

Sloane stiffens against me. I realize that sounded harsh when I didn't mean it to. I'm just so fucking tired, and the constant worry about messing this new life up is manifesting exactly what I *don't* want to happen: messing it the fuck up.

"I'm sorry, love. I didn't mean that the way it came out."

"It's okay," she says, but the brightness in her tone comes off forced.

"No, I'm serious. You're not a burden, if that's what you think."

"It's okay," she says again as she casts a brief smile up to me before she turns her attention back to her laptop. "I get it. All your hard work has been worth it, though. The initial reviews from opening night are great."

She pulls the computer closer so I can see the reviews she's been reading. But it takes me a moment to turn my attention to what she's trying to show me. I don't know whether to press her on this obvious deflection, or if doing so will make her retreat even more. In the end, I figure it's likely I'll just make things worse if I open my uncaffeinated mouth on the topic, so I squeeze her arm instead and read the reviews over her shoulder. They might be early and a little biased, as most are from loyal regular customers, but I can tell by the detail and enthusiasm that we're off to a good start. And as Sloane points out particular passages and comments, I know she's proud of it too, even if my words just now delivered a sting I didn't intend.

"What have you got planned for the morning?" I ask when we've read through a few reviews together.

"I think I'll meet up with the girls for coffee. It would be nice to see them a few more times before they leave town," Sloane replies, but something about the way she says it makes me think this is an impromptu plan she just came up with to get out of the apartment. "After that, maybe I'll run some errands, I'm not sure. What about you?"

"I've gotta head to 3 in Coach when brunch is over. Jenna texted that they've had some problems with one of the exhaust hoods." I let my fingers drift through Sloane's hair, the waves still faint from last night. "How about you meet me there at four? Come in the back, through the kitchen. We can go somewhere and grab a drink."

"Yeah. That sounds good." Sloane rises and gives me a brief smile when she turns my way, but there's a tightness in it before she lays a kiss to my cheek and takes her empty bowl to the kitchen. "I'd better get ready."

With a final flash of a smile, Sloane picks up Winston and disappears down the corridor with the cat growling in her arms.

I contemplate following her into the shower. Maybe I should press her against the cold tiles and bury myself into her tight heat and kiss every drop of water from her face until she knows without doubt that she is *not* a burden. But I don't. I worry that when she needs or wants space, she won't ask for it, and I'll push too hard. I'll push her away.

I rest my forehead in my hands and stay like that for a long while, thinking about all the things we should discuss tonight when we can relax with a couple of drinks. We'll find a private table at a quiet bar and talk it through just like we agreed at Fionn's. And then we'll come back to our home, and this morning's conversation will just be another brick in the foundation of a life we're making together.

When Sloane appears from the corridor with her skin flushed from the heat of the shower and her hair damp, I'm still at the table, a second cup of coffee nearly finished.

"Four o'clock at the restaurant, yeah?" I ask as I rise from my chair.

She nods, her smile bright, but the tightness she can't hide from me remains. "I'll be there."

And though she kisses me goodbye, and tells me she loves me, and casts a smile over her shoulder as she goes, that thin mask still remains to follow her out the door.

"*Feckin' eejit*," I say to myself as I drag a hand through my hair and flop down on the couch.

I made up this fucking game on a whim just to keep her around, and now I give her the impression that I think the whole thing is just a giant pain in my ass. And even worse, I make out like having her in my life is a fucking burden.

It's not. It's the furthest thing from it. I just can't bear the thought of losing her, which is exactly what's going to happen if I don't get my shit together and we talk this stuff through.

So that's what I resolve to do.

I haul my ass up and go to the gym down the street, then come back for a shower. I spend some time looking up some ideas for the New Year's Eve menu, which is still a few months away but I know will creep up fast. Winston keeps watch as I do some chores and make lunch and give him a slice of bacon that he hasn't earned, because he's kind of a dick. Then I'm headed to 3 in Coach, giving myself just enough time to make it there after the staff have all gone so I can see if this fan is something I can fix myself before Sloane arrives.

I enter through the back door and disarm the alarm, then head down the dark, windowless corridor to the kitchen.

Everything is sparkling clean, all the utensils and pots and pans where they should be for Tuesday lunch when the restaurant will be open again. As I scan the prep area, my gaze snags on the framed sketch hanging on the wall, the one that Sloane left for me that first day she came in. A faint smile passes over my lips as I remember the blush in her skin and the panic in her pretty eyes. It was the first time I really let myself believe she might want something more than friendship, but she didn't know *how* to make it happen.

A sudden noise from a darkened corner startles me and I whip around to see David sitting in the steel chair we set out for him next to the dishwasher.

"*Jesus feckin' Christ*," I hiss as I bend at the waist and slap a hand against my heart as its chambers flood with adrenaline. "What the hell are you still doing here?"

David doesn't answer me, of course. He's not spoken a single word since we found him in Thorsten's mansion. His vacant gaze is caught on the floor as he rocks a slow rhythm in his chair, something he seems to do on the rare occasions when he's agitated.

I walk over to him and lean down enough to scrutinize his expressionless face. He seems to calm a little when I lay a hand on his slumped shoulder. Nothing else appears amiss about him.

"Thank fuck I came, mate. Hate the thought of you spending the night in here."

I leave him to look at the schedule of shifts on the whiteboard. There's a note for the line cook Jake to drive David home after brunch. Jake is our newest staff member here, having relocated from Seattle six months ago, and he's been nothing but reliable so far, so this level of fuckup is unusual and definitely something I'll give him shit for on Tuesday.

When I've got David settled with a glass of water, I focus on the task at hand, flipping the switch for the fans. One of them doesn't turn on. There's not much I can see with the filter shielding the mechanism from view, so I gather my tools from the office and head to the electrical panel to kill the power for that section of the kitchen. Once I've dismantled the casing, it doesn't take long to find the source of the problem—a disconnected wire. It takes a little fiddling to get everything put back together, but it's a pretty straightforward job and I get it all finished just a few minutes before four o'clock.

"I'll be right back, David," I say, my brow furrowing as his gentle, metronomic rocking resumes. "I'm just going to turn the breaker on, then as soon as Sloane arrives, we'll get you home, okay?"

I don't know how much he comprehends. Nothing changes in his demeanor.

Shaking my head, I turn away and gather my tools to store them in the office. With a flip of the kitchen switch in the breaker box, I turn the power to the fans back on.

When I return to the kitchen and round the stove, I stop dead.

The cold muzzle of a gun presses to the center of my forehead.

A deep chuckle and the smooth, unfamiliar voice of the man holding the Glock clash with the panic that floods my veins. "Well, well," he says. "The Butcher of Boston."

I raise my hands as the muzzle presses harder to my face in warning.

"And your little Orb Weaver will be here any minute too. As tempting as that party of three sounds, I'd really like to spend some quality time together, just you and me. So, you're going to make her leave."

A key slides into the lock of the back door as the click of the safety releases on the gun pointed at my face.

"If you don't, I'll kill her," he whispers, taking a step backward toward the shadows that envelop the corner of the room. He shifts the weapon, pointing it toward the door for the corridor, the one Sloane will walk through any moment. "And I'll enjoy every second of making you watch."

KEYS

Sloane

I slot my key into the lock at the service entrance of 3 in Coach and push the heavy steel door into the shadows of the corridor. When I slip it into my pocket, I keep my hand around the cool metal. Aside from the one to Lark's apartment, I've never had someone else's key before. Knowing how much the restaurant means to Rowan and his brothers, the ridged metal feels sacred to me. I like to hold it against my palm, to know that I mean something to Rowan too, enough that he wants me to share this place with him.

I know Rowan has been incredibly stressed with everything going on. I've felt him close down from time to time, and whenever I questioned him on it, he said he just wanted to leave the problems at work and forget about them for a while. That made sense, and I've tried to create the same safe place for him that he's always made for me. Our own little realm where the outside world disappears for a while. But this morning was the first time I felt the picture shift in a way that had my guts twisting and my heart crawling into my throat. Until now, I'd not asked myself if the burden that weighs him down is *me*.

I have to keep reminding myself to take him for his word, that he didn't mean it that way, even though my insecurities keep rattling around in my head like insects pinging against panes of glass. If he said I'm not a burden, then he's being honest . . . right? We all say things we don't mean. It will just take a day or two to shake it, and things will get better once Butcher & Blackbird is fully up and running.

I press the key tighter in my palm. It's proof. He and I are not temporary. Our circumstances are, and they'll pass in time.

"Rowan," I call out as I near the kitchen. "I found this place online that looks pretty cool, with a rooftop patio. Maybe we could . . ."

My voice trails off as I enter the room.

Rowan is standing with his hands braced against the edge of the stainless steel prep counter, his shoulders tense, his head bent. When his gaze collides with mine, it's wracked with darkness and defeat.

"What's wrong. . . ?" I ask as I slow to a stop and take him in. My heart surges with worry. Every spark of intuition tells me everything about this is very wrong. "Did something happen with the restaurant? Are you okay?"

I start to approach him, my hand raised to touch his arm, but he straightens abruptly and backs out of reach. My feet halt instantly. My heart rate doubles.

"Are you okay?" I ask again.

His voice holds no kindness, no warmth, not even familiarity when he says, "No, Sloane. I am not okay."

My throat collapses around the words I want to say. Heat erupts beneath my skin, burning every inch of me from the inside out. My gaze bounds between the confines of Rowan's dark, sharp stare, its edges bordering on lethal. "What's going on?"

"What's going on is that you need to go home."

"Okay . . . I'll just get an Uber—"

"No. To Raleigh. You need to go back where you belong."

"I don't—" A sudden burst of emotion chokes my throat. My nose burns. A sting floods my eyes. "I don't understand."

Rowan drags a hand through his hair and breaks his gaze away before he takes another step backward, clearly agitated that I'm lingering here. I'm desperate to take a step closer, to just touch him and make whatever this is stop before it all disintegrates in my hand like a castle of sand swept out to sea.

"Did I do something? If I did something, you need to tell me. We can talk it through."

He pinches the bridge of his nose as a frustrated sigh empties from his lungs. "You didn't *do* anything Sloane, this just isn't fuck-ing working. And I need you to go."

"But . . . I thought you said we would do what normal people do. Talk to one another. Make it work."

"We're not '*normal people*,' Sloane. We can't pretend to be some-thing we're not. Not anymore. I told you this back in April, on the tenth. I said that I never wanted to be like everybody else."

I shake my head, trying to claw my way through confusion and into my memories. "I don't remember—"

"Tenth or the thirteenth. Whatever. It's just like I told you in the car on the way to the gala. I said even then that the restaurant was the only thing that made sense in my life. But it doesn't matter.

What matters is that there are some things we can never have. I can never have a normal life. Neither can you. We're monsters in this world."

I know I'm not a normal person, but I don't feel like a monster. I feel like a weapon. The final justice on behalf of those who can't speak, delivering punishment for those who don't deserve clemency. But maybe Rowan is right. Maybe I've just been deluding myself about my reign of vengeance, and I'm every bit the monster as the prey that we hunt.

I'm caught on these questions when Rowan lets out a frustrated sigh, like this is taking up too much of his time. The hurt of it twists and burns in my chest.

"My restaurants are all that really matter," he says, pointing toward the dining room before pressing his finger to the stainless steel counter. "I need to keep my focus here. Trying to have both these places and a relationship is not feasible for me. So you need to leave. Go home."

Rowan's hard stare doesn't let up. It drills right into the depths of me. It doesn't waver as the first tear falls from my lashes to carve a hot line down my cheek. He doesn't even blink when the next ones quickly follow.

"But . . . I love you, Rowan," I whisper.

Rowan isn't warm, or kind, or anything but cold and clinical when he says, "You think you do, but you don't. Because you *can't*."

My mind is spinning. My heart is crumbling into ash. Part of me wants to run as much as he wants me to. Run and run until I don't even know where I am anymore. Until I can't feel this pain.

But I plant my feet.

"I'll go, if that's what you want," I say, my voice tight and small. "But I need you to tell me something first, please."

"What."

"I need to know why I'm unlovable."

It's the first time I've seen even the slightest hint of hesitation in Rowan since I stepped into this kitchen. But in an instant, he swallows it down. And nothing else comes.

My anger blisters beneath the weight of this imploding loss. "Tell me."

I'm met with nothing but a lightless stare. Tears flood my vision until I can barely see Rowan through the watery veil.

"Just be honest with me. Why can't you love me? What's wrong with me? *Tell me*—"

"Because you're a fucking psycho, that's why."

Rowan's words hit me like a slap. The tears stop. My breath stops. My shattered heart. Even time. The moment of silence between us feels eternal, a pain that's carved right into whatever is left of my soul, his words branded there forever. I know in an instant they'll follow me, a ghost that will never let go.

Rowan folds his hands into tight fists as he leans a little closer, as though trying to force this revelation through my eyes and into my brain. "You kill people and cut bits of them off and make an elaborate show out of stringing up some batshit-crazy map that no one can figure out but you. Then you gouge out their fucking eyes and make them into decorations. I know I'm no fucking saint, but that shit is next-level insane. *That* is what's wrong with you, Sloane. You're unhinged. You're going to crash and burn. You'll take me with you if I let this keep going. So you need to *fucking leave*."

I take an unsteady step backward, then another, and another.

Discomfort registers for the first time in my hand, and I realize I've been gripping the restaurant key so tightly that it's bitten into my skin. I pull it from my pocket and stare at the silver resting on the red marks in my palm.

My gaze lifts, not to Rowan but the sketch I drew last year. It's framed near the door to the front of the restaurant, right where Rowan can see it as he works, where it's safe from the heat and humidity in the kitchen. Just like I thought it was safe in his skin. Like I was safe in his heart.

But I'm not.

When my attention drags to Rowan, I hold his eyes for the last time.

I give myself just one breath to remember every detail of his beautiful face. His full lips. That scar I wish I could kiss. His navy eyes, even though their glare cuts right through me.

In the next breath, I turn my hand and let the key slide from my skin and fall to the floor.

I say nothing more as I pivot on my heel and leave 3 in Coach.

I run the whole way back to his apartment. Twelve blocks. Three flights of stairs. It's only when I take my set of house keys from my pocket and burst into the living room in a mess of sweat and uneven breaths that I let myself cry again.

I'm a fucking psycho.

I thought he was just like me. I thought we were the same. It might have started with a game, but even from the beginning, it felt like so much more. Like I'd finally found a kindred soul. All these years, these crazy experiences, the longing and loneliness of the in-between—I thought it added up to something brighter on our horizon. We were getting closer, weren't we?

It's what I let myself believe.

How could I have been so wrong all this time?

I love Rowan. Right down to my fucking core. I love the future I saw with him, and now he's ripped it right out of my grasp.

What if this is always what was waiting on the other side of the mountain? Just a jagged cliff to fall over?

It takes me a long moment to realize I've moved from the center of the room to Rowan's sofa. I don't know how long I've been sitting. I don't even know how much time has passed since I arrived. It feels like my head is stuffed with cotton, a fuzzy barrier between my thoughts and the world.

I blink and look at Winston, who sits across from me on Rowan's favorite chair, his eyes a slash of yellow in his plush gray fur.

"You're probably even more psycho than me. You're named after a fucking undead cat," I say to the feline as another burst of tears crawls up my throat. I toss a defeated wave in Winston's direction before I drop my head into my hands and fucking *sob*. "So yeah, like, I totally get it with the whole *look of death* thing you've got going on, but you're still getting on a fucking plane and coming with me because I'll be damned if I go back to Raleigh alone."

I cry a flood of tears that feels never-ending until something soft grazes my hand. My damp palms slide down my face and Winston stares up at me, his gentle purr a rumble of comfort. When I lift my arm, he climbs onto my lap and lies down. "So, I admit I'm a psycho and now you want to be friends? I guess that tracks."

We sit like that until my tears eventually slow, just me and the cat and the vibration of his purr against my thighs. And after a long while, when the knowledge that Rowan could come back at any moment eats away at my thoughts enough to dominate them, I set the cat aside and rise.

"If we're getting on a plane, we're going to do it looking hot. And I don't mean in a trash-fire kind of way," I say to Winston as he stares at me, seemingly disgruntled that his warm human bed has moved.

I head to the shower, turn it up until it's scalding. Every one of Rowan's products goes down the drain, because my *fucking psycho* energy is real in the moments when I'm not a snotty, sobbing mess. Then I dry my hair, do my makeup, promise myself I won't cry again so I don't ruin the best eyeliner job I've done in a while. I even put on some fake lashes, because *fuck it*. If I'm going to be a psycho, I'm going to be the hottest damn psycho Logan International Airport has ever seen.

Of course, some of that perseverance ebbs away when I book the next flight out of town and pack up my shit.

By the time I call Lark, my determination is nearly gone.

"Hey, Gold Star Tits, how are you?" she asks, her voice a chime of bells.

A deep breath streams through my nose. "Um. I've been better."

"Why? What happened?"

"Rowan," I say, blinking back the tears. "He broke up with me."

"*What?*" There's a long stretch of silence. I nod, even though I know Lark can't see me. "No . . ."

"Yeah."

A sound of anguish bleeds into the line from Lark's end of the call. Whatever glue holds my heart together enough to keep it beating softens with the sound of Lark's distress on my behalf. Jagged points of pain lance me from the inside out, scoring muscle and bone.

"He couldn't have . . . You can't be serious . . ." Lark whispers.

"Dead serious, unfortunately," I reply, putting the phone on speaker as I sit on the couch and pull Winston onto my lap. "I just booked a flight back to Raleigh. I want to get out of Boston right away. Can I stay at your place for a little bit until I figure out what the fuck to do with the tenants in my house?"

"Of course. Always. As long as you want. Text me your flight details and I'll change my flight so we can leave together." A string of swears and disbelief flows from Lark as I text her my flight number. When the details come through, she repeats the information before she heaves a long sigh. "Oh, sweetie, there has to be some kind of mistake. That man *loves* you."

My huffed laugh is bitter and sardonic. "That's what I thought too. But he made it pretty clear that he doesn't. I'm a *'fucking psycho,'* apparently, and therefore can neither love nor be loved. I guess that's not news. Turns out, I'm too psycho even for him."

"That's what he said to you? And you didn't pluck his eyeballs out and flush them down the toilet?"

A faint smile passes over my lips and fades away just as quickly as it appears. "I probably should have."

"What else did he say?"

"I dunno, some weird stuff," I reply, trying to remember the recent details that already seem hazy beneath the pain. "He said I needed to go home, and at first I thought he meant here, to the apartment. But then he said 'no, to Raleigh.' When I asked why, he wouldn't give me a reason at first, just that it wasn't working between us and that the restaurants had to take priority."

"But I thought it *was* working."

"Me too." I pick at Winston's fur, replaying every word of our breakup, even though I'd give anything to forget them all. "I asked him to talk it through together. That was something he'd said at Fionn's place, that we would talk about stuff like normal people do."

"That sounds reasonable and pretty non-psycho to me."

"Yeah. Same. Then he said something kind of strange." My brow furrows as I open the search function on my home screen and type in the word *lobby*. It brings up a message from Rowan as one of the options, and I press on it to open his text. "He said that he 'never wanted to be like everybody else.' He claimed specifically that he'd told me that on the way to the Best of Boston gala on April tenth."

"Okay . . . what's weird about that?"

"I don't remember him saying that. Not ever. And the gala wasn't on the tenth."

Lark pauses. She's probably thinking I've lost my shit, and she might be right. "Maybe he got the date wrong?"

"But the gala was two days before his birthday, on the twenty-seventh. Don't you think that's kind of strange that he wouldn't remember that?"

"Sweetie, I dunno. If he's in the midst of a breakup and obviously stressed about restaurant shit, he might have gotten the dates wrong."

"I guess, but then he corrected himself and said the thirteenth.

It's the *way* he said it, the way he put it all together. It was just weirdly specific," I reply, scrolling through messages he and I shared around those dates. "He said something else about our conversation in the car on the way to the event, that the restaurant was the only thing that made sense in his life. But I'm positive he never said that."

"Hun, Sloane, I love you. I love you more than anyone, sweetie, but he might not fully remember all the details. I mean, he's clearly fucked in the head if he's going to give you up, so who knows what's going on upstairs, you know?"

Lark keeps talking, explaining every reasonable theory for why he could have said what he said.

But I don't hear a word as I push the cat from my lap and rise to my feet.

Because I'm staring at a text I sent him at the end of March, the same day he'd called and asked me to be his date for the awards.

> Do you think this gala will have an ice cream buffet? If so, I should probably let them know that you only accept freshly milked semen

My blood turns to shards of ice in my veins.

I remember holding that white tub in my hands in Thorsten's kitchen as I read the homemade label to Rowan.

April tenth to thirteenth.

I know what he said on the way to the gala. I remember it as clearly as I remember the warmth of the kiss he'd pressed to my neck in the lobby, the tingle of electricity in my skin when he'd taken my hand across the leather seat during the drive. *At least one thing is going right at 3 in Coach,* he told me. *Stuff inevitably goes wrong. It just . . . feels like a lot lately.*

Lark is still talking when I say, "I have to go," then disconnect the call.

My fingers are cold and numb when I open the app for the camera I installed in the restaurant kitchen.

My stomach churns as I take in the details on the screen.

"No . . ." Tears flood my vision. "No, no, *no* . . ."

I clutch at my heart as it shatters for a second time. Blood drains from my limbs. The edges of my vision darken and I press my eyes closed tight. A sound of anguish tumbles past my lips as my knees buckle, my phone dropping from my hand. I know the horror I just saw is real. But there's no time to fall apart.

What if you're not fast enough?

I don't answer that question. I can't. The only thing I can do now is try.

I swallow the lance of pain and steady myself to take one turn in the middle of the room. My gaze lands on my leather case where I keep my scalpel among my pencils and erasers.

Hands shaking, I pick up my phone and dial the Unknown Caller, a contact whose name I never entered into my phone. He answers on the second ring.

"Spider Lady," Lachlan says. "What's the occasion?"

"I need a favor. Urgently," I reply as I whip my case from the side table and stride toward the door. "You have as long as it takes for me to run twelve blocks."

"Sounds fun. I like a challenge. What do you need?"

"I'll tell you what I know," I say, already descending the stairs by twos. "And you're going to give me everything you can find on David Miller."

FINESSE

Rowan

The sharp edge of the mandoline lays against my inner forearm between the ropes that bind me to the chair. My palms face upward in curled fists, my short nails digging into my flesh as I brace against the pain I've already endured and that which is yet to come. Ragged breaths saw from my chest and I grit my teeth. I know what's about to happen. Blood already pours from two other wounds, and he's determined to get the perfect slice this time.

The blade catches in my skin and peels it from the flesh beneath.

I swallow a scream as David pushes down to resist my futile struggle and glides the mandoline toward my elbow until a thin strip of my skin is cut away. He tosses the bloodied tool onto the prep counter where it skids to a halt next to his gun.

Then he tears the flap of skin free from my arm with a merciless tug as the sound of my distressed cry fills the room.

"You know, I developed a taste for this at Thorsten's," David says as he leans close until he takes up all the space in my vision.

He grips my hair with one hand and wrenches my head back to smile down at me. His once-vacant eyes are not fucking vacant anymore. They are *ravenous*. And they're pinned on me. "Did you develop a taste too?"

Blood drips across his fingers from the sliced skin pinched between them. I thrash in my chair but can't escape his hold.

"Just a little nibble," he says.

I press my lips tight. A choked growl of protest vibrates in my throat as he smears my bloody skin across my lips.

"No?"

His counterfeit pout turns into a reptilian grin.

David's tongue slides out between his teeth and he lays the skin across it like a veil, holding it out for me to see. He closes his lips around it, lets it wiggle against his triumphant smile.

Then he sucks it into his mouth.

Eyes closed, his jaws work slowly, like he savors every bite as he rolls it between his teeth.

His audible swallow turns my stomach.

"Such a delicacy. So very rare." He turns away to the table and drags a bottle of Pont Neuf across the stainless steel counter. "You know what else is rare?"

My answer is only ragged breaths.

"A woman like Sloane," David says.

I'm going to be fucking sick.

I have never, *never* felt like this. Like there's an empty pit in my stomach. Like I'm falling into it from the inside out. So helpless. So fucking desperate. That look in her eyes when I told her I didn't love her, it haunts every breath I take. Those goddamn tears rip me apart.

"Not many people would do what she did for me," David says as he spins the corkscrew into the bottle. It squeaks with every metronomic turn of his hand. "But then, that's her way, isn't it. Just like she protected that friend of hers, the Montague girl. So strange how that teacher just suddenly disappeared from their boarding school, don't you think? People do have a funny way of conveniently disappearing around the Montagues."

"Leave her alone," I grit out.

"Though when I dug and dug *and dug* for answers, it seemed as though there were already rumors swirling about the things he did to the girls there. Terrible things. Depraved things. Deviant things. But at least he did one *good* thing—he made the Orb Weaver. A beautiful monster."

The cork pops free of the bottle.

His voice drips with feigned innocence when David says, "Do you think she would want to do those deviant, depraved things with me?"

My vision reddens with rage as I thrash in the chair. "*Leave her the fuck alone,*" I snarl.

David sighs as he pours himself a glass of wine. "I don't think she wants to either. But I'll *make* her."

I erupt within my restraints, unhinged. Wild. Insane.

But I go nowhere.

"Maybe I'll take my time," he continues as he unwinds the cork from the metal spiral. "Make her trust me. Maybe I'll even make a miraculous semi-recovery. You know, not so much that I don't still tug on her little black heartstrings, but just enough that she can convince herself into fucking a lobotomized man. Or maybe I've used up all my patience already. I've been waiting for this moment for so long, you know. Maybe I'll just follow her all the way back to 154 Jasmine Street. I could break into her house and bring her a doggie bag. Feed her little pieces of you and then fuck her until I tear her apart, until she's nothing more than another piece of bloody, pulverized meat destined for the trash."

He saunters closer until he's right in front of me, his gaze caught on his wine as he swirls it in the glass and then takes a sip.

"Either way," he says as a smile sneaks across his lips, "the sound of her begging will be a beautiful symphony. A masterpiece."

My throat clogs. My eyes fucking sting.

I know there's no reasoning with him. There's no bartering. I have nothing to offer. But I try anyway.

For her.

"Please, *please*, just leave her alone. If you want begging, I'll fucking beg. If you want money, you can have everything I own. If you want to cut me up into a thousand pieces, you can. Do whatever you want with me. Just please leave her be. *Please*."

David leans closer. His eyes scour every inch of my face. "Why would I do that, when I can have you both?"

A flash of movement. Silver in the dim light.

Pain erupts in my wrist and agony spills from my lips. I look down to where the corkscrew is buried in my flesh, twitching with every beat of my heart.

"The Pont Neuf," David says as he holds his glass beneath my bound arm. Blood trickles into the wine. "It's nice, but a little bland for my taste. I like something full-bodied."

He leaves the corkscrew in my arm as he takes a long sip. When David's eyes fix to mine, they're hazy, half lidded. His slow smile is exultant.

"So much better," he whispers, and swirls the wine and blood together before drinking more down. "That little tang of iron really adds another dimension to the mix. As insufferable as that pretentious old windbag was, I must admit—Thorsten really was on to something. And all this talking? Well . . . it's made me hungry. I bet you're famished too."

David turns away toward the counter where the mandoline lies in a smear of blood on the stainless steel.

It's Sloane's face I see when I drop my chin to my chest and close my eyes. It's her tears I feel when sweat slides down my face to drop on my lap. I think about how fucking beautiful she was when I told her I didn't want her, her skin radiant with the pain of my words. I watched her heart shatter, and I twisted that knife for nothing. Because I'll never be able to save her. Not from this. Not from him.

I can only hope that she disappears the way I know she can. They way she should have, from the first moment I let her out of that cage.

I'm thinking about that day I met her in the bayou when I notice David go still in the periphery.

When I drag my gaze from my lap, he's still standing at the table where the mandoline is, but his posture is different. Stiff. Tense. He pivots a slow turn with his back to me, his head angled at the length of the prep table to his left and then the counter on his right.

"Looking for something?" a voice says from the shadows.

Shock and confusion. Desperation and fear. It all crashes into my chest as Sloane steps into the light, David's gun raised in her hand.

She's so fucking beautiful. So brave. The gun doesn't waver in her hand as she keeps it trained on him and walks forward to stop enough to the side that I can see her clearly. Her skin glows with a light sheen of sweat. Hazel eyes rimmed with black liner and thick lashes flick to me.

Her face is expressionless as she takes in my bloody arm and the corkscrew embedded in my wrist.

She looks to David. A slow smile creeps across her lips.

"Hello, David. I'm so happy we finally have a chance to talk," she says.

And then she lowers the gun.

"I was wondering when you'd finally make your move."

Her smile takes on a dark edge. A *sharp* edge. One that slips right between my ribs.

Sloane doesn't look at me. Not even a glance in my direction. She keeps all her attention on David, warmth and wonder in her eyes, that fucking dimple a shadow next to her lips.

I want to rip his fucking skin off.

"I admire your work," she says. "The South Bay Slasher. I assume you befriended Thorsten while you were in Torrance, am I right?"

David smirks before raising the glass to his lips and taking a long sip of wine, then he sets it on the counter next to the mandoline and crosses his arms. "So, you've been stalking me. Can't say I'm entirely surprised."

Sloane shrugs. "I like to know who's out and about."

"I know. I've been doing some stalking of my own. I'm aware of the caliber of prey you hunt. You're here to kill me."

"If I was," she says as she raises the gun and examines the barrel, "I would have done it already."

David lets his gaze travel the length of Sloane's body. There's a flash in his eyes, a flicker of all the things he wants to do to her, all his depraved desires. "I was watching your special little moment with this asshole a couple of hours ago, don't forget. I know pain when I see it. You could say it's my specialty."

"And it was a very convincing performance, wasn't it." Sloane shrugs and keeps her finger on the trigger as she rests her elbow against her hip and points the gun toward the ceiling. "I've been watching you too."

"Little lies will catch you in a web, Orb Weaver. You should know that better than anyone," David says through the dark, predatory smile that creeps across his lips. "I shut down the security cameras."

Though David edges a little closer to her, Sloane remains relaxed. Nothing about her stance changes when she says, "Tsk, tsk, David. You must not have counted all the video feeds. That one there?" she says as she points the Glock to a camera in the corner of the room that's aimed toward us, its red light still on. "That one is mine. I've been watching the whole time."

David's smile falls as he realizes she's right.

Sloane's smirk is triumphant as she gives him a wink. "Like I said. If I wanted to, I would."

In a whip of movement, she aims the gun at David, the muzzle pointed at his forehead. He stiffens and drops his arms.

"*Pow, pow, pow,*" she says in a staccato rhythm. Her grin spreads before she lowers the weapon to her side. "Just kidding."

I can see only David's profile, but he can't hide that gleam in his eye.

He's fucking enraptured.

And Sloane eats it up, her face lighting in an indulgent smile. "Did you befriend Thorsten to find me?" she asks with a flirty tilt of her head.

"More like to defend myself. I had an idea you might come for me someday. I figured if I made friends with someone like us, I might have a buffer every August when people of our . . . nature . . . tend to wind up dead. Of course, Thorsten didn't know he was being hunted, so I suggested I could pretend to be his fucked-up servant for the night while he scratched his itch with the serendipitous appearance of two seemingly perfect victims." David takes a drink and studies her before he leans against the counter. "You know what they say: teamwork makes the dream work."

Sloane beams. "Indeed. But sometimes it takes a while to find the right team."

David tips his glass in her direction. "Very true."

"Blackbird . . ." I say.

She sighs and pins me with a lightless glare. "Stop with the 'Blackbird' already."

"*Sloane*, love, *please*—"

"Love?" Sloane's head tilts. Her eyes are black in the dim light. "*Love . . . ?* You really thought that's what this was? You said it yourself—I'm a fucking psycho, remember? A monster. This isn't love. It's boredom. It's competition. And by the looks of things," she says as she lets her gaze travel from the corkscrew and down the steady drip that flows to the pool of blood on the floor, "I've already won."

I shake my head. My voice is only a strangled whisper when I say, "He is going to do brutal things to you, Sloane."

"Oh, you mean like maybe he'll wax poetic while pounding balls-deep into my ass? Is that the kind of thing you're thinking of?" Sloane rolls her eyes. "I think I've proven I can handle that."

Every pain in my body is eclipsed by the one in my chest as my heart incinerates. She watches it happen, just the same as I did to her. But I don't sense even the smallest shred of remorse or regret, only disgust in the way her lip curls before she looks away.

Sloane's expression smooths as her eyes lift to David. "You know, I'm really in the mood to tear up the town, if you catch my drift," she says to him with a wink.

His returning smile is ravenous.

I beg, but it's like they can't hear me. Thrash in my chair, but they don't see.

Tears burn my eyes. I know what he'll do to her, my beautiful Sloane. He'll fucking destroy her. Strip bits of her off. Eat them in front of her, just like he's done to me. And so many other horrible, hideous, fucking monstrous things that I can't bear to imagine, but I imagine them anyway.

Even if he lets her walk out of this room alive, she'll never survive the night.

"What do you have in mind?" David asks.

"How about we finish up here and go have some fun? I have some ideas. Maybe Kane Atelier would be a good place to start."

Bile churns in my stomach as David grins and lifts his glass. "To a night out on the town." He knocks back the rest of the bloodied wine and sets the empty glass on the prep table.

"Here, take this." Sloane's hand lifts as though it's caught in slow motion, her palm open and the Glock resting on it like an offering. "I don't really like guns."

David's eyes flash with anticipation as he reaches for the weapon, his gaze fixed on the deadly prize.

The moment his fingers graze the grip of the pistol, Sloane's other arm moves in an upward slash. There's a flash of silver, something hidden in her hand.

David recoils in reflex. Blood sprays across the Glock as it falls to the floor. He launches for her with his other hand, but Sloane is too fast. Her downward strike slices his other wrist. David roars in frustration, but the growl becomes a wail of pain as she kicks out his leg and sends him to his knees.

As he falls, her scalpel is waiting.

It slides into the notch in the hollow of his throat, the sharp edge pointed upward. David's weight splits the flesh in two up the length of his throat as Sloane holds the blade steady between her hands.

It comes to a stop against the point of his chin, deep against the bone.

David coughs a gurgling, desperate breath through the gaping slit. A rush of blood sprays across Sloane's face. She doesn't blink as she lets her gaze travel over every detail of his pain and fury, her smile dark and triumphant as his dimming eyes glare back.

"I don't really like guns," she repeats, and grips his hair in a tight fist. She pulls the blade free with her other hand. "Too loud. No finesse."

She plunges the scalpel into his eye. David's scream is nothing but a sputtering burst of crimson spray.

Then she lets him fall to the floor.

Blood spreads in a thick pool over the tiles. Sloane stands with her back to me as she watches David's desperate movements slow and still, and even when they stop, she remains there, staring down at him as though she needs to be sure he won't get up again.

"Are you okay?" she asks without turning around, her voice a quiet rasp.

I survey my bleeding arm where the skin has been flayed from the throbbing flesh beneath. My cheek and ribs pulse where I've taken his early blows. The corkscrew still ticks with the quickened beat of my heart, but it probably looks worse than it is.

"I wouldn't mind getting out of this chair, but yeah. I'll be fine."

Sloane nods, then falls into silence, her gaze still pinned to the body on the floor.

"Sloane . . ."

She doesn't move.

"Sloane, love—"

"No."

"Um . . . Blackbird?"

Still nothing.

". . . Peaches?"

Her head whips to the side and she pins me with a glare over her shoulder. But there are tears there too, streaking through the blood splashed across her cheeks. "I told you I'd cut you if you called me that again."

"Blackbird it is." I give her a weak smile.

There's worry in her eyes as she takes me in, but hurt too, and it fucking consumes my soul.

"Love, I—"

"Shut up," she snaps, and pulls her phone from her pocket. A heartbeat later, the sound of its ring precedes my brother's voice.

"Well done. My friend Conor is right outside. Do you want him to come in?" Lachlan asks.

"No. Thanks for sending reinforcements though."

"You okay?"

"Sure." Sloane watches me over her shoulder. Tears still glass her eyes, even though the look she gives me is fucking lethal. "Your asshole brother needs . . . skin. I could use help with clean-up too."

Lachlan chuckles. "Fionn is already on his way. I know some people for cleanup—give me an hour for that. Conor will watch the door until they get there." There's a pause, and when Lachlan speaks again, his voice is soft and serious. "Thank you for looking after my brother, Sloane."

"Log out of my video feed. I don't want you to watch in case I change my mind and kill him myself."

"Do me a favor and give him a big sloppy kiss instead," Lachlan says.

She responds with an aggrieved grunt and disconnects the call before tossing the phone on the prep table with a clang.

She turns to me then, her eyes blazing and her arms crossed. "I'm counting this as a win."

"That's fair."

"That's three for me. Best of five."

"Deserved. Totally."

"And I'm still very angry with you."

"I get it, love."

"I want to stab you."

"Yeah, that makes sense. Please not my dick though. Or my balls. Or my pretty face."

Sloane's lips tremble. Her hard expression crumbles and recovers to a stoic mask, only to fall a second time. The red spatters and streaks on her face are so achingly beautiful, her tears so fucking agonizing. "You broke my heart."

"I know, love. I'm sorry. I'm so fucking sorry. You know I only did it to get you away from him, don't you? I had to get you out of here or he was going to kill you."

The tears in Sloane's eyes shift and shine as they gather at her lash line. "I am not unlovable." She jabs her bloody finger in my direction, punctuating every word. "I am very fucking lovable."

I'm desperate to just touch her, even for a moment, as though seeing she's okay is not enough. "Love . . . please . . . just let me out of this chair so we can talk properly."

Sloane's forehead crinkles as she tries to hold on to her ferocity and fails, and when I give her a little smile, she can't help herself— her gaze drops to my scar and lingers there.

"Come on, Blackbird. Let me up so I can prove to you that I fucking love you to pieces. Maybe I'll take that first aid kit by the door too if you don't mind."

Her ferocious glare returns.

"Or I'll just bleed out on the floor, that's cool . . . but getting out of the chair would still be aces. Preferably with no stabbing."

After another long moment of hesitation, she approaches and starts working the knots free, first the ones that bind the chair to the support post of the counter and then those looped tight around my limbs. The last rope to fall to the floor is the one that straps my impaled wrist to the armrest.

I erupt from the chair the instant it's gone.

Pain is dulled by need as I yank the implement free and grab Sloane as she backs away, crushing her to me in a desperate embrace. And I thank every god I never pray to when she wraps her arms around my body. She buries her face into my chest and dampens my shirt with all the fears she's kept buried.

"I thought I was too late," she says, over and over. "I'm so sorry, Rowan. It took me too long to figure out your clues."

I take her face in my palms and stare down into her wide hazel eyes. An ache chokes up my throat as I savor this moment to just look at her, to feel her warmth against my skin. I came so close to losing *everything*. But she's here, with her ginger scent and black eyeliner smeared in streaks down her skin, her freckles dotted with specks of blood. Creases line her forehead and her furrowed brow as her gaze bounds between mine.

She's never been more beautiful.

"Not too late, Blackbird. Right on time."

She tries to smile, but it doesn't come. Her dimple is only a faint depression on her skin. And I know the lies I told her are the most dangerous kind, because I weaponized her real insecurities. Even if I said them only to save her, cuts like those still run deep and heal slowly.

I lower my head and hold her eyes, keeping her face steady between my palms. "You have never been unlovable. You were just waiting for someone who will love you for who you *are*, not for who they want you to be. I can do that, if you'll let me." I press my lips to hers and taste salt and blood but pull away before the kiss deepens. "I fucking adore you, Sloane Sutherland. I wanted you from that first day at Briscoe's. I have loved you for years. I'm not stopping. Not ever."

Sloane's gaze drops to my lips and remains there. She nods.

"You might be psycho," I say with a grin as her eyes narrow, "but you're *my* psycho, and I'm yours. Got it?"

When she lifts her eyes from my lips, she finally smiles. "You're still kind of the worst."

"And you still love me."

"Yeah," she says. "I do."

Sloane rises on her tiptoes and folds her hands around my nape, drawing me closer until her forehead presses to mine, her breath a sweetly scented caress on my lips.

"I really fucking do," she whispers. "And you're going to have to try harder than that to get rid of me, because I'm not going anywhere."

"Neither am I, Sloane."

When Sloane pulls my lips down to hers, I know it. I feel it in every beat that throbs in my raw, bleeding flesh. That the world could turn in every direction and shatter every reality, but there's no other life than the one we choose to build.

PIGMENT

Sloane

"We're going to be late," Rowan says. But he doesn't care. Not really.

Because his hands are threaded into my hair and his head is tossed back as I swallow his cock.

"Jesus, Sloane. How are you so fucking good at this?"

I hum my satisfaction into his flesh and cup his balls with my free hand as I thrust my fingers into my pussy with the other. When I moan again, he looks down, his eyes black with desire.

"Fuck, I love watching you touch yourself," he hisses.

My eyes flutter closed as I swirl my touch over my clit. Precum threads across my tongue.

"You'd better make yourself come, because I am right on the fucking edge and we need to *go*."

I slow the motion of my fingers, slide my lips to the crown of his erection, and grin.

My insolence is met with a growl. Rowan's hand darts to my throat and catches the giggle that begs to be set free.

"Are you being a brat?" he asks as I run my tongue along the underside of his erection and pin him with my most innocent eyes. His hand tightens. "Have you forgotten the last time you were a brat?"

I shrug, even though I most certainly have *not* forgotten. When I decided to push his buttons and disregard most of his orders while riding his cock a few weeks ago, he kidnapped me as I was coming home from drinks with Anna, blindfolded me, and strapped me down on a table in the restaurant to eat a full range of delicacies off my naked body. He edged me for *hours*, drizzling caramel sauce across my nipples to suck it off as he fucked me, dripping cold whipped cream onto my genital piercings before licking them clean. Every time I begged for mercy, he laughed.

"Good girls get rewards," he'd said as he turned down the vibration on the anal plug he'd pushed into my ass after he tied me down. He slowed the rhythm of his strokes as he thrust into me, pulling me back from the brink of an orgasm. "Brats receive punishment."

He'd slid out of me, jerked off until he sprayed his cum in warm spurts across my chest, then started all over again.

It probably had the opposite effect of what he had intended, because I had *the best* time that night.

"That's your answer?" he says now, his eyes lethal and dark. "Just a shrug? That seems pretty bratty to me."

I sigh and lick my way back to the crown of his erection as I cup his balls.

"I might have lied about the appointment time," I reply as I stroke the length of his cock and lavish the tip with a swirling lick. "We have an extra hour."

My eyes stay fused to Rowan's face as this information settles into his endorphin-flooded brain.

"Oh, thank fuck," he finally says, and plunges into the heat of my mouth. "Make yourself come or I swear to God I am going to steal you away to some remote cabin and punish you for three days."

Rowan Kane, always threatening me with a good time.

He loosens his grip on my throat but keeps me steady as I kneel before him and take his cock as deep as I can. It hits the back of my throat and my garbled, choked sounds spur the rhythm of his thrusts. With my other hand, I drive my fingers into my pussy until they're coated in my arousal and the cum he already spilled into me earlier.

My slick fingers withdraw, and then I move my touch to Rowan, finding the pleated rim of his ass. He shudders as I massage the tight ring, and then I push a finger inside.

"Oh holy shit, Sloane—"

"Are you using your safe word?"

"*Fuck* no."

I grin and add a second finger, gently stroking until I find the touch that makes him tremble. "What a good boy," I coo, my tone saccharine. "And good boys get rewards."

My lips seal around his cock and I suck.

An uninhibited sound of pleasure rumbles from Rowan's chest as I fuck him with my fingers and swallow his erection. With my other hand, I circle my clit, climbing closer to the orgasm I know he'll demand of me. And as I feel his body coil tight, that's exactly what he does. *Demands.*

"Blackbird, you'd better come right the fuck now because you are *killing me* and I swear to fucking God—"

I fall apart with his cock plunged to the back of my throat, my whimpering moan a vibration that surrounds his length.

His words set me off every time.

A breath later, Rowan growls as his hot cum floods my mouth. I swallow every drop and draw out his pleasure until I'm sure he's spent, a thin sheen of sweat glistening across his naked chest with his shuddering breaths.

"We've gotta go," I say with a devious smile as I withdraw my fingers from his ass. "We're going to be late."

Rowan gives me a flat glare that doesn't last, then presses a kiss to my forehead before we clean ourselves up, get dressed, and rush out the door.

Every step we take in the warm June sun has my heart hammering, not with anxiety, but with excitement. If Rowan is nervous, he doesn't let on. He tells an animated story about Lachlan from when they were teenagers as we walk the city streets, our fingers interlaced, my other hand braced around the largest scar on the inner surface of his forearm. The night it happened, Fionn had meticulously treated the wound and used Dermagraft to replace the missing tissue, and Rowan was diligent about taking care of it from that night on. And soon, the scar will be transformed into something beautiful.

He'll love it. I know he will.

We stop at Kane Atelier on the way to our appointment, entering the shop to the scent of leather and the sound of indie music. I tamp down a grin as I wonder if Lachlan ever listens to Lark's music, and when I glance at Rowan beside me, I think he might be wondering the same.

"You old twat. What are you working on?" Rowan says as Lachlan wheels his worn swivel chair away from his desk and tosses what looks like reading glasses next to the hide he's carving.

"Custom saddlebags for a biker's Harley. If I couldn't kick your ass myself, he would gladly do it for me," Lachlan fires back. "And I'm only two years older than you, dipshit."

"Then why are you wearing old man glasses? You look like you're about to do a crossword puzzle and fall asleep in your La-Z-Boy recliner," Rowan says with a wink at me.

"Fuck off. What do you want, you feckin' asshat?"

"Actually it's me, I have a little request," I say as I take a step closer to Rowan's brash older brother.

"Ah, the spider lady, coming to ask me for a favor," Lachlan says with a devious grin as he leans back in his chair.

"Actually, I'm calling in a favor."

"Oh really? What favor is that."

"Saving your little brother."

"If I remember correctly," Lachlan says, tapping one of his ringed fingers on his chin, "I helped clean up your rather messy murder scene before erasing any record of the existence of a certain David Miller from the annals of serial killer history. So, I'd say we're even. You're welcome."

I roll my eyes and Rowan smirks next to me. "Fine. A favor for Lark Montague in that case."

There's a beat of hesitation before Lachlan emphatically says, "*Fuck* no."

"Come on," I reply, my voice bordering on a whiny plea as I take another step closer. "Lark is moving to Boston the same week that we're going to be away. Just help her get her stuff into her new apartment, please. She doesn't have much."

"Why doesn't she have much?" Lachlan asks, his brow furrowed, his voice stern. Rowan and I exchange a fleeting, confused glance before I refocus on Lachlan.

"Um, she travels light, I guess . . . ?"

Lachlan's gaze darkens as though this is insufficient information before he smooths his reaction beneath an apathetic mask. "Fine. But don't expect me to stick around when it's done."

"Of course not."

"And I'm not going to show her around the city or some shit."

"Absolutely not."

"We're not like, friends. She can't call me for . . . milk."

"Okay . . . I'll let her know not to call you for milk. Done."

Lachlan grunts. I grin.

"Thank you," I say as I walk over and give him a hug I already know he won't return. "You won't regret it."

"Yes, I will."

"Okay then."

I give him a kiss on his stubbled cheek to the sound of Rowan's delighted snort and then back away.

"Thanks for that, bellend. We've gotta run," Rowan says with a teasing grin that Lachlan returns with a flat glare, but he still rises from his chair. He walks us out of the studio and onto the street, and we make plans to get together for dinner next week before he presses his forehead to Rowan's as he always does. And then we're off, heading to our appointment hand in hand, taking our time to enjoy our simple company and the mounting excitement for what's to come as we weave our way to our destination.

The little brass bell rings at the top of the door as we enter Prism Tattoo Parlor.

Laura, the owner of the shop, greets us warmly and gives Rowan a consent form to complete as she and I finalize details about the design I gave her, our voices hushed so that Rowan can't hear the specifics. When everything is signed and the design is printed on the transfer paper, Rowan takes a seat in Laura's chair.

"Sorry, Butcher, but I don't trust you as far as I could throw you," I say as I step behind him to lower a blindfold over his eyes. Laura smirks as she preps Rowan's arm and transfers the stencil across his scar.

"You wound me," he says.

"Right," I snort. "Did you or did you not follow me for three days in California just so you could cheat your way into winning a game?"

"I did not cheat. And besides, I lost. *Miserably*, I might add. I still can't eat ice cream."

I grin and take a seat next to him so I can watch as Laura starts to lay down the first black lines in his skin. "Maybe we'll start a desensitization program for you. I have some ideas."

"Now you're talking."

It takes a few hours, but the picture comes to life on Rowan's arm, a design I made myself and worked with Laura to refine so it would cover his scars and fit the contours of his musculature. And before long, she's cleaning the fresh tattoo off, wiping away the excess ink and the dots of blood to reveal the final image. We share a bright smile across Rowan's body, one artist to another, as he peppers us with questions we don't answer.

"Okay, pretty boy. Time to check it out," I say as Laura takes one of Rowan's biceps and I grab hold of the other. We guide him to his feet and over to a full-length mirror. I stand next to him as Laura pulls the blindfold free and he gets his first look at the tattoo that encompasses the length of his forearm.

"Holy fucking shit," he says, not taking his eyes from the design as he steps closer to the mirror and twists his arm from side to side. He absorbs every detail, both in the mirror and on his arm directly, his sharp gaze bouncing to me every few seconds. "It's amazing, Blackbird."

The raven's black feathers shimmer with hints of indigo, its eye otherworldly and opalescent as it looks into the distance. It stands clutching a polished chef's knife, light a bright reflection on the blade. Behind the bird and its sharpened perch is a background of graffiti-like spatters in bursts of vibrant color.

"The colors are epic, Laura," he says, glancing over at her with an appreciative smile.

She grins. "Thank you, but your girl here is the one who came up with it. I just brought her design to life."

Laura hands him the reference drawing on her iPad, the original that I sent her two months ago when Rowan first suggested a cover-up for the scars. He stares at the image and swallows. It takes him a long moment before he turns his gaze to me.

"Color?" he asks. He points to the image without taking his eyes from mine. "You did this?"

I shrug, the start of an ache forming in my throat when I take in the hint of a glassy shine in his eyes. "Yeah. I guess I did."

Rowan hands the iPad back to Laura and crushes me in a tight embrace, his face buried against my neck. He says nothing for a long while. He just holds on.

"You did color," he whispers, but he still doesn't let go.

I smile in Rowan's arms. "What can I say, Butcher. I guess you brought it out of me."

PLUCKED

Rowan

"You know, Blackbird, even though I suggested it, I honestly didn't think I'd enjoy hunting together as much as I would competing against you," I say as I clean off my butcher knife with a bleached cloth.

Sloane laughs but doesn't turn around, her focus too taken with the colored sheets of dyed muslin that she attaches to the fishing line with glue. "I'll take a guess. Is it because your favorite part is not actually the killing, but winding me up?"

"Pretty much." I grin when she gives me a flash of a teasing glare over her shoulder, and then I drop my gaze to the tiny nicks in the sharpened blade in my hands. I slide my cloth in one more pass over the edge before setting the knife aside with my other tools. A bone saw. Meat slicers. And my favorite, a Damascus steel Ulu knife that Sloane gave to me from Etsy for my birthday. "But I did enjoy it. Very much. I like working with you."

"I like working with you too. I think we should catch the Forest Phantom together next year, even though I technically won, because I am the ultimate winner, just in case you forgot. And you probably deserve a runner-up prize anyway since you didn't even vomit this time," she says as she reaches up to point to the eyeballs hanging in fishing line over Dr. Stephan Rostis's head. "Go, you."

"I'm never going to live that down, am I."

"Probably not, no."

While Sloane continues to glue her last few sections of precut cloth, I work on my own final preparations. And then I just sit back and watch my Blackbird, no longer wielding her art in monochrome, but in vibrant Technicolor.

When she's done, she stands back and surveys her canvas behind the body. The three layers of her web are mixed with bursts of color. Hues of jeweled greens in one layer. Blues in another. Reds and purples in the last, each one meticulously dyed by her own hand. It's a stunning installation that radiates like panes of stained glass from the suspended body, his arms and legs outstretched. Rigging him up from the walls and ceiling has been my biggest contribution, aside from slicing off a few choice pieces of flesh for Sloane's skin ornaments that she's sewn within the layers of filament and muslin. But the art? That's all her.

"Beautiful, Sloane," I say.

"Thanks," she replies warmly, but she doesn't turn around, or she would see that I'm not staring at her canvas, but at *her*.

As her gaze remains fixed to the layers of color, I change playlists on my phone. "The FBI is going to be so fucking confused. You're evolving, not devolving. And I'm not sure they're going to finally figure out that the webs are maps now that there's color involved."

"You'd think it would help," she says on the heels of a little laugh, then shakes her head and shrugs.

"One thing has stayed pretty consistent though . . ."

"What's that?"

I jerk a nod toward the body when Sloane turns to face me. The question in her eyes rapidly dissolves into suspicion. When she folds her arms across her chest, I raise my hands in apology, though I'm not sorry at all for what I'm about to say. And she knows it.

"*What*," she says flatly.

I point to the not-so-good doctor, whose blood trickles down his face in drying streaks. "Left eye hole. Always a little gouge-y."

Sloane guffaws a laugh, but it wanes when I shrug. A sliver of doubt etches a crease between her brows. "It is not."

"I'm sorry to say, *it is*."

"You're so full of shit."

I drag my stepladder in front of the body and gesture toward it. "See for yourself."

Sloane's lips part, her cheeks flushed with rising frustration. *Fucking adorable.* Flustered Sloane with her feathers ruffled and her talons ready? That's always my favorite version. And I savor every moment, from her fierce glare to her determined steps as she stomps to the ladder to get a closer look.

"Rowan Kane, you fucking weirdo with this left-eye-hole shit, *I do not gouge, I plu*—"

Her irate tangent stops dead as she takes in the bloody hole, then looks down to me, then back again. Though I manage to bite down on a laugh, there's no hiding the amusement in my eyes, not from her.

"What the fuck is that?" she asks, pointing to the dead doctor's face.

"I dunno, Blackbird. Maybe you should check it out. Unless . . ."

"Unless what?"

"You're not squeamish, are you?"

At this, her laugh breaks free, though it's short and unsure. "How's the ice cream looking these days, Butcher? Managed to crack into some cookies and cream yet?"

"Ouch, Blackbird," I say with a hand over my heart. It thunders beneath my palm. "Wounded, yet again."

Sloane grins, her dimple popping out next to her lip, and then she focuses on the lifeless face before her, the eyes rimmed with blood and the features slack. She reaches her gloved fingers to the left eye socket and pulls out a small, round packet wrapped in tape.

"See?" she says as she balances the mystery on her palm and descends the ladder. "*Plucked*. I plucked it right outta there."

"You did. Almost like you've done this before. Elite-level plucking."

She stops in front of me, her eyes glittering with amusement as they bound between mine. "What is this?"

"I think the trick with a present is usually to open it," I say as I press a kiss to her forehead in reply to her eye roll. She takes the tissue I offer and begins wiping the blood from the tape. "Make sure to clean it all off, though. Important documents inside."

Sloane's face crinkles, her pretty hazel eyes narrowing as she tries to reconcile my words with the small size of the package. "Documents . . . ?"

"*Life-changing* documents, actually. So, yes. Be careful."

With a final, suspicious glance in my direction, Sloane shifts her focus to the ball of tape and cleans every ripple in the cellophane until it's free of blood. Once it's finished, she peels off the strips of sticky plastic, setting each one aside until she can unfold the outer layer of protective paper.

Inside is a folded paper napkin. And inside that, another taped present.

"Oh my God, Rowan. You kept this . . . ?" she asks with a chuckle of disbelief as she reads my handwriting scrawled below the logo of a melting ice cream cone on the napkin.

> Butcher & Blackbird
> Annual August Showdown
> 7 days
> Tie-breaker by rock-paper-scissors
> Best of five
> Winner takes the Forest Phantom

"Hold on a second," I say when she's read each line out loud. "It's missing something. Hand that over for a second while you unwrap the other one."

"What are you up to, weirdo?"

"Maybe I want to blow my nose on this highly sentimental piece of tissue. Just hand it over, Blackbird."

Sloane laughs and shakes her head with confusion, but she passes the napkin back to me and I take my pen from next to my tools to write out a new line, all the while sneaking glances at her to keep watch on her progress as she unwraps the other gift. Like it has every moment I've been with Sloane, my heart fucking pounds the entire time, like it's going to carve itself free of its cage of bones.

When she's about to pull the final piece of tape from the wrapping around the gift, I place my hand over hers, the napkin folded between my fingers. If she can feel a tremor in my flesh, she doesn't say.

"I fixed it," I say, my eyes flicking to the napkin. "Read that first."

She holds my gaze for a moment before she takes the paper and unfolds it, her movement careful and slow. I watch her eyes shift over the words. Her lips press tight. When she reads it out loud, her voice is unsteady.

"Marry Sloane Sutherland and love her forever, if she'll let you," she whispers.

Those big hazel eyes are glassed with tears when she looks up at me. I take the little napkin back. She pulls the last piece of tape from the black cloth and unfolds it to reveal the engagement ring, a blue-gray sapphire set in gold with delicate leaves that climb toward the stone.

And I drop down on one knee.

Sloane swallows. A burst of nerves floods my veins and I'm about to launch into all the things I want to tell her when she says, "Did you just propose on a napkin with a ring you stuffed in a guy's eye hole?"

I blink. My mouth opens. Nothing comes out for a moment that feels about as long as eternity.

"You know, it seemed pretty cute in my head, but in hindsight . . . maybe it's too much?"

She shakes her head.

"Not enough?"

She shakes it again, a few tears jostling free of her lashes.

"Just right?"

"It's fucking *perfect*," she sobs.

"Oh, thank Christ." A long breath whooshes from my lungs as I press my palm to my chest. I clasp my hand over hers, the ring clutched in her shaking grip. "I thought for a minute that I had royally fucked it up."

Sloane makes some kind of strangled squeak. She starts bouncing. First just little bobs, but they get bigger with every second that passes.

"You seem excited, love."

An unintelligible, garbled sound escapes her lips.

"Shh. Man-guy is trying to propose here."

"*Rowan*—"

"Sloane Sutherland, my beautiful Blackbird. From the first moment I met you, you changed the course of my life. I can't remember anything being fun or exciting or new without you. I can't remember feeling anything but numb until you burst into my world in your smelly little cage of orzo pastas," I say, smiling when her laugh breaks free amid her tears. My grip firms around her trembling hand. "I can't envision the future without you in it. And I don't want to, not ever. So marry me, Sloane, and we'll go on crazy adventures forever, and fuck shit up, and be best friends and do karate in the garage and make love every day and grow old together. Because I can't imagine anyone I'd rather spend all those moments with than you."

I pull the ring from her grasp and hold it at the end of her finger.

"What do you say, Blackbird? Will you marry me?"

Tears streak across her freckles as she nods, her voice tight when she says the words I've been waiting months, maybe even years, to hear. "Yes, Rowan. Of course I'll marry you."

I slide the ring on her finger and she no more than glances at it before she barrels into me, nearly knocking me to the floor as she grasps my face between her palms and peppers my skin with whispered yeses and desperate kisses.

"I love you, Butcher," Sloane whispers when she pulls away to look into my face. Then she slants her mouth to mine.

She doesn't have to say it, because I feel it in every touch and weighted glance. It bleeds into the kiss she presses to my lips, as though it lives on her tongue when it sweeps over mine. But those words still sink into my chest, another layer of an unbreakable foundation.

Sloane slows our kiss and when we part, she grasps my hand to tug me to my feet. As soon as I'm up, she drags me toward the darkened corridor that leads to the exit off the kitchen and the doctor's collection of expensive cars. "Now let's go do karate in the garage."

"By 'karate' do you mean I'll bend you over the hood of Dr. Stephan's Porsche and fuck you blind until you beg me to stop?"

Sloane tosses a wicked grin over her shoulder. Her dimple pops out next to her lip as she gives me a wink and leads me toward the shadows. "Follow me and find out, pretty boy."

Maybe I was right. We're not normal people. We are monsters.

But if we're monsters, we'll thrive in the dark.

Together.

THE PHANTOM

The city disgusts me.

The scent of the polluted sea. Exhaust from a passing bus. The breath of people who spill their putrid thoughts into the vile air. The city is a cesspool of decay.

Now the men of Sodom were wicked exceedingly and sinners against the Lord.

I swallow the distaste for this environment that has engulfed me for the past week. My gaze drifts from one end of the street to the other, but it always returns to the door across the street and the curve of gold letters on the glass.

My watch alarm beeps. Twelve noon.

Lord, I ask for your blessings to be poured out onto me, your humble servant. Lift my hand against my adversaries. Send back upon them every wrongdoing and injustice they have loosed upon me, your faithful disciple.

Amen.

I open my eyes and resume my vigil from the cafe patio. My

tea has cooled; the book splayed before me remains unread. My fingers tap in time to the music that echoes in my head. A hymn, one my mother used to sing.

Let sinners take their course,
And choose the road to death

The door opens across the street. A tall man with an athletic build holds it open for a woman with raven hair. Her gaze flicks to her surroundings. THE KILLERS, her black T-shirt says.

My blood heats.

But I, with all my cares,
Will lean upon the Lord;
I'll cast my burdens on his arm,
And rest upon his word

As they step onto the sidewalk, the couple turns to speak with another man who lingers behind on the threshold of the door. Black tattoos cover his hands and his muscled arms. He's not as tall as the first man but more powerful in build. The protector. The fighter. I can tell—the way he stands, the way he grins, the coiled readiness in every move. A snake, always ready to strike.

They exchange words I can't hear, smiles I can't feel. The second man clamps his hand over the shoulder of the first. Their foreheads press together before they separate. The first man then walks away hand in hand with the woman. He places a kiss on her temple and she grins. I watch them stroll down the street and turn the corner. For a long moment, my gaze remains there, trapped on their absence as though I haunt their footsteps, a ghost lurking in their shadows.

I settle deeper into my chair. I refocus my attention where it needs to be.

On Kane Atelier.
I seek his blessing every noon,
And pay my vows at night.
Rowan Kane took my brother.
And I vow to take his.

SKULLDUGGERY

Sloane

Rowan Kane is up to no good.

As usual.

I can tell. I don't know *how* I know, but I do. Over the last few days it's been lurking in his little glances. I've seen it in the way he's looked at his phone and hammered out a message, or the devious little glint in the smile that follows. He might try to hide it, but it's there. I can sense it. It's like a faint trace of smoke on the wind. A flash of light on a blade. Whispers in shadows.

He's *scheming*.

My eyes narrow as he loads the dishwasher. If he can feel my gaze drilling into the side of his face, he doesn't let on. When I clear my throat, he doesn't look up. I fold my arms across my chest and lean against the counter, but he still doesn't acknowledge that I'm staring right at him. He said once that he always notices me, and it wasn't a lie. I'm positive this whole oblivious act has to be bullshit.

So I wait until he finishes with the dishwasher and then takes a sip of his coffee before I announce, "I call skullduggery."

Rowan sputters and coughs. When his watering eyes finally land on me, he's clearly fucking delighted.

"Skullduggery? Does this mean you're going to put on a sexy pirate costume and fuck me while you're wearing an eye patch?"

"No."

"What about if I wear the eye patch?"

"Still no."

"What about if I throw in a stuffed parrot?"

"*Rowan*—"

"Love," he says with a warm grin that lights his eyes with amusement. He sets the mug down and approaches, grasping my wrists and tugging my arms from their firm hold across my body. "What kind of skullduggery are you worried about?"

"I don't know," I reply as he wraps my arms behind his back and lays a kiss on the pulse that surges in my neck. "Why don't *you* tell *me*?"

His lips drag up my skin in the way he knows ignites my ticklish streak. When my body squirms in response, he pushes me back against the counter. "Blackbird, the only shenanigans I'm up to are the kind where I'm in your pants."

"You mean like, kidnapping me again?"

"Umm, I was thinking more like *right now*, but that can be arranged."

Rowan's grip tightens on my waist and he lifts me onto the counter as he catches my lips in a demanding kiss. With my arms wrapped around the back of his neck, I kiss him back with desire that matches his, reveling in the glide of his tongue over mine and the caress of his calloused hands as they dip beneath the hem of my shirt to warm my bare flesh. But my thoughts? They are still wrapped up in a question.

"What are you up to?" I ask when I pull back just enough to form the words against his lips.

"Making out with my fiancée," he says, and dives back into the kiss.

I manage to pull back and break the kiss despite his best efforts to keep it going. My eyes narrow with a suspicious glare. "You're deflecting."

"I'm not." One of his hands roams to my breast and he toys with my nipple piercing in a way that has my pussy aching for attention. "I answered your question. I'm making out with you and then I'm going to fuck you on this here countertop," he says as he gives the polished granite a slap. "Pretty direct response."

"Are you scheming to kill someone?"

"What?"

"You know, murder. That thing we're good at. *Oh my God*, you're going after the Forest Phantom, aren't you? You're going to kill him before the annual game."

"Love—"

"Just *tell me*. That's it, isn't it? I bet you've already got him locked away somewhere. You're probably going to have him up on the statue in Boston Common riding that horse with George Washington by morning—"

"*Blackbird*," Rowan says, his palms a sudden warmth on my cheeks. His eyes shift between mine, and though he's amused, I can tell he's a little worried too. "Though I find your paranoia adorable and I'm filing that George Washington idea away for later, you're way off course here." He presses a kiss to my forehead before pulling away to level me with a serious gaze. He seems to come to some conclusion as a lengthy sigh passes his lips. "Is this about the wedding?"

The wedding.

Every time I think about the wedding, my heart rate spikes. The room seems to close in, as if all the air has been vacuumed out and I'm left with nothing to breathe. It's not the thought of marrying Rowan that gets me. He's my best friend. I love him more than anything. It's the enormity of the task that we've barely even started since he proposed six weeks ago, and especially the presence of guests. Two in particular. Do I invite my parents? Would they even bother coming? If I don't, will it look bad when Rowan knows half the city and probably wants a bunch of his friends to attend? They've been nothing but kind to me, but won't they wonder what's up when I have Lark and maybe her family but no one else? Won't that look weird? Won't *I* look weird?

"Sloane? Is that the issue?" Rowan presses, his voice soft.

"No . . ." I lie, even though I hate the thought of lying to Rowan about how I feel. But I don't want him to think the wrong thing, that I'm changing my mind. And besides, I am still convinced he's up to *something*.

"Do you think the wedding *might* have something to do with it?"

I shake my head.

"Here's what I think," Rowan says as he lowers his hands to the countertop on either side of my hips, caging me in. "I think you're stressed about planning this thing out. You're putting too much pressure on yourself. And now you're seeing trouble where there isn't any."

"But you're always trouble. So maybe I'm seeing pretty clearly."

Rowan's grin turns rakish. "I'm *delightful* trouble. As for skullduggery, like I said, my scheming is pretty straightforward. Fuck my fiancée. Make her come. Send her away on her spa vacation with a couple of hickeys on her pretty tits."

"Hickeys? Seriously?" I can't help but giggle as his hands climb beneath my shirt, towing it up my body until he lifts it off and discards it on the floor. Rowan's eyes stay riveted to my chest as he pulls the cups of black lace down with an appreciative groan.

"Damn straight," he says as he toys with one of the piercings, tugging gently on the little bar. I bite down on my lip to trap a whimpering moan, and Rowan's eyes immediately dart to my mouth and hook there. "Hmm now, Blackbird. You're not keeping your sounds from me, are you?"

I swallow. "Winston will start growling."

Rowan might laugh, but we both know it's true. Winston has taken a liking to me and has used that as a convenient excuse to attack Rowan when he thinks I'm in mortal danger.

"I'm willing to risk a few more scars on my arse," Rowan says before laying a bite to my neck that draws a gasp from my parted lips. "I'll lock him in the bathroom if I have to. But all those little sounds you try to hide? They belong to *me*."

My hands thread into his hair as Rowan kisses his way down my throat and across my chest to lavish my nipple with attention. He swirls his tongue over every curve and angle of the piercing before gripping it between his teeth to give it a delicious tug.

"Goddammit, I really love it when you do that," I hiss as his fingers toy with the zipper of my jeans. He drags it down with agonizing slowness, as though he can hear every thought in my head that screams at him to move faster.

"When I first saw these piercings through your bra at the gas station, I nearly fucking died," Rowan says as he plays with one

331

of the little hearts, coaxing my nipple into a firm peak. "I swear I had a hard-on for the rest of the drive to Fionn's."

My giggle becomes a gasp when he leans down to suck on my breast. "I know. You kept shifting around in the seat. You looked miserable."

"I *was* miserable. I needed to touch you." He lays a kiss on my neck, presses in on my body. "I needed to know everything about these fucking little hearts. And to think, I didn't even know about the other decorations."

I grin as Rowan nips my earlobe. "I thought you might like the nipple piercings. You spent enough time staring at my boobs in the diner. It was kinda cute how hard you tried not to."

Rowan groans against my neck before he pulls away to look in my eyes. "Blackbird, I have a question."

"Okay . . ."

"Did you get the hearts for me?"

Blush crawls beneath my skin, and Rowan's eyes dart down to my cheeks to soak it in. "Maybe a little bit."

He swipes a hand down his face before resting his forehead against my shoulder. "I love you so fucking much that it physically hurts me," he says as I laugh. When he straightens, Rowan tugs me off the counter and sets me on my feet. "I got something for you too. I've been saving it for a special occasion. Get naked and stay right here."

"What are you—"

"Just trust me," he tosses over his shoulder as he heads down the hallway to the bedroom. I start to undress as Winston's growl precedes the sound of the bathroom door closing. And then a few moments later, Rowan appears from the dimly lit corridor, stalking toward me with a new purple vibrator and a bottle of lube in one hand.

. . . A purple vibrator that matches his outfit.

A dragon onesie costume.

"Rowan Kane, what the *fuck*," I say as I cackle with disbelief.

"I'm not Rowan. I'm Sol," he growls as he stalks closer. His ravenous gaze pins me and doesn't let go. I take a step backward and then another, every laugh that escapes me only feeding the hunger in his eyes. "And I'm going to breed you, little human."

"You are so weird," I say on the heels of a shriek as he surges forward and I run around the end of the island, narrowly avoiding his reaching grip.

"Try to escape all you want, my little human. I will still catch you."

I cackle as I keep the island between us and creep toward the end closest to the corridor in the hopes I can make a break for it toward the bedroom. "Why are you like this?"

"A sentient dragonman knows not why it is a talking dragon. Only that it must make little dragonlings with its two dicks." Rowan tries not to smile as I giggle maniacally. "*Run*, human."

I squeak and take off for the corridor, but I don't make it more than ten steps before he's got me. He lifts me from the floor and into his arms as though it's effortless. "For a dragon, you're not very scaly, *Sol*. This will be more like being fucked by a velveteen rabbit."

Rowan snorts a laugh as he tosses me onto the bed. "A half-boiled rabbit at this rate. This is not breathable fabric."

"Take it off then, you weirdo."

"No way. I'm committed to the bit, Blackbird." He clears his throat and resumes his booming dragon impersonation when he says, "On your hands and knees, little human."

I do as he says, laughing the entire time as I bend over. But the laughter dissolves into a loud moan as he plunges his cock into my pussy with a single stroke.

"Fuck, Sloane. So fucking wet for me, every single time," Rowan says as he glides out and thrusts back in again, the soft fabric pressing against my ass cheeks every time he bottoms out.

"You're really doing it," I say as I look over my shoulder and grin. His hair is already clinging to his damp forehead beneath the hood where two little orange horns are sewn. "You're fucking me in a non-breathable velveteen dragon suit."

"Damn straight I am," he grits out, not breaking the cadence of his thrusts as he grips my waist with one hand and opens the bottle of lube with the other. I watch as he drizzles the thick liquid onto the crack of my ass. "And I'm going to fill this perfect cunt and then this tight little hole before I pass out from heat exhaustion."

I snort a laugh and brace my head against my arm, pushing my ass up higher as he slides the toy through the slick lube to press it against the pleated rim. With a deep breath and a little push of the toy, it slips past the resistance.

"Oh my *God*," I moan into the sheets as he pushes it in deeper, slowly, inch by inch. Every thrust in my cunt is deep and slow as he guides the vibrator in until I'm filled, until I feel like I couldn't possibly take more.

Then he turns it on.

We both pause, as though any movement we make will push us over the edge before we're ready to take a breath and dive. Rowan hisses a string of swears and I try to relax, but it becomes impossible when Rowan starts to resume a pace of slow, languid strokes. His rhythm becomes faster, his thrusts deeper. He turns up the level of vibration on the toy, and then he isn't just fucking me. He's *claiming* me, like no one else ever could. He grips my breast with one hand, my hip with the other, and ruts into me with merciless, carnal need.

"Touch yourself," he grits out. "Make yourself come. Fucking scream my name, Sloane. Let me hear how I fucking destroy you."

I do everything he asks.

I bring my fingers to my clit, slick with arousal and lube, and roll my touch over the triangle piercing as I cry out Rowan's name. An electric surge blankets my flesh, like all the energy of my body is siphoned from my limbs until it explodes in my core. My pussy cinches tight around Rowan's erection and I fall apart as a growl rips free from his chest. He pulls the toy from my ass and pushes his length in its place as he shudders, emptying the rest of his spend into the tight heat.

"Fuck," he hisses when he catches his breath and slowly withdraws. When he's slipped away, he keeps his hands on my flesh, separating my ass cheeks so he can watch as the cum drips free. "I thought I could go another round, but I need six bottles of Gatorade first."

"Maybe we should do the pirate costume next time."

"You be the pirate, I'll be the parrot."

"You are so fucking weird."

"But you love me," Rowan says as he shimmies off the bed to take off the dragon costume, his body slick with sweat.

"I do."

Rowan grins and leans down to kiss my temple before heading to the bathroom to free Winston and return with a damp cloth. Winston hisses and takes a swipe at Rowan's bare calf in retribution, but Rowan manages to dodge the perpetually disgruntled feline before he climbs back onto the bed to clean my skin with reverential strokes.

"Are you excited to go away for the weekend?" he asks, his gaze trapped on the motion of his hand as he runs the cloth over my inner thigh.

"Yeah, it'll be fun. I'll miss you, though."

Rowan smiles as he casts a fleeting glance up to meet mine. "You'll just miss my dragon cosplay. Admit it."

I grin and fold my hand around his nape to draw his lips to mine. The kiss lingers, sweet and slow, until I pull back to admit, "Maybe I'll miss that too."

"Knew it," he says with a grin before he backs away and offers a hand to help me off the bed.

I don't have much time to shower and get the last of my belongings packed before Lark calls to let me know she's waiting on the street below. Rowan wraps me in a tight hug and peppers my cheeks with kisses before he's pushing me out the door with instructions not to get eaten by a shark, despite my protests that it's early October and I have no intentions of getting in the frigid water at Cape Cod. And then I'm rushing down the stairs of the old brick building, bursting out into the sunshine to be greeted by Lark's even brighter smile.

Within twenty minutes, we've picked up Anna and are heading to the Leytonstone Inn, a boutique spa hotel overlooking Newcomb Hollow Beach. It takes us a little over two hours to reach the inn, and we manage to avoid the Thursday-afternoon rush hour traffic to make it just in time for dinner and a few glasses of wine before we crash out in our rooms. In typical Lark fashion, she's got an outing planned for first thing in the morning, a scenic sunrise hike along the Sand Cliffs before we're back at the hotel for lunch and afternoon yoga, which I'm terrible at. Surprisingly, Anna is even worse, and we spend most of the time trying to hold our shit together and not disrupt Lark's laser focus. We spend the evening eating and drinking and laughing. Laughing so much more than I thought I could.

Saturday is a full-on spa day, much more my speed than the yoga. It starts with a sauna session. Facials. A full-body scrub. And before lunch, a massage session with the girls in a room with a view of the beach.

"You should come back here before the wedding," Lark says as the masseuse works on my shoulder where the muscles are still tight from the fall at Harvey's house in Texas. "Get all the kinks worked out."

Anna snorts. "Work them in during the evening, out during the morning."

"Dragon onesie," Lark and I say in unison with a round of giggles.

"Have you settled on a location for the wedding?" Anna asks, her voice muffled where her face is pressed into the hole of the massage table.

"Not yet."

"This could be a good spot. Nice and chill. Quiet."

"Your dress fits the vibe too," Lark chimes in. As soon as I told her that Rowan had proposed, she dragged me to her aunt

Ethel's house to lay claim to what she announced was a "gold-star-tits dress." And she was right. Ethel's vintage lace dress had been lovingly stored away in her enormous, museum-like home and was in near-perfect condition. Ethel herself made the minor repairs and adjustments within two days of our visit, but it already fit every curve on my body as if it had been made for me.

"True," I reply. "You might be on to something. I do really like it here."

Lark senses the hesitation in the way my voice grows quieter with my final words. "But . . . ?"

"But the guest list is really stressing me out. And like, all the other shit. Flowers and music and *blah blah blah*. And if my parents come, they're so particular, you know? I don't know if it would fit their tastes."

"Does it fit *yours*?"

Yeah, it really does. The thought of something intimate and small at a comfortable, boutique beach inn sounds perfect. But every time I remember how Rowan shone as bright as a star at the Best of Boston gala, surrounded by friends and acquaintances, the doubts creep in. Maybe he would prefer something big, something grand. Maybe he wouldn't want something small and intimate at all.

I don't answer Lark as these thoughts tumble through my mind.

"I'll be right back, girls," Anna says after we slip into a long silence. "Need a quick bathroom break."

"Ooh, me too, I'll come with," Lark says.

I don't move as they leave and the door closes behind them with a quiet snick, too absorbed in the feeling of tight muscles finally releasing beneath the masseuse's expert touch.

"I'm just going to get more oil," she says after a few moments of silently working my left shoulder. I mutter a relaxed thank-you, and after some rustling and rummaging behind me, she returns to resume work on my back.

"How's the pressure?" a voice says.

A familiar voice. One that is definitely *not* my masseuse.

I shriek and roll off the table, the towel clutched to my body as I come face-to-face with my not-masseuse.

Rowan Kane.

"*What in the ever-loving fuck.*"

"Hey, Blackbird."

I stare at him, mouth agape, before I dart a wary glance around the room. The massage therapists are gone. My friends are clearly in on whatever the fuck this is. It's just me and the smirking Irishman, looking hot as fuck in a leather jacket, a motorcycle helmet laying on the table where Lark was a few moments ago.

"What the fuck are you doing here?" I ask.

Rowan hops up onto the table next to his helmet as he rubs the stubble on his chin. He casts his gaze to the windows, trying and failing to conceal the delight in his eyes. A nonplussed shrug is his first response as he keeps his attention trained to the sea.

"I dunno, I just thought maybe you'd like to get married this weekend. Kinda seemed like a nice spot."

Words refuse to make it from my brain to my tongue. Only one is able to make it out alive. "What . . . ?"

"You know, that ceremony where we say some vows and exchange rings and you look smoking hot in a beautiful dress and I look pretty dapper in a fancy suit. Then we eat cake, have a little dance, a bit of a craic, take bets on whether Lark and Lachlan will hook up, go back to our room to have some mind-blowing post-wedding sex, and then you're stuck with me forever. That kind of thing."

"*. . . What . . . ?*" A sudden ache chokes up my throat as pieces start snapping into place. He arranged this whole spa thing with Lark as an engagement present. When I asked him about his work schedule for the weekend, he seemed to skirt around the details, though I didn't think much of it at the time. Then there was that whole lingering sense that he was scheming. "*Skullduggery.*"

"Maybe a little bit."

"But you said I was way off course."

"You were."

"You said you were only scheming to get into my pants."

"No lies spoken."

"Then what the fuck is this?"

"Clearly, additional skullduggery. Minus the parrot."

I have so many questions that they seem to short-circuit my brain entirely. All I can manage is to shake my head and try to swallow the burning fist that closes around my throat. And Rowan can see it. His eyes soften as they flow across my face.

He slides off the table and approaches as though closing in on a wild creature, moving with careful and slow steps until he's able to grasp my elbows as I keep the towel clutched to my chest. "Love," he says with a faint smile. "I know you're freaking out a bit about the whole planning part. So, I thought if we just did it, right here and now, we won't have to overcomplicate things. We do it the way we want, with our close friends and family and *that's it*. Nobody else. Just small. Everything is here if you want it. And if you don't, that is fine too."

My voice sounds small when I ask, "The dress is here?"

"Yep."

"What about Fionn, and Lachlan, and—"

"And Rose, and auntie Ethel, someone for hair and makeup, and everything else we need, it's all here."

"But who—"

"Conor can do the ceremony. Lachlan can walk you down the aisle. He said he'd be honored to escort the spider lady."

My eyes well with tears. I bite down on my lip to keep it from wobbling, but it's impossible when Rowan traces it with his thumb, tugging it free from the grip of my teeth.

"The weather is supposed to be perfect. We can do it at sunrise, if you want. Right out at the water. Or we can do it another day. Plan it another way. I just thought . . ." Rowan's gaze drops from mine, as though he can't hold the connection between us. He shuffles his feet. Crinkles his nose. When he meets my gaze, his eyes shine. "I just want to marry you. I want to do it without you torturing yourself over what anybody else wants. I just care about you and me."

This man. Sometimes it feels as if he'll never stop cracking my heart to fit more of himself inside.

His features grow hazy beyond the watery film that covers the world when I blink. "For real?"

The first thread of hope and relief weaves into Rowan's expression. "Yeah, Blackbird. For real. Only if you really want to."

I don't even let him finish his sentence before I've caught Rowan in a desperate hug. "Yes," I whisper. "Yes, I really want to."

"Oh, thank fuck," he says as he lays his chin on my shoulder and wraps me in his arms. "I was having another ring-in-the-eye-socket moment of doubt there. You're *sure*?"

I nod my head against his chest.

"Extra sure?"

"*Rowan—*"

"Okay, great, well, on that note, gotta go."

In a flash of movement, Rowan has released me to grab his motorcycle helmet and stride toward the door.

"What the *fuck*?" I ask.

"Bad luck the day before the wedding," he says as he tosses me a cheeky smile when he pauses on the threshold. "Love you, Peaches. See you tomorrow."

The door is shut before I've even managed to move from my place in the center of the room, but I still call out after him. "*I'll cut you.*"

"Empty threats," he calls back as his footfalls stride away down the hall.

By the time Anna and Lark return with champagne and giddy smiles and laughter, I feel as if I've been struck by a hurricane.

And that feeling sticks with me all the way through the rest of the day and into the night and straight through to the next morning. Like I'm caught in a storm. And it's frightening, but maybe exciting too. Like I can't wait to see what it looks like on the other side, how the world might change in its wake. Maybe I'll be swept away by the winds and land someplace new, somewhere I never expected to be.

As the minutes tick down, and my hair and makeup is done and the dress is on, that storm concentrates in the depths of my heart, and it lives there in every beat as I take Lachlan's offered arm and wait by his side for the doors to open. Once they do, we'll walk out to the deck that's bathed in the morning light. We'll take the stone path to where Rowan waits on the sand cliffs overlooking the sea, and then I'll marry my best friend. The love of my life.

Lachlan keeps my hand pressed tight to his side in a way that makes my heart ache as he jerks a nod toward the doors ahead. "You sure you want to marry that *eejit*? There's no escaping him if you do."

"There was never any escaping Rowan Kane. I didn't want there to be," I say as I turn my smile to Lachlan.

Lachlan lets out a low and thoughtful hum. His dark blue eyes seem a little lighter than usual. A little softer. "You're kind of all right, Spider Lady."

"You're not so bad either. Most of the time, anyway," I reply as I turn my attention ahead. "Kind of a dick to my best friend, though."

"*Feckin' Christ.* I helped her *move.* Have you seen the size of her couch? You said she didn't have much stuff—"

"Still a dick. Sort it out."

Lachlan grunts and shuffles his feet. "For a methodical, reclusive serial killer, you're pretty feckin' brazen."

"It's my wedding day. What if I just embrace it? Boss around my brothers-in-law, marry the Boston Butcher, eat some cake. Sounds pretty great, actually. So, yeah. You need to dance with Lark. Bride's orders."

"Then I hope you enjoy watching me hate every minute of it."

"Lachlan Kane, you're just like your brother," I say as I turn a beaming, lethal grin toward him. "Always threatening me with a good time."

Lachlan scoffs but turns his gaze away too slowly to hide the little glint of delight in his eyes. "Yeah, Spider Lady . . . You're kind of all right."

The music starts up. The doors open. Lachlan's other hand lays over mine.

I take one breath.

And then I walk from the shadows and into the sun.

A TEASER FROM

LEATHER & LARK

BOOK 2 IN THE RUINOUS LOVE TRILOGY

Lachlan

Claire Peller looks just the same as I remember her. Hair scraped away from her face in a high ponytail. A bleached, predatory smile. The minimalist lines of a black suit. It's all a pristine veneer over a deeply hidden desire to make everything messy.

Claire grins and turns her attention to Rowan. "Hi, Rowan."

He gives her a single nod, but there's no warmth in his simple response. Claire doesn't give a shit. In fact, she feckin' loves it. She turns her gaze to Sloane and Rowan preempts whatever she's about to say when she sucks in a breath. "This is my wife, Sloane. Sloane, Claire."

"It's a pleasure," Claire says. Sloane only gives a tight smile but Claire barely notices, her focus already shifting to Lark.

"And this is Lark," I say as I bow my head in her direction. "My wife."

An incredulous laugh bursts from Claire and my blood turns to fire. She looks between us as though waiting for the punch line, one that doesn't come.

"You're *married*?"

"Yep."

"Lachlan Kane," she says and shakes her head. "I never thought I would see the day. A lot has certainly changed since that Halloween party two years ago." There's a cutting edge to Claire's voice that's meant to leave wounds. But when I meet Lark's eyes, there's only an unreadable mask watching me back. I should probably feel relieved that she seems unscathed, but part of me is a little disappointed, as much as I don't like to admit it.

"Yeah. Well, see you around," I say with finality as I turn back to my food.

"Yes, definitely," Claire says as her phone rings. "I'll stop by the shop sometime. We can catch up properly."

Before I can protest, Claire accepts the call and her heels clack across the slate floor as she leaves Butcher & Blackbird. I shake my head, focused on my food until I sense tension in the air and look up.

Lark and Sloane exchange some kind of silent conversation.

Sloane raises a single brow.

Lark's eyes narrow.

Sloane sighs and shrugs.

And then Lark is sliding off the booth. She stands and hikes her ridiculously huge bag up her shoulder.

"Well, this was fun. Gotta run," she says as she beams a smile bright as a feckin' laser at Sloane and Rowan. When it lands on me, that smile feels like it could slash my skin open. "See you at home."

And then she's striding out of Butcher & Blackbird, her energy trailing after her like a comet.

Rowan laughs and shakes his head before he takes a sip of his drink. "Unless you want to be bailing her out of jail, you'd better go get your wife."

I lean back in my seat and tap the ring on my index finger against my glass as I try not to look toward the door. My focus lands on Sloane instead, who masks her smile with a bite of food. A sinking feeling coats my chest. "What are you on about?"

"Go get her before she knifes Claire, you *bellend*," he says.

"Nah . . . she . . ." I look toward the door and then to Sloane, her eyes full of sparks. "What . . . ?"

"Listen," she says, laying her palm flat against the table as she finally meets my eyes. That bloody dimple flashes next to her lip. It's like her bat signal for mischief. "Lark Montague might be cute as a button, all *shiny happy ra-ra cheerleader* shit, but bitch is fucking vindictive. I love her to death and beyond, but let's just say that particular unicorn doesn't shit rainbows."

I still can't reconcile her words with the woman I think I know. "*That* Lark . . . ? *Let's cover everything in sparkles and sing a song* Lark . . . ? You're telling me she has a legit spiteful streak? Like . . . she's not just a walking catastrophe but *on purpose* malicious . . . ?"

They both laugh. Fucking *laugh*.

"Lachlan," Sloane says, shaking her head, "I'm going to give you this one because you're hopeless and I pity you."

"Thanks . . ."

"Lark Montague doesn't just have a 'spiteful streak.' She takes the idea of retribution and makes it into a full-on glitter parade of vengeance."

Rowan points his fork toward her. "She rigged a glitter bomb in my car for the time I made Sloane cry and told her to go home. I spent a grand getting the car detailed and I still find glitter on a daily basis."

"When we were in boarding school, this girl named Macie Roberts called one of Lark's friends a 'skanky cum bucket.' So

Lark got into Macie's room and spent an entire night writing *I'm a skanky cum bucket* in fabric paint on literally every item of clothing Macie had, even her underwear."

"Tell him about the sequins."

"Sequins?" I ask as the two snicker.

Sloane's brows hike as she pushes a bit of food around her plate. "A few years ago, Lark was living with her boyfriend at the time, a guy named Andrew. One weekend while Lark was out of town, he and their mutual friend Savannah hooked up at Lark and Andrew's apartment," she says as an irrational tidal wave of anger sweeps through me. "A couple weeks later, Lark broke into Savannah's house while she was sleeping and spelled *cheating bitch* on her face with Gorilla Glue and sequins. She stole Savannah's bottle of nail polish remover and her phone and computer so she had no choice but to go out and buy more to get the glue off. Even once the sequins were gone, you could still see the marks. It was pretty awesome."

I can't deny I kind of love the ballsiness of that plan. I almost smile, but then I catch the exchange of a dark look between Sloane and Rowan. "What is it?"

"Well . . . Lark will neither confirm nor deny her involvement, but two months later, Andrew died in a freak fireworks 'accident,'" Sloane says with air quotes.

"You think Lark . . . murdered someone . . . ? *That* Lark?"

Sloane shrugs.

"Don't know why you're still sitting here when she's probably slicing Claire's face off to make into a kite, but it's your bail money, I guess," Rowan says, and in a heartbeat I'm halfway to the door.

The sound of Rowan and Sloane's laughter follows me out to the street.

I lurch to a stop on the sidewalk, craning my neck to look past pedestrians. I listen for Lark's voice, which always carries like chimes on the wind.

Nothing.

I pivot a single spin before I follow my gut and head east.

Phone clutched so tight in my hand it might snap, I bring up Lark's number where it's saved to favorites and tap it.

Straight to voicemail.

"Feckin' banjaxed *bollocks*," I hiss, and the memory of her laugh slaps me. She would make fun of me for saying that. Tease me until I'm forced to turn away to hide the smirking grin that begs to break free every time she pushes my buttons. Then she'd fire some snarky comment at me about Budget Batman and put her walls back up, just like I try to keep mine from falling.

But this time, the problem isn't the barriers between us. It's not what will happen if we let each other in.

It's what she's letting *out*.

I take off running. *She can't be far.*

ACKNOWLEDGMENTS

Thank YOU for taking the time to come on this crazy journey with Rowan and Sloane, and for spending time in their world. I hope you enjoyed the wild ride. It was an absolute JOY to write this story, and I had the best time bringing these characters to life. I hope that joy came through on the page for you.

Endless thanks to my agent, Kim Whalen, and everyone at The Whalen Agency for always being such an incredible source of support and guidance. Kim, you've championed me and my work since our very first conversation, and I am so grateful for everything you've done to bring *Butcher & Blackbird* and the Ruinous Love Trilogy to readers all over the world. And to Mary Pender and Orly Greenberg at UTA, I'm so excited to partner together and discover new ways to bring this story to life! Thank you for falling in love with these characters as much as I did.

To Sierra Stovall, Hayley Wagreich, Andrew Rein, and the entire team at Zando: Thank you for asking me to hop aboard the pirate ship and sail the seas with you. I've never been so excited to get on a boat in my life (and anyone who has ever sailed with me can verify that). I can't wait to see what we conquer next!

In the UK, I am so grateful to the team at Little, Brown UK, particularly Ellie Russell and Becky West, who have been enthusiastic supporters of the Ruinous Love Trilogy from the moment they first got it in their hands. And in Hungary, a special thanks to András Kepets, who set in place the first domino that brought these partnerships to life.

Big thanks to Najla and the team at Qamber Designs, who created the stunning covers for all three books in this series. It has been an absolute pleasure to work with everyone on that team—they did an amazing job of capturing the essence of these stories!

Such huuuuge thanks to the amazing ARC readers and social media supporters of *Butcher & Blackbird* for taking the time to come on this journey with Rowan and Sloane. It means so much to me that you want to be part of this story's life and evolution. Your videos, messages, pictures, drawings, and comments keep me going every single day. I had really no idea where this would end up, and it's been THE MOST FUN ride because I'm on it with you.

Extra special thanks to Arley, who is always my go-to for sharing early chapters and whose feedback made *Butcher & Blackbird* into a better story. Arley—you really helped me find the balance I was hoping to achieve, and I thank you! And to Jess for being an early champion of Rowan and Sloane and for always checking in on me. You always seem to pop up when I need your little boost of sunshine the most. Jess, your calming energy and unwavering support mean the world to me!

I'm so fortunate to have made friends with some incredibly talented authors along the way. Their guidance and encouragement have helped me get the most out of the crazy ideas floating in the "glitter brain soup" in my head. To Trisha Wolfe: your willingness to share advice helped me push through, even in the early days when I was like, "What the fuck even is this story?!"

And to my friend Lauren Biel, who helped me get THE MOST out of David. When I was like, "Is this lobotomized guy a step too far?" Lauren was like, "ABSOLUTELY NOT." This pint of cookies and cream is for you, you hot bitch. Please check out Lauren's dark hitchhiker romances—start with *Hitched*! And Lauren—where the hell is my boxcar man?!

Last, but certainly not least, to my amazing boys: my husband, Daniel, and son, Hayden, who help carve out time so I can write, bring me coffee and smoothies, and give the best hugs. I love you, my boys. (Hayden, don't you dare read this. I'm talking to the universe.)

ABOUT THE AUTHOR

#1 *New York Times* and *USA TODAY* bestselling author and TikTok sensation with works sold worldwide in over eighteen languages to date, **Brynne Weaver** has traveled the world, taken in more stray animals than her husband would probably prefer, and nurtured her love for dark comedies, horror, and romance in both literature and film. During all her adventures, the constant thread in Brynne's life has been writing. With nine published works and counting, Brynne has made her mark in the literary world by blending irreverent dark comedy, swoon-worthy romance, and riveting suspense to create genre-breaking, addictive stories for readers to escape into.

Instagram: @brynne_weaver
TikTok: @brynneweaverbooks
Facebook: facebook.com/groups/1200796990512620
Goodreads:
goodreads.com/author/show/21299126.Brynne_Weaver